CHOICE OF ENEMIES

A NATHAN MONSARRAT THRILLER

M. A. RICHARDS

Mechanicsburg, PA USA

Published by Sunbury Press, Inc.
105 South Market Street
Mechanicsburg, Pennsylvania 17055

www.sunburypress.com

For information about special discounts for bulk purchases, please contact Sunbury Press Orders Dept. at (855) 338-8359 or orders@sunburypress.com.

To request one of our authors for speaking engagements or book signings, please contact Sunbury Press Publicity Dept. at publicity@sunburypress.com.

ISBN: 978-1-62006-662-1 (Trade Paperback)
ISBN: 978-1-62006-663-8 (Mobipocket)
ISBN: 978-1-62006-728-4 (Hard Cover)

Library of Congress Control Number: 2015956422

FIRST SUNBURY PRESS EDITION: January 2016

Product of the United States of America
0 1 1 2 3 5 8 13 21 34 55

Set in Bookman Old Style
Designed by Crystal Devine
Cover by Amber Rendon
Edited by Janice Rhayem

Continue the Enlightenment!

For Young Hee: Patience, Perseverance & Pulchritude

"A man cannot be too careful in the choice of his enemies."
—*Oscar Wilde*

"It is best to win without fighting."
—*Sun-tzu*

I. THE DELTA

IN THE COOL OF THE AFRICAN DAWN

In the cool of the African dawn, six armored Suburbans bulled through the sodden Delta jungle toward Bonny Island. In their wake, whirlwinds of red dirt billowed upward toward the crown canopy. Inside the vehicles, frigid air filtered the jungle stench of rot and decay. Felix Sanhedrin, a twenty-five-year veteran of covert operations in Africa and the Middle East, sat on the rear bench of the convoy's second Suburban like Allan Quatermain returned to the Dark Continent. White linen slacks, a blue Oxford shirt, a silk ascot, and a freshly pressed, khaki bush jacket adorned his thin frame. A device more computer than chronometer rested on his left wrist. His felt slouch hat boasted a faux leopard-skin band, and his canvas jungle boots gleamed. A Glock 19 nested in a leather holster on his right hip.

Sanhedrin's new boots rested atop two green, canvas duffel bags stuffed with Benjamin Franklins, and he carried with him, like a talisman, the blessings of the Mandarins who guided the operations of the Central Intelligence Agency in Langley, Virginia. Despite their stated policy to never negotiate with the enemies of the United States, Sanhedrin had convinced the éminences grises to ransom his assistant, Nathan Monsarrat, from the rebel group called Fighters Against Terror in Africa, or FATA.

He issued orders like a young boy presenting Santa Claus with his Christmas list. "First rule: I'm in charge, and my word is law. Second rule: we take only Monsarrat with us. Final rule: my money's bought your silence. Neither you nor your shooters nor your medics will speak of this mission to anyone. Never repeat, never. *Capish*, my new friend?"

Next to Sanhedrin, Mark Palmer wore funereal black, a shooter's vest, tee shirt, tactical pants, jungle boots, baseball cap, Nomex gloves, and sunglasses. Years beneath the African sun had braised his face and arms. He was clean shaven, and his hair was cut in a brown bristle. Military tattoos covered both his forearms, and blue veins latticed his knotted muscles. He carried an M4 rifle, a brace of Heckler and Koch P30 pistols in nylon holsters

1

strapped to his thighs, a combat knife, commo gear, and four P30 magazines looped onto his belt. The shooter's vest held extra M4 mags.

He spoke with a soft, Southern drawl. "Five by five, Mr. Scarnagh. No worries. We were never here."

Sanhedrin had declared himself to Palmer by his work name, Fineghan Scarnagh. He operated under the letters F and S, keeping with the monograms on his shirt cuffs. Felix and Fineghan. Sanhedrin and Scarnagh. "You should call me Fineghan. After all, we're in the same line of work."

"What line of work would that be, if you don't mind my asking?"

"I'm an independent oil consultant. I work with firms in Africa. Occasionally in Russia. Often in the Middle East."

"Funny we haven't met before, me being the chief of security for the biggest oil services company in Africa," Palmer offered.

Sanhedrin prided himself on his light touch. "I'm a traveling oil gun for hire."

Palmer smiled politely. "Have you worked with my company previously, Fineghan?"

Sanhedrin admitted that he had not experienced the pleasure. "What about you, Mark? How'd you get into the oil business?"

Palmer gestured toward the two men in the front of the Suburban. "We're specialists—Frank, Joe, and me. We have skill sets that oil companies find attractive."

"Former army?" Sanhedrin asked, although he had memorized the personal history of every man and woman in the convoy.

Shafts of golden sunlight as thin as reeds cast shadowed patterns on the hardscrabble road. Joe Marinelli drove the Suburban, while Frank Rollins navigated in the shotgun seat. They might have been clones of Palmer. They wore the same clothes and carried the same equipment, save each sported a mustache, closely trimmed beard, and hair plaited into a single braid, blonde for Rollins and brown for Marinelli.

"Afghanistan, Iraq, Yemen, Somalia, Eritrea, South Sudan," Palmer replied. "You name it, if it's in the shit, we fought there."

"Rangers for Joe and me," Rollins answered.

"Scrolls, not tabs," Marinelli added. "Mark was a Special Forces light bird. Compared to him, Frank and me are cub scouts."

Compliments bored Palmer. "Monsarrat also claimed to be an independent oil consultant. Like you, he worked in Africa, Russia, and the Middle East."

"You know him?" Sanhedrin inquired.

"We met a few times in Abuja and Lagos. Port Harcourt, more often."

"It's a small world, isn't it?"

Palmer recited his sums for Sanhedrin. "In my small world, people who claim to be independent oil consultants are usually CIA spooks. Not that I have anything against spooks, other than they can't be trusted."

"I'm sorry for your hard times," Sanhedrin commiserated, "although I'm not your usual independent oil consultant."

"Roger that," Palmer agreed, "you carrying a Glock on your hip."

"It's just window dressing," Sanhedrin answered modestly. "Did you have a problem cashing my check?"

"Your payment sailed through the bank."

"Is it my couture that bothers you?"

Palmer had attempted to trace the background of Fineghan Scarnagh. His head hurt from banging it against the maze of brick walls he had encountered. "Truthfully, I smell Agency all over you."

Sanhedrin brushed his fingertips across the holster. "My cologne upsets you?"

In the front of the Suburban, Rollins and Marinelli eyed the dirt road for threats while listening hard to the conversation. Each bore scars from prior Langley operations.

"In my experience," Palmer continued, "when the Agency runs an operation, things usually turn south real fast, and the shit splatters everyone involved, save the boys and girls from Langley. So I'm only asking for confirmation."

"Confirmation of what, exactly?"

Palmer exuded patience. "Confirmation this is Langley's operation."

"Me? An Agency spy? Perish the thought!" Sanhedrin protested.

Palmer's distrust of the man next to him increased each time he uttered a sentence. "If you say so, Fineghan. What about Monsarrat?"

"I have no clue," Sanhedrin deadpanned. "We've never met."

In Palmer's weltanschauung, the most dangerous spooks supplied the glibbest answers. "Yet, you're here to ransom him from the rebels."

"Like I said, Mark, I'm a traveling oil gun for hire. I take the shit jobs nobody else wants or can pull off."

"You're also a specialist?"

"In my own area of operations."

Sanhedrin rubbed a smudge of dirt from the toe of his right boot against the driver's seat. "Tell me about Monsarrat."

"He's a big, smart, tough guy."

"It sounds like you were friends."

"I wouldn't say friends," Palmer corrected. "More like professional associates. I was sorry to hear the rebels took him from the oil rig, but until you called my bosses, I had no brief to go after him."

Sanhedrin appreciated men with military backgrounds. They accepted their roles without the *sturm und drang* civilians brought to operations. He prodded the conversation in a new direction. "How many shooters are you holding in reserve?"

"A half dozen with the Blackhawks, a few miles from our destination. If the balloon goes up, they'll ride to our rescue like Valkyries with rotors."

"Let's hope none of us is headed for Valhalla," Sanhedrin sniffed.

Beyond the road, tawny animals skittered in the bush, while colorful birds perched in the canopy's high tree branches. Inside the armored vehicles, shooters checked their weapons and pulled on balaclavas. Doctors and nurses inspected their sedatives and intravenous drips. Drivers steered an erratic conga line through ruts steep enough to snap the chassis of a Suburban. Navigators alternated between 7x50 power binoculars and their naked eyes to sweep the jungle for ambushes.

Across the dirt roads of the Delta, FATA rebels stretched wires at axle height and buried IEDs inside the garbage that rose from the flat, wet land like mountains of refuse. They named the highest mounds after the ruling politicians and generals. Mount Abacha. Babangida Hill. Gowon Peak. Occasionally, rebels poured jerry cans of gasoline onto the mounds and set them afire. The stench of burning garbage carried inland as far as Port Harcourt, and flaming refuse drifted on evening breezes toward the Cameroon border.

In their manifesto, FATA professed to represent the political aspirations of all the weak peoples of the Delta oppressed by the powerful desert tribes, the multinational oil firms, and the National Oil Company. In pidgin communiqués, they claimed to fight against the corruption of the government and to struggle for an equitable redistribution of the vast wealth brought into the country by the industrialized world's unslakeable thirst for its sweet crude. To achieve their goals, they kidnapped foreign oil workers to exchange for ransom.

They operated from a ramshackle compound on the banks of the Bonny River. A hundred yards from their base, Rollins keyed his mic and peered through the darkened Plexiglas windows. "Tangoes with Kalashnikovs at twelve, three, and nine o'clock."

The radio sputtered. "Four tangoes with AKs on our six."

Sagging barbed wire strung between splintered wooden stakes demarked the boundaries of the compound. A tripod-mounted M2 machine gun squatted atop a platform of logs in the middle of the dirt road. Teenage sentries stood behind the crude barricade, weapons cradled in their arms like 7.62 mm wands of death. They watched the passage of the six Suburbans with the baleful eyes of youth.

"Those punks could wreak some kind of havoc with that Ma Deuce, if they maintain it," Marinelli offered. "A .50 caliber demands respect."

"Half starved, three quarters drugged, and strapped to a Chinese AK-47," Rollins agreed. "These kids are already dead. It's only a question of how many people they'll kill before they keel over."

For Sanhedrin, racking jitters announced the proximity of danger. "Are you a deep thinker, Frank?"

"Understand your enemy, sir," Rollins advised. "His strengths, his weaknesses, and, most of all, his motivations."

"What I don't understand," Sanhedrin admitted, "is why Abuja tolerates the rebels."

"It's a question of balance," Palmer explained. "FATA earns serious money from kidnapping foreigners. It makes even more cash selling stolen crude on the black market. When the politicians are satisfied with their kickbacks, they leave the rebels alone. When they're unhappy, they send in the generals. Their army, though, is more corrupt than competent, and the rebels invest their money in small arms, rigid-hull inflatable boats, and shoulder-fired missiles to discourage helicopters from entering their Delta airspace. They're also highly motivated, even if they have no formal training. The two sides fight, no one wins, and the status quo ante returns."

Oil dominated life in the Delta. It stained the sky with a sulfuric miasma and soaked the ground with a gelatinous sludge. When the Suburbans entered the compound, their tires sank into the muck. Palmer, Rollins, and Marinelli donned their balaclavas as the drivers pulled the armored vehicles into a tight circle, like a wagon train in a John Ford movie. A dozen shooters exited the Suburbans and established a box perimeter. Doctors and nurses in crisp uniforms followed.

Sanhedrin waved his slouch hat as he entered the security of the box. "Nathan, today is your liberation day! Fineghan Scarnagh is here to rescue you!"

Across a muddy clearing, Nathan Monsarrat squatted on his hands and knees. Kidnapped four and a half months earlier from an oil rig forty miles offshore in the Gulf of Guinea, the deep-cover operative was now skeletal with dysentery, enervated by malaria, and beset by a gallimaufry of lesser jungle diseases. He weighed sixty pounds less than the day, fifteen years earlier, he exchanged his undergraduate innocence for the arrogance of the Central Intelligence Agency.

Relief topped the chart of his emotions at the arrival of the convoy, followed by anger. Even by the cautious standards of the Agency, his rescue had taken far too long. Disgust concluded the trifecta. In typical Sanhedrin fashion, the immediate action of his boss had been to identify his work name like a débutante presented at a cotillion ball. Still, he offered silent thanks for his arrival. He would have embraced equally a den of Cub Scouts or a klatch of shuffleboard players, if they possessed the firepower to free him from the rebels.

Above Monsarrat stood Blessed, the FATA leader, an Ijaw with biceps the size of footballs and the color of ripe eggplants. Raised tribal markings scarred his face, chest, and thighs. Knotted strips of red and white cloth around his forearms paid homage to Egbesu, who protected warriors from bullets and knives. His right hand rested on his captive's head, as if Monsarrat were a faithful pet, and he pressed a rope leash against his throat like a hangman's noose.

Prior to his capture, Monsarrat had radiated a middle-America respectability. An inch over six feet, he possessed a thick mop of unruly, brown hair and weighed five pounds below two hundred. His unblemished skin shone with health, and his crisp, brown eyes flashed with energy. The muscles of his chest and arms were firm. His six pack rippled. He carried himself as if he were still a three-letter athlete at the university in his native Iowa, football in the fall, basketball in the winter, and baseball in the spring, in the days when jocks proudly wore their padded jackets with the Churchillian "V" sewn over the heart.

Sanhedrin grimaced as his boots squelched through the muck of the clearing. "You've had your fun, Blessed. Get him off his knees."

The Ijaw flicked the fingers of his left hand, and two dozen rebels spread across the clearing, their Chinese weapons pointed at the box perimeter. He inhaled deeply the brimstone of fancy white man's cologne and spat to remove the bitter taste. "I wan' my muny. Yuh gib my muny, I gib yuh *obobo canda*."

A rapacious ego, a sharp intelligence, and a dearth of emotions had carried Sanhedrin to the top of the Central Intelligence Agency. Still, he lusted to join the elite ranks of the Mandarins and planned to launch his gambit by rescuing Monsarrat. His strategy would fail, however, if the deep-cover operative died in the Delta. "I won't tell you again, Blessed. Get him off his knees."

The second-in-command of the rebels, a tall, lean Ibani named Innocence, took the rope leash from Blessed. The scars on his forehead marked him as a member of his clan's ruling family. His bald skull gleamed with sweat, and a sadistic fire burned in his black eyes. Jagged nails capped his long fingers. He jerked the leash hard, pressed his foot against Monsarrat's neck, and grunted a single word like a challenge. "Nuh."

Monsarrat flopped like a gaffed fish. Blood dripped from his throat, where the harsh rope scraped his flesh raw. He tore at the leash, but the Ibani gripped it too tightly.

Blessed grabbed Monsarrat's matted hair and lifted his face from the sand. "Yuh gib my muny, I gib yuh *obobo canda*," he repeated.

"His name is Nathan," Sanhedrin replied. "Not white boy."

Innocence slapped the back of his right hand into his left palm. The sound cracked in the quiet morning. "Nuh, nuh Nathan. *Obobo canda*."

The Ijaw spat again. "I wan' my muny."

Sanhedrin spoke as if offering a cup of tea. "You've made your point, Blessed. You know I won't buy him if he's dead."

"Yuh gib my muny."

Sanhedrin raised his hand. Rollins and Marinelli removed the duffel bags from the Suburban. They crossed the clearing and dropped them before the Ijaw.

Blessed unzipped the canvas bags and withdrew thick stacks of crisp Benjamin Franklins. He waved the bills toward Innocence, a broad smile spread across his huge face. "My muny!"

Innocence dropped the rope. "Dis time, we gib yuh *obobo canda*. Nex' time, *obobo canda* de'd man."

Monsarrat pushed himself upright and stood unsteadily, as if acquiring his land legs. He brushed his hands, removed the rope from his throat, and dabbed the blood with his fingers. He gazed at the two rebels with a clinical dispassion. He wanted to strangle them and watch saliva bubble on their lips as the breath escaped their lungs. He wanted to enjoy his reflection in their black eyes as death took them.

When he spoke, his voice rasped. "I'm going to kill both of you, very slowly, with my fingers around your throats."

"Not another word, Nathan," warned Sanhedrin.

Monsarrat assayed his clean clothes and scrubbed skin, as if he were a ghost and the rescue an elaborate hoax. "Rosalinda's at the hut, Felix. We have to take her with us."

Sanhedrin turned to the two shooters. "Get him to the vehicles."

Rollins and Marinelli carried the protesting Monsarrat across the clearing. Sanhedrin led them into the box and gestured for the medical team. "Take good care of him, Doc. I need him in the office stat."

"Forget the damn doctor, Felix," Monsarrat insisted. "You have to find Rosalinda. I won't leave her here."

"I don't know who you mean, old buddy, but we only have room for one passenger on this trip."

"Don't be obtuse," he snarled. "Rosalinda Santiago is the nurse from the oil rig. She saved my life."

"We'll come back for her," Sanhedrin promised. His words rang as falsely as a wooden nickel. "I only paid for one hostage today, and our friends don't seem the types to offer a two-for-one special."

Despite his weakness, Monsarrat twisted free from the two shooters. "You ordered me to visit the rig, Felix. I wouldn't have been stuck in the middle of the Gulf of Guinea if it hadn't been for you, and I would have died in this shithole if it hadn't been for Rosalinda, so I'm not leaving her."

On the abbreviated ladder of Sanhedrin's virtues, patience occupied a low rung. "A lot of people dedicated a lot of time and a lot of money to arrange this little escape. No arguments, Nathan. You're coming with us."

Two nurses gripped Monsarrat's wrists, and a doctor slid a needle into his arm. "It's Lorazepam, son. You'll sleep just fine."

Monsarrat sagged as the intramuscular injection entered his bloodstream. The nurses led him to one of the two Suburbans outfitted for the medical team and hoisted him onto the rear bench.

Sanhedrin's bony fingers tapped his watch. "How long before he needs another shot of that junk, Mark?"

"A few hours, but he's very weak, so the one injection may be good for your entire flight home."

Sanhedrin considered his cover story. "I heard he's a stubborn son of a bitch. Four and a half months with these FATA assholes was probably just time out for him."

Palmer had observed the familiarity of the interactions between Monsarrat and the man he knew as Fineghan Scarnagh with a sense of satisfaction. They definitely shared history, and he was sure the Agency played a large role in their lives. "Hard to see how being a guest of the rebels could be pleasurable for anyone."

Sanhedrin noted he had maintained silence during the trade. "No words of greeting for your professional associate?"

"Just following your orders. Your money for our eternal silence."

"The longer I work with you, Mark, the more I like you."

Eighteen weeks earlier, on Easter Sunday morning, FATA rebels in three fast, rigid-hull, inflatable boats had sped from the mouth of the Bonny River into the Gulf of Guinea. Beneath a cloudless sky, the dual diesel engines of each thirty-six foot RHIB, muffled and capable of fifty knots, quickly covered the forty miles to the oil rig. The rebels fired the M60 machine guns across the placid waters for entertainment, until they exhausted the ammunition.

While the galut of European rig managers, drillers, derrick hands, and roughnecks, plus a baker's dozen Asian galley hands, and a nurse attended the Sunday church service in the rig's chapel, the rebels swarmed the ladders. On the upper platform, they dispatched the security guards. Innocence and half the force raided the stores for food and supplies. Blessed and the remainder of the rebels burst into the chapel. The giant Ijaw compared each European to a five-by-seven-inch photograph. When none of the white faces matched the picture in his hand, he posted two rebels as guards and stormed from the chapel to search the rig.

An unobservant man, Monsarrat had avoided the service in favor of an extra cup of coffee in the mess. When the rebels assaulted the platform, laughing, yelling, and firing AK-47 rounds, he checked his Tag Heuer watch and cursed his laxity. Three hours remained until his helicopter rendezvous, but he could not summon the pilot. His cell phone sat atop the bunk in his cabin, three hundred feet across the exposed platform. Also in the cabin, inside the ditty bag he had carried from Abuja for the weekend visit, was his Glock 30 pistol.

In lieu of portholes, the mess offered pastel murals of pink clouds in blue skies above a cerulean ocean laced with white breakers. With only a single hatch for access and egress, the rectangular room provided fewer escape options than a prison cell on Alcatraz Island. Monsarrat closed his eyes. In his mind, he scanned the rig. The open platform offered no place to hide, so reaching his room undetected was out of the question. Outside the mess, the gangway ran in two directions. Leeward led to the platform. Windward ended sixty feet further at an emergency ladder that descended to the structure's small boat berth, a grid of steel planks extending twenty feet into the Gulf of Guinea.

He opened his eyes. In the Hobson's choice between the trigger-happy attackers on the platform or the requiem sharks in the warm waters of the Gulf, he preferred the pelagic killers. If the heavens smiled upon him, he could steal one of the boats that had ferried the attackers to the rig. He crossed the mess and pushed open the hatch, willing silence upon the heavy door. He stepped into the gangway, and the wooden stock of an AK-47 crashed into his forehead.

The rebels stripped Monsarrat of his possessions and dragged him, bleeding and unconscious, to the platform. Blessed ripped off his shirt and wiped the blood from his swollen face. He held the picture next to him and chortled. The rebels carried him to the chapel, laid him on a pew, and bound his hands to his ankles with thick strands of rope.

With Monsarrat secured, they lashed the Europeans together with a long rope. A separate rope bound the Asians. They led their captives from the chapel to the boats. In their wake, they half carried, half dragged the semi-conscious Monsarrat. At the berth, they tossed the Europeans over the gunnels into the hull of the first boat. They dumped the Asians into the second RHIB. Innocence supervised the loading of the pilfered goods into the third RIHB. He slapped Monsarrat conscious, pressed the muzzle of AK-47 against his forehead, and barked orders in pidgin. Rebels threw Monsarrat over the gunnel of the third boat, among boxes of food, cases of water and beer, and packages of toilet paper and towels.

Blessed arrived moments later, pulling a Filipina by her black hair with his right hand. He tossed her into the boat and dropped the photograph onto Monsarrat's chest. "*Oyinbo*, yuh dun lib' now wit' de nurse wuman."

In the compound, Blessed forced Monsarrat onto his hands and knees and exchanged his bonds for a leash. Each morning, as the tankers berthed in the Bonny River estuary filled their holds with light, sweet crude, the rebels led him around the compound like an unloved pet. The harsh rope burned his neck and throat, while his hands and knees bled into the muck. At noon, he ate the day's single meal, pounded yam and cassava, from the ground like a Delta dog. At night, he slept inside a rancid thatch hut.

To keep track of the days, he devised a simple calendar, each morning inserting a bent stalk of straw into a corner of the thatch hut. To keep his mind sharp, he recalled statistics of favorite baseball teams. He pictured the crystalline waters of Hawaiian beaches and New Hampshire mountains spackled with fragrant wildflowers. Telepathically, he urged his boss, Felix Sanhedrin, to launch a rescue mission. Unwilling to depend upon Sanhedrin, he prayed for divine intervention, to rise like Samson in the Temple of Dagon, to rip asunder his rope bonds and smite Blessed with the jawbone of Innocence.

Only Monsarrat's desires challenged the leadership of Blessed. The Ijaw demanded absolute compliance from the rebels. His initiation into FATA of the teenaged boys and girls stolen from Delta villages began at dawn and ended at dusk in a savage ceremony of rape. Monsarrat, forced to attend the obscene rites, understood why the rebels embraced cruelty like a religion. Inflicting pain onto their victims was retribution. It was a salve for their own sufferings.

When the European oil companies ransomed their skilled workers, Blessed shook with laughter, but when the governments of the impoverished Asian countries abandoned their citizens, he ranted threats of vengeance. Shortly after the final European departed the compound, he dragged his trophy prisoner to the clearing. The rebel leader placed his thumbs on Monsarrat's cheekbones and his index fingers on his suborbital ridge, then pressed until his eyes bulged. "*Obobo canda.* Yuh wutch now. *Obobo canda* dun be gud boy now."

He passed the leash to a young rebel. She appeared no older than twelve. Her flat, brown eyes were deep holes. They radiated the vacuity of a corpse.

The dozen remaining captives kneeled in the clearing. Filthy rags gagged their mouths, and the ubiquitous thick ropes bound their wrists and ankles. The thirteenth Asian, the Filipina nurse, sat apart. Blessed strode across the clearing and ripped her stained uniform from her brown body as if peeling skin from a banana. He raped her quickly before his fighters and the condemned Asians, as if the violent act were a chore to finish before lunch. When finished, he spit on his hands and washed himself as the rebels fired their weapons into the air. Naked, the nurse shivered, her arms wrapped modestly around her small body.

Monsarrat pulled the rope from the hands of the young rebel. He crossed the clearing, removed his tattered shirt, and wrapped it around the Filipina, holding her tightly until Innocence pressed the muzzle of an AK-47 against his temple. "Dis time, *oyinbo*, yuh live. Nex' time, I kill yuh de'd."

He yanked the rope tight against Monsarrat's throat and dragged him to the young rebel fighter. He slapped her face with the back of his hand. "Yuh wutch gud now, gurl. Nex' time, yuh nuh watch, I kill yuh."

Blessed approached the line of captives. The machete in his mammoth hands appeared as inconsequential as a plastic condiment sword, but when he brought the sharp edge of the jungle knife down upon the limbs of the first Asian, arms tumbled and legs sputtered like brown and red Catherine wheels against the iron sun. Monsarrat screamed for Blessed to stop, but the young girl jerked the leash hard against his throat.

Explosions of AK-47 rounds signaled the approval of the rebels. Blessed passed the bloody machete to his deputy. Innocence moved with a feline grace toward the second Asian and quartered him with an exact series of blows. The rebels again fired their weapons. Blessed passed the jungle knife from one young fighter to the next, applauding as they hacked the remaining Asians to offal.

When the feral dogs descended upon the piles of flesh and bones, Innocence hauled Monsarrat to join them. He forced him to squat on his haunches. "*Oyinbo*, yuh dun eat now wit' de dogs."

Monsarrat pulled at the rope leash until he could gasp a few words. "Go fuck yourself, asshole."

The rebel deputy gouged a bloody furrow across Monsarrat's left cheek with his long, jagged nails. He ordered the rebels to beat him for his indolence, and they complied with youthful abandon. Monsarrat absorbed the bashing of AK-47 butts against his head and the kicks delivered to his stomach and groin, until he was certain the next strike would stop his heart or explode his head.

Blessed intervened before the final blow. The FATA leader slung him over his broad shoulder, whispering soothing salves. "*Obobo canda*. How yuh manage? *Obobo canda*, suffah man. *Obobo canda*, sojah man."

At the hut, he removed the Filipina's rope leash from the stake and dragged her inside. "Nurse wuman yuh dun care fuh muy *oyinbo* now."

The first shivering wave of malaria struck Monsarrat not long after the feral dogs dragged off the remains of the Asians. His eyeballs swam in pools of blood, and his internal organs swelled. Anemia weakened him, and jaundice yellowed him. He shook, as if possessed by the trickster Eshu.

Rosalinda Santiago saved him.

The Filipina had signed a contract to serve on the rig in the Gulf of Guinea for two years, after graduating at the top of her class from a prestigious Manila nursing school. The company paid more in one month than she could earn in twelve working for a Manila hospital, and as the eldest child of her family, she bore the responsibility of caring for her aged parents and younger siblings. In her mid-twenties, she stood five feet tall and wore a silver Saint Agatha medal around her neck. Her black hair was thick. Her brown eyes were shaped like almonds. Her nose was flat, and her lips curled upwards, as if she were considering a particularly nasty joke. She spoke with a strong Batangas accent.

Blessed brought small bottles of tonic water to break Monsarrat's fevers, their yellow labels the color of his skin. He crooned and pried open his jaws.

Rosalinda stopped him. In her sing-song accent, she addressed the FATA leader like a recalcitrant child. "He needs real medicine, not bubbly water, you fool. Do you want him to die?"

He threw her against the thatch wall. "Nurse wuman, yuh nuh tawk, yuh dun care fuh muy *oyinbo*."

Undaunted, she demanded, "Give me paper and a pencil."

When the writing instruments arrived, she listed a dozen items in her bold penmanship. "I don't care if you can't read. Take this list to a pharmacy in Port Harcourt. Bring me the medicines immediately, or this man will die before the sun sets tomorrow."

In the night, old women from Delta villages entered the hut to bath the foul secretions from Monsarrat's body with viscous water. Like withered crows, they muttered imprecations in a cackling patois of sorcery.

Rosalinda chased them away and yelled for Blessed. "Keep those witches away from him, and bring me the medicines!"

In reply, he knocked her to the ground and stormed from the hut. He returned before dawn the next morning with a brightly colored plastic bag from a Port Harcourt pharmacy. "Yuh dun kill suffa man, nurse wuman, I dun kill yuh."

The bond between the two captives grew stronger as Rosalinda nursed him through the bout of malaria and healed him after his beatings at the hands of Blessed and Innocence. For his part, Monsarrat protected the Filipina with a ferocity rivaling a father's defense of his daughter. Nights, when she sobbed as if the deluge of her tears could create a flood to carry her home, he comforted her with false promises. Until the morning of his rescue, when Blessed dragged him to the clearing while Innocence bound her wrists and ankles to a pipe outside the thatch hut with lengths of rope.

Palmer watched the door of the Suburban close behind the unresisting Monsarrat. He signaled for his shooters to return to their vehicles, and, in reverse order from their arrival, the drivers broke the circle and drove toward the compound's exit.

Settled again inside the second Suburban, Sanhedrin patted Palmer on the knee with an avuncular familiarity. "I hope we have the opportunity to cooperate again."

Ignored by the rebels, the convoy passed the crude, log barricade and turned away from the river. Deep in the Delta jungle, smoke from cooking fires rose in curlicues. Palmer glanced at his watch. "Twenty minutes until the airfield."

"You and your boys did outstanding work this morning."

"I'm happy Monsarrat is a free man again."

Like most very successful, highly egocentric men, Sanhedrin viewed the world through the filter of his own disdain. "Of course, you'll be even happier when the second half of my payment arrives in your bank account tomorrow morning."

During his military career, Palmer had served under commanding officers as calloused as old warts, but had never met a man like the one seated next to him. "Monsarrat called you Felix. More than once."

"What's that, Mark?"

"When Monsarrat said that he wouldn't leave without the nurse, he called you Felix. Not Fineghan."

"Perhaps you misheard?"

"Not much chance of that."

"Maybe Monsarrat misspoke. He is, after all, delirious."

Palmer snapped his words like a whip. "Of course, Fineghan. He's delirious."

"Of course," Sanhedrin agreed.

Three miles to the west, in a circular clearing beneath the canopy, six shooters protected two Blackhawks marked by large, red crosses against white backgrounds and the livery of the oil services company. The rotors beat angry clouds of jungle dirt. The medical team ferried Monsarrat from the Suburban to the helicopters, and the crew hoisted him into the hold of the lead dustoff. Sanhedrin, Palmer, a doctor, and two nurses joined him, while the six shooters mounted the second Blackhawk.

Sanhedrin sat in a webbed seat. He secured the four-point safety harness and inserted an orange and green foam plug into each ear. "You oil wallahs live well on the plantation, Mark. You have the best toys money can buy."

The lead pilot waited for the Suburbans to depart the clearing, then lifted the Blackhawk, nose downward, from the ground. The vibration of the airframe shook Monsarrat awake. His eyes focused upon a nurse with a smile as starched as her uniform. He flashed the victory sign. When he tried to speak, his voice croaked. "Am I going home?"

She bent to hear him better as she cleaned his wounded hands and dabbed salve onto the rope burns. "All the way to Virginia, dearest."

"Rosalinda, too?"

Her voice sounded faint and willowy to Monsarrat, as if carried beyond the penumbra of his hearing by a slow breeze. He reached for her words, but they slipped through his fingers, and he slept again.

At the private airfield, Palmer delivered his promise of an uncomplicated departure. The Blackhawks touched down at the far end of the runway, near a Gulfstream 650 marked by livery identical to the helicopters. "Your people in Virginia will remove Monsarrat from the plane and fuss with the feds. My people will refuel and return home."

They shook hands. "Should I be surprised if we run into each other again?"

"Like you said, Mark, it's a small world," Sanhedrin answered.

Returned to the United States and the embrace of twenty-first century medical care, Monsarrat's body slowly recovered from the Delta ordeal, although he could not vouch for his mind. Toward the end of his recuperation in Virginia's horse country, the Agency sent Felix Sanhedrin to him.

He wore a gold cotton turtleneck and a silk Nehru jacket the color of a tropical sunset. His summer wool slacks were sharply creased. Birkenstock sandals adorned his feet. A bejeweled medallion on a sterling silver chain rested above his breastbone. "The Mandarins salute you and greet you," he began. He might have been addressing Rome's senators from the steps of the Forum. "They appreciate your sacrifices and offer you whatever assignment you choose, within reason, of course. Specifically, after your recuperation, you can remain at Langley with full honors and ride a desk, or you can continue your oil analyst cover and return to the field. Africa, the Persian Gulf, Russia, South America, it's your choice."

Monsarrat admired Sanhedrin's equanimity as much as his courage in couture, but he countered with a third option. "Thank the Mandarins for me, Felix, but tell them I choose retirement. I want a full pension and a generous medical disability."

"You sure, old buddy? You could ride this incident all the way into the senior ranks of the Agency."

"I want a new career, too. Something stimulating but not at all dangerous."

"Anything specific, Nathan?"

Monsarrat felt the pressure swell behind his eyes, as it often did when speaking with his boss. "I'll get back to you."

Before departing, Sanhedrin tapped Monsarrat's cheek. "It's healing nicely, Nathan. Very distinguished, like you fought a duel to protect the honor of a young maiden."

More pleasant were the Saturday visits of Abigail Houghton, office colleague and secretary to Felix Sanhedrin. Monsarrat had long considered Abby a fellow conspirator against the machinations of their mutual boss, but during his recovery in the Virginia countryside, their relationship evolved from colleagues to friends and, with the blessings of the medical staff, to lovers. He chose Abby as his Beatrice, and he confessed his guilt at abandoning Rosalinda in the Delta to her.

Two years younger and six inches shorter than Monsarrat, her sharp cheekbones and the slight tilt of her eyes proclaimed her Tartar heritage. Her cornflower eyes radiated energy. Deep dimples accented her peaches-and-cream complexion, and her brilliant smile exploded white between her lush, red lips. She wore her blonde hair in a plait that fell between her shoulder blades. Tennis sculpted her body with hard muscles. She had been married for ten months to a Kiowa pilot, whose bird had gone down in a sandstorm fifteen miles from Ali Al Saleem Air Base, the tent stippled, arid rock north of Kuwait City that had served as the gateway to the wars in Iraq. She no longer wore her wedding band.

"Felix thinks you should stay with the Agency," she stated.

"Felix needs someone to empty his inbox, even from halfway around the world," he replied. "He's too busy climbing the ladder of success to take care of business."

"He says you have a bright future with the Agency."

"Working with Felix, my future has a very short shelf life."

"You could work for someone else, in another office."

His head ached. "I want out, Abby. I want my life back."

"I'm going to miss you, Nathan."

Monsarrat had always relied on his paranoia to illuminate the right path. In the Virginia countryside, he discovered inspiration. "Quit the Agency and come with me, Abby. We could move somewhere warm. No more winters. No more traffic jams. We'll play tennis year-round."

She stroked his face. Her cool fingers lingered on his furrowed cheek. "I believe you're feverish, baby. You can't leave the Agency. Langley is in your blood."

He closed his eyes and felt his head sink into the soft pillow. "If I stay with the Agency, my blood's going to end up all over the walls of some foreign shithole."

"Sleep, baby. You're just tired."

The following week, the Mandarins once more dispatched Sanhedrin to the Virginia horse country. He wore a white Oxford shirt open at the neck, a double-breasted, navy-blue blazer, grey slacks, and cordovan penny loafers without socks. He oozed modesty. "For your retirement package, Nathan, I've arranged a position in the oil industry. Ridiculous salary, generous expense account, first-class travel, exotic hookers."

Monsarrat didn't trust his former employers. Most of all, he suspected Sanhedrin guilty of deceit, the greatest of the Agency's multitude of venial and mortal sins. He didn't want to be coerced into performing his patriotic duty a few years down the road. "I want something collegiate, Felix. A university professor. Maybe economics. Or political science. Nothing esoteric."

"No can do, old buddy. You don't possess the academic skill set to fulfill the role."

Most of Monsarrat's strength had returned. He felt ready to spar with his soon-to-be former boss. "You're the magician. You can do it."

Sanhedrin patted his hand. "I'll look into it, Nathan."

Monsarrat grabbed his bony wrist. "I want you to tell me what happened to Rosalinda."

Sanhedrin shirked physical contact. He tried to free his hand, but Monsarrat held him tightly. "Who's Rosalinda, old buddy?"

Monsarrat squeezed harder. "You promised me in the Delta that you'd get her away from Blessed and his psychopaths."

Sanhedrin tapped Monsarrat's hand. "I have no recollection of that conversation, old buddy. Perhaps you imagined it? After all, you were feverish."

Monsarrat pulled him closer. "I would have been dead if she hadn't taken care of me. You have to ransom her. I'll pay."

"Tell me again, Nathan. Who is she?"

Monsarrat released him. Sanhedrin upset was less likely to be helpful than Sanhedrin happy. "Her name is Rosalinda Santiago. She was the nurse on the oil rig. She kept me alive in the Delta. I can't abandon her, Felix. I owe her."

"I understand, old buddy. It's a point of honor." He rubbed his hand. "I'll see what I can find out."

"You have to move fast. She won't last much longer, not as a prisoner of FATA."

"I'll see what I can do, old buddy."

The following day Sanhedrin wore a grey suit with pinstripes. The gold chain of a watch fob stretched across his vest. "I asked a contact in Malacañan Palace to look into your nurse. I'm afraid he gave me some unpleasant news."

Monsarrat felt his chest constrict. "Tell it, Felix."

"Manila has written off all the Filipinos on the oil rig, including your friend, Rosalinda."

"Easier for Manila to claim she's dead than to push for her release," Monsarrat grumbled. "Is there proof?"

Sanhedrin was a master in question avoidance. "I asked my contact at our embassy in Abuja to investigate. He'll get back to me soon."

"Pressure him. You know what our pen pushers are like when they go overseas."

"You need to be patient, old buddy."

"Don't lecture me on patience, Felix. I spent eighteen weeks with those sadistic FATA sons of bitches. One hundred and twenty-six days on my hands and knees in the Delta, while you attended diplomatic receptions in Georgetown."

"Negotiating with illiterate freedom fighters offers unique challenges," Sanhedrin stated. He passed Monsarrat a blue plastic folder. "Now for some happier developments, old buddy. Felix has come through for you yet again. Sign on the dotted line. I have to admit, I'll miss working with you."

Monsarrat suspected he would hear from him as soon as he needed a favor. "Seriously, Felix? You can't do better than Greylock College? It's a second-tier liberal arts college in the middle of the Berkshires."

Sanhedrin shrugged. "The oil job is still open, old buddy."

Monsarrat scribbled his signature across dotted lines and joined the administrative ranks of Greylock College as Dean of Undergraduate Studies, a still-young man who suffered from headaches, depression, malaria, and guilt.

Weeks later, on the morning of the Columbus Day holiday, he left a sleeping Abby to meet Sanhedrin in a Dupont Circle café. Autumn had arrived in the District of Columbia. He wore a sweatshirt from the college. Sanhedrin sported a tweed jacket with elbow patches and a tartan deerstalker. They sat at a table by a window in the rear of the café that afforded both a clear view of the entrance.

Sanhedrin appeared rueful, but his manner was ruthless. "My contact in Abuja went the extra mile and kidnapped one of the FATA rebels. As soon as the black hood dropped over his head, the little punk pissed his pants. Then he started talking."

Monsarrat sipped his coffee. "Don't sugar coat it, Felix."

"Blessed killed Rosalinda fifteen minutes after the convoy departed the compound. I'm sorry about the sad news, old buddy, but at least you have closure."

The report confirmed Monsarrat's worst fears. "You're confident the intel's accurate? Your contact isn't trying to get you off his back?"

Sanhedrin tasked. "You haven't been gone that long, Nathan. Even the probationers at the Farm know better than to feed me bullshit."

He pressed his fingers against his forehead, as if his head ached, to prevent Sanhedrin from noticing the liquid welling in the eyes. He remembered the Filipina's courage and her despair, her loyalty and her loneliness. He remembered her rape and how she kept him alive in the Delta. "I should've taken her with me."

Sanhedrin spoke as if admonishing a slow staffer. "You were my mandate. No one else. You know it's how we work."

His fist banged against the table. "It's not how I work. She saved my life, and I deserted her. I'm no better than you."

Sanhedrin stood and picked up the tartan deerstalker. "I respect your pain, old buddy, but don't bite the hand that pulled you out of the Delta. Make your peace. Move on."

Only the passage of time, aided by Abby's ministrations, lessened the weight of his guilt. As he trained himself to relax, he came to appreciate the tolerance of the college and learned to accept his neighbors, colleagues, and students. Like a burn victim accepting a graft of skin, he gradually adapted to the persona of Dean Monsarrat. Yet, he could shed his remorse no easier than a lapsed Catholic could relinquish his catechism.

II. BLESSED

AN HOURGLASS OF SAND

Nathan Monsarrat had not planned to tip his hourglass of sand at Greylock College in western Massachusetts. A week beyond his fortieth birthday, he sat in his third-floor corner office and stared at the neat stacks of files that Doris Lambert, his secretary, had placed on the rosewood desk earlier in the morning. Outside his windows the Berkshire kingdom blazed with the autumnal colors of oak, maple, and birch leaves. The campus reminded him of his native Iowa, albeit more liberal than pastoral.

Campbell Hall, the college's granite crown of higher education, housed the administrative functions of the college, including the Office of the Dean of Undergraduate Studies, the position Monsarrat had occupied since leaving the Central Intelligence Agency two years earlier. He enjoyed his new life in academia, despite the often infuriating faculty meetings and the constant griping of his colleagues, who always capitalized on opportunities to take offense at slights, either real or imagined, but always insignificant.

The door to his office remained open to staff and students. Publicly, he professed a policy of accessibility. Privately, enclosed spaces poked him with hot needles of claustrophobia. Although he had regained his health and weight, the irrational constrictions along with occasional bouts of malaria offered reminders of his Delta imprisonment. He called through the open space. "Doris, what time does the Disciplinary Committee meet?"

In response, she engaged the intercom. Doris embraced decorum. "From two until four, Dean. In the Conference Room. It's your last appointment of the day."

"Do you have the file?"

"I put it on your desk this morning. It's the blue, plastic folder with the red flag on the tab in the upper left corner of your desk, exactly where you requested it."

Monsarrat imagined her head arcing like a vigorous scythe. She undertook her actions with bravura. "Do I have a lunch appointment, Doris?"

He heard a faint trace of exasperation in her reply. "Your schedule is open. Would you like me to reserve a table at the Faculty Lounge for you?"

A walk in the bracing autumn air might stimulate his appetite. He might chance upon a professor preparing an upcoming lecture, or a student studying for an exam. He could exercise at the gym. He really wanted a drink, despite the fine, crimson worms of early dissipation that had begun to mar his features like thin webs of shame. He believed he had earned his fondness for bourbon. "No, thank you. I'll grab a sandwich at the Student Center."

"As you wish, Dean," she replied and clicked off the intercom.

A compendium of undergraduate antics filled the Disciplinary Committee folder. A freshman accused of beating his roommate for leaving his soiled clothes on the floor. A senior apprehended shoplifting CDs from a local music store. A sophomore caught defacing library walls with anti-war graffiti. A junior charged with sexually harassing his French III instructor. An entrepreneurial student alleged to have imported a hooker from Springfield to ply her trade in his dormitory room.

He closed the folder and studied the Tag Heuer on his left wrist, a replacement for the watch stolen by the FATA rebels. Two hours until lunch. He reopened the folder. A case of plagiarism. An incident of cheating on a proctored test. A dozen complaints of drunken behavior. An equal number of complaints for violations of quiet hours in the dormitories. So many incidents for such a small college. Monsarrat believed that the geographic isolation of the students contributed to the plethora of cases.

He closed the file again and glanced at his gym bag in the corner of the office. The delicate chirping of the beige telephone on his desk annoyed him. On his first day at the college, he had requested a telephone with a more robust ring but still awaited its delivery.

He picked up the receiver. "Yes, Doris? What is it?"

"A caller on your private extension, Dean. Would you like to speak with him?"

Monsarrat heard the peeve in her voice. She offended easily. He had considered firing her, but the talent pool in the Berkshires was thin, and the community of secretaries rarely forgave assaults upon its ranks. "Who is it? Professor? Student?"

"His name is Franklin Seleucid from the Educational Placement Services in Boston. He'd like to speak with you about an African student interested in the college."

He shuddered as she spoke the given and family names, chilled by the "F" and "S," as if an ill wind had blown from the hilltops. "How does he have my private number?"

"I'm sure I don't know, Dean. If you speak with him, you can ask him directly."

Early in his tenure, Monsarrat had attempted to discern the thin line separating flippant Doris from practical Doris, but the border was porous, and he had abandoned the effort. "Put him through."

He heard the line click as she made the transfer. In a voice resplendent with bonhomie, he announced, "Good morning. Dean Monsarrat speaking."

"Good morning to you, Dean Monsarrat. Franklin Seleucid from the Educational Placement Services in Boston here. Thank you for taking my call."

Monsarrat had always suspected that Sanhedrin, like a dormant disease, would one day infect his new life. "It's been a long time, Felix. You're still on the side of angels?"

One hundred miles to the east, Sanhedrin replied, "It's Franklin, Dean."

Felix Sanhedrin was ten years older than Monsarrat, six inches shorter, fifty pounds lighter, and one thousand percent more Machiavellian. If the Lord had smiled upon Sanhedrin only once, it was to grant him the gift of arrogance. Monsarrat had worked diligently to remain on the good side of his former boss. He hadn't coveted Sanhedrin's long knives protruding from his back.

No matter under which name Sanhedrin traveled, Monsarrat considered him a mercury blob. The man was incapable, through constitution or training, of providing definition. A conversation with Sanhedrin was an exercise in Delphic obscurity. "My apologies, Franklin. How may I help you?"

"We're a new company, very small and very selective, an elite agency you won't forget, once you work with us. We provide clean solutions to oily situations," he explained. "We specialize in placing highly motivated students from Africa in small, liberal arts colleges throughout New England. Our clients are the sons and daughters of wealthy families."

He allowed the dean to grasp the fiscal importance of his statement. "We advise our clients on the best placement for their academic experiences in the United States. We have an exemplary prospect who specifically requested to study at Greylock College. In fact, he insists that he will attend no other school. I'd like to discuss his placement with you. Are you free for lunch tomorrow?"

Monsarrat shifted the receiver between his hands, as if weighing the pros and cons of accepting the invitation. On the obverse, the five hundred miles separating the college from the Agency provided a barely acceptable buffer zone from his former boss. On the reverse, it always proved safer to confront Sanhedrin than to allow him to slink through the shadows, like a hot-breathed, bony assassin. "I could meet you for lunch at 1:00 p.m. tomorrow."

"Tomorrow at 1:00 p.m. Should we meet on campus?"

Monsarrat wanted to keep Sanhedrin as far from his academic colleagues as possible. Complications trailed him like the dirty train of a bridal gown. "Why don't we meet in town? There's an excellent Lebanese restaurant called Sidon on the corner of Main and Pine Streets. You can park your car in the public lot."

"I'm sure you'll be excited by my student, Dean. He presents an excellent opportunity. Who knows? He may only be our first venture together."

"Until tomorrow, Mr. Seleucid."

He dropped the phone into its cradle, pressed the intercom, and passed the information to Doris to enter into the office's digital calendar. He opened the Disciplinary Committee file. A moment later, he closed it.

He pressed the intercom again. "I'm taking an early lunch."

"Very well, Dean."

Monsarrat imagined her glower. Doris, he decided, was efficient but cold-blooded. She would get along well with Sanhedrin.

He picked up his gym bag and strode out of the office. Crossing the campus, he greeted colleagues and students. Holbrooke Gymnasium, a two-story box of red brick and tall, glass windows, housed a well-equipped gym. In the faculty locker room, he hung his academic suit in his locker, changed into exercise clothes, and entered the weight room. He worked the free weights, more reps with lighter loads to lengthen the muscles, thirty-pound dumbbell curls, a dozen lifts with his right arm, followed by a dozen lifts with the left arm. He switched focus from biceps to triceps and supplemented the iron with sit-ups and push-ups. Monsarrat worked out with an exactitude lacking in other areas of his life.

He considered his brief conversation with Sanhedrin. His former boss might be enjoying a second career in academia in eastern Massachusetts vice his own reinvention in the western hills of the state, but he didn't believe in coincidences. Neither could he envision Sanhedrin, a grasping man with tentacles reaching into every aspect of the oil industry, working in such an anodyne venture as placing foreign students in American colleges. He doubted there could be enough money involved to interest him, although as president of Educational Placement Services he could conduct Agency business under the cover of academic activities, open accounts in foreign lands with tolerant banking laws, and use the front company to launder funds. The possibilities for a man of Sanhedrin's illicit talents were endless.

Monsarrat switched out the dumbbells for a one-hundred-pound barbell. The iron felt light in his hands. When he doubled the disks, the heavier weight released his paranoia. He welcomed its prickly return. A healthy measure helped his critical thinking. The sweet spot was to maintain the balance between sharp analysis and cold fear.

He spread a towel on the floor. If Sanhedrin hoped to impose upon his knowledge of Africa, he would throw him through the door of the restaurant. Images of Blessed, his machete and rope leash and talismans and tribal scars, haunted him like the shades of dispatched memories demanding final resolution. He recalled Innocence, the feral dogs, and the tumbling limbs of the Asians. He remembered Rosalinda holding his head in her hands as he shook with malarial fevers.

He crunched his rectus abdominus muscles with increased intensity. After the two hundredth repetition, he tucked his chin onto his knees and breathed deeply. He flipped onto his stomach and stiffened his arms. The line of his back formed a smooth incline. He bent his elbows parallel to the floor, so the square of his chin rested centimeters off the ground. He finished one hundred push-ups, flipped onto his back, and began the second of his six sets of sit-ups and push-ups.

He walked to the treadmill, set the timer for forty-five minutes, and left the incline flat. During the first minutes, he jogged slowly, gradually increasing speed and the degree of incline. Running purified him, as if he were a penitent burning Africa from his marrow, one gorgonian memory at a time.

Recuperating in Virginia, Monsarrat had asked his former boss why he needed four and a half months to finalize his release. Sanhedrin's reply, that he used the time to collect intelligence on FATA, a group that posed a threat to the oil interests of the Agency, had upset him. When he objected to being used as an opportunity, Sanhedrin reminded him that they were both soldiers in the army of Langley.

"Except I fought the war in the slime and the shit, while you wore thousand-dollar suits and ate lunches with oil executives at The Hay-Adams."

Sanhedrin replied with an infuriating insouciance. "Each of us fights with the gifts the good Lord bestowed upon him. My gifts are cerebral. Yours are physical."

Monsarrat had wanted to physically leap from his bed and throttle him. He was surprised that the urge still remained strong.

The treadmill's timer chirped. The revolving belt slowed to the pace of a slow jog, and the degree of incline flattened. The timer chirped a second time, and the belt halted its revolutions. Monsarrat breathed deeply. Sweat poured from his body. His heart pounded. His muscles throbbed. He felt powerful.

"You're making the rest of us look bad, Nathan. How are we supposed to impress the coeds when you're doing your shtick?"

"Good to see you, Marty," Monsarrat said. "Canceling your classes again?"

George Martins stood four inches taller than five feet, but carried himself like a heavyweight boxer. He had bulked his chest and shoulders and neck, which created an image of imbalance upon his stalk legs. When not in the gym, he gravitated toward corduroy jackets and pants. He wore his hair in a bristle cut and, keeping with the vintage image, wore a neat mustache and beard. His wife, a small woman with a walnut pageboy haircut, taught first grade at the local elementary school. Monsarrat had met her at a college party. She stood by her husband's side, nodding and smiling at his witticisms. She glanced at her watch often. She regularly looked over her left shoulder toward the foyer of the house, as if she hoped for a rescue.

An associate professor of English, Martins possessed an arcane expertise on John Steinbeck. He served on the Disciplinary Committee and usually voted with Monsarrat, an indication that they followed the same ideological lines, or that he simply preferred to cast his vote with the highest ranking person in the room, a proven strategy for advancing through the academic ranks.

"I am steeling my sympathetic tendencies against the pleas of the not-yet-educated," Martins answered. "Honestly, we have too many cases to cover in only two hours. Either we stop busting so many little twerps, or we add more time to the schedule."

Monsarrat was curious. "Which do you suggest, Marty?"

Martins warmed to his topic. "Of course, there is a third way, a standing disciplinary committee. The faculty members would serve for a semester, without any teaching responsibilities. Members could not leave for their end of semester vacations until the dockets had been cleared. Abracadabra! No more backlogs."

Monsarrat thought the proposal had merit but knew it would never be approved. The small college could not dedicate so many of its faculty to pursuits beyond classroom instruction. He suspected that Martins had canvassed the other members of the committee and received their support before tossing out the idea as a hybrid, half in jest, half in earnest. "A third way, Marty? Shades of Vietnam? Are you shooting for a position in the Political Science Department?"

"I'm resuscitating discredited theorems from past generations as recycled weapons in the current culture wars, until they are once again tossed onto the mulch of disuse."

Monsarrat stepped off the treadmill. He reached for his towel and a liter bottle of water. "What does that mean, Marty? Are you even speaking English?"

"It's election season, Nathan. Radicalism is returning to the campus. Power to the people. Death to pigs. Our brothers and sisters are growing out their Afros. White chicks are burning their bras. Asian daughters are deserting the library. Asian sons are tossing Forbes into the trash."

He wondered how far Martins would carry his riff. "What about white dudes, Marty? What are they doing?"

"Going to the gym, pumping iron, drinking beer, getting ready to commandeer the revolution. Or at least look good when the sisters and the white chicks and the Asian daughters come to sweep them away. For white dude revolutionaries, it's all about using political means to achieve their aims of twenty-eight varieties of pussy."

Martins solemnly proclaimed, "Power to the people, my Howard Johnson brother."

Monsarrat toweled the sweat from his face. "Give me a break, man. Were you even alive during the sixties?"

"Sure, I was in diapers, but I absorbed the energy of the moment through my mother's breast milk. Happenings. Be-ins. Sit-ins. Woodstock. Free love. Age of Aquarius."

He opened the bottle of water and drank half of the liquid in a long draught. "What are you teaching this semester? Sex and Revolution?"

"Something like that. I call it The Politics of Literature. The students study Stokely Carmichael, Abbie Hoffman, Gloria Steinem, Malcolm X, Che Guevara, and Angela Davis. They read about their parents in college. I think they're jealous."

"You keep pushing the envelope, you'll end up in the dock, like Copernicus," he warned. "We're in the heart of conservative western Massachusetts. We're not radical leftists like our cousins in Boston and Cambridge."

"Academic freedom, Nathan. Can't touch me. I'm tenured."

He steered their conversation back to firmer ground. "I'll consider your proposal, but the problem lies in the realm of public perception. If we go to a standing disciplinary committee, will potential students and their parents think we're a lawless campus? Will we see a decline in the number of applications for admission?"

"If we maintain the status quo, we may be skewered for not taking firm action," Martins countered. "Shirking our responsibilities. Sticking our heads in the sand."

Monsarrat was certain that Martins had wanted to say 'up our asses' but had suppressed his word choice at the last minute. "We could increase the number of our meetings, but that could also create the impression that our students are out of control."

"Fucked if you do. Fucked if you don't," Martins intoned. "Either we're proactive or reactive. I say the former is the better choice."

He drained the bottle of water. "George Martins, love child of Abbie Hoffman and Angela Davis. Power to the academics."

When Martins flinched, he felt like a bully. "C'mon, Marty, stand proud, man. It's an idea worthy of discussion."

"Yeah, it's a good idea."

"You wanna grab lunch after your workout? Anywhere but the Faculty Lounge. We can go over the cases before the meeting."

"Okay, let's do Mexican at the Cantina on Main Street."

"Better visuals than food."

"Don't tell me you're one of those purists who goes to a restaurant to eat?"

He had not wanted to offend Martins. He needed his support. "How long will you work out?"

"Just a few laps on the track today. Gimme an hour. I'll meet you at the Cantina."

By the door to the men's faculty locker room, he tossed the empty bottle of water into the recycling bin. He showered, changed into the uniform of dean, hung his gym clothes in his locker, and shoved the bag into the cramped space to pick up before heading home later that afternoon.

At the restaurant, he sat at the bar and ordered a Corona. He tossed the lime wedge onto the counter and ate a handful of nacho chips. He began his second Corona as Martins arrived. They ate at the bar and analyzed the election season. Monsarrat disdained politics but listened politely as Martins skewered the candidates of both parties. He would have rather discussed the Red Sox or the Patriots.

The Disciplinary Committee meeting started on time and finished ninety minutes late. The members grumbled, but Monsarrat insisted they finish the cases. Martins supported him, as he had all afternoon. At the conclusion of the meeting, he floated his proposal. Monsarrat thanked him and promised to consider it, but knew that he would only perform an academic kabuki before rejecting the idea while praising it as a fine example of bold thinking, exactly the sort of creative audacity needed from the faculty. He welcomed the win-win outcome. During his career with the Agency, happy endings had been as rare as virtue.

When he returned to Campbell Hall, only the janitors remained in the building. In his office, he scanned the e-mails that had arrived during his absence. He fingered the business card the dean of students, a recent divorcée with a doctorate in Jacobean theater and an office across the hall from his own, had passed him at the start of the meeting. A question mark with a heart beneath the curved line followed her cell phone number. He studied the card like a conjurer shifting bones before feeding it to the shredder. Until recently, the Agency had been his mistress. Commitments to women had rarely lasted beyond a holiday weekend, until his friendship with Abby developed into a long-distance relationship.

Beneath yellowed pools of arc light in the dedicated lot behind Campbell Hall, he unlocked the door to his Jeep, drove to Holbrooke Gymnasium, and retrieved his gym bag. On Main Street, save for a few restaurants, bars, and coffee shops, businesses were shuttered. He knew he should eat dinner, yet he wanted a drink. Food only provided cover.

He turned onto Elm Street and parked in front of Ralph's, a local watering hole. An eponymous neon sign illuminated the entrance to the bar. The town and the gown mixed along Main Street, but on Elm Street, Ralph's customers preferred to drink with people they had known since childhood. Out-of-town students sensed hostility. Local students, even those who lived with their parents in the town, experienced resentment. Faculty departed before finishing their drinks and never returned. Despite his tailored suits, silk ties, custom-made shirts, and hand-lasted shoes, Monsarrat had been accepted by Ralph Sanders, the owner and bartender, a hard man an inch shorter, twenty pounds lighter, and ten years younger.

The first time he had stepped into the bar's dark interior, Monsarrat sat alone at the rail and sipped shots of Wild Turkey. Ralph poured his drinks with the charm of a proctologist, until Monsarrat commented on a framed photograph of Chuck Norris by the cash register. The actor's signature was as bold and strong as his celluloid roles.

"You know Chuck?"

"I met Mr. Norris," Ralph answered in a voice colder than the shots of frozen vodka he served with a side of cherry licorice, Ladies Special, 8:00 p.m. until closing, every night.

"He came through here?"

"Fuck no. I had the honor in Fallujah. Back in 2006."

"You're a Marine?" Monsarrat avoided the past tense, which was only used when a grunt had gone onto his eternal reward.

Ralph wore the bristled crew cut of the jarhead. "You know Fallujah?"

"Al-Fallujah. Ar-Ramadi. Hadithah. Ar-Rutbah. Al-Jid. Al-Qa'im," Monsarrat agreed. "I'm still shaking the sand from the Western Desert out of my crotch."

Ralph examined him. "You're not a Marine."

"No, sir, I am not, but I had the honor of sharing time in Al-Anbar with some of the finest men and women to grace the uniform."

"The Army sent you to Fallujah?"

Monsarrat had not spoken about his time in Iraq to anyone at the college. The facts did not fit the cover of dean. Yet, he felt an immediate affinity with Ralph, as he did with most veterans of the Al-Anbar campaign. "I went for the hunting."

Ralph snorted, a rolling baritone laugh. "That's rich. We hunted ragheads every minute of every day in the desert. What did you hunt?"

A dozen customers sat in the bar. Some drank steadily. A few watched the Red Sox lose to the Orioles on a fifty-inch plasma television. Others engaged in a favorite local pastime, excoriating the hated New York sports teams.

Monsarrat spoke softly, so that only Ralph could hear his words, "*Mujahedin.* Mostly al-Qaida and foreign fighters. Every shit bird we could send to his seventy-two virgins."

"Christians in Action?"

"Sir, gentlemen never discuss religion, politics, or women."

Ralph supplied the punch line. "Good thing we're not gentlemen."

He poured a double shot of Wild Turkey and passed it to Monsarrat. "You did some righteous work over there. It's on the house."

Monsarrat entered the bar and took his usual seat at the rail. He tilted his head toward the regulars. They never exchanged verbal greetings, only nods and raised hands. He had learned their names through the osmosis of proximity. He recognized their odors, how they held their cigarettes, the slouch of their backs as they hunched over their boilermakers. Conversation in the bar interfered with the business of drinking. Occasionally, the gregarious cheered when the Red Sox scored.

Ralph poured a double shot of Wild Turkey. "What's the news from the hallowed halls of academia, Dean?"

"Same shit, different day, Ralph. Same as it ever was."

"Roger that, Dean. May the good Lord bless us and keep us from radical change."

Monsarrat swallowed the bourbon and savored the sweet burn in his throat. He placed the double-shot glass upside down onto the bar. "Don't stop now, Ralph. You've hit the sweet spot."

On the television, a gaggle of former baseball players discussed the Fall Classic. "Who do you think will take the Series?"

"Fuck me if I care. I lost interest after the Dead Sox choked."

"An autumn event as regular as leaves turning," agreed Monsarrat.

Ralph poured the second double shot. "As long as it ain't the Spankies. I hate those New York clowns almost as much as I hate Osama bin Laden and Mullah Omar."

The second glass of Wild Turkey joined the first on the bar. He dropped a twenty dollar bill next to it. "Death to all shit birds."

Generous tips bought goodwill. Ralph leaned across the bar. "Coupla guys came into the bar today, late afternoon, just in time for the before dinner rush."

Monsarrat knew Ralph did not subscribe to the philosophy of gossip. "Local guys?"

He might have read the description from a police report. "Different accents. Dressed too nice. Oxford shirts. Pressed khakis with creases. Dock shoes. Blazers. Fifty-dollar haircuts, styled and blow dried. No facial hair."

He felt the electric surge of paranoia. "Sounds like upscale clientele, Ralph."

Ralph filled a third shot glass. "Upscale from somewhere not here. They had a bad smell to them."

Monsarrat left the bourbon on the bar. "What did they smell like?"

"They smelled like feds."

He dispensed with jocularity. "What are you not telling me?"

"They sat at the bar. One guy made a call on his cell phone. He talked like he was inside a bubble."

"You blended into the background, just part of the woodwork?"

"I'm a yokel with a buzz cut," Ralph agreed. "Harmless. Probably brainless. Drink my profits, go home, beat the wife, kiss the dog."

"Enough foreplay. Tell me."

"They talked about the dean. Not any dean. A specific dean."

"No names?"

"No names," Ralph agreed, "but I thought you might be interested."

"A female dean? Male? Old? Young?"

"No details, but they discussed access and egress points and securing a perimeter. They talked about getting back to Boston in time for dinner."

"Feds, you say?"

"Just a feeling, Dean. The kinda sensation that kept me alive in Iraq."

Monsarrat picked up the shot glass, swallowed the bourbon, and placed the glass upside down on the bar. He covered it with a second twenty dollar bill. "Obliged, brother."

"Drive carefully, Dean. I've got to think about my publican's license."

Monsarrat guided the Jeep down Elm Street. He halted at the stop sign, flicked the directional signal, turned onto Maple Street, and bore right at the fork onto Cartwright Road. Number 24 was set back from the pavement by a large yard. Maple, oak, elm, and a smattering of birch trees provided shade. In another week, the palette of their leaves would carpet the lawn with fallen colors.

The trip from his house to the college consumed less than fifteen minutes. He enjoyed the privacy his two acres of land offered. Security lights on the house and the two-car garage set to an automatic timer illuminated the property. As he steered the Jeep into the driveway, motion sensors lit a dozen powerful perimeter spotlights. If his neighbors had been closer, they surely would have complained.

He parked the Jeep before the detached garage. He had converted the interior space into a weight-training area with benches, barbells, dumbbells, and mats. A canvas heavy bag reinforced with duct tape hung from a ceiling beam by a stout chain. A speed bag was tethered on an elastic rope between the ceiling and floor.

He ignored the upright flag on the rural route box at the bottom of the driveway, picked up his gym bag, and unlocked the three deadbolts on the front door. Inside the house, he dropped the locks, tossed the gym bag onto the maple floorboards, and crossed the foyer to the security node. In its pale glow, he tapped a twelve digit alphanumeric code, then scanned the whorls of his right index finger. The diodes flashed green.

Monsarrat had augmented the security system with digital cameras designed to record in all light and weather conditions onto detachable drives. With help from an acquaintance in the Boston Field Office of the FBI, he received licenses to possess and carry a small arsenal of weapons. A Glock 30 protected the bedroom. A second Glock 30 defended the living room. He placed Smith & Wesson seven-round .357 Magnums in the bathroom and in the garage. An HK45 rested in a kitchen drawer. In the center console of the hardtop Jeep he locked a five-round .38 Smith & Wesson Special. He preferred forty-five caliber pistols and either .38 or .357 magnum revolvers for dependability and stopping power. He found fifty caliber handguns unwieldy, nine millimeter pistols temperamental, forties a poor compromise, and long guns unsuited to concealment.

In his bedroom, he hung his suit and tie on wooden hangers. He cleaned his shoes, placed them on a dowel rack, and tossed everything else into the clothes hamper. In the bathroom, he donned a pair of sweat pants and a sweatshirt. He removed his leather briefcase from the closet, tossed it onto the bed, and spun codes into the dual combination locks. Two years earlier he had modified its interior to provide structural stiffness, a holster, and loops for a brace of magazines. He took a Glock 30 and two full mags from the night stand. He checked the action and the loads before placing them into the briefcase.

He placed the briefcase on the floor next to the bed but did not close the locks. Ralph's story had loosed his paranoia from its dormancy. In the morning he would cross the Rubicon and carry, for the first time, a weapon into Campbell Hall. He felt vaguely stained. To hear the sound of a voice in the big house, he spoke aloud. "The first time is hard. Popping your own cherry is difficult."

In the kitchen, he poured a generous amount of Wild Turkey 12 Year Old into a cut crystal tumbler and fixed a simple dinner, four ounces of linguine with butter and garlic sauce. He read the first chapter of a Douglas MacArthur biography. A few minutes before midnight, he rinsed the dishes and placed them into the dishwasher. In the bathroom, he flossed and brushed his teeth. Before turning off the bedroom light and sliding beneath the blankets, he checked that the Glock remained within reach. His final thoughts before sleep centered on the same questions he had entertained since listening to Ralph's report.

Why would two heavy hitters arrive in western Massachusetts less than twenty-four hours prior to his luncheon meeting with his former boss? Why would two heavy hitters need to discuss access and egress points? Why would they need to secure a perimeter? Why had Sanhedrin called him?

A DEAN ENJOYING A LATE AUTUMN MORNING

Monsarrat parked on Main Street ninety minutes before his luncheon meeting with Sanhedrin to canvas the surrounding area for the heavy hitters. He checked the revolver's load, locked it in the center console, and stepped out of the Jeep. He deposited quarters into the parking meter and checked his watch, a dean enjoying a late autumn morning in western Massachusetts beneath a cloudless, blue sky.

Briefcase in his left hand, he pushed open the door to Josephson's Jewelry and greeted the owner. He slipped off his Tag Heuer. The jeweler screwed a loupe into his right eye while Monsarrat stared through the store window into the street. He removed the loupe, shrugged, and returned the watch. Monsarrat thanked him, slipped it onto his left wrist, and walked out of the store.

After purchasing a pack of gum and a get-well card in Schubert's Pharmacy, he crossed the street to the post office. Before approaching the counter, he scribbled a few words onto the card, sealed the envelope, and addressed it to his home. He bought a book of stamps at the counter and dropped the card into the mail slot.

He made the heavy hitters in Nash's Coffee and Tea Emporium. They shared a table in the bay window, diagonally across from the entrance to Sidon, but had traded their pressed khakis and dock shoes for jeans and work boots. The first added a grey New England Patriots sweatshirt, the second a black Boston Red Sox jacket. They wore University of Massachusetts baseball caps, and au poivre stubble pebbled their cheeks and throats. Patriots Sweatshirt stared out the window as Red Sox Jacket sent text messages on his cell phone.

Monsarrat understood the challenges of mounting an observation post in a small town. Static surveillance was always difficult, but the heavy hitters were not amateurs. He made them because he had looked for them. To be sure, he stepped into Nash's. At the counter, he watched them in his peripheral vision, and in their eyes saw bright recognition. Patriots Sweatshirt continued to stare out the window, but Red Sox Jacket increased the tempo of his texting.

He ordered a double espresso and loitered by the register until he received a demitasse cup with a sliver of lemon peel perched on the rim. He dropped two dollars into the tip glass, chose a table in the rear of the store, and glanced at the sports pages of the Boston newspaper. He sipped the espresso and noted that the heavy hitters had switched roles. Red Sox Jacket stared out the window. Patriots Sweatshirt sent more text messages on his cell phone.

He checked his watch, laid down the newspaper, and finished his espresso. Their stares drilled into his back as he crossed Main Street. He hefted the briefcase and entered the restaurant two minutes before one o'clock. Eight tables for couples and twice as many four-person tables filled the floor. Patrons occupied half of them.

The proprietor greeted him. "*Marhaba*, Professor Monsarrat. It's been far too long since I have gazed upon your handsome visage."

Monsarrat knew better than to correct the Lebanese on the differences between dean and professor. "*Marhabatain*, Asif, my friend. How is your family?"

"*Al-hamdulillah.* Praise to Allah for his gifts. We are all well."

"Your son is still the top scorer for his soccer team?"

"His feet are blessed, Professor. He kicked in his mother's stomach. If he keeps kicking so well, his coach says he will be a candidate for a full scholarship to the University of Massachusetts. *Insha'allah*, even better, an Ivy League college."

Monsarrat clapped him on the shoulder. "He's a good boy, Asif. Allah has surely smiled upon you."

The restaurateur pointed toward a small table in the rear. "Your luncheon companion is waiting for you, Professor."

Monsarrat had seen Sanhedrin as soon as he stepped into Sidon. "When did he arrive?"

The Lebanese shrugged. "Maybe five minutes ago. No more."

Monsarrat rubbed his thumb and index finger together, a gesture Asif well understood. "He's an important friend of the college."

"We will serve you well today, Professor. You have my word."

Monsarrat walked through the dining room. He placed his briefcase onto the floor, to the right of the chair, and offered his hand. "Mr. Seleucid? I'm Nathan Monsarrat."

Sanhedrin pushed back his chair and stood. He shook Monsarrat's hand. "It's my honor, Dean. I've heard quite a bit about you."

"All good, I trust?"

"Excellent, Dean, all excellent."

Monsarrat beamed down at the smaller man. His former boss could have been a Cambrian fly cast in resinous amber. He appeared not to have aged since their last meeting. To mark the academic occasion, he wore a Herringbone jacket with leather buttons and a rolled lapel, a linen shirt with an orange ascot of jacquard silk, Italian jeans, and suede harness boots.

He smiled upward, like a searchlight sweeping the night sky. "Shall we look at the menu, Dean? I am ravished."

Monsarrat took his seat. He dropped the cloth napkin onto his left thigh and picked up the menu. "How was the drive from Boston, Mr. Seleucid?"

"Call me Franklin, Dean. I feel like we're old friends already."

"As if we've known each other for ages," Monsarrat agreed. He wondered how long they would continue the charade. "I'm Nathan. No need for the title."

He signaled for the waiter, a tall, lanky blond with watery-blue eyes he recognized from the college. "An Almaza. My friend would like a Heineken."

"Good memory, Nathan." With the public introductions concluded, Sanhedrin ditched the persona of Franklin Seleucid. "How are your instincts these days?"

Monsarrat recited the curriculum vitae of Educational Placement Services, founded on January 1, 2010, by Dr. Franklin Seleucid, EdD in early childhood education, and located on Commonwealth Avenue in Boston. Claimed losses to the IRS of $87,500 dollars for the most recent calendar year. Personnel included Seleucid, a secretary, a full-time assistant, and a part-time assistant. The landlord, Upper Commonwealth Realtors, provided janitorial services.

Sanhedrin focused on the cash flow. "Start-up costs. We'll be in the black within two years. Good work though. You're still fast."

"The Internet is a wonderful tool, Felix. No one has a right to privacy."

"Anything else about my business you would like to share with me?"

Monsarrat described the two heavy hitters drinking coffee in Nash's. He did not mention Ralph.

Sanhedrin fingered the menu. "I thought my boys were professionals, but you made them right away. I suppose I'll need to look for new help."

"Do the Berkshires frighten you, or are you in trouble again?"

Sanhedrin leaned back in his chair. "Troubles galore, but not from the bucolic Berkshires, old buddy. My current business clients are a tad heavy handed when they want to make a point."

"Why do business with them?"

"They pay half the costs in up-front cash."

"Did you leave the Agency, Felix, or is the educational consultant gig a new cover?"

"Just like you, old buddy, I'm out. Congress squeezed our budgetary balls again, and the Mandarins waved retirement bonuses. Not as sweet as your medical disability checks, but the scribbling was on the wall. Take the money today, or take a hike tomorrow."

"With only your pension for company."

"That's exactly correct," Sanhedrin confirmed. "Bit of a no-brainer, really."

"Why the new career in education? You've got contacts with every oil executive in every nasty country in the world. Why not work for them and make some serious scratch?"

The waiter placed two bottles of beer and two glasses on the table. Sanhedrin handed the glasses back to him. "Real men drink beer from bottles, son."

Monsarrat picked up the menu. "Are you ready to order, Franklin?"

"You first, Dean."

"I'll have the kalamar mezza, the lamb kabobs, and another Almaza."

Sanhedrin examined the menu. "Give me the baba ghannouge mezza and the chicken kabobs. I'll take another Heineken, too."

The waiter accepted the menus and took their orders to the kitchen.

Monsarrat drained half the Almaza. He would have preferred shots of bourbon, but could not afford to be fuzzy in the presence of his former boss.

Sanhedrin watched him closely. "I was in Roppongi a while ago, in the private dining room of my favorite Kobe beef restaurant, talking to a few samurai friends about the Saudis, trying to figure out how to convince the princes in Riyadh to quit playing grab ass with the Chinese and get into bed with the Nipponese."

Monsarrat remembered the establishment, discreet even by Tokyo standards. The waitresses were young and demure, the food excellent, and the cost of a dinner triple a month of paychecks from the college.

"We were draining bottles of Johnnie Walker Blue," Sanhedrin continued. "One samurai was moaning about his newest mistress, a Eurasian with the original name of Suzie. Half Saigon, half Paris. He said she was a guilty pleasure, the hottest pussy he ever had. Her slanted snapper washed fifty years off his life. She was a mega-dose of Viagra."

He drank his Heineken. "Suzie was acting her age, which might have been twenty-two but was probably closer to eighteen. She wanted a specific piece of jewelry that she saw some bimbo actress wear in a Japanese fashion magazine, except the gewgaw was a fourth century jasper necklace from the Kofun period borrowed from the Kyoto National Museum. Sizzling Suzie didn't care. She wanted it all for herself, and she wouldn't spread until she got the piece."

"Why not buy her a high-end knockoff?"

Sanhedrin tapped his Heineken on the table. "My question exactly. The samurai said the little vamp would know the difference. I asked why he didn't buy the original from the museum. He said they didn't sell pieces from their collections."

Monsarrat finished the Almaza. His former boss possessed an exquisite sense of pace and timing. He was blessed with the gift of the bard.

"I suggested that he have the piece stolen," Sanhedrin continued. "His eyes lit up. He just about yelled, 'Toro! Toro! Toro!' You would have thought I was the genius who invented the theory of relativity. He dragged me out of the private room into a more private hallway. He promised I would be a hundred thousand bucks wealthier if I could get him the necklace by the end of the week."

He finished the beer. "I had six days. I delivered the necklace in five. I put out thirty-five thousand total expenses to secure the piece. Another five thousand to validate its authenticity. I thought I would clear sixty big ones for a few days of orchestrating the gig, but the samurai got misty eyed and blubbery, thinking of crawling between those young Eurasian legs again, and tossed in the forty thousand in expenses as a bonus."

Monsarrat smiled appreciatively. Sanhedrin had always been fond of money.

"It was more scratch in less time than I could make as an oil expert. Fewer headaches, too. The only other ways I know to make

that kinda fast cash is to sell drugs, weapons, or little girls. It's
not that I am opposed to those lines of work, but I don't
particularly enjoy the company of the clients. They're vicious,
sadistic, and completely without moral compunctions. If they
want to keep your business relationship quiet, they kill you, but
they take their sweet time doing it. They make your FATA buddies
look like schoolboys in short pants."

Monsarrat grimaced at the mention of his Delta captors. He
hoped his former boss had not noticed.

The waiter served their food and cold beers. He took away their
empty bottles.

"Later that night, I'm in the lobby bar of my hotel, as
anonymous as could be, among the little Asians in their grey suits
and the fat Gulfies in their bathrobes with handkerchiefs on their
heads."

He spoke as if political correctness had never infected the
Agency. "I'm thinking of my bank balance, I've got a hard-on the
size of a Polaris missile. Should I hire a high-end hooker? Order a
bottle of Blue and a fat Cubano? Then it hits me. La lumière. An
epiphany."

"Tell it."

"My new profession. Fixer nonpareil."

"You did it all your life for Uncle Sam."

"Oil boys, weapons wallahs, sex traffickers, intel peddlers. All
those fat fucks with big bucks need someone quiet, dependable,
smooth, fast, and unobtrusive to clean up their messes. Someone
subtle to get in, get out, no fuss, no mess."

"They need someone like you."

"Fuck that, Nathan. They need me."

Monsarrat chewed his kabobs. He didn't want to offend Asif.
He felt Adam's rectitude, knowing better but unable to stop
himself from taking a bite of Eve's apple. "Business is good?"

"Business is excellent, old buddy. Business is fucking
booming."

"How did you come up with the Educational Placement
Services cover?"

"I have friends in Personnel. They created a legend for me.
Just like they did for you, except mine is off the books. The
Agency thinks I'm fishing for marlin in Key West."

"The less the Agency knows, the happier I am," Monsarrat
agreed.

Sanhedrin finished the mezza, drained his second beer, and
called over the waiter. "Clear our dishes, son, and bring us each

an espresso. My friend likes a slice of lemon peel on his demitasse cup."

The blond boy appeared nervous, as if the Lebanese had leaned on him to ensure his two customers left the restaurant as happy as stuffed pashas. "What other services do you offer, Felix?" Monsarrat asked. "Other than fencing jewelry for Yakuza in expensive suits?"

"Diversified services for discriminating clientele. You like how it sounds? I'm thinking of putting it on my business cards."

"Very pithy."

"I cater to men and women, Asians, Occidentals, Blacks, Caucasians. I'm an equal opportunity fixer nonpareil."

"How do you find your clients?"

"Recommendations. I do a job, the client is satisfied, he tells a friend. Or she tells a friend. Don't look so surprised. Women with money desire discretion. They want to know who their husbands are screwing and who's screwing their boy toys. They want to discredit a competitor. They want to blackmail an enemy. They want vengeance. They're just like men. On the outside, they're upstanding members of their communities. On the inside, they're venal sleazebags."

Monsarrat was not surprised. Pol Pot and Hafez al-Assad paled next to some of the women he had known at the Agency. "What do your staffers do for you?"

"They're part of the educational cover. I work alone and subcontract as the job dictates. Mostly retirees, like you and me. Good people from friendly agencies, Americans, Brits, Israelis. Professionals who make me comfortable."

"You pay a percentage or a flat fee?"

"The latter. They do the job well, I pass them an envelope."

"All cash?"

"My clients prefer to work outside of the banking system. They pay me in cash, I pay my people in cash. Nobody's tried to stiff me yet. I explain at the start of our cooperation that any attempt to fuck me will result in a greatly increased bottom line for them."

"It's just a matter of time."

"Probably you're right," he conceded. "I'll burn that bridge when I come to it."

The waiter served two demitasse cups of espresso, Monsarrat's with a peel. "Excellent service. I'll be sure to tell Asif."

The boy sputtered. "That would be great, Dean Monsarrat. That would really be great."

Sanhedrin watched the exchange like a father disappointed by the mistakes of his son. "Saint Nathan. Patron of students, waifs, the lost and lonely, the dazed and confused."

Monsarrat tapped his watch. "Is the point in the production where you explain why you're visiting your old Agency buddy, who has nothing to offer you?"

"Enough about me," Sanhedrin agreed. "Are you enjoying academic life, Nathan? Happy as dean? Enjoying the solitude of the Berkshires?"

Monsarrat swam in the shoals of ambivalence. He had yet to decide upon a succinct answer. "The faculty and students are interesting. The hours are good."

"It sounds like you're playing the Kubler-Ross game, old buddy."

"Are you tugging at my delicates, Felix?"

He sat comfortably on the seat of judgment. "You're too young for the role of retiree in the Berkshires. You were one of our best and brightest. You went up against the nastiest scumbags and walked away smiling. Not a hair out of place."

Monsarrat glanced around the room. Most of the luncheon diners had already departed the restaurant. "I didn't walk away from the Delta. I was carried out."

Sanhedrin offered his angelic smile. "I don't need a lecture, Nathan. I rescued you."

"You took your sweet time about it, too."

"I'm surprised, old buddy. I would have expected more gratitude from you."

"Gratitude? Is that another FATA thug?"

"Don't you wonder how your old friends from the Delta are faring?"

"Are you talking about FATA or your prospect who wants to study at my college?"

"I'm talking about getting your own back. Making things right."

"You're talking about revenge?"

"The dish best served cold."

Monsarrat felt the probe beneath his fifth rib, his former boss as Joab, the Lebanese restaurant as the forest of Ephraim. "You came to me, Felix. What do you want?"

"You misunderstand, old buddy. I have something to offer you."

"Tell me quickly, without the big words. Remember, I'm just a simple dean."

Sanhedrin maintained his own pace. "I'm offered a job. I accept it. Or I turn it down. I'm an independent kind of a guy. Most jobs I accept. The jobs I turn down, I offer a good reason. There's no need to piss people off. Except as time goes on, I start to receive offers that I can't turn down. Maybe the risks are high, but the money's too good. Maybe the people making the offer won't accept any answer other than yes."

"Maybe you should get out of the fixer business and stick to educational placements."

His body language expressed disdain. "Most jobs, I locate. I purchase. I deliver. Half the fee up front. Balance on completion, plus expenses. Customers pay up. Slap me on the back. Offer me a cigar. Some jobs, I do a bit more. I charge more. Same end result."

He signaled the waiter and pointed to his espresso. "You want another, Nathan?"

Monsarrat shook his head.

Sanhedrin held up one finger. "You think the waiter understands sign language? He doesn't look too bright."

"You know how my attention wanders."

"Fact number one," Sanhedrin continued. "Some clients are difficult by nature. They're demanding. They're distrustful. They're Russian."

Monsarrat almost felt badly for him. "That's too much greed, even for you."

"As I said, Nathan, sometimes I receive offers that I can't turn down. A Russian comes to you with a request, you say yes. You say no, you wake up dead in a Brighton Beach dumpster with your balls in your mouth and your dick up your own ass. Except, all that gruesome shit happens before a Russian gorilla empties a magazine into what used to be your skull."

"Who's your client?"

"You know better than to ask that question."

"Which Russian scares you so badly you need to send heavy hitters to the Berkshires?"

"I'll take the Fifth, Nathan."

"What's on your mind, Felix?"

"Now you've asked the sixty-four-thousand-dollar question."

"Then give me the answer."

The waiter served Sanhedrin his second espresso. He placed the two empty cups onto his tray. "Would you gentlemen care for dessert?"

"Just bring the bill, son."

Monsarrat coughed politely.

"Fact number two," Sanhedrin acknowledged, "some clients are inherently dishonest. You remember what it's like to have a Russian goombah sitting across the table from you?"

"I'm retired, Felix. I'm not senile."

He recited the events as if he were calling the play-by-play of a baseball game. "I'm in my office when I get a call from the assistant of a wealthy collector of nativist art, a Russian from St. Petersburg, the cold one, not the Florida one. The collector's learned that a late-first-century Nok terracotta, a naked woman holding a spear, is for sale. She's a huntress with a large head, almond eyes, open mouth, round butt, and tits like howitzer shells. She wears a rope around her throat like a necklace. The Russian collector wants this terracotta very badly."

Monsarrat knew *biznesmeny* well. "When rich Russians want something very badly, they usually get it very quickly."

"The assistant tells me to walk down Commonwealth Avenue to a local coffee shop. I'm to look for a large gentleman wearing a blue suit and carrying a brown attaché case. He also tells me that if I am not sipping an espresso within ten minutes, the large gentleman will come to me. I understand that our meeting will be more pleasant if it takes place in public. So I beat feet to the coffee shop."

"Russians are experts in offering only one choice," Monsarrat commiserated.

"You got that right, old buddy."

Monsarrat's paranoia rattled its cage. He knew the terracotta was bait. He needed to discover the trap his former boss had set. "Go on, Felix. You have my complete attention."

"I make it with plenty of time to spare. At least thirty seconds," Sanhedrin continued. "Large does not begin to describe the Russian. He's the size of the Moscow *oblast*. The coffee cup in his hand looks like a thimble. He gestures at a chair, pushes an espresso toward me, passes me the attaché case, and tells me to open it in that snide, nasal tone Russians use when they're trying to be polite."

"You mentioned a Nok terracotta? Nok as in the Jos Plateau?"

"Afraid so, Nathan."

"Did the Russian say who has the Nok?"

Sanhedrin ignored the question. "I open the case and find a black cell phone and neat stacks of Benjamins. The cell phone's a burner, programmed to call only my new Russian pal. The Benjamins are a fifty-large deposit for my services, with an identical briefcase to follow after the Nok's delivered. Expenses refunded with receipts."

"How much for the Nok?"

"I asked the same question, old buddy. He passes me a piece of paper with a six-figure sum, how much of the client's money I'm authorized to spend and not a ruble more."

Sanhedrin swallowed the espresso as the waiter placed the bill on the table. He dropped a credit card onto it. "Here you go, son."

Monsarrat read the name, Franklin Seleucid.

"The large Russian instructs me to contact the seller, negotiate the price, verify the terracotta's bona fides, and orchestrate the exchange. When I deliver the Nok, I'll receive the second payment of fifty thousand dollars."

"If it's so simple, why do you need me?"

"Patience, old buddy. All will be known in good time."

Monsarrat suspected that he would be told little. His former boss never shared.

"The Russian passes me a second piece of paper with the seller's name and location. You can imagine my surprise."

"Not yet, but I'm looking forward to when you let me in on the secret."

"The next day, I contact the seller and negotiate a mutually acceptable price."

"You're good to go. Make the exchange."

"That's exactly why I'm here," he declared. "I want you to make the exchange for me. I'll reward you generously."

Monsarrat's paranoia warned him to leave the restaurant, but Sanhedrin had planted his hook too deeply. He repeated his question. "Who has the statue?"

"It's a Nok terracotta. Take a guess."

"Don't play coy."

"It's in Port Harcourt."

For the briefest of instants, Monsarrat thought his former boss had made a joke, before he remembered that he fully lacked a sense of humor, but even for a man of Sanhedrin's ego, it was an enormous request. "You want me to go back to the Delta?"

"Not like last time, old buddy. No oil platforms. No rebels. Just the seller in a hotel. You verify the authenticity of the terracotta. You give me the good word, I transfer the funds. You collect the Nok, deliver it to me, then treat yourself to a good meal. Or buy a Porsche."

"You make it sound easy."

"Even better, before you return home, you could make an excursion into the Delta, visit the rebel compound, stuff a couple of willie pete grenades up the asses of Blessed and Innocence, watch them burn like sacramental candles, and go back to the Berkshires with the greatest gift of all. Revenge."

"The dish best served cold," Monsarrat mumbled.

Since arriving at the college, he had attempted to suppress his memories of the Delta, an effort akin to squeezing a balloon. When he sublimated the desire for revenge, ennui claimed him. Or night terrors. More than two years onward, he had finally achieved a precarious balance. Or had become anaesthetized to the stealthy battles raging within his psyche. "Any other inducements you would like to share with me?"

"Think about it. Let's see if academia has slowed your steel trap of a brain."

"If you spend the Russian's money on a knock-off Nok, he'll be upset with you."

"Upset, my ass," Sanhedrin snorted. "Remember the dumpster in Brighton Beach? When I meet my maker, I'd like it to be under more dignified circumstances."

"If you wind up in the dumpster, I'd be shoved in right after you. If I were to agree to work with you."

"Which is why we cannot afford to make a mistake."

"There is no we, Felix. Don't think you're gonna get lucky because you bought me a skewer of kabobs."

"Kabobs today. A briefcase with fifty large tomorrow."

"You're offering me half of your fee? It's not like you to be magnanimous."

"I understand your reservations, old buddy."

"I don't think you're being fully truthful with me. I think you'll be paid far more than a hundred grand. I think it'll be closer to half a million. Ten percent of that much money would be easier for you to write off."

Sanhedrin appeared offended. "I think it's a generous proposal. I certainly wouldn't offer it to anyone else."

He felt the familiar pressure swell behind his eyes, the signal that he had been in the presence of his former boss too long. "Thanks for the offer, but you'll need to find someone else. I'm not interested."

"Pay attention, Nathan," Sanhedrin ordered. "Do us both a big favor and say yes. I need the statue, and you need the money, not to mention the closure that your visit to the FATA compound will give you."

Monsarrat looked for the waiter. "We should do this again soon. I'll call you when I'm in Boston."

Sanhedrin possessed an uncanny ability to exploit an opponent's weakness. "Remember loyalty, Nathan? Watching each other's back? I taught you everything you knew about the Agency, and when you wanted to start a new life, I found this job for you. Hell, I even did my Hercules shtick and pulled your chestnuts out of the Delta fire after you let Blessed capture you on the oil rig."

"You took your damn sweet time to get me out."

"You owe me, buddy. I need to deliver the statue to the Russian, and you're the person with the best qualifications for the job."

"I can give you a dozen names of people more qualified than me."

"You're the only one I trust."

Monsarrat had never before seen humility in the same room with his former boss. "How would I verify the terracotta's authenticity? The only Nok I've seen is the fake I bought for two bucks from a scam antiquities dealer."

"An expert on Nok art in Cambridge met the seller and confirmed the terracotta. He tagged it with a digital marker. Five minutes of work cost me ten thousand bucks, plus airfare."

"Why didn't he bring the Nok back with him?"

"Well, Nathan, he's an academic. He gives lectures and writes learned articles. The two-thousand-year-old Nok is a national treasure, and smuggling is beyond his skill set."

Monsarrat understood Sanhedrin's predicament. The cultural icon, most likely, had been stolen from a museum. His former boss couldn't hire a packing company to wrap it in soft paper and ship it across the Atlantic Ocean. He needed someone familiar with the corrupt bureaucracy to smooth its exit from the country. "Why don't you collect the Nok, cut out the middleman, and keep the cash for yourself."

Sanhedrin offered a pained expression. "The large Russian made it very clear that I am not to leave Boston until the collector holds the Nok in his hands. Now you understand why I need your help, old buddy?"

Monsarrat also understood the presence of the two heavy hitters. "The job doesn't sound like it's worth fifty thousand dollars."

"You know everything I know, old buddy."

"Not quite, Felix. You know the name of the seller."

"You're like a dog with a bone, Nathan."

"Flattery doesn't answer the question."

"It's close hold information, old buddy, but his name is Rehovoth Okeri. He's a very nice politician from Port Harcourt."

The name tickled Monsarrat's memory. "Did he steal the Nok?"

"It's been in his family for generations, but he has a cash flow problem now."

At least, Monsarrat thought, the police would not be looking for the statue. "Tell me again. What will I do for my fifty thousand dollars?"

Sanhedrin leaned across the table and clapped his shoulder. "Welcome aboard, Nathan! We're gonna be a great team. It'll be old times again."

"I didn't accept your offer, Felix, I'm just waiting to learn what I have to do to earn the fifty thousand dollars."

"Your job is to prevent Okeri from pulling a bait and switch. Only if you're 110 percent certain do you instruct me to transfer the money into his account. When he receives confirmation of the deposit, he gives you the Nok. You deliver it to me. I pass it to the large Russian, who gives me the second briefcase. We both get rich."

Monsarrat slipped into the mindset of his former life. "What are the logistics?"

"You fly from Boston via Europe to Abuja, maybe sixteen hours with the stopover. You charter a private jet for the flight to Port Harcourt. You do the job, retrace your steps, and return home. Forty-eight hours, maximum seventy-two. Call in sick on Friday. You'll be back in time for work on Monday, barring unforeseen circumstances."

"It's the unforeseen circumstances that ruin the best-laid plans."

"Not my plans, old buddy. I ain't Ted Mack, and this ain't no amateur hour."

"What are the contingencies?"

"Big boy rules. What you need, you take. Big boy risks. Big boy rewards," Sanhedrin stated. "What the situation warrants, you do. No Agency handcuffs. No congressional oversight. No inspectors with halitosis exhaling in your face."

"Backup available?"

"Negative. Complete self-reliance."

"What if I bring in my own help?"

"It's your choice, how you want to slice your banana."

His paranoia howled like a Berkshire banshee. He doubted the job would be the smooth, in-and-out affair Sanhedrin envisioned. He hoped it would not be a fubar. When the waiter delivered the credit card receipt for signature, he wrote $100 across the tip line. As he scribbled an illegible signature, he remembered the waiter's name. "Here you go, Luke."

The waiter beamed. "Thank you very much, gentlemen."

Sanhedrin slipped the receipt into his shirt pocket. "The tip cost more than the lunch."

"It's the price of doing business in the Berkshires, but you can surely afford it."

"How can you be so certain, old buddy?"

"Because I'm about to make you very wealthy."

"In that case, consider today's lunch as your birthday present, slightly belated."

"Very good of you to remember."

"The big four-oh, right? A great year. Life begins at forty."

"As long as it doesn't end before forty-one," Monsarrat replied.

AS GUILTY AS A HUSBAND CHEATING

Monsarrat departed the college under the cover of visiting an older brother in northern Iowa who had fallen off a ladder while pulling leaves from the rain gutter of his house. The injuries were serious but not life threatening. His colleagues had been sympathetic. Even Doris offered a wan smile. Leaving the campus, he felt as guilty as a husband cheating on his wife. It was an emotion he had not experienced since his earliest days with the Agency.

Packing followed a ritual as arcane as the instructions in Leviticus for offering *omer*. Shirts and pants to the side. Underwear in one pile, socks stacked separately, handkerchiefs between them. Toiletries in a leather kit next to shoes. A cornucopia of pills to battle the *P. falciparum* and *P. ovale* mosquitoes spilled across the pillows, although to prevent a relapse of malaria Mefloquine required weeks of ingestion before it could battle the sporozoites and merozoites in his bloodstream, which would eventually twist his muscles into pretzels and bend his spine into a hillock. He considered Doxycycline and Atovaquone useless and Chloroquine as effective as the tonic water Blessed had offered him in the Delta.

He had departed the Lebanese restaurant with Sanhedrin and walked to a blue Maserati GranTurismo. The two heavy hitters followed at a discreet distance. His former boss unlocked the doors with an electronic fob and passed him two items: a Manila envelope and a small light device that resembled a fragile dental probe.

"What is it, Felix?"

"It's a doohickey. It has an official name, but I know how little you enjoy the minutiae of technology."

Monsarrat slipped both into his briefcase. He had known many colleagues in the Agency who had confused technical means with flesh and blood ends, but Sanhedrin had not been one of their ranks. "What's it do?"

"It will verify the digital marker tagged onto the terracotta. Don't pack it in your suitcase. Don't let it get confiscated in an airport."

"What's to stop Okeri from placing the digital marker on a fake Nok?"

The question pleased Sanhedrin, as if Monsarrat were a perspicacious student. "Switching the marker would not be difficult, but once removed it would no longer function. It would be for decoration only."

"What's my response if Okeri tries to rip me off?"

Sanhedrin had already considered the possibility. "If you determine that the Nok is a fake, then you must convince Okeri to deliver the genuine terracotta to you immediately. My Russian buyer will have his own experts to verify the statue's authenticity. I don't look forward to one of his bone crushers telling him that the object of his Slavic desire is a cheap imitation."

Monsarrat considered the Brighton Beach dumpster. "If Okeri removes the digital marker from the genuine Nok, how can I verify its authenticity?"

Sanhedrin pointed to his briefcase. "The digital marker will leave traces on the Nok that the professor verified. The doohickey will identify them."

"What if Okeri paid your expert to verify a fake Nok?"

Sanhedrin scoffed. "He teaches teenagers about African art. He doesn't live in our world."

"Why do you trust him?"

"I don't trust anyone, old buddy, but don't delude yourself into believing that Okeri can turn my expert against me," he stated. "Still, if you encounter difficulties in Port Harcourt, you'll have to earn your fee the hard way. You used to be quite good at that sort of thing. Just come back with the authentic Nok."

Monsarrat conceded that Sanhedrin was probably right about the expert on African art, but probably, while an acceptable option to a Langley desk jockey, got operatives killed in the field. "What has Okeri been told to expect?"

Sanhedrin passed him a glossy 8x11 inch photograph of the Nok. "My representative will meet him in the lobby of the Hotel Paradise in Port Harcourt on Sunday morning. The rest of it you already know."

Monsarrat studied the picture before slipping it into his briefcase.

Sanhedrin removed a laptop from the GranTurismo. "In our day, geeks never got the girls. The guy who programmed this computer gets more ass than a toilet seat."

"You want me to e-mail you updates?"

"You pop the cover, turn it on, and supply the password. It's programmed to do only one thing. It links to my computer. If you try to do anything else, surf the web, read your e-mail, check the weather, watch porn, even play a game of solitaire, think of the opening scene from the old television show with the self-destructing tape."

"What can I do with a link to your computer?"

"You can send me a specific message, and I can transfer the money into Okeri's account," Sanhedrin replied. "Then you can send me an all's-well signal and scoot back to the loving bosom of the Commonwealth of Massachusetts."

"You'll meet me in Boston?"

"You clear the secure zone at the airport, and I'll be waiting with bells and whistles."

"As long as you'll have my money, Felix."

Sanhedrin handed him a 3x5 index card. An alphanumeric password and the message were written on it. Monsarrat studied the card and passed it back to Sanhedrin.

"Give them to me, Nathan."

Monsarrat closed his eyes and repeated the information.

Sanhedrin wrote a cell phone number on the back of his business card. "If anything goes south between now and deplaning in Boston, call me immediately."

"You'll send the cavalry?"

"I'll do what I can, but bottom line? You're on your own."

Monsarrat wrote on the back of his own business card. "I've been there before, Felix."

"What is this, old buddy?"

"My fee and the day and time when one of your assistants will deliver half of that sum to me. Large bills. Hundreds are better than fifties. Less bulk. I'll provide you with an accounting for reimbursable expenses when I deliver the Nok."

Sanhedrin turned the card over, front to back, back to front. "Oh, Nathan, Nathan, Nathan. My old buddy. What are you trying to do to me?"

Monsarrat gestured toward the heavy hitters. "No tricks, Felix. You don't want to worry about me slipping up behind you, despite your protection."

Sanhedrin sounded disappointed, as if a trusted friend had attempted to deceive him. "It's twice the sum we agreed upon, Nathan."

"I didn't agree to anything. You made an offer. This is my counter-offer. It's non-negotiable."

"It's a large sum of money."

"Find another patsy. On such short notice."

"I'm surprised, Nathan. I've never thought of you as rapacious, but as you say, it is short notice. In forty-eight hours, you'll have the first tranche."

Monsarrat locked the suitcase and spread Sanhedrin's documents across the blanket. A well-stamped tourist passport for Evan Walsh. Credit cards in the same name. A Massachusetts driver's license with an address in one of Boston's exclusive suburbs. Round-trip tickets seated him in Lufthansa's business class from Boston to Abuja via Frankfurt. Elastic bands bound four thousand dollars and another four thousand equivalent in euros, for expenses. Business cards introduced him as the director of acquisitions for a private museum in Cambridge. From the Ministry of Culture in Abuja, he carried a letter of guarantee graced with officious stamps that certified the loan of the Nok terracotta for the Cambridge museum's upcoming exhibit, *Art of the Terracotta*.

The excellent quality of the documents, a Sanhedrin trademark, reassured him, but he thought his former boss had agreed too quickly to his demands. Either he was more afraid of the Russians than he admitted or there were aspects to the job that he had not explained. Or both. His former boss doled out his intelligence like a miser contributing to the Sunday charity plate, but the information Sanhedrin did not want to share was exactly what he needed to know.

He placed the laptop, the Walsh documents, and the traveling money into a European leather valise with a strap. He felt comfortable with the loop over his wrist, like a leather handcuff. His flight to Abuja departed that evening. He opened the safe and ran his fingertips across the fifty thousand dollars the two heavy hitters delivered exactly forty-eight hours after Sanhedrin had departed the Berkshires for Boston. He secured the safe, set the security alarms, locked the house, put his suitcase into the back of the Jeep, placed the leather valise onto the passenger seat, and drove toward the Lee Interchange. Before entering the Mass Pike, he pulled onto the shoulder of the turnpike plaza and made two calls.

Abby answered on the first ring. "Guess where I am, big boy?"

"On your couch, eating chocolate chip ice cream, and watching old movies?"

"That's for tonight," she replied. "One more try?"

"Buying a French maid's uniform and a buggy whip?"

"That's closer, but not quite right. Although you might want to bring them with you next weekend."

"I surrender," he said. "Where are you?"

"At the Kennedy Center, buying two tickets for Verdi's *Aida* at the Opera House."

Monsarrat stifled a groan. "One ticket for you, one ticket for me?"

"You better like it, Nathan. They're damned expensive seats."

He would have preferred two fifty-yard-line tickets to the Redskins game at FedEx Field but was too smart to share his thoughts. "Should I bring a tux?"

"I thought you would wear your French maid outfit."

"You owe me, Abby."

"Somebody's cranky."

"You can work your way back into my good graces right now."

"Over the phone? I charge $8.95 for the first three minutes and then $7.95 for each additional minute. Heavy breathing is extra. Major credit cards accepted."

He waited for her laughter to fizzle. "When did Felix quit the Agency?"

She laughed again. "Felix hasn't left Langley, at least not as of thirty minutes ago. He was sitting in his office when I said good-bye to him."

"Are you sure?"

"Of course, I'm sure," she answered. "What's wrong, baby? Why the sudden concern about Felix?"

"Did you know he came to see me at the college this week?"

"I know his schedule, Nathan. He was at Vauxhall Cross in London with his SIS friends. It was his boondoggle of the month."

His paranoia red zoned. "Okay, Abby, my bad. I have to run to another meeting. Love you, babe."

"From bureaucracy to academia," she teased. "Out of the pot and into the fire."

He waited a minute before making his second call. Why had Sanhedrin lied to him about such a verifiable fact? Was his former boss becoming operationally lazy? Did he hold him in such low regard that he had tossed a salad of mendacity? Had he unwittingly agreed to play the role of a sacrificial pawn in another convoluted Felix Sanhedrin production?

Explanations were as substantial as coils of smoke. He punched the international access code into his cell phone followed by a series of digits and waited for the call to connect in Port Harcourt, more than five thousand miles and five time zones distant.

In his soft, Southern drawl, Mark Palmer asked, "On schedule, Nathan?"

Monsarrat had never worked with Palmer but knew him professionally. The former Special Forces lieutenant colonel oversaw the safety of close to six hundred American and European executives and their families, plus another four hundred skilled and unskilled laborers. They had developed a respectful relationship, based on mutual acquaintances and shared experiences. During his recuperation in the Virginia countryside, Monsarrat received a message from Palmer, sent through friends in Langley. "When you are ready to settle accounts, I'll be here."

Monsarrat understood retribution. He knew personal reasons had prompted Palmer to send his message, but the knowledge did not diminish his appreciation for the offer.

On a humid Sunday evening a month before the start of his own captivity, two of Palmer's executives had dined with a group of tribal chiefs and politicians inside the Hotel Paradise in Port Harcourt. A dozen FATA rebels in Land Rover Defenders riddled the hotel's security checkpoint with their Chinese AK-47s and sped along the curved drive to the entrance of the hotel. At the first crack of the gunfire, Palmer hustled the two executives to the helipad in the rear of the hotel and loaded them into the hold of the company's Twin Star helicopter. Four members of his team joined them. The Rolls-Royce engines spun the rotors, and the bird lifted off the helipad.

Palmer divided the remainder of his shooters into two units. The first unit shredded the Land Rovers with M4 rifles. The surviving rebels fired wildly toward the hotel as the second unit in black, fully armored Suburbans with smoked windows braked broadside to the smoldering vehicles. When the panicked rebels ran, the shooters cut them down. In less than five minutes, they prevented the kidnapping of the two oil executives and killed a dozen rebels.

Six days later, on a bright Saturday morning, FATA rebels fired a dozen 81 mm mortars toward the oil service company's compound. Four shells fell within the walls. Two failed to detonate. The third destroyed the visitor's dugout along the third base line of the softball diamond, but the final mortar pierced the ceramic roof of the recreation center. Three children and one mother were killed. Others were injured, some seriously.

"Wheels down in Abuja at fifteen-forty hours tomorrow. The Lufthansa flight from Frankfurt."

"My boys and I will meet you as you deplane. We'll escort you through Immigration and help you pass by Customs without the usual shakedown."

He had wired the payment into Palmer's account after their initial conversation. "You received my presents for you and your staff?"

"Very generous. Travel well, and I'll see you tomorrow afternoon."

Monsarrat closed the connection and steered the Jeep onto the turnpike. At the Auburn Interchange, he paid the toll, exited onto Interstate 290, and passed through Worcester to Interstate 495 before Chelmsford. He turned onto Route Three and followed the Everett Turnpike to the Somerset Parkway in Nashua, New Hampshire. He locked the Jeep in a park-and-ride lot, retrieved the valise and the suitcase, and caught an express bus to Logan Airport in Boston. Ninety minutes later, he checked in as Evan Walsh for the Lufthansa flight, received his boarding passes and luggage claim, endured security, and cleared Immigration.

A chit allowed him round-trip access to the Senator Lounge, where he drank bourbon until the monitor flashed his boarding call. He took his aisle seat in business class, placed his valise on the empty seat next to him, and accepted a flute of Champagne from the hostess. During the seven-hour flight, he declined the meal service in favor of nip bottles of bourbon. His nerves torqued as the plane descended into Germany. In Frankfurt International Airport, he walked the antiseptic hallways until he found the lounge.

He spoke to a dour Hessian standing like a black-vested sentry behind the rail. "*Guten Morgen, mein Herr.* I hope you serve bourbon."

The German said, "*Natürlich.* We have many American customers. What do you prefer?"

Monsarrat placed a twenty dollar bill on the counter. "Whatever's on the top shelf. A double. No ice."

"*Es wird mir ein Vergnügen sein.* It will be my pleasure."

Monsarrat did not believe him but accepted the glass. "*Vielen Dank.*"

He drank double shots until the flight for Abuja boarded. Once on the plane, his luck fled. A large woman wearing a hat rarely seen beyond the boundaries of Ascot occupied the seat next to him. Waves of expensive perfume rolled off her ample chest. He took the aisle seat and squeezed his valise into the seat pocket.

Before the cabin crew began the safety checks, she introduced herself in the particularly difficult accent of the dry northern states. "My name is Mrs. Olufunke Ademola. Olufunke means that I am loved. My husband is Chief Adunbi Ademola. He is as pleasant as his name. I am from Abuja. I am a Christian."

She offered her hand and waited for Monsarrat to introduce himself.

The prospect of conversing with her during the six-hour flight filled him with dread. He accepted her fleshy appendage, as thick and heavy as an ironwood war club. Her hands were gardens of rubies, emeralds, sapphires, and diamonds, each stubby finger weighted by a ring bearing an oversized precious stone.

He discovered inspiration. "It is my pleasure, Mrs. Ademola. I am Dr. Peter Smith from Boston."

"A medical doctor? Or a professor in the university?"

"An anesthesiologist, Mrs. Ademola."

She sniffed her approval. "What brings you to my country, Dr. Smith?"

"My son by my first marriage works in Abuja." He knew how Nigerian women of a certain age and social class enjoyed detailed explanations.

"Your wife has passed onward?"

Monsarrat shook his head. "We divorced."

"Divorce is the work of the devil," she declared. "Now you are remarried?"

"Happily so."

"And where does the young man work?" she pursued.

"He's a diplomat in the U.S. Embassy."

"Then he is a spy," she proclaimed.

Monsarrat smiled wanly. "He enjoys Abuja very much."

She nodded, as if everyone enjoyed her city, even American spies.

Monsarrat feared for his inspiration. "My husband is already with him. I had to attend a medical conference in Frankfurt, so I'm looking forward to seeing them both again."

Rolls of flesh wobbled on her throat. "Your husband?"

He began to relax. Perhaps his plan would succeed. "This trip is also our honeymoon. We were married last June. Same sex marriage is legal in Massachusetts."

The cabin crew began its presentation. When the seat belts and flotation devices had been returned to the overhead bins, Mrs. Ademola called for the stewardess. She whispered in her ear.

The stewardess agreed. "Six-A is free, madame. You are welcome."

Mrs. Ademola unfastened her seat belt. Her left hand held onto the brim of her hat. She stood and extended her right hand to Monsarrat, then thought better of it. "I wish you a good trip to my country, Dr. Smith."

Monsarrat stood for her to pass. He watched her sway down the aisle before retrieving his valise and placing it on the empty seat. He drank nips of bourbon and tried, but failed, to sleep. He critiqued his primary and contingency plans, analyzed his research on Nok terracotta statues, and reviewed everything he remembered about Port Harcourt, the Hotel Paradise, and Mark Palmer. He reexamined all he knew about Blessed, Innocence, and the FATA compound.

He cared naught for justice but sought vengeance, not only for his own torture and imprisonment, but for the murder of Rosalinda. Two years earlier, he had abandoned her. Before he returned to Massachusetts with the terracotta statue, he would avenge her.

Information on Rehovoth Okeri had been as plentiful as a Thanksgiving harvest. The scion of the royal family of Bonny, he bore the honorary title of Amanyanabo. The leader of his people, he had led a short-lived, bloody uprising as a young man against the government forces in the Delta. The military retaliated savagely, destroying villages, killing children and the elderly, and raping girls and women. In the aftermath of the failed rebellion, Okeri switched his focus from insurrection to politics and reaped greater successes in the halls of power than he had on the fields of battle. He also gathered vast amounts of wealth.

In Monsarrat's experience, successful African politicians from traditional royal families did not need to sell cultural icons to finance their lifestyles. The country's light, sweet crude and endemic corruption guaranteed their accumulation of cash. Also in his experience, his former boss was constitutionally incapable of honesty, and his story of the Nok raised malignant questions. He hoped the answers he found in Port Harcourt would be benign.

His nerves tightened, as if twisted on a rack of his own dread. He feared he was striding toward a battle where the outcome was uncertain and the odds did not favor him.

He aligned the legion of nip bottles standing like centurions on his tray table into a tighter formation. Their red and yellow labels reminded him of the color of his own malarial eyes during his Delta captivity. As the plane began its descent toward Abuja International Airport and the massive girth of Mazu Rock filled the curve of the horizon, the stewardess swooped them into a plastic bag. He hoped their defeat was not an omen.

An Immigration official in a faded and patched green uniform scowled at the arriving passengers. He gestured them toward chutes, one for citizens of West African nations and the other for foreigners. Additional Immigration officials sat on three-legged stools in open booths at the end of each chute. Standing before the second chute, wearing sunglasses, a cotton Aloha shirt, black cargo pants, and plastic sandals, Mark Palmer looked more like a tropical tour guide than a former Special Forces officer.

He greeted Monsarrat. "It's good to see you again, Nathan. How was the flight?"

Monsarrat was already sweating in the heat and humidity beneath the airport's dormant ceiling fans. He shook Palmer's hand, as dry and as hard as granite. "Not enough bourbon."

He added, "It's good to see you, too, Mark."

Palmer scrutinized his appearance. "It's a bitch of a flight from the East Coast. We can get you some coffee on our plane to Port Harcourt. First, let's guide you through the formalities."

He led Monsarrat to the far end of the hall, took his documents, and added a thick envelope to them. He rapped on a dirty window until the Immigration official looked up from his newspaper then waved the envelope. "Pavlovian reactions. The lazy bastards see an *oyinbo* with an envelope, they positively exhibit signs of life."

The official slid open the window and took the documents. He opened the envelope and offered a smile of blackened stumps. He stamped Monsarrat's passport, handed the documents to Palmer, and slid the envelope into his tunic.

"Fifty bucks still goes a long way in this country."

"Not as far as a dentist," Monsarrat muttered. During his time in the Berkshires, he had wiped the visceral ugliness of the country from his memory, but the buried images now awakened like the undead in a B-grade horror movie.

They waited for the luggage to appear. After half a desultory loop, the carousel stopped. Passengers pulled bags from the opening in the wall. Additional suitcases appeared. Gripping his valise, Monsarrat pushed through the crowd and grabbed his suitcase. When Palmer reached for it, he held it tight. "Just lead me out of here."

They walked to the front of the green line. A Customs official in a once-blue uniform scarred with stitches pointed to the table. Monsarrat placed the suitcase on the dented metal slab, and Palmer laid a second envelope on top of it. The official nodded and slid the offering into his tunic and waved them forward. In the public area stood three casually dressed men. Monsarrat remembered it was Saturday in Abuja.

Palmer didn't bother to include surnames. "Nathan, meet Todd. He's my deputy. Because he's so damn good at his job, I punished him and put him in charge of security for our Abuja office."

Todd stood six feet tall. He wore his blond hair in a ponytail, secured by an elastic band. His pale moustache drooped over his upper lip, and his flattened nose appeared to have been on the wrong end of a hard left jab. When he removed his dark glasses, his brown eyes showed a sharp intelligence. "Pleased to meet you, Nathan."

Palmer introduced the rest of the party. "Frank and Joe work for me in Port Harcourt."

A vague familiarity shrouded the two men. As Monsarrat shook their hands, a wisp of memory tickled him, then dissipated like fog in the morning sun. He blamed jet lag and too much bourbon.

Frank said, "Looking forward to working with you."

Joe nodded in agreement. "Heard a lotta good things about you, Nathan."

Todd reached for the suitcase and led them out of the airport. Beggars beseeched them with plastic cups. A red patina of desert sand stained the buildings. Pits like the work of an avant-garde artist marked the canvas of the walls. The humid air stunk of garbage and jet fuel. Beneath a "No Parking - Penalty Enforced" sign at the curb, two armored, black Suburbans with smoked windows idled. Todd walked to the rear of the second Suburban and placed Monsarrat's suitcase in the storage compartment. He, Frank, and Joe climbed into the vehicle.

Palmer followed Monsarrat into the first Suburban. "Nathan, our driver is Sean. Bob is riding shotgun. They're from our Abuja office."

They wore the uniform of the day, and their skulls gleamed like polished cue balls. Sean donned an Orioles baseball cap and a set of headphones. He spoke into the mouthpiece and listened to the reply. "Off we go."

"We should be at our airfield in ten minutes," Palmer explained. "The flight's an hour and fifteen minutes, give or take. Nice plane. Gulfstream 550."

"Your employers are generous with their perks."

"When you decide to leave academia for the real world, give me a call."

Monsarrat peered through the smoked windows. "I'm pretty sure this doesn't qualify as the real world, Mark."

"Enjoy the ride, Nathan. I'll brief you when we reach the plane."

The Suburbans exited the airport onto Umaru Musa Road. Monsarrat noted the police dozing beneath tattered golf umbrellas, ragged protection against the brutal African sun. Feral dogs sniffed at them. Prostitutes stood by the side of the road, their blouses opened, exhibiting their wares.

The small convoy turned north onto a private road, smooth and freshly painted. After two miles, the Suburbans reached a well-maintained perimeter fence. A large sign warned of security dogs and electrified wires. Four guards stepped out of their gate house and walked toward the Suburbans, M-4 assault rifles cradled across their chests.

Sean released the door locks, slid down his window, and showed his identification. The guards each opened a door and peered into the vehicle. They cleared the second Suburban, and the entrance gate rolled along its tracks. On the tarmac, waves of heat shimmered off the Gulfstream's two Rolls-Royce turbofans. The noise and fumes from the engines, added to the heat and humidity, curdled the bourbon in Monsarrat's stomach. Two young men in linen camp shirts, tan trousers, and brown dock shoes stepped off the ramp. They wore sunglasses and sported brown crew cuts. Save for a difference of one's cropped beard and the other's inch in height, they appeared identical.

Todd passed the suitcase to the bearded twin. He shook Monsarrat's hand, waved to his Port Harcourt colleagues, and returned to the Suburban. The two armored vehicles circled the jet and drove toward the gate house.

Inside the plane, Palmer introduced the crew members. "Nathan, meet the twins, Pete and Paul. Pete's neat, and Paul's tall. It's a silly mnemonic, but the best way to tell them apart."

He added in his soft drawl, "Two coffees, please, boys. Mine's black. Nathan?"

"The same."

"Anything stronger?"

Monsarrat considered the private stock of an executive jet. "Too close to game time."

They settled into leather seats. Pete delivered the coffee from the gallery in thick ceramic mugs emblazed with the oil service company's livery. "Watch yourselves, sirs. We're about to lift off."

The interior of the cabin was quiet and the vibration minimal. Monsarrat closed his eyes and imagined life as an oil executive. He appreciated the amenities and the obscenely generous salaries, but neither could compensate for the requirement to work in the Delta.

"Try the coffee, Nathan."

Monsarrat opened his eyes. "I'm good, Mark. Give me the brief."

Palmer explained his preparations. "Four suites at the Hotel Paradise, two flanking your suite and one directly across the hall from it. Your suite is wired for sight and sound, voice-activated video cameras with sensitive mics and long-life batteries. We adapted the locks on the doors so they can only be opened by us, not by the hotel staff. We have commo gear and silenced weapons. We've practiced the transition from our suites into your suite. We're fast and smooth."

Training overcame exhaustion and alcohol. Names and mission specifics were banished from the enclosed space. "You'll recognize the seller?"

"I'm an old Delta hand, Nathan, and I always do my homework."

"My bad. I'm just tired."

"Apologies not necessary."

Monsarrat hoped for a smooth transaction but anticipated the O.K. Corral. "How many shooters will you bring to the party, in case unpleasantries arise?"

"Eight, including me," Palmer answered, "but I expect your seller will keep a low profile. Best case scenario, he'll act rationally and arrive alone."

"Worst case scenario?"

"I don't think there is one. He won't bring attention onto himself, pawning national treasures to an *oyinbo*," Palmer continued.

Monsarrat granted him the point. "Just grins and giggles, okay? Let's say he arrives with bodyguards and insists they accompany him. How do we play the scenario?"

"One or two bodyguards is not a problem. Three straphangers is still manageable. Beyond four, though, the space becomes crowded and more difficult to control."

"I'll make sure the numbers stay low."

"You must leave the locks in the suite open. I don't want my boys to waste time kicking down doors."

"Are your boys disciplined?"

"They're former military, Nathan. They understand the chain of command."

The Gulfstream's engines thrust the jet down the runway and into the sky. Their energy pushed him into the leather seat. He felt the bump of the wheels folding into the fuselage. "I'll need a weapon in the hotel room."

"If memory serves, you're fond of the Glock 30?"

"It's one of my favorites."

"On the desk is a combo fax, scanner, and printer, acquired for its enormous printing capacity. Pull out the paper holder. The

Glock is inside, fully loaded and suppressed. If the situation heads south, don't deliberate. Shoot first and make sure no one is able to answer questions later."

Monsarrat appreciated professionalism. "It'll be my call, Mark."

"No argument. We'll monitor you, video and audio. When you want the cavalry, give me a go word or a hand signal."

"How about heel of the palm pressed against the forehead? Either hand."

"Good enough," Palmer agreed. "What's the go word?"

"Glitch," Monsarrat answered. "As in I hope we don't have one."

The plane leveled at its cruising altitude of 51,000 feet. The coffee mug in Monsarrat's hand was steady. "After the exchange, how do we go forward?"

"We rendezvous outside the hotel with the rest of the team, two dozen shooters with SAWs, Ma Deuces, and M4s," Palmer explained. "The boys set the ambush yesterday outside the FATA compound. A dozen 81mm mortar rounds will soften them up, and when they're running through the muck like headless chickens, we'll set off the claymores. We mop up and get you and your statue to the airport."

"Blessed and Innocence belong to me. I want the honor of the coup de grâce, putting bullets between their eyes," Monsarrat insisted.

"It's your party, Nathan. Your pièce de résistance."

"It's a solid plan of attack, Mark."

"Train hard, fight easy, I say."

Hearing the detailed preparations, his nerves began to loosen and his muscles started to relax. "If the room needs cleaning, do you have a contingency in place?"

"I have a crew to sanitize it."

He was curious. "In whose name did you register at the hotel?"

"An Aussie named Jamie Ferguson, but don't order room service."

Monsarrat understood his concern. "The fewer people who see us, the fewer problems to fix."

The cabin soothed him with a blanket of white sound. He thought he could stay aloft for a very long time, contemplating the philosophy of opposites, the ying and yang of hell in the Delta below and heaven in the skies above.

He realized that Palmer was explaining the transformation of the FATA since his release from the Delta compound. "Blessed got true religion, or someone offered him a more lucrative business model. The number of rebel attacks on oil installations has decreased and kidnapping attempts have slowed to once or twice a month, and those attempts have been so rankly amateur, I'm convinced FATA has not been involved. At the same time, politicians and generals from Abuja started to arrive at the compound with suitcases."

"Payments for stopping the raids?"

"If the visitors had been from the oil companies, maybe, but politicians and generals? Blessed should have been paying them to stay out of the Delta."

Monsarrat acknowledged the point. "If Blessed were buying them off, he would have gone to Abuja. So why the visits to the Delta?"

Palmer admitted that he did not know. "Any change in FATA behavior, I need to understand why. I increased surveillance on the compound. Six weeks after the visits began, a team of watchers followed Blessed and Innocence, dressed in their Sunday best, to Port Harcourt Airport. Frank, Joe, and I picked them up at the terminal, where they loaded a dozen suitcases onto a plane bound for Abuja. Frank and Joe stayed with them while I braced a few officials with white envelopes to learn where the two psychopaths were headed."

"The luggage was full of cash from the politicians and generals?"

"Once I learned they were headed for Frankfurt, I bought three tickets on the same flight. We had a tense moment in Abuja when we changed planes and lost sight of them, but thirty minutes later they were back at the gate. I figured they were on the tarmac eyeballing the transfer to make sure the suitcases didn't vanish."

Monsarrat considered that rebels might not be as stupid as they appeared. "How much money did they carry?"

"Judging by the size of the suitcases, I'd say between one point five and two million, depending on the denominations, in dollars or euros. Nobody carries naira to Europe."

"Why fly to Germany with so much cash? To buy weapons? Invest in real estate?"

"Frankfurt wasn't their final destination. A pair of stiffs in suits met them in the terminal. They transferred the suitcases to a private jet and went wheels up."

"It takes planning and a willingness to spend serious money to buy that kind of service," Monsarrat noted. "Blessed and Innocence don't reach that level of sophistication."

Palmer agreed. "Seems like they had an angel whispering in their ears."

Monsarrat thought of Sanhedrin.

"We dropped a few Franklins and discovered that they flew to Vaduz," he continued. "No one goes to Lichtenstein with so much cash save for one reason."

"They opened an account."

"Whatever went down in Vaduz, it happened fast. Blessed and Innocence returned to the Delta less than twenty-four hours after they went wheels up from Port Harcourt."

Monsarrat returned to his original question. "What is FATA doing for the politicians and the generals to earn that kind of money?"

"It bothers me, not knowing," Palmer admitted. "We might want to have them answer that question before we blast their compound into the stone age."

"They could be trafficking teenage boys and girls. Or drugs."

"I'm just hired help, Nathan. If you want to shoot first and ask questions if they're still alive, I'm with you. If you're curious and want to pull out their molars first, I'll hand you the pliers. As long as we agree on the bottom line. I still have a mother and three little kids who need to be avenged."

Monsarrat knew curiosity was an indulgence. "Why tell me the story?"

Palmer offered a generous portion of his Southern charm. "Just jawing, Nathan."

"I doubt that, Mark, but I didn't come all this way only to collect a statue," he replied. "Whatever games Blessed and Innocence are playing in Vaduz don't concern me. Before I go wheels up for Massachusetts, though, I'll send both of them to hell."

Pete came to collect their coffee mugs. "We've begun our approach, gentlemen."

The Gulfstream touched down smoothly at a private airfield. The jet taxied to the end of the runway, where a pair of Suburbans waited at the edge of the tarmac. Monsarrat held onto his valise and followed Palmer down the ramp. The humidity clung to him like an oppressive weight. He felt as if he were forcing a path through quicksand. The sun fried his skin, and the heat scorched his lungs.

"Port Harcourt welcomes you, Nathan."

Monsarrat watched Frank carry his suitcase into the second vehicle before climbing into the lead Suburban, where Palmer again made introductions. "Nathan, our driver is Bill. Dave has shotgun."

They dressed in tee shirts, tactical pants, jungle boots, and sunglasses. Both wore tactical vests with ceramic plates. Clips secured a pair of Mossberg 500 shotguns with pistol grips and six-shot side saddles to their seats. Each strapped a Heckler and Koch P30 pistol in a nylon holster to his thigh and attached a three-inch push knife in a hard nylon sheath to his belt.

Monsarrat shook their hands. "How long to the hotel?"

"Not far in distance. Go-slows are the problem, but since it's Saturday, we may make speed," Bill answered.

Monsarrat stared out the darkened window. Decay fed upon the urban landscape like testamentary blight. Mounds of garbage as high as two story houses bordered the road. Concrete buildings sagged. Behind crumbled exterior walls, unfinished houses squatted like stumps of broken teeth. Hand-painted billboards, faded by the elements and torn by the restless, offered hair straightening and money exchanges.

His task was simple. Ascertain the validity of the Nok. Signal Sanhedrin to transmit the funds to Okeri's bank account. Travel through the Delta jungle, attack the rebel compound, and kill the FATA leaders, plus every rebel with them. Return to Massachusetts with the Nok, collect the remainder of his payment, and seek peace in the guise of Dean Monsarrat.

A single doubt grew stronger, until it pounded like a vengeful sledgehammer. If Sanhedrin's contact had passed false intelligence about the death of Rosalinda two years earlier, if she were still alive, if she remained on the rebel compound, she would surely die in the attack, ripped apart by mortars, claymores, and 5.56 mm slugs.

A HULKING, EVIL CASTLE

The Hotel Paradise hulked like an evil castle on a hill above the center of the city. The two Suburbans drove through the security checkpoint to the entrance of the building. Palmer led Monsarrat directly to his suite, showed him the suppressed Glock 30, pointed out the hidden cameras and microphones, and opened the cooler filled with bottled water, sandwiches, and snacks. "If you need anything, just smile for the cameras or sing for the mics."

Despite the efforts of the air conditioning, spores of mold stained the walls. Monsarrat removed the leather kit from his suitcase and carried it into the bathroom. He brushed his teeth with bottled water and swallowed aspirin. After shaving and showering, he inspected the Glock. Its proximity reassured him.

He woke early on Sunday morning, groggy from ragged sleep, repeated his ablutions, and dressed in a short-sleeved bush shirt, khaki cargo pants, and ankle-high canvas boots. At the desk, he turned on the laptop, confirmed the wireless connection, put the computer to sleep, and placed Sanhedrin's doohickey next to it. He again checked the Glock's slide and magazine. He paced, reversed direction, moved a single chair before the desk, and turned to the wall. "I'm heading to the lobby."

He played with coffee and toast while waiting for Okeri to arrive. At the front of the restaurant, Frank and Joe paid more attention to their eggs than to him. When Joe leaned forward to emphasize a verbal point, he tapped the table twice with his right index finger, then laid his palm flat on its surface, the signal that Okeri had arrived with a sole bodyguard.

As if contemplating an existential koan, Monsarrat focused his full concentration on the entrance to the restaurant. He experienced the familiar singularity of purpose when an operation morphed from the theoretical to the actual and instincts fueled by adrenaline and balanced by experience replaced the tedium of research and preparation. His first thought, as he turned in his chair and absorbed the full force of an explosion of confusion, that a suicide bomber had hurled him into a Nigerian hell, was quickly surmounted by his curiosity about Okeri, if he were in league with the two rebels or just another cog in Sanhedrin's machinations. His third thought centered on the desire for vengeance in multiple acts against his former boss for his deceit, against Palmer for his naiveté, against himself for his gullibility, but mostly against Blessed and Innocence for his Delta imprisonment and, especially, for Rosalinda.

Like a black hole, the mass of Blessed absorbed the light of the room. Trailing in his gravitational force, Innocence carried an aluminum photography case. They wore polyester suits with sagging jacket pockets. In a traditional greeting, Blessed threw his arms above his head. "*Obobo canda*! How manage deze days? Suffah man c'mon back tuh me!"

Monsarrat thought Blessed did not seem surprised, as if he accepted his appearance in a Port Harcourt hotel as a rhythm of nature akin to the dawn, the dusk, and the tides. Or as if he considered his presence as a sign of Egbesu's favor. Or as if he had been told to expect him. Innocence wore his only emotion, a caustic scowl of defiance, disgust, and hatred on his scarred face. He appeared ready to drop the aluminum case and pull the weapon from his jacket pocket.

Monsarrat's right hand itched to hold the suppressed Glock. Instead, he offered it and a promise. "Good morning, Blessed. I'm going to make you a wealthy man."

The giant took Monsarrat's white hand between his two ebony palms. He chortled at the disparity in their size. "I already welty, suffah man. I wear European suits made for me. One fittin'! Innocence wear European suits. One fittin'! Wat you wear, suffah man?"

Monsarrat felt the sweat drip beneath his shirt. Speaking took an act of divine will. "We'll go to my room. In fifteen minutes, you'll be even more wealthy."

Innocence glared at Monsarrat but spoke to Blessed. "Why yuh trust suffah man? Yuh fuhget he spit on us wit' his funny muny? Wat he gunna do tuh us tuday? How he gunna steal frum us dis time?"

Blessed swept Innocence aside as easily as if he were swatting a mosquito. "I fuhget nuttin'. We no do no business in dis place. We go wit' suffah man. We make everytin' right."

The elevator shook like an old dog in the rain. Monsarrat recited a silent prayer for the complacency of the two rebels. He wanted payback so badly, he considered killing the two men inside the cage. They stood in such close proximity their arms would entangle if they tried to clear their weapons.

Innocence had provided Monsarrat with an epiphany. Sanhedrin had allowed him to rot in the Delta for eighteen weeks while he exchanged the Agency's ransom money for counterfeit bills. His former boss had banked the authentic greenbacks and bought his freedom with fake money. For Sanhedrin, who could grasp a nascent opportunity like no else, his captivity had been a divine stroke of luck, a foolproof scenario to deepen his pockets.

He ushered the rebels into his suite, leaving the door slightly ajar. "Make yourselves comfortable, gentlemen. This will just take a minute."

Blessed settled his huge frame into the chair. Innocence stood above him. Monsarrat sat behind the desk and flexed his fingers, like a pianist preparing for the ivory keyboard. When the screen woke, he typed the password into the laptop. "Before I transfer the money, I need to examine the Nok."

"Show it tuh 'im, Innocence. Let suffah man look at it."

"Dis *oyinbo* cheat us. His muny no gud. We try tuh buy guns 'n bullets, the big Roosan man, he laff at us. He call us stoopid niggah boys. Wat yuh plan tuh do tuh him, Blessed?"

"Maybe we take dis man wit' us. Maybe we keep him dis time fuhevah. Maybe I gib him tuh yuh. Yuh beat him like a wuman."

Monsarrat listened to their argument with detached interest. The rebels would soon understand that they were dead men. "Why don't we conclude our business before you decide how to dispose of me?"

"Yuh take dis muny, Blessed, den you kill dis suffah man. Yuh sell dis old stat'chue tuh sum udder *oyinbo* sum udder day. Dis suffah man gonna be a de'd *oyinbo*."

Blessed fixed the primal power of his intensity upon Innocence. "Yuh gib hin dat case. Yuh gib sojah man dat case now."

Innocence released his grip. "Yuh do be safe wit' it, *oyinbo*."

He placed the case on the desk and pushed open the locks. The statue, resting in a nest of crumbled newspapers, matched its photograph. He located the digital marker, slid the switch on the doohickey, and ran the red light over the surface of the statue. When it flashed green, he turned off the device and placed it aside the terracotta.

Innocence was suspicious. "Wat dat, *oyinbo*?"

He took a sensual pleasure in the certainty the two rebels had mere minutes to live. Vengeance would soon be his, justice no longer delayed, justice no longer denied. "It's my magic wand. I wave it, and you get rich."

He carefully secured the locks and carried the case to the far corner of the room, where it would be safe from the ensuing carnage, and returned to the desk and typed Sanhedrin's message into the laptop. With the tip of his finger hovering above the enter key, he felt a righteous strength.

"Wat wrung wit' yuh, suffah man? Why yuh makin' noises?"

His smile burst like the sun shattering a rain cloud, a kid in the candy shop smile. "What you are watching, Blessed, is the blooming of a shit-eating grin."

"Wat yuh say, suffah man?"

Monsarrat hit the enter key. "I say that you are now a wealthier man."

The rebel leader ripped the laptop from his hands. When he squinted at the screen, his laughter boomed, an explosive sound. Mucous ran from his broad nostrils. "*Obobo canda* dun big, big muhstake. *Obobo canda* dun add a big, big zero fuh me. *Obobo canda* dun makin' me welty, welty, welty wit his big, big, big muhstake."

He handed the laptop to Innocence. "Yuh look, Innocence. Yuh look at *obobo canda*'s big, big, big muhstake."

Innocence stood over Blessed and giggled. "Oh, suffah man be stoopid man. Oh, suffah man be moh stoopid t'an stoopid niggah boy."

Their reactions confirmed Monsarrat's suspicion that Sanhedrin had not planned to pay the rebels for the statue. His former boss had schemed to steal the Nok and bank his Russian client's money. He had lied to him about Okeri, and he had maneuvered him like a front rank pawn into a small, enclosed space with his Delta captors, confident they would never leave the hotel room alive.

"Yuh look for muy bank now, Innocence. Yuh look for suffah man muny in muy bank."

Innocence removed a smart phone from an inside pocket of his suit pocket. His fingers flew around the small screen, but after a moment his expression of glee faded into despair. He held the phone next to the laptop. "Nuh muny, Blessed."

"Whut yuh say, nuh muny? Yuh see suffah man on dis machine. He sen' me muy muny. My muny in muy bank."

Innocence shook the phone at Monsarrat. "*Oyinbo* dun it one muh time! *Oyinbo* dun rob dis muny! Dis *oyinbo* gonna be de'd *oyinbo*."

Blessed stood and threw the chair across the room. "I wan' my muny. Where my muny?"

"Suffah man stole all dis muny!"

The rebel leader howled. "Nuh suffah man gunna take muy muny!"

"Yuh kill dis *oyinbo*, Blessed! Yuh kill him de'd!"

Monsarrat pressed the heel of his palm against his forehead. He spoke calmly as he reached for the Glock. "Glitch. It's a glitch. Just a glitch. I'll fix it."

He pulled the Glock from the machine as Palmer and three shooters burst into the room from the adjoining suites. Two more came through the hallway. Their suppressed weapons hissed. Blessed absorbed the assault of bullets from four weapons. Rounds from the fifth and sixth knocked him to his knees.

Innocence dropped to the floor and curled into a fetal position as Monsarrat pressed the suppressed Glock between his eyes and reached into his pocket for his weapon.

"You stay right here. Don't go anywhere."

Palmer closed the door to the hallway. "Frank, sweep the suites. Grab Nathan's suitcase. Make sure you don't even leave dust. You have five minutes, but do it in less. Load the Suburbans and wait for us downstairs."

Monsarrat handed Innocence's .50 caliber Desert Eagle to Joe. "If that bastard so much as flinches, clean his ears with a bullet."

He crossed the room and kicked the rebel leader onto his back. Blood frothed from his mouth and stained the brown hotel rug crimson. His lungs labored, and his wide eyes stared at the ceiling, as if seeking answers from a plaster heaven.

"You put a rope around my neck, you son of a bitch. You led me on my hands and knees. You treated me like a dog."

He felt gratification at the fear in Blessed's eyes. He put his foot on his neck and crushed his face into the rug. "I said I would kill you with my fingers around your throat, but I was wrong. I'm going to crush your windpipe with my boot."

Palmer watched the rebel thrash. "The bastard's too damned big to die."

Grunting his agreement, Monsarrat fired the suppressed Glock. The first bullet killed Blessed. The second and third were insurance.

Palmer threw him a towel. "Your boots, Nathan."

Monsarrat cleaned the gore and dropped the cloth onto the dead rebel.

"Take his weapon," Palmer ordered. "Bring over the little one."

Joe withdrew a second Desert Eagle from the dead man's jacket, then dragged the terrified rebel deputy next to the bloody corpse.

Monsarrat slapped him twice with the butt of the Glock, two fast movements with his right hand. "You remember those poor Asians you hacked into pieces before you fed their body parts to the dogs? Their souls need to drink your blood before they can go to their eternal sleep."

Innocence held his hands before his face, fingertips pressed together, and whimpered in the patois of the Delta.

"I believe he is praying."

Monsarrat jerked down his hands. "You have something to tell me?"

"Sojah man nuh wanna talk. Sojah man wanna kill Innocence de'd."

"I can kill you fast, or I can kill you slow. It depends on what you have to tell me."

"Stick with the plan, Nathan."

"I came for the statue, Blessed, and Innocence," he replied. "I need five minutes with this son of a bitch, then you can drop me at the plane and head to the FATA compound. They're your fight now, not mine."

He turned to Joe. "Hog tie him. Wrists to ankles. Make it tight."

Joe kicked Innocence onto his stomach, withdrew plastic zip cuffs from his cargo pants, and in a smooth motion pulled the rebel's arms behind his back and yanked them upwards. The rug muffled his howls.

"Need a hand, boss."

Palmer helped him cuff his wrists and his ankles. They connected the two plastic manacles with a third zip cuff and rolled him onto his side. "What now?"

Cold discipline replaced hot emotion. "Wait in the Suburban. I'll meet you downstairs in a few minutes."

"We're staying, Nathan."

"Suit yourself, but don't interfere."

He sat cross-legged on the rug, inches away from the rebel, and smelled the uric stench of his fear. "You wet yourself, Innocence."

"Sojah nuh wanna kill Innocence!"

Monsarrat pointed to the Glock. "If you answer my first question correctly, I'll ask you my second question. If you answer that question correctly, I'll ask my third. So on and so forth. If you answer all my questions correctly, you will live, but the first time you lie to me, I will shoot your balls off."

"Sojah man nuh wanna kill Innocence!" he repeated. "Sojah man and Innocence work fuh de same man. De big, big CIA man."

Monsarrat slapped him. "Don't waste my time."

The rebel spit blood onto the rug. "Innocence tell sojah man big, big CIA secret. Sojah man nuh kill Innocence."

He slapped the rebel again. "Time to choose, Innocence, live or die. Why are the politicians and generals paying so much money to FATA?"

Tears spilled from his eyes. "Sojah man CIA. Innocence CIA. Same! Same!"

Monsarrat pressed the Glock into his eye. "Last chance to answer my question." Innocence's sobs blotted his words.

"Say it again."

The rebel spoke in staccato bursts. "De pol'ticians and de gen'rals gib Blessed big, big muny tuh fight de fut washahs. Tuh fight de Mus'im brudders. Nuh muh fightin' wit de oil men. Dey prumise Blessed after de reb'lution he gunna be de big, big gen'ral in de bran' new army of de Delta. Dey prumise Blessed gunna be min'ster of de oil."

Monsarrat thought the story preposterous, which made it plausible, from an Agency standpoint. "Which revolution?"

"De CIA reb'lution. De big, big CIA man gib big big muny to de pol'ticians and de gen'rals fuh de reb'lution tuh fight de fut washahs. One day he cum tuh de Delta fuh Blessed. He cum wit' big, big guns."

The ability of the Agency to delude itself never failed to amaze Monsarrat. "Had you ever seen him before?"

"De same same CIA man cum to de Delta tuh buy sojah man."

Behind him, Monsarrat heard Palmer softly whistle.

"De big, big CIA man open de strong bottle. Blessed, Innocence, big, big CIA man drin'. T're, f'oh times. Blessed git de runny tummy. He guh tuh de hole. Big, big CIA man whispah. He prumise Innocence one day fas' his liddle CIA man cum tuh kill Blessed. He nuh trus' Blessed. He say Blessed stoopid man. He say Innocence smaht man. He prumise Innocence gunna be new leader of FATA in de reb'lution. He prumise Innocence gunna be de big, big gen'ral in de bran' new Army of de Delta. He prumise Innocence gunna be de new min'ster of de oil. He prumise Innocence big, big muny."

The Agency had not altered its approach to recruitment since the glory days of Cold War honey traps. Offers of power, sex, drugs, weapons, and money followed by threats and violence. He shifted the Glock to the center of Innocence's forehead, atop his tribal markings. "Talk faster. Tell me about the revolution."

Pain contorted the rebel's face. "De FATA fighters gunna help de pol'ticians and gen'rals kill all de fut washahs in de gubernment and in de army and in de police in de Delta. We gunna make a new gubernment for all de God fearin' Christ'in people."

"When does the revolution start?"

"De fuhst day of de new year de fut washah pres'dent gunna die. De fut washah min'sters gunna die. All de fut washah pol'ticians and gen'rals frum de nort' gunna die. De new gubernment gunna be all de Jesus fearin' Christ'in people frum de sout'."

Monsarrat laughed. The Agency loved its games.

"Yuh gunna free Innocence, sojah man. Yuh gunna free Innocence now."

"Sure, Innocence. I'll set you free."

He spoke over his shoulder. "Hand me a knife and a towel, Mark."

Palmer passed him a three inch push knife in a scabbard. "Small cuts only, Nathan."

Monsarrat snarled, "What did you say?"

"Nothing drastic, just enough to make him talk."

"I'm paying for your muscle, not your advice."

He gagged the rebel's mouth with the bloody cloth, drew the push knife from the scabbard, and sliced the fleshy lobe from his right ear. "If you lie to me, I'll cut you into small pieces, starting with your dick."

Strangled sounds erupted from Innocence's throat. He tried to press his shoulder against the wound, but the blood spurted.

Monsarrat pulled the towel from his mouth and tossed the severed flesh onto his chest. "Tell me about the statue."

The rebel strained against his plastic restraints. "Blessed cum bahk frum de hole. He ful' wit' de anger. He say big, big CIA man nuh moh gib him bad juju. He say now big, big CIA man make him sick wit' bad, bad drin'. He say befuh big, big CIA man cheat him with de nuh gud muny tuh buy de suffah man. De big, big CIA man say he nuh drin' nuh gud. He say nuh muny nuh gud. De muny sojah man muny. Sojah man muny nuh gud. He prumise Blessed big, big gud muny. He say he wan' stat'chue in mus'um. He say Blessed mus' tak' de stat'chue. He gib Blessed dis stikah. Blessed mus' put dis stikah on de head of de stat'chue. He say his liddle CIA man gunna cum fuh de stat'chue. He gunna look for dis stikah. He see dis stikah, he gib big, big gud muny tuh Blessed."

He repeated, "Big, big gud muny tuh Blessed."

Monsarrat thought Sanhedrin deserved both a Pulitzer and an Oscar.

"Sojah man gunna say tuh big, big CIA man. Innocence de man in de Delta. Innocence gunna kill all de fut washahs. Big, Big CIA man wan' anudder stat'chue in de mus'um, Innocence gunna git it fuh him. Fastah dan Blessed. Bettah dan Blessed. Innocence gunna be de big, big gen'ral in de Army of de Delta. Innocence gunna be min'ster of de oil. Innocence gunna be de boy of de big, big CIA man."

Monsarrat slit a strip of cloth from the rebel's suit jacket. He wrapped it around his head to bind his wounded ear.

"Sojah man gud man."

He pressed the tip of the knife hard into the rebel's crotch. "You're wrong, Innocence. I am a very, very bad man. Do you believe me?"

He nodded vigorously.

"Speak carefully. One wrong answer, and you'll squat to piss. Tell me you promise."

"Innocence prumise!"

Monsarrat understood the Okeri and the terracotta had been red herrings waved by Sanhedrin. The Amanyanabo had never owned the statue. Still, he pressed the rebel. "Where is Rehovoth Okeri? Why didn't he come with the statue today?"

"Dat man, him de uld man! Him de bad, bad man! Him de pol'tician man!" Innocence protested. "He nuh de stat'chue man. Blessed de stat'chue man. Blessed tak' de stat'chue in de mus'um. Okeri, he nuh gud man. Him de pol'tician man! Him de fut washah man!"

Monsarrat slapped his face. "Okeri's not from the North. He's not a Muslim."

Innocence cringed like a beaten dog. "Him de man wit' de fut washahs. He one fuh dem. He nuh gud man. He nuh man fuh gud sojah man."

Monsarrat thought Innocence truly confused by his mention of Okeri. "Last question, Innocence."

"Sojah man gud man!"

He asked the only question that mattered to him, the reason he had agreed to Sanhedrin's proposal. "How did Rosalinda die?"

When the rebel shook his head, blood soaked through the bandage and painted the rug in a red arc. "Who dat? He de fut washah man?"

He struck him with so much force that an electric jolt shot from his shoulder to the tips of his fingers. Innocence collapsed onto the floor, his head at an odd angle. For a moment, Monsarrat thought he had killed him, but Innocence gathered himself and offered a glare of demonic hatred.

"Easy, Nathan," Palmer drawled.

Monsarrat hauled Innocence into a sitting position and again pressed the tip of the blade into his crotch. "Rosalinda is the

Filipina nurse who took care of me in your stinking compound. How did she die?"

"De nurse wuman? Blessed dun kill her!" He chortled at the memory. "Blessed dun kill de gurl wit' his big, big stick. Blessed dun kill de gurl de'd."

Monsarrat wanted to slit the rebel's throat more than he wanted to breathe, but the story of Langley's plot was plausible and, as much as he wanted both rebel leaders dead, he knew better than to betray an Agency operation.

"De gurl cry! De gurl cry tuh live!"

Monsarrat wrapped his hands around the rebel's throat, knowing he could not kill him but wanting to drag him to the dark brink of death. The more Innocence thrashed, the harder he squeezed, until he felt the tip of Palmer's suppressed Glock against his temple and heard his cold words.

"Let him go, Nathan."

"Back off, Mark."

"Can't do that, Nathan. Drop your hands."

"You'll shoot me to save this piece of shit?"

"I don't like it, but orders are orders."

Monsarrat hauled Innocence upright. "Live again, you son of a bitch, but know that one day I will find you. I will tie you to a chair. I will cut off your toes, your fingers, and your dick, feed them to the dogs, and watch you bleed out and die."

"Nevah, sojah man! Sojah man nevah kill Innocence!"

Monsarrat grabbed the Glock and swung the butt into the rebel's head. Innocence collapsed, the cloth binding his wounded ear dripping blood into the rug.

He cleaned the push knife, his hands shaking with barely contained anger, and handed it and the pistol to Palmer. "Why do you want him alive?"

"Personally, I agree with you. I want him dead, but my people feel differently."

"You knew Okeri wouldn't show up. You expected the two FATA rebels."

"It's all about the intel."

"You played me."

"All's well that ends well."

"Not from where I stand," Monsarrat countered. "I've been screwed by the Agency more times than I can count, but I never expected you to shaft me."

He sent Sanhedrin the final message, although he knew all was far from well, picked up the aluminum case, and followed Palmer into the hallway. The elevator shuddered as it descended to the lobby. The Suburbans idled outside the hotel, as if impatient to distance themselves from the abattoir. He placed the aluminum case and the valise on the rear bench of the second vehicle and sat next to them, like a mother protecting her young.

Palmer climbed into the navigator seat and issued a terse command to Joe. "Get us to the airfield fast."

Monsarrat leaned forward. "What happens to your plans to raid the FATA compound?"

"It'll be done, just not today."

"You'll wait until after the revolution?"

"You heard Innocence. He enjoys Langley's protection. He's the new leader of FATA, and he's part of their plans."

"Plans for what?"

"I can't say, Nathan."

"Can't or won't?" he demanded. "What is your oil consortium planning?"

"I can't say, because I don't know," Palmer replied. "I'm just a shooter."

Monsarrat struggled to maintain composure. "Rosalinda kept me alive in the Delta, but those bastards raped and killed her. I waited two years for payback, and you stopped me."

"I feel for you, Nathan, but I can't help you."

"Sooner or later, Innocence is a dead man. If you get in my way again, I'll kill you, too."

"Let it go, Nathan."

Monsarrat wanted information immediately but had no way to obtain it. Threats would be like water off a duck's tail to Palmer, and bribery would be futile effort for a professional dedicated to his employers. His chances with Sanhedrin, who in the throes of success often suffered from verbal dysentery, would be better. He also possessed the statue, an invaluable bargaining chip.

The Suburbans cleared the security checkpoint at the oil company's private airfield and drove onto the tarmac to the idling Gulfstream 550. Monsarrat followed Palmer out of the vehicle, carrying the aluminum case and the valise. Joe passed his baggage to Paul and held up his hand in a gesture of farewell. As soon as they strapped into their seats, the jet rolled down the runway.

The Gulfstream lifted off and gained cruising altitude. After the landing gear retracted, Paul brought him a slab of hard, white foam, a permanent marker, and a utility knife. "Is this what you requested, sir?"

"Put it on the table. I'll need a trash can, too."

Monsarrat opened the aluminum case and carefully removed the terracotta. He threw the newspapers into the trash can. With the marker, he traced the statue's outline onto the foam and repeated the procedure with the doohickey. He carved the markings with the utility knife and placed the foam into the aluminum case. The statue and the doohickey fit the spaces perfectly.

He tossed the debris into the trash can, closed the case, and placed it by his seat. "Is there a shower on board?"

Palmer pointed toward the galley. "Whatever you need—soap, shampoo, towels—the boys will get for you."

Monsarrat shaved, brushed his teeth, and showered. He changed into traveling clothes and handed the stained items to Paul. "Can you take care of these for me?"

"I'll burn them when we're back on the compound."

Slightly more than an hour after lifting off from Port Harcourt, the Gulfstream landed at the private airfield in Abuja. Monsarrat and Palmer reversed their actions of the previous day. They greeted Todd and climbed into the waiting Suburbans. The small convoy covered the distance to Abuja International Airport quickly. Todd escorted Evan Walsh's suitcase through security and onto the baggage loading dock, while Palmer checked him onto the flight, slipping envelopes thick with naira to airline employees and Immigration officials.

Before the jetway, Monsarrat gripped Palmer's shoulder. "Innocence killed Rosalinda. I'll be back for him."

"I hope you won't wait two more years."

"You took my money, and then you screwed me."

Palmer's sigh carried the weight of confession. "Hell, Nathan, I would have helped you kill Blessed for free. Just not Innocence this time."

Six hours after its departure, the Lufthansa jet touched down in Frankfurt. In the lounge, Monsarrat again embraced his paranoia and changed his routing. "Will my suitcase be on the new flight?"

"Not to worry, Mr. Walsh. We have enough time to make the connection to New York," the representative promised.

He slept through the nine-hour flight. In John F. Kennedy International Airport, the statue caused little curiosity. In the Green Line, he handed a Customs official his declaration form. He walked to the taxi rank with a jauntiness he had not felt for many months. In the back of the cab, he instructed the driver to take him to the Plaza Hotel. He retrieved his cell phone from the valise and dialed Solomon Grinnell.

The former yeshiva *bocher* answered on the first ring. "*Nu?*"

"I used to work for your father," Monsarrat began. "Back in the day. As his adviser."

Grinnell's father, David, had been a cobbler in Williamsburg who had never employed more than a hammer and tacks, but the Biblical reference was Monsarrat's standard greeting.

Grinnell spoke as if he had just emerged from a casting call for heavily accented Brooklyn thugs. He peppered his conversations with Yiddish, Hebrew, and Arabic slang. "You wanna buy a diamond, *habibi*?"

"I'm looking for something dignified, not ostentatious. Something practical, but powerful. Something that sends a message."

"You leave it to me, my friend. I know what you like."

"Why don't you bring it to your favorite restaurant? The flowery one? In ninety minutes?"

"Expedited service costs extra. On a Sunday evening, no less."

"Ninety minutes, Solomon." He closed the connection and awaited the call from his former boss, who would be displeased that the Nok had not arrived in Boston.

When the cell phone rang, the screen showed the number from Sanhedrin's business card. "The flight out of Port Harcourt was delayed. I missed the connection in Abuja."

Disappointment tinged his reply. "You switched flights in Frankfurt."

"We were rerouted to Miami."

"You flew into JFK. On time. No delays. A little more than an hour ago."

"What do you want, Felix?"

"I would have thought that answer to be obvious, Nathan. I want you here, in Boston, right now, handing me the statue."

"Yeah, about the Nok. Looks like we'll have a slight delay in our delivery schedule."

"How much of a delay, Nathan?"

"Gotta take another call, Felix. I'll be in touch." He severed the connection, slid the battery from the case, and dropped the pieces into the valise. He did trust cell phones.

On Sunday evening, traffic into Manhattan flowed easily. The Plaza Hotel conjured fond memories for Monsarrat of afternoons in the Oak Bar, drinking bourbon with oil company executives whose expense accounts reached as deep as their drilling projects. The driver stopped beneath the draped flags at the Fifth Avenue entrance. Monsarrat paid him as a bellboy carried his suitcase into the lobby. At the bell desk he received a claims check. He carried the aluminum case and the valise to the Rose Club. The maître d' led him to a table at the rear.

"I'm expecting a friend. About my size, a little heavier, thick, black hair with lots of brilliantine. He looks like a South Korean politician with a *yarmulke*."

He slipped the twenty dollar bill into his pocket. "I'll look for him."

The Rose Club was a compromise between a London gentleman's club and a Parisian boudoir. Monsarrat ordered a bourbon and a seafood Cobb salad from a waitress who spoke as if she were auditioning for the role of Kate in a Broadway production of *The Taming of the Shrew*.

The maître d' escorted Grinnell to the table between the delivery of the bourbon and the salad. The New Yorker wore a black suit and a white shirt with an open collar, as befitting Hassidic couture. A leather laptop bag hung from his broad shoulder. While most of his religious brethren shopped at Sears, Grinnell wore Armani suits and tailored shirts. Upon first sight, he was often mistaken for an Italian businessman, or a French cop, until the *tzizit* of his *tallis* hanging beneath the hems of his jacket and the silken *yarmulke* perched upon his brilliantine hair were noticed.

Monsarrat had met him through a Mossad contact based at the United Nations, when they lured a Libyan diplomat with oil connections and a predilection for young boys into a honey trap. Grinnell had supplied the boys, and Monsarrat had admired his discretion. Two months later, he purchased from him a five round .38 Smith & Wesson Special, identifying numbers removed, for a nervous American oil executive who had slept with the wife of a Venezuelan colleague.

Grinnell lived and worked among his fellow Hassidim but possessed the soul of a Russian mafia *vor*. He and three brothers owned a small diamond exchange on 47th Street, between Fifth and Sixth Avenues, in the Diamond District. In certain social circles, he was renown for his artistry turning handguns into collectibles bejeweled with diamonds and precious stones.

Monsarrat stood and shook hands with him. The Hassid placed the leather laptop bag on the floor, then summoned the waitress.

"Dearest, bring me a Johnnie Walker Blue. And whatever it is that my friend is eating."

The waitress eyed him with a cold menace but held her tongue.

"Will you pick around the shrimp, Solomon?"

Grinnell lifted his left shoulder in an exaggerated shrug. "*Insha'allah*. The Lord will guide me."

"How are you, Solomon? You're looking very prosperous."

"*Baruch ha'shem.* Business is good. It's been a long time, *habibi*. I heard you had a few problems a while back? Something African?"

"I retired. I'm a dean now. Greylock College in the Berkshires."

One of Grinnell's bushy eyebrows arched. "*Oy.* An academic with special needs?"

Monsarrat shrugged. "I take on the occasional odd job for friends."

Grinnell handed him a white envelope. "Whenever you feel the need to visit the *sherutim*, fill this envelope with $5,000. Plus any gratuity you feel appropriate."

"Dollars and euros together?"

"As long as I don't lose on the exchange rate, Nathan."

Monsarrat pushed back his chair. "Excuse me, my friend. I need to use the men's room."

He took the aluminum case and the valise with him. In the privacy of a toilet stall, he placed the dollars and euros into the envelope. He included five one hundred dollar bills as a tip for expeditious service and added an extra thousand dollars.

At the table, he placed the envelope between them. "Five thousand equivalent and an extra five hundred for your kindness on a Sunday evening."

"Conducting business at night upsets my wife. She prefers me to remain at home with her and the children."

Monsarrat nodded sympathetically. "What did I purchase, Solomon?"

"Just like before, Nathan. A clean five round .38 Smith & Wesson Special. Plus two boxes of hollow point bullets, in case you want to take down a Middle Eastern Emirate."

Monsarrat tapped the envelope. "I added an extra thousand dollars to the envelope. I need a ride."

Grinnell was already punching a number into his cell phone. "To where, *habibi*? Uptown? New Jersey? Westchester?"

"New Hampshire. Just over the Massachusetts line."

Grinnell's other eyebrow arched. "You'll cover gas and tolls, in addition to the thousand?"

"Of course."

Grinnell's accent intensified when he addressed the cell phone. "Moishe, I need you to bring the Audi to the Plaza Hotel with a full gas tank. You have a passenger."

He listened for a moment. "Take her home and give her a good-night kiss. I want you here before I finish my salad, and you know how quickly I eat."

He severed the connection as the waitress brought his food. He held up the glass of Johnnie Walker Blue. "*L'chaim*, my friend. May you prosper in your new career."

The Hassid carefully ate his salad, picking around the shrimp.

"The Lord is guiding your fork, Solomon."

"Blessed be the name."

Monsarrat smiled at the mention of the Ijaw.

"Something amusing, Nathan?"

Monsarrat had never discovered the font of his inspiration. He was simply gratified that it kept appearing. "What do you hear from Sanhedrin?"

Grinnell finished his salad. He arranged the shrimp into a small mound. "Funny you should ask. A business associate also inquired about Felix a while back."

"A Russian gentleman?"

"I don't think that gentleman applies to this individual. Russian, though, yes."

"What did he ask?"

Grinnell poked the shrimp with his fork, and the pile collapsed. "He was interested in Felix's *bona fides*. He wanted to know if he were trustworthy."

"An interesting question from a Russian."

"I told him that Felix was an expert in his field and left it at that. Are you involved with Sanhedrin? Is he the reason you need my services?"

The chirping of Grinnell's cell phone spared Monsarrat from answering the question. The Hassid listened for a moment. "Moishe is here. Get going. I'll cover the check."

Monsarrat shook his hand. He gathered the laptop bag, aluminum case, and valise.

Grinnell eyed the luggage. "You're not light on your feet anymore."

Monsarrat admitted the critique had merit. "One last thing, Solomon."

"Name it, *habibi*."

"Let me know if you hear anything more from your Russian friend about Sanhedrin."

The Hassid held up an admonishing finger. "Sanhedrin is a dangerous man, Nathan, but these Russians make him look like a puppy. You upset them, and very bad things happen to you."

At the bell desk, the driver greeted him. His clothes were the same color as Grinnell's, but more polyester than Armani. "You're Nathan, right? I'm Moishe Goldman. You wanna go on a ride?"

He stood an inch shorter than six feet and weighed perhaps two hundred pounds, all of it hard. His slightly flattened nose added to the intensity of his accent. The flat bulge between his black jacket and white shirt suggested a nine millimeter weapon. His large knuckles were scarred. "I've never been to New Hampshire."

Monsarrat shook his hand and felt its strength. "You box, Moishe?"

"Light heavyweight," he admitted. "I've added a few pounds since I stopped."

"Are you as good with that nine millimeter as you are with your hands?"

He smiled modestly. "It's a tie."

Monsarrat retrieved his suitcase. He pointed to the Audi A8, and the bell boy placed the suitcase into the trunk. He tipped him and slid the aluminum case and the valise onto the rear bucket seats.

Streetlights illuminated their route. "I thought we'd go up the Henry Hudson, take the Cross Bronx, pick up I-95, and cruise to New Hampshire. The Audi cruises well."

"Before New London, go north on I-395. You get close to the Massachusetts border, I'll tell you where to pull over."

"Got it, boss."

He gave Goldman three hundred dollars. "For gas and tolls. And coffee. A lot of coffee. Don't be shy about stopping."

"Yes, sir, boss. You want, I'll grind the beans myself."

Grinnell had provided a nylon hip holster for the well-maintained revolver. He spun the cylinder, loaded five rounds of brass-jacketed hollow point bullets, replaced the weapon, and left the zipper open. He dropped the laptop bag into the passenger door's pocket, close to his right hand.

Goldman watched him. "Expecting trouble, boss?"

"I have a bad habit of pissing people off."

"Believe me, boss, I know what you mean."

Monsarrat closed his eyes. He thought about Sanhedrin and the terracotta. Sanhedrin and Blessed. Sanhedrin and Innocence.

"Would you like music, boss? I got rock 'n' roll. I got classical. I got opera. I got country 'n' western. I got jazz. I got all the music guys of your generation like."

"Surprise me."

Goldman spun dials and punched buttons. Monsarrat recognized "Cumberland Blues." When they stopped for coffee across the Connecticut line, he noted that Goldman removed the keys from the ignition.

They passed aged industrial cities strung like rusted trinkets the length of Long Island Sound. At Old Saybrook, they crossed the Connecticut River. Twenty minutes later, Goldman exited onto I-395. Approaching the Massachusetts border, Monsarrat felt the presence of Sanhedrin, as if his former boss were a vengeful Shakespearean shade striding through the shadows of the empty border.

"Take the next exit. Bear right at the bottom of the ramp. Go straight for two hundred yards. You'll have a choice of all-night gas stations. I'll need a can of lighter fluid, a box of kitchen matches, and one of those aluminum cooking trays. And another coffee."

Goldman pulled the Audi into a space in front of a mini-mart. He returned in a few minutes and passed Monsarrat a plastic bag, along with a cup of black coffee.

"We gonna have a barbeque, boss? You want me to pick up steaks? A few cold brews?"

Monsarrat gestured at the pumps. "You need gas?"

"I'm a frugal guy. Less money on gas, more money for me. I can make it to New Hampshire in this baby. Gas is twenty, thirty cents per gallon cheaper there."

Monsarrat placed the aluminum cooking tray and the other purchases on his lap. "North of Putnam, you'll see a sign for a rest area. Pull into it slowly. It will be very dark."

"You got it, boss."

The Audi covered the distance quickly. Goldman steered the car into the empty rest area, and in the glare of the car's headlights, Monsarrat saw a picnic table. "Park the car, but leave the headlights on. Lock it, and come with me."

He slid the Smith & Wesson beneath his belt and carried the valise and the plastic bag to the table. The grill was filled with bottles and cans, and the metal bars were rusted. He took the documents from the valise, tore the papers into small pieces, made three loose piles in the aluminum tray, and sprayed the piles with lighter fluid.

"We gonna play with fire, boss? Get a little bit of pyromania action going?"

Monsarrat lit a kitchen match and dropped it onto the first pile. The lighter fluid ignited, and the paper curled into ash. He repeated the procedure twice, wrapped his hand inside the plastic bag, and crushed the ashes.

He didn't need to ask him if he carried a knife. "Give me your blade."

He accepted a five-inch dagger and sliced the binding of the Walsh passport. He cut the data and visa pages into small squares, soaked them in lighter fluid, and burned the papers twice before crushing the ashes.

Old habits only slumbered in his memory. He passed everything to Goldman. "Sprinkle the ashes across the grass. A little here. A little there. Don't dump them all in one spot. Toss the rest of the crap into two or three garbage cans."

"Like a *goyishe* cremation ceremony, boss?"

When Goldman returned, he unlocked the doors. "Fast work, boss. Just under fifteen minutes."

In Massachusetts, I-395 changed its numbers to I-290. The Audi passed through Worcester and merged onto I-495. In Chelmsford, Goldman turned onto Route Three. Beyond the New Hampshire border, Monsarrat instructed him to take exit number eight. "At the bottom of the ramp, drive into the park-and-ride lot."

"No need to catch a bus, boss. I'll take you where you want to go."

"Drive around the lot, Moishe. First clockwise. Then reverse direction. Go slow."

"We looking for anything special, boss?"

"Special, no. Out of the ordinary, yes."

"Like what, for example?"

"Like thugs in cars waiting for a bus that won't arrive until morning."

Goldman finished the first loop. He put the Audi into a tight turn and drove in the opposite direction. "No thugs, boss."

Monsarrat knew that if Sanhedrin were involved, appearances deceived. "Two rows to the right, toward the middle. Stop at the Jeep."

He fit the suitcase into the trunk and laid the aluminum case onto the rear bench. He laid the laptop bag with the revolver and his personal items on the passenger seat.

Goldman stood next to the idling Audi. "You need me for anything else, boss? I gotta get back. My mom likes me to be home by sunrise."

Monsarrat handed him a Benjamin Franklin. "For coffee, Moishe. It's a long ride."

The brake lights of the big car flashed in the darkness as he climbed into the Jeep. He drove down Amherst Street until he found a hotel. At the registration desk, he filled out the form and gave three hundred dollars to the clerk, a young man with moguls of scarlet acne on his cheeks. "I left my credit card case in the kitchen."

The clerk passed him the room key and a cash receipt. "It's not a problem, sir. Cash or credit card for one night. Either is okay."

In the room, he switched on the television. The twenty-four-hour weather channel predicted excellent meteorological conditions for the new day. He confirmed the Nok and the doohickey were no worse for wear of the trip and inspected the Smith & Wesson and its arsenal of hollow point bullets. He did not need to bring down a Middle Eastern Emirate. A small former boss would suffice.

LARGE BILLS, USED BILLS, REAL BILLS

Monsarrat again slept poorly and woke before dawn. Sanhedrin had stalked his dreams. He shaved, showered, dressed, and conducted a final inspection of the hotel room. At the registration desk, the rosaceous clerk returned his deposit, minus the charge.

In the Jeep, he watched the pink glow of the new day as he reconstructed his cell phone. The thought of waking Sanhedrin so pleased him that he dispensed with the usual pleasantries. "Large bills. Used bills. Real bills."

"Good morning, Nathan. Mind telling me where you are?"

"Greenfield. Come alone. At noon. If you're sixty-one seconds late, or if I make any of your muscular friends, I'll put the Nok under my wheels and turn it into terracotta dust."

"You're a tad dramatic this morning, old buddy."

"I'll give you exact directions later."

"Changes to our plan are unwarranted, Nathan, but I'll bring the second installment of your fee to Greenfield at noon. I'll give you the money, and you'll give me the statue."

"One more thing, Felix."

"Yes, Nathan?"

Monsarrat trusted his instincts. "Tell your heavy hitters to get away from my house. Tell them if I see them in the Berkshires again, I'll shoot them."

"Done. Anything else?"

He had much to discuss with his former boss but only one item that would not hold for a few more hours. "My fee has increased."

Sanhedrin objected. "I offered you fifty thousand dollars, but you twisted my arm, and I agreed to double it. Now you're jacking me for more money? You're going down a dangerous road, Nathan."

"Save the despair for someone who cares. Delivery of the Nok will now cost five hundred large."

"Half a million will put me so deep into the red, I'll look like a college loser in a slasher movie."

Monsarrat severed the connection. He drove the Jeep toward Vermont, dotting the I's and crossing the T's of his plan. On Route

101 in Keene, he stopped for coffee and made a phone call to an acquaintance in the Boston Field Office of the FBI. At Winchester, he turned south onto Route 10 and arrived in Greenfield two hours after ending the conversation with his former boss. He liked to arrive early for a contentious meeting, and he expected his encounter with Sanhedrin to be hostile. He wanted to feel comfortable in his environment, especially if there was a possibility that he would shoot someone, or that someone would shoot him.

He parked the Jeep on a dirt shoulder alongside a grassy paddock, one hundred yards from the entrance to a preparatory school, facing south. Fifteen minutes before noon, he dialed Sanhedrin's number but did not allow him the opportunity to speak. "Route 10. Cross the Mohawk Trail."

Eight minutes later, he pressed redial. "Horse paddock on Bernardston Road. You have seven minutes."

At the approach of noon, a blue Maserati cut across the opposite lane of traffic. It rolled to a stop six feet from the Jeep. Sanhedrin stepped out of the GranTurismo. He wore a black cotton tee shirt, black jeans with a silver belt buckle, and black hi-top sneakers. Monsarrat thought he looked like an elf with a bad attitude.

He held up his hand. "Sit on the hood, Felix."

"Absolutely not. This is a GranTurismo. No one sits on the hood of my Maserati."

Monsarrat's shirt hung over his belt. He lifted the hem to reveal the pistol and holster on his hip. He let the shirt fall.

Sanhedrin sat on the hood of his car. "Are you planning to shoot me, Nathan?"

"You come alone?"

Sanhedrin nodded.

"No friends? No heavy hitters?"

Sanhedrin shook his head.

"Throw your car keys over your head. I want them to land behind the Maserati."

"I do not have keys. I have a sophisticated electronic fob that locks and unlocks the door, arms and disarms the alarm systems, and starts the ignition. I can not throw it into the dirt."

Monsarrat tapped the holster.

Sanhedrin threw the fob over his head. "You need to show some respect."

"Toss me your cell phone, Felix."

"Is this necessary?"

"Reach into your pocket slowly. Use your fingertips."

Monsarrat caught the cell phone. He removed the back panel, took out the SIM card, and snapped it in half. He reassembled the device and threw it back to Sanhedrin.

"Your second cell phone. Same drill."

Sanhedrin started to argue, thought better of it, and tossed his second cell phone.

Monsarrat repeated the procedure. "Sit on your hands, Felix, and remain rigid."

Monsarrat picked up the fob at the rear of the GranTurismo and put it into his pocket. He completed the circle and leaned against the hood of the Jeep. He had not seen backup. If Sanhedrin had brought his heavy hitters, they were good enough to remain out of sight.

"May I get off my hands, Nathan? You know I have circulation problems."

Monsarrat had known him since his first day at the Agency. He was neither handsome nor imposing. He projected neither an aura of power nor wealth. At best, he was unassuming and banal. At worst, he was evil. He lacked the chromosome that supplied humanity. "Sure, Felix. Lord knows I don't want you to suffer."

Sanhedrin rubbed his wrists and elbows. "You're looking well, old buddy. I trust the trip went smoothly, all flowers and kisses?"

"Are you asking if I have the Nok?"

"I am asking that exact question."

"It's in the Jeep. The doohickey verified its authenticity."

"Excellent work, Nathan. May we make the exchange? Statue for cash?"

Monsarrat was curious. "Is it the real thing, Felix?"

Sanhedrin exuded innocence. "You said the doohickey verified it."

"The doohickey scanned the sticker," Monsarrat agreed, "but when it beeped, it was the first time, because there never was an expert on Nok art from Cambridge. You gave the sticker to Blessed and told him to place it on the statue during your last trip to the Delta, when you launched your plan to have me kill him, so Innocence could take his place as leader of FATA and the Agency's pet rebel *jefe*. You used the rigamarole of the sticker to distract Blessed, so the big bastard would focus on the doohickey instead of the weapon pointed at his forehead."

Sanhedrin was angelic. "I haven't spoken to Blessed in ages."

"Too bad, Felix, since the next time you talk to him, it'll be in a séance with a medium."

"Is Blessed dead?"

"You know he is."

"What about Innocence?"

"He'll be fine. He's missing an earlobe. I wanted to kill him but something came up."

Sanhedrin appeared pleased. "There's no need for remorse. Blessed was a bad man."

"You don't have to tell me about Blessed. The big bastard wanted to kill me."

"I suppose that was to be expected, Nathan, seeing how you turned off his lights."

"You make it sound like I flew all the way to Port Harcourt to whack him."

Sanhedrin beamed compassion. "That's what you did, Nathan. You flew to Port Harcourt. You acquired the Nok. You whacked Blessed. You flew home."

Monsarrat fought his swelling waves of anger. "Why do you want Innocence alive?"

"Did you get the fever in the Delta, Nathan? You're babbling."

"Okeri was a no-show. You sent Blessed and Innocence to take his place."

"How did they come to the Nok?"

"You know the answer."

"Pray, Nathan, enlighten me."

"From a museum," Monsarrat replied. "Why did you feed me the line about Okeri?"

"I'm sure I don't know what you're talking about, old buddy."

Monsarrat altered the degree of his attack. "Blessed told me the ransom money he received two years ago was fake. He blamed me."

"I still don't know what you're talking about."

"He wanted to drag me back to the Delta with a rope around my neck as punishment, right after I transferred the cash for the Nok into his bank account."

"What were the chances of that happening? Blessed beating you mano a mano?"

"You left me to rot in the Delta for four and a half months," Monsarrat accused. "Then you fed me a crock of fairy tales about the special circumstances of my ransom."

Sanhedrin tsked. "I don't understand. All I did was provide you with a generous reward for expediting the acquisition of the Nok."

Monsarrat bulled forward. "Your reward was a quarter million Agency dollars."

"Are we still discussing the statue, Nathan?"

Monsarrat's fingers itched to hold the Smith and Wesson. "How much was my ransom?"

Sanhedrin made vague hand motions. "It was a long time ago, old buddy."

Monsarrat remembered for him. "You brought two duffel bags to the Delta, but less than a quarter million dollars in Benjamin Franklins. It took you eighteen weeks to gather the money, because you had to buy small quantities of counterfeit dollars to avoid attracting attention to yourself. I figure it cost about twenty-five thousand bucks at ten cents to the dollar to buy the fake money, so you pocketed around $225,000 in authentic Agency cash."

"You were delirious with malaria, Nathan. How could you possibly remember such small details?" Sanhedrin asked in his blameless voice. "I believe you are suffering from PTSD, old buddy."

Monsarrat wanted to keep his former boss on his heels. "Do the Mandarins know you ripped off their money? They get pissy when employees steal from them."

Sanhedrin offered his mantra. "I still don't know what you're talking about, Nathan."

Monsarrat shared the hard knot of his suspicions. "The Mandarins don't like senior staffers to blow operations for personal gains, Felix. Treason incenses them."

"I'm sure the Mandarins will be pleased by your concern."

"How did Blessed know to attack that particular oil rig on that specific day, Felix? At that exact time? When I was aboard? Who gave that big bastard my photograph?"

"What photograph, old buddy?"

"The one taken of me at the ambassador's New Year's party in Abuja. The one Blessed gave me on the oil rig."

"I'm starting to worry about you, old buddy."

"You planned it, Felix. Your fingerprints are all over the operation. Attention to minutiae. Bottom line greed. You told Blessed to kidnap me from the oil rig, stole the Agency's cash, and gave him the fake money. You knew that stupid bastard wouldn't be able to differentiate between a good bill and a bogus bill."

Sanhedrin mimed applause. "It's a fascinating theory, Nathan, but I still don't know what you're talking about. I didn't arrange your kidnapping, I didn't collect funny money, I didn't steal from the Agency, and I didn't leave you to rot in the Delta. I rescued you."

By the length of Sanhedrin's denial, Monsarrat knew he had discovered a weakness. His former boss might be afraid of

Russians, but the Mandarins also scared him. "Blessed tried to buy weapons with your fake money. The dealer laughed at him. When you arranged for the big bastard to steal the Nok, you told him that the bogus money belonged to me, and he was so stupid he never bothered to ask how I could have given you the fake bills while I was on my hands and knees in the Delta with a leash around my neck."

"You have so much anger, Nathan."

"You were my boss, and you betrayed me! You sold me to that big bastard, so you could pad your own bank account. I should put a bullet in your head and let you bleed all over your shiny car."

Sanhedrin's concern deepened. "Are you cold, Nathan? Do your muscles ache? Should I take you to the emergency room? Your eyes have that yellowish-reddish malarial tinge."

Monsarrat made a show of considering his options. "Public executions are messy. I should just tell your Russian client that you ripped him off. You remember the dumpster story, Felix?"

"From whence this hostility, old buddy?"

Monsarrat enjoyed Sanhedrin's discomfort. "My change of plans, Felix? I went to New York. The large Russian in the blue suit? My friend knows him. They know his *vor*."

Sanhedrin admitted his mistake. "Sometimes I talk too much."

"If my friend doesn't hear from me by sunset, he'll deliver a message: Felix Sanhedrin ripped off your boss, transferred the money into his own account, and delivered a five-dollar imitation Nok."

Sanhedrin tsked again. "The Nok is a national treasure."

"Your large Russian friend won't care. Even if the Nok is the real thing, he won't appreciate your creative accounting, keeping his money for yourself."

"Your fantasy is extremely detailed, Nathan. Shrinks say that's a worrisome sign."

"Once the large Russian hears my friend's story, he'll want his money back. You know how unreasonable Russians are when it comes to their women, reputations, and bank accounts."

Sanhedrin yawned and raised his hand to cover his mouth.

Monsarrat remembered his own distress signals in Port Harcourt. One verbal. One physical. He wondered if Sanhedrin were wired, or if his heavy hitters were watching with powerful binoculars, so well hidden he had been unable to make them. "Hands down, Felix. If you move them again, I will shoot you."

"My bad, Nathan, but can we make the trade now? I really need to return to Boston."

He squared the circle and repeated his earlier question. "Why did you tell me to expect Okeri?"

"He was the seller."

"If he was the seller, why did Blessed and Innocence come to the hotel with the statue?"

"I'm sure I don't know, Nathan, since I wasn't there. Maybe you should ask Innocence. You can't ask Blessed. You killed him."

Monsarrat discovered that he enjoyed cross-examining his former boss. "I did ask him. He swore that you told Blessed to steal the Nok from a museum. He also swore that they had nothing to do with Okeri. Finally, he swore that you promised he would be the next minister of oil, after the Agency overthrows the current government in Abuja."

Sanhedrin's laughter was mirthless. "Is that why you let him live, Nathan, after everything he did to you in the Delta? You thought he belonged to the Agency? I'm sorry to tell you, old buddy, but academia's made you soft."

Monsarrat wanted to throttle Sanhedrin with his hands, as he had tried to do to Innocence. Instead, he peppered him with accusations. "You lied about quitting the Agency."

Sanhedrin fidgeted on the hood of the Maserati. "I didn't lie to you, Nathan. I'm just waiting for the Human Resources people to process my paperwork."

"The Educational Placement Services and fishing for marlin were fantasies?"

"Absolutely not," he protested. "The Boston gig is up and running nicely, and the Agency is not aware of it. As for the Keys, I enjoy a long weekend in Hemingway country."

Listening to Sanhedrin temporize, Monsarrat realized he had overlooked the obvious. When Palmer had claimed that he would have done the job for free, he assumed he referred to his own need for vengeance, but he didn't need the extra money, because Sanhedrin had paid him to keep Innocence alive. "You hired Palmer to make sure I killed Blessed and let Innocence live."

Sanhedrin appeared offended, as if he had been vilified as a Greek with gifts. "Mark Palmer? The oil gunslinger?"

"Did you tell Palmer to whack me if I insisted on killing Innocence?"

Sanhedrin exuded compassion. "You have a serious problem with your paranoia, old buddy. You're seeing enemies instead of your friends."

"My paranoia responds to the barometric pressure of the bullshit surrounding me."

Sanhedrin, Monsarrat knew, abhorred loose ends. He also recognized that upon delivery of the terracotta statue, he would become the very definition of a loose end. "Why didn't you hire Palmer to pick up the statue?"

"Okeri was paranoid. He didn't trust Palmer. He wanted an outside middleman. I wanted someone who knew the environment. Voila. I thought of my old Agency buddy."

"Drop the fairy tales. You may have plans for Okeri, but they never included the statue."

Sanhedrin pantomimed the letters T-I-M-E in the air, followed by a question mark. "Can we make the trade now?"

"You have my cash?"

"In the trunk."

"You know the drill, Felix. Sit on your hands."

He opened the trunk of the Maserati with the fob, removed a garbage bag, and closed the lid. "Really, Felix? Isn't a plastic bag just a bit déclassé?"

"My circulation?"

Monsarrat nodded.

"I have to tell you, Nathan, I am more than a little pissed off by your extortion. We had a deal. You need to learn to keep your word."

"Spare me the righteous indignation, Felix."

"I never thought of you as a greedy man."

"I see you still have the ability to talk out of multiple sides of your mouth."

Sanhedrin started to reply, but Monsarrat tapped his hip. "You talk again without permission, and the price doubles to an even million."

Sanhedrin blinked his eyes in Morse code.

"Go ahead, Felix."

"Why are you jacking me, old buddy?"

Monsarrat considered the multiple answers to the question. He decided to share a parable with his former boss. "I'm a nice guy, so I'll give you something extra for your money. You'll appreciate the irony, I trust."

"I'm a captive audience."

"When Innocence thought he was going to die, he told me the most fascinating story, hoping it would extend his miserable life."

"Pray tell, old buddy."

"Let's say you're in a swanky London restaurant with one of your friends, who comes up with the bright idea of overthrowing a Muslim government and installing a friendlier group of Christians who will guarantee access to a country's oil."

"Did Innocence offer that fairy tale all by himself?"

Sanhedrin's reaction confirmed Monsarrat's suspicions. "Who do you work for, Felix? The Agency? The oil companies? Both?"

"I told you, Nathan. I am a spook and a businessman."

Monsarrat recognized the glean in Sanhedrin's eyes. The verbal dysentery had begun its infection. He hastened its journey with an additional question. "A businessman who helps oil companies overthrow governments?"

"I'll bring the Agency around, but it will take time. Revolutions are expensive propositions. The Mandarins won't sign on until we have partners with deep pockets on board."

"Who's the mysterious we, Felix?"

Sanhedrin climbed onto his soapbox. "We are a group of concerned Americans who fear that our country has lost her moral compass. We worry about weakness in the White House. We are concerned by the corruption in Congress and on the Supreme Court. We want to return our country to her former greatness."

Monsarrat was impressed. Sanhedrin had delivered his lines perfectly. "You call yourselves Sons of Liberty Redux?"

Sanhedrin shook his head. "We are patriots who wish to rebuild America."

"All that work must cost a bundle of cash."

"We are tired of prostrating ourselves before countries we should bomb back to the stone age. We seek to remove our shackles and liberate ourselves from the oppression of our own making. We are creating a proud and strong America, a resurgent America, an America that will bow to no other country. If threatened, we will destroy that threat. If denied our legitimate aspirations, we will take what we need."

Monsarrat whistled softly. "How much Kool-Aid did you drink, Felix?"

Sanhedrin glowed with patriotic fervor. "The Christians think like us. They want what we want. Decent lives. Bright futures for their children. The current ministers and generals in Abuja, though, are desert Muslims. They do not want what we want."

"They don't think like us?"

Sanhedrin did not require prodding. "They work against our interests. They provide aid and sustenance to our Salafist enemies and support Islamist insurrections throughout Africa. Worst of all, they sell our oil to the Chinese."

Monsarrat wondered how many enemies his former boss could juggle at one time. "Which is worse, Felix? Oil supporting the fundamentalists? Or oil supporting the Chinese?"

"We need to stop playing defense and switch to offense. This is our coming-out party. We get rid of the Islamists, install a Christian government, and use the north of the country as our base of operations. The Agency destroys the Salafists in the Maghreb and the Sahel and negates the threats to our democracy. The oil companies get light, sweet crude. The Christians get political power. Everyone goes home rich and happy."

"Except for the Northerners."

"They don't count. They are not our friends."

"They're desert Muslims."

"You're fast, Nathan. You earn a gold star for comprehension."

Monsarrat needed to keep Sanhedrin talking for a few more minutes. "You're wasting your talent, Felix. You should be scribbling screenplays in Hollywood."

"There are still happy endings in this world, Nathan, if you're creative."

"Don't write your Oscar acceptance speech yet. Your Christian friends aren't exactly trustworthy. Loyalty is not one of their strengths."

Sanhedrin pondered the advice. "Honestly, Nathan, I don't give a rat's ass if they don't have a sash full of Boy Scout badges. As long as I'm paying more money than anyone else, I can buy all the trust I need. As long as I carry better weapons than anyone else, I'll have all the loyalty I want."

"You ignore the Agency's first catechism at your own peril."

"Please, Nathan, don't tell me you've found true religion?"

"Bribery is temporary, but blackmail is forever," Monsarrat quoted. "Remember, Felix? You preached it."

"Use your impressive grey cells and tell me what could be more permanent than money from the big oil companies."

Monsarrat felt humbled by the fervor of Sanhedrin's hubris. "I almost died in the Delta two years ago and almost got killed Sunday in Port Harcourt, just for money?"

"A revolution is a chessboard with multiple moving pieces. Everyone has a role. You are a pawn, Nathan, and pawns serve the big boys in the back rank."

"Pawns are foot soldiers."

"There you have it," Sanhedrin agreed. "Sacrifice is your fate, old buddy."

"What are you, Felix? The king?"

Sanhedrin's denial was prolix. "More like the bishop, powerful but hidden. One minute subtle. The next minute slashing across the board to capture the enemy. More maneuverable than a knight, not as rigid as a rook. More of a power broker than the queen, neither as visible nor as targeted. All in all, the ultimate player."

The more Sanhedrin expounded, the faster the seconds ticked. "What's the endgame, Felix? After you knock off the desert Muslims and give the Christians a new government?"

Sanhedrin swallowed the bait like a hungry fish. "Oil is only the beginning. When our work is finished, our country will be stronger and prouder than at any time since we dropped the atomic bombs on Hiroshima and Nagasaki. We will hold our heads high, and our enemies will cower."

"You didn't need to twist arms to convince your oil friends to donate to the cause. They must have jumped at the chance to protect their interests. They must have stumbled over each other to be the first to shove money into your bank account."

"It is a brilliant plan, Nathan, if I may be immodest."

"You don't want FATA blowing up oil pipelines, so you bought Blessed, but at some point he became too greedy or too uncontrollable or both, so you decided to get rid of him and put Innocence in charge. He's smarter than Blessed and more easily controlled."

Sanhedrin clapped his hands together slowly, like an audience of one at a private screening. "Bravo. Superb. If you add a libretto, you'll have an opera fit for a Medici."

"You ever worry about your allies, Felix? They're masters of the double-cross. One morning you're the great, white bwana, the next afternoon you're the centerpiece in a voodoo ceremony for Baron Samedi."

"I can take care of myself, Nathan."

"You a very competent guy. No arguments from me."

Sanhedrin smiled demurely.

"I don't know if you're good enough, though."

Sanhedrin's smile did not waver.

Monsarrat ticked off facts, one finger at a time. "First, you steal the Mandarin's money. Second, you rip off a Russian. Third, you plot to overthrow a government."

"What's your point, Nathan?"

"Which leaves me with a wealth of options," Monsarrat concluded. "To which of these fine fellows should I rat you out? The Mandarins? The Russians? The desert Muslims? Can you appreciate my dilemma, Felix?"

Sanhedrin's smile was rictal. "Tread carefully, Nathan. Cause and effect, you know."

Monsarrat made a show of considering his choices. "If I go to the Mandarins, they might suspect I was your partner."

Sanhedrin nodded politely.

"If I choose the desert Muslims," he continued. "They might think I'm part of the plot."

"You're running out of options, old buddy."

"I'll have to stick with the Russians. They're the least of the three evils."

"If I go into the dumpster, old buddy, your body parts will be next to mine."

Monsarrat accepted the possibility. "Granted, it's a calculated risk."

"What do you want, Nathan? Bottom line?"

"Aside from four and a half months of my life, my health, and half a million bucks?"

"Exactly, old buddy. Aside from all those temporal concerns."

Monsarrat thought his former boss needed to study the fine art of playing the long game. He needed to enroll in a Delta immersion course.

"You looking for a job that pays better than academia? Work for me, Nathan. It would be just like old times, except with better money and none of those torpid staff meetings."

"I don't think so, Felix. I don't like you."

"Since when is that a precondition in our line of work?"

"What I want, Felix, since you're asking, is closure."

"You've got that, old buddy. Blessed is dead."

Monsarrat disagreed. "Full closure. Blessed was only one part of the equation."

"What's the other part, old buddy?"

Monsarrat took the Maserati's fob from his pocket and heaved it across the road. "Put your hands on top of your head and get in the Jeep. You know the drill."

Sanhedrin watched the fob sail across the blacktop and fall beyond the dirt shoulder. He crossed both arms high before placing then atop his head. "Now, now, Nathan. How am I supposed to drive home?"

A geyser of dirt erupted three feet to Monsarrat's left. Sanhedrin slid fast off the hood of the Maserati and pointed to the revolver. "Take the piece from the holster with the tips of the fingers. Hold it in front of you."

Monsarrat followed the instructions. "A sniper, Felix? In Greenfield?"

"Squat down. Drop the weapon. Put your hands behind your neck. Elbows out. Stand up, walk ten feet backwards."

"I feel like a kid in gym class getting ready for jumping jacks."

Sanhedrin examined the Smith & Wesson before slipping it into his waistband. "It's clean. Did you plan to shoot me?"

"Maybe in the meat of the thigh. No permanent damage."

"I believe it's best if we agree to a timeout, Nathan. Our own Nipmuck agreement. You stay in the Berkshires, and I won't visit you. You don't come after me, and I won't come after you, but if I see you, I'll kill you. Agreed?"

"If I see you first, can I kill you?"

"Not gonna happen, Nathan."

Monsarrat knew he was slightly ahead of schedule, so he asked another question, confident that Sanhedrin would answer. The verbal dysentery had yet to leave his system. "How did you know I was in New York, Felix?"

"You activated the Walsh passport, you became a big, fat target. I tracked you all the way, although I had to convince the airline to allow you to switch your flight in Frankfurt."

He considered the information, then asked another question. "Who's the sniper, Felix? Anyone I know?"

"The sniper and his spotter," Sanhedrin corrected. "You met them in the Berkshires. Their instructions were to let you make them. I wanted you confident. When you're paranoid, Nathan, you're the best I've ever seen. When you're confident, you're sloppy."

Monsarrat feigned shame. He wanted his former boss to feel munificent in his superiority. "Hubris is my Achilles heel."

"You can put your hands down, Nathan. You can also take the Nok and my laptop from your Jeep and place them next to the Maserati."

"You don't want the bag of cash?"

"It's Monopoly money. My original offer was fifty thousand dollars, and that's what I delivered to you before you left for Port Harcourt. I'm not giving you another penny. Did you really think I would let you blackmail me?"

"I can keep the fifty thousand?"

"Of course, Nathan. I always uphold my commitments."

Monsarrat succumbed to curiosity. "How much money will the Russian spend for the Nok, Felix? If you're paying me fifty thousand, it must be worth at least a quarter million."

Sanhedrin snorted. "You're way off base, old buddy. Your fifty thousand is chump change. The statue's worth a hundred times that amount. Maybe more."

"Not a bad haul," he admitted.

"All of it tax free."

Monsarrat placed the valise and the aluminum case next to the Maserati. "Where do we go from here, Felix?"

"Walk backward to your Jeep. Stop at the hood. Throw your cell phone across the road. Just like you did with my fob."

Monsarrat complied.

"Now the second cell phone."

"I'm a dean. I can't afford to carry a second cell phone on my salary."

Sanhedrin laughed. "Get in your Jeep and drive back to your college, Nathan. Stay away from me, stay away from the Russians, and stay away from the oil company boys. In fact, stay on your campus and don't leave western Massachusetts. Keep your nose clean, and mind your own fucking business."

"Not a problem," Monsarrat agreed. "When does your revolution start?"

"Wheels are in motion, old buddy."

"The Christian express has left the station?"

"On time and at speed, fully staffed, and generously funded."

Monsarrat checked his watch. "I hope you make your appointment, Felix."

"I will if it doesn't take too long to find the fob."

"Sorry about that," Monsarrat apologized. "It seemed like a good idea at the time."

Sanhedrin waved away the *mea culpa*. "Before you leave, I want to be one hundred percent positive that you understand today's lesson. I want you to know what will happen to you if you forget to call your friend in New York."

"What's that, Felix?"

Sanhedrin again crossed both arms high. A second geyser of dirt erupted in the same spot. "If you fuck with me, you will die."

Monsarrat had expected the second bullet. He did not flinch. "Thanks for the advice."

"Good-bye, Nathan. I hope I won't see you again."

Monsarrat drove south. In the Jeep's rear-view mirror, he saw Sanhedrin walk across Bernardston Road. He dropped the Maserati's fob into the cup holder. He doubted Sanhedrin would find the garage door opener before the FBI arrived.

On schedule, a black Impala passed him, heading north. From his time with the Agency, he held the Bureau in low respect. Still, the grey suits had their uses.

III. INNOCENCE

APRIL FOOLS' DAY

Early shoots of green, purple, and gold crocuses spread like an iridian blanket across the campus of Greylock College. The vernal probes poked their tips through crusted snow beneath the eaves of the academic buildings. Icicles dripped in the warmth of the spring sun, and Frisbees spun through the crisp, blue skies. On April Fools' Day practical jokes abounded, and the weather was the cruelest cut of all. With the approach of dusk, the temperatures dipped below freezing, a raw wind blustered, and a fresh covering of snow fell from leaden Berkshire skies. The following morning students traded board shorts for down parkas and packed snowballs to target the hardy few brave enough to drive onto the campus.

On the final day of the month, winter capitulated in a snit of cold rain, but by the second Monday of May, chthonic faculty members shed their heavy wool scarves for the ritual tweeds of the academic mysteries. The glorious scent of spring blooming in western Massachusetts soothed restless spirits. Courtships sprouted across the picturesque campus. Study week followed the conclusion of classes and led to final examinations. Parties raged like wildfires in dormitories. The campus police responded to complaints with alacrity, and the Disciplinary Committee's ledgers bulged with end-of-term cases.

Monsarrat gazed out the open window of his office. Yellow-bellied sapsuckers knocked, and dark-eyed juncos twittered. The dull bass of druid music reverberated across the common. Students in varying degrees of undress tanned on towels, separately, enjoined, and entwined. A few dedicated souls jotted notes into the margins of textbooks. Usually not a covetous man, he envied their innocence.

On his desk, two Loony Tune folders awaited, a recent attempt by Doris to focus his attention. Daffy Duck held the cases for the afternoon's Disciplinary Committee meeting. Bugs Bunny concerned an upcoming recruitment trip through the southern states. Neither file interested him, despite the nostalgic packaging. He felt like a lethargic Elmer Fudd.

When the phone rang, Doris answered it. He awaited her arrival. Lately, she delivered her messages in person, as if ascertaining that he had not absconded with the furniture or fallen asleep at the desk on the college's time. He practiced smiling.

She knocked on the door. "Dean Monsarrat, you have a call from Professor Martins. Shall I tell him you're busy?"

He did not welcome her displeasure. "Put him through, Doris. By all means."

George Martins spoke as if he had rehearsed his speech. "Nathan, for this academic year's final meeting of the Disciplinary Committee, we must take firm action in the neo-Nazi case. We cannot allow students to paint swastikas and "The Fourth Reich Will Arise!" on the door of the Hillel room. The ADL will be all over us. We must make an example of these young fascists."

"All three have been suspended, Marty. We'll vote on their expulsion today. I'm confident the outcome will be unanimous."

"We need to turn the case over to the district attorney to try the little bastards for spreading hate crimes."

Monsarrat remembered their conversation at Holbrooke Gymnasium earlier in the academic year. Perhaps the bristle cut associate professor of English was wooing a female member of Hillel. "They'll wear the stigma of expulsion, Marty. If the feds want to prosecute them, it won't be our problem."

"What about the Anti-Defamation League?"

"No media circus, no comments, no interviews, no well-placed sources, or we'll be in court answering lawsuits from parents."

He had developed a distrust of the media during his time with the Agency, one of the few aspects of his former life not discarded after leaving Langley.

Surrender flavored his answer. "As long as justice will be served."

Monsarrat wanted allies, not enemies, and helped Martins climb off his soapbox. "We expel them and we're seen as taking a strong stand against intolerance, hatred, and bigotry. Soon enough, they'll be sitting in the dock while a judge reams them."

"No press release from the college?"

"Negative, Marty."

"How about a statement from the president to the faculty and students? An open letter on the website saying that sort of behavior will not be tolerated?"

He considered the proposal's merit. "It's a good idea. The president could comment at the top of her remarks at the graduation ceremony. The media will pick it up, too."

"A reaffirmation of inclusion vice exclusion?"

Monsarrat agreed. "You're on a roll now, Marty."

"I can start a petition and have a thousand signatures by graduation."

Monsarrat did not doubt his ability. A college campus loved drama, especially during final exams. "Let me whisper into her ear. It might save you a lot of grunt work."

"You mean save my energy for other types of grunting."

He chose the high road. "Thanks for the call, Marty. I'll see you this afternoon."

He sensed rather than heard Doris approach. She stopped at the door, as if the threshold were a mined border and his office a demilitarized zone. "I need your itinerary, Dean, so I can make plane and car and hotel reservations for you."

"Will do, Doris."

She radiated disapproval. "I need it soon."

He attempted levity. "Aye, aye, skipper."

She spun on her flat heels. He heard her huff at her desk. He had failed to discover the source of her enmity but suspected that his presence annoyed her.

His e-mail program stuttered, "Read me. Read me." The subject line stated in uppercase letters, MP FOR NM. A message from Mark Palmer surprised him, since their parting the past autumn had been caustic. Men like Palmer initiated contact to achieve an objective. They did not waste oxygen discussing old times, but marched to the rhythm of well-defined orders. Seize a hill. Assassinate a village leader. Convince a dean of undergraduate studies to undertake a mission inimical to his own interests. Monsarrat admired his abilities, but Palmer belonged on the far side of the Atlantic Ocean.

He read the message quickly, then a second time more slowly. Perhaps Palmer had forgotten that their parting had been neither warm nor friendly.

Dear Nathan, I hope this message finds you well. You will remember, I trust, our mutual friend in whose mouth butter would not melt. You last spoke with him in the company of our revered associate, who unfortunately passed away shortly after presenting you with a doll from a private collection.

Some months ago, our friend described his anticipated cooperation with your former employer, who has since enlisted the partnership of a consortium of influential businessmen for whom I work. Unfortunately, our friend has reneged on our arrangement. Since you know him so well, I would like to discuss with you options for resolving this issue before it becomes sticky.

The consortium, he knew, was Palmer's employer, while sticky was a euphemism for bloody.

I will call soon. In friendship and respect, Mark.

He glanced at his telephone, as if it were a block of plastique. Friendship and respect were qualities he did not associate with Palmer.

He closed the e-mail and flipped through the cases to be discussed during the afternoon's meeting. Aside from the Hillel incident, the infractions were collegiate, freshmen drinking beer, sophomores smoking pot, juniors plagiarizing from the Internet, seniors driving too fast on campus.

When his cell phone rang, the screen showed only an "unavailable" announcement. He accepted before voice mail took the call. "Dean Monsarrat," he announced, as if the title were a suit of armor.

"Good to hear your voice, Nathan."

Monsarrat answered truthfully. "Your e-mail surprised me, Mark. Are you in the neighborhood?"

"Close enough. Our nation's capital."

Since leaving the Agency, Monsarrat had avoided the District of Columbia, save for his visits to Abby, as an early Christian would have skirted the Colosseum of ancient Rome. "My sympathies."

"Can we discuss my message?"

"Over the phone?"

Palmer laughed politely. "Not likely. You feel like a power lunch in Georgetown?"

"Maybe lunch without the adjective, but not down there."

"Are there restaurants where you live?"

Banter tired Monsarrat. "Not like the big city, but we manage."

"Is Friday good for you?"

"Shall we meet inside the Cantina on Main Street at thirteen hundred?

"Mexican?"

"It passes," Monsarrat admitted. "Is your visit business or personal, Mark?"

"A bit of both, actually."

"So you'll write this trip off against expenses?"

He accepted the challenge. "Lunch is on me, Nathan."

On Friday, the final day of the academic year, he dressed in faded jeans, running shoes, a white Greylock College tee shirt, sunglasses, and a blue nylon windbreaker with the college's logo imprinted on the chest and sleeves. The zipper worked as smoothly as the trigger on the Smith & Wesson that he had placed into a discrete leather holster, butt forward, looped over his left shoulder and secured to his belt. He preferred a cross-draw, especially if he had to unzip the windbreaker with his left hand. It was an inelegant option, but he did not wish to meet Palmer without a weapon.

Shortly before noon, he walked up one side of Main Street and down the other. He saw SUVs and pick-up trucks filled with suitcases and boxes. He saw trailers attached to sedans. He spoke with students and met their parents. At half past twelve, he pushed the sunglasses on top of his head and entered the Cantina. He sat at the bar, chatted with the bartender, and examined the patrons. He appreciated small, crowded spaces. Only a rank amateur would attempt to shoot him in a packed restaurant, and Palmer was a consummate professional.

At ten minutes to one o'clock, he took a table in the rear of the dining room. Five minutes later, Palmer entered the restaurant. He wore slacks, loafers, a white oxford shirt open at the neck, and a blue blazer with nautical buttons. The black frame of his sunglasses hung from the top button on his shirt. A slight bulge broke the smooth drape of the jacket. He approached Monsarrat like a boxer at the weigh-in ceremony prior to the fight, appraising his opponent.

He offered his hand. "You're looking well, Nathan. Enjoying academia?"

Monsarrat shook it. "Very much so."

When he took his seat, Palmer shrugged to release the pressure on his shoulder holster. "Port Harcourt, in case you're curious, is still a nasty place, but my employers pay me an obscenely inflated salary. Another two years, I can retire and spend my days fishing."

Monsarrat gestured toward his shoulder. "You don't trust me?"

"It's only a nine. Is that a .38 banging your ribs?"

Monsarrat smiled in confirmation. "A small one."

"May I make a suggestion?"

"Of course."

"We close the book on the Delta and start fresh in the Berkshires. At least, until you hear my proposal."

"The reason for today's lunch."

"I want you to know that I still feel badly about Port Harcourt."

"Personally?"

"Professionally, too," Palmer stated. "I want Innocence dead, but my desires don't carry a lot of weight with the people who sign my paychecks."

Monsarrat considered the proposal. "Let's try to make it through lunch without shooting each other."

A waitress took their orders and returned with their beers, a Sol for Palmer, a Pacifico for Monsarrat. She set a platter of nachos in the middle of the table. Around them, parents and students spoke of vacation plans, grades, and home responsibilities.

Palmer tore a chunk of nachos from the platter. "I like the United States. I appreciate it even more after spending so much time outside the country. I like small towns, like this one. People are nice to each other. The streets are clean."

Monsarrat ate a nacho and waited for Palmer to conclude his oratorio.

"I like our democracy. I like our lifestyle. It's a country worth fighting for. It's a country worth bleeding for. I'm not ashamed to say I'm a patriot. It's an old-fashioned word, but I believe in it. God, country, and service to both."

Monsarrat recalled Johnson's tribute to patriotism, the last refuge of the scoundrel. "You mean your time in the military?"

Palmer drank half the bottle of Sol and dabbed his mouth with his napkin. "My life was painted in blocks of black or white. Either you accepted it, or you got out."

"You got out," Monsarrat observed.

"After twenty years, a friend hooked me up with my current employers. We're a good fit."

He ate another nacho. "I believe in the new mission. It allows me to serve, on a different playing field but using the same skill sets."

"It pays better, too."

If Palmer heard cynicism in Monsarrat's reply, he ignored it. "I don't do it simply for the money. I do it to keep our lifestyle safe, just as I wore the uniform to protect us from dangers foreign and domestic."

"Keeping the country safe by keeping the oil flowing?"

"I'm not a policy wonk, Nathan. I'm a shooter. I call things as I see them, and I see us as a nation of demanders. We demand gas for our cars. We demand electricity for our air conditioners. We demand oil. We demand steady supplies of everything."

Monsarrat remembered Sanhedrin's speech in Greenfield.

Palmer finished his beer and signaled for another round. "You're not keeping up."

Monsarrat lifted the Pacifico. "I'm absorbing the ambiance."

When the waitress delivered the beers, she gestured at the platter. "Nachos okay?"

"Excellent," Palmer promised. "The best I've had in a long time."

Monsarrat watched her toward the kitchen. "Are you flirting with the waitress, Mark?"

Palmer shrugged. "I don't lie unless it's necessary. I prefer to shade the truth."

Monsarrat understood the art of shading, as well as the subtleties of truth. "When did you last eat nachos?"

"A long time ago. You can't get them in Port Harcourt."

The waitress returned, carrying platters of food. She placed the taco dish before Palmer and the burrito dish before Monsarrat. "*Buen apetito.* Enjoy your lunch, gentlemen."

Monsarrat poked the burrito. "The food's not bad, especially for a small town in the Berkshires, but I'm not sure I would travel all the way from Port Harcourt for the tacos."

Palmer leaned toward Monsarrat. "Why are you carrying a piece, Nathan? Like you said, it's a small town in the Berkshires."

"I could ask you the same question, Mark. Who scares you?"

"In my job? It's a long list."

He pondered the admission. "Anyone special at the top?"

"Right now, your former playmates from Langley concern me."

"I know how you feel," Monsarrat admitted.

Palmer asked his own question. "Do I make you nervous, Nathan?"

"Anyone associated with Sanhedrin makes me nervous."

He shrugged. "You've lost me. Who's Sanhedrin?"

Monsarrat did not want to believe that Palmer would deny the obvious. "Felix Sanhedrin is a completely malevolent, thoroughly reprehensible, extremely dangerous, Agency sociopath."

"A lot of Langley people fit that description."

"You'd know him if you met him, and you would never forget him."

"You think I know him from Port Harcourt?"

"Just before I went wheels up in Abuja, you said that you would have done the job for free," Monsarrat explained. "At the time, I thought you meant payback for the FATA attacks against your people, but you didn't mean free for the pleasure of taking out Blessed and allowing Innocence to live. You meant that you didn't need the money I sent you, because Sanhedrin had already shoveled cash into your bank account. If I hadn't called you, you would have initiated contact with me."

Palmer snapped a taco between his teeth and chased it with a long swallow of Sol. "He called himself Fineghan Scarnagh."

Monsarrat recognized the nom de guerre. "He carries an address book of work names, with the conceit that each given name starts with an F, and each family name begins with an S. Fineghan Scarnagh. Felix Sanhedrin. One and the same."

"Scarnagh contacted me through my employers, who gave me the green light to work with him. When he told me the two outcomes he wanted, I was hot to trot," Palmer stated. "First was a statue. Second was a dead Blessed. I told him I didn't know anything about art, but I would gladly whack the big bastard."

"You thought your new friend Scarnagh was legitimate?"

"Very few people from the Agency fit that particular adjective."

"True words."

"Scarnagh said you'd arrive in Port Harcourt for both the statue and Blessed."

"Sanhedrin," Monsarrat corrected.

"Of course," Palmer agreed. "I was to cover your six and provide the necessary intelligence and tools. You were not to know of my contact with him."

"He told you that Blessed had the statue?"

"Just the opposite. He intimated that obtaining the statue and killing Blessed were two separate actions. You had lead on the first. I had lead on the second."

Monsarrat appreciated Sanhedrin's skills in compartment-alization. "What were his instructions for Innocence?"

"He insisted that I keep him alive. I thought the orders were odd, but my employers told me to not ask questions."

Monsarrat thought his former boss had chosen his hired help wisely. "You insisted on staying in the hotel room with me to protect Innocence?"

"It was a difficult order to follow," Palmer admitted. "Although it might work out to our mutual advantage."

"I don't follow."

"I need to reach into my right coat pocket."

Monsarrat placed his right hand on his own chest, the tips of his fingers inches from the leather holster. "Do it."

Palmer retrieved a white envelope and dropped it on the table. "A check made out to you."

"You're returning the money I sent you last fall?"

"It's listening money if you reject my offer, which I hope won't happen. If you agree, it's an advance on a job I'd like you to do."

Monsarrat pushed the plate of burritos to the edge of the table and signaled for another round of beers. The waitress delivered the two bottles, looked at the faces of her customers, and walked away without speaking.

He remembered Sanhedrin's admission that he preferred to subcontract to professionals who made him comfortable. Retirees like himself. Shooters like Palmer. He felt the heat of an epiphany. "The statue and Blessed were the second time you worked for Sanhedrin. The first time, you helped him ransom me from the Delta."

"Two years ago he wrote my employers a generous check to rent me and my boys for the day," Palmer acknowledged. "Initially, I thought he was a dilettante in a silly suit, but I soon realized he was the real thing, a genuinely nasty piece of work."

"You hid behind your balaclava and stayed quiet," Monsarrat accused. "You let him sedate me. You let him abandon Rosalinda to the rebels, and they killed her."

"My marching orders were to provide cover when he ransomed you and keep my mouth shut. He was adamant on that point."

"You were a good soldier, just following orders?"

"It's what I do. I'm not a Langley cowboy."

"Sanhedrin paid you well? The money assuaged your conscience?"

"In my defense, Nathan, I didn't know Rosalinda existed before you said her name in the compound. If our roles had been reversed, you would have done the same."

Agreeing with Palmer pained Monsarrat. "Sanhedrin was so pleased with your work on the ransom that he came back to you for help with the statue."

"Affirmative, but I told my employers I would be loathe to work with him a third time."

"He has that effect on people."

"Are we good, Nathan?"

Monsarrat supplied the answer Palmer needed. He wanted to hear the proposal. "Go on, Mark. Tell me about our mutual advantage."

"Your semester ends today?"

"Exams closed this morning. On Monday, we start the first of our summer sessions."

"Are you scheduled to teach a course?"

"Deans administer. Professors teach," he replied. "What's on your mind?"

"I want to offer you a job."

"I don't need money. I do quite well with my salary and my pension. Not oil cartel well, but western Massachusetts well."

"Indulge me, Nathan. I told my employers you would say just those words, but they insisted I put the offer on the table."

Monsarrat experienced a flush of déjà vu and wondered if Palmer's narrative would obtain the sophistication of Sanhedrin's tale. "I'm listening."

"It's a homework assignment. You teach a few people a lesson, school them in the simple economics of trying to screw the American people and fuck with our way of life."

"Well, that's a come on, if I ever heard one."

"Got your attention, do I?"

"Tell it."

Palmer pushed aside his plate of tacos and reached for the bottle of Sol. He swung it in a crescent, like an alcoholic pendulum. "Sometimes my employers have found it beneficial to work with your former associates to achieve our mutual goals. You know, support for friendly governments and guarantees of preferential access to crude."

"Foreign Policy 101."

He began at the end and worked back to the beginning. "When the White House talks to my employers, they like to mention the three P's: public-private partnerships. But it's more like padding politicians' pockets. Washington, Abuja, there's no difference. The game's the same. You play with oil, you get dirty."

"Cheap electricity, gas, and heating oil means votes for the president and his party, every two years in November."

"Light, sweet crude heats the East Coast during its long, cold winters. People want to stay warm and cozy inside their homes, and they don't want to pay a lot of money for that privilege. So our government feeds Abuja niblets of American power, allows our defense contractors to sell the Nigerian military outmoded weapons systems that places them eons beyond the capabilities of their neighbors."

"In turn, the oil consortium receives preferential treatment, which translates into profits for shareholders."

"Symmetry in a perfect world."

"Except your world is out of balance," Monsarrat concluded.

"My employers snuggled up real close to the past military dictatorships," Palmer agreed, "and for the last five months, they snuggled up real close to the new democratic government. For the consortium, there's no difference between the former, who quoted surahs from the Qur'an, and the latter, who read scriptures from the Bible. Both were corrupt and brutal, but only the junta sold us oil preferentially."

"What changed?"

"Langley orchestrated the coup that brought the current government into power, but it could not have happened without the cooperation of the consortium. The Agency promised my employers a larger slice of the oil pie at deeply discounted costs in exchange for their support, but the consortium now views the democratic government as too venal. It's an opinion the Agency does not share."

"The Mandarins and the oil wallahs are spatting, so soon into their marriage?"

"More like ripping it apart," Palmer answered. "The consortium believes that the Agency betrayed them."

He signaled the waitress and pressed three twenty-dollar bills into her hand. "For the check, okay? Keep the change. Just give me the receipt."

She returned quickly. Her smile as she handed him the receipt was forced.

Palmer slipped the paper into his wallet. "Feel like a walk, Nathan? A bit of exercise after lunch?"

Monsarrat folded the white envelope and slid it into the back pocket of his jeans. "How much time do you need to tell your story, Mark?"

"It's a complicated tale."

Monsarrat suspected that Sanhedrin would appear at some point in Palmer's narration, like an unwanted houseguest. "Oil, the Agency, and Abuja. I'm sure it's a story of tangled intricacies."

ALLEYS OF A HOSTILE ENGAGEMENT

The spring sunshine warmed the college town. Behind their sunglasses, both men appraised the movements on the streets as if they were stalking the alleys of a hostile engagement, wary of ambushes. Monsarrat led Palmer to Greylock Common, the small park beyond Main Street. A granite statue stood in the middle of an emerald plot of grass, surrounded by a low fence. Around the broad plinth were chiseled names of the wars in which the sons of the town had fought. A needle adorned with a marble wreath rose from the pedestal. A quote from *The Red Badge of Courage* filled a marble plaque, "It was not well to drive men into final corners; at those moments they could all develop teeth and claws."

Palmer examined the statue. "Your town needs a second monument, Nathan. We've had a number of engagements since Korea."

Monsarrat sat on a wooden bench in the shade of an oak tree. "We're a liberal college town. Our elected officials do not believe in the glory of war."

"Do they believe in honoring those who made the ultimate sacrifice?"

"I'll mention it at the next council meeting."

Monsarrat had come to appreciate the slow pace of the Berkshires. He watched a pair of grey squirrels languidly chase each other around an oak tree. They reversed direction and roles, the pursued now pursuing the pursuer. He felt an affinity.

Palmer joined him on the bench. "Something bothering you, Nathan? It's a hell of a grimace you're wearing."

"Thinking about work, Mark. It may not be important, but it is surely persistent."

"Are you enjoying the life of an academic? I'm only asking because you seem, for lack of a better word, unfulfilled."

"You came to that conclusion during lunch?"

Parker remained stoical. "I don't possess special powers of divination. I just observe."

The two squirrels sat on the haunches before the bench, waiting to be recompensed for their entertainment. Monsarrat flicked his foot. "Not today, fellas. I didn't bring any peanuts."

The squirrels disappeared. He wished the magic would extend toward Palmer. "I have job security. I've almost stopped seeing Delta killers under my bed."

"I think you miss the life, Nathan. I saw your eyes in Port Harcourt. They were burning. Now? They're glazed with torpor."

"Maybe you're projecting?"

"I'm not trying to shrink your head, I'm just talking, one bush rat to the next."

An apropos image, he thought. Port Harcourt was renowned for its voodoo rituals. "Tell me about the homework assignment."

"My employers appreciated the quality of your work last fall. When you whacked Blessed, our world became a better place. The number of rebel attacks plummeted after your coup de grâce. Company profits rose."

Two joggers approached the bench, heaving words between them like medicine balls. From the opposite direction, a bicyclist pedaled, chunky tires humming. Monsarrat wagered that the bicyclist would veer first and allow the joggers the right of way. The strong acquiesced to the weak in the college town. Citizens sowed patience and harvested decency.

"You'll be gone a week, maybe two, definitely no longer than a month. Flat fee, no difference if it takes you twenty-four hours or thirty days, but you'll receive a one hundred percent bonus if the work is concluded satisfactorily within seven days. Fifty percent if within two weeks."

"It's a generous offer but one hundred percent of exactly what?"

"Two hundred thousand dollars, in addition to the check."

The bicyclist swerved to avoid the joggers.

Monsarrat empathized. Bigger, stronger, faster, smarter, he had been avoiding conflict like a virgin running from vice since assuming his collegiate responsibilities. He thought of the envelope in his back pocket. He thought of two hundred thousand additional dollars and the completion bonus. He thought of torpor. "Who defines satisfactorily?"

"The terms of the contract," Palmer answered. "Sign the dotted line, Nathan. Not only for the money, which is generous, but personally, I'd like to work with you again."

Monsarrat would have been flattered if he were not so cynical. Compliments between professionals were as rare as hen's teeth, but like an Abrahamic host, he felt he owed his guest the courtesy of listening to his story. It might be a pleasant experience, like hearing a Southern writer read aloud his works, full of imagery and grace. "Pitch it, Mark. What do I have to do to earn that kind of money?"

"My employers belong to a consortium of American oil companies. No foreigners. Our Venn sectors may overlap occasionally, but our bottom line is that foreigners cannot be trusted beyond small areas of commonality."

He summarized the upheavals in Abuja, the orchestrations of the consortium, the machinations of the Agency, their marriage of convenience, and the January coup. "From the start, we sought different outcomes, economically and politically, but shared a few common goals. We both wanted the military dictatorship gone, and the northern leaders back with their goats in the desert sands. We both spouted the usual pabulum about democracy and human rights, a more level playing field, and a transparent business environment, but the Agency wanted a more reliable security partner, and the consortium desired a more reliable supply of crude."

"Also less expensive?"

"Profits are the bottom line."

Monsarrat remembered Innocence begging for his life, spewing a tale of CIA money, CIA proxy armies, and CIA revolutions. "You wanted Christians in charge of the country. You wanted a dictator who looked to Rome, not Mecca."

"An indelicate analysis, but accurate," Palmer agreed. "For years, the military dictatorship had allowed Salafists to use the barren north as their base of operations in the Sahel and the Maghreb, in exchange for very large deposits into their Geneva bank accounts, but the power of the Salafists had expanded so greatly that they demanded control of the Delta, as well as the desert. The threat to Nigeria's strategic location and its vast reserves of oil became an existential threat to the security of our own country, as well as a challenge to the bottom line of the consortium."

"So the Agency and your employers rang in the New Year with a revolution and a new government."

"On January the first, we installed leaders in Abuja who would work with us, a new president, new ministers, and new generals, each and every one a God-fearing, Southern Christian, save for a token Muslim Northerner who was tamer than a house cat."

"What went wrong?"

Palmer laughed. "What didn't go wrong? The Agency's job was to own the new leaders and supply them with money. Our task was to train them in the realities of twenty-first-century oil markets, re-haul their production facilities, and send the light, sweet crude to America."

"The Agency dropped the ball?"

"Drop-kicked it would be more accurate," he responded. "The day after we set up the new government, our allies started sleeping with the competition."

"Back to square number one."

"It gets worse."

"Why am I not surprised?"

"After a few months, the consortium asked the Agency to teach the new leaders a lesson, make an example out of one or two, show them who's in charge, but Langley refused. The Agency was happy with the government's soldiers roaming the north, kicking the shit out of the Salafists, who they saw as anyone not wearing a cross on a chain and a tee shirt claiming to be a janissary for Christ."

"Payback is a bitch."

"The Agency advised the consortium to exercise patience and consider long-term strategic goals."

Monsarrat understood frustration. "It sounds like a Langley kiss-off."

"The politicians inside the Beltway are obsessed with lines in the sand, not extracting oil from the sands," Palmer agreed. "A few of the most influential consortium members flew to Washington and spoke with a coven of senators and cabinet secretaries. They all passed the buck to the national security advisor, who advised that nothing was more important than containing the Salafists and stated that it doesn't matter if Abuja lifted its skirts like a cheap hooker. He told them to stop complaining and start counting profits."

The government's willingness to sacrifice the consortium's interests did not surprise Monsarrat. Since the attack on the Twin Towers, the business of Washington was no longer business, but the destruction of the new generation of terrorists whose sole purpose was to bring down the government of the United States. "Despite being screwed by Abuja, the oil wallahs still have profits?"

"Of course," Palmer deadpanned. "The consortium always makes a profit, but the return on its investment is chump change compared to expectations."

Monsarrat saw the light at the end of the tale but not his role in it. "It's a great lesson in civics, but where does my homework assignment fit into the story?"

He delivered his lines like an actor on cue. "The consortium needs you to help send the new government home and kick out the competition."

Shake his hand, rise from the bench, walk away from the recruitment, his paranoia shrieked, but a sticky curiosity adhered him to the wooden slats. "The consortium plans a second coup, but without the Agency?"

Palmer sidestepped the question neatly. "Your homework assignment is to present a simple proposition to a person of interest. If he accepts, you engage in a bit of babysitting."

"What if he refuses?"

"You kill him."

"Go back to your office, plan your recruitment trip, go to the gym, have a drink, just don't keep warming your backside on a park bench listening to the charm of a Southern killer, his paranoia railed. "Wet work is messy, but if that's your choice, take him out. You're good enough, and you're proximate."

"Wet work is the last resort," Palmer clarified. "In any case, the person of interest lives far from Port Harcourt."

"Who is he? Where is he?"

"Not yet, Nathan. Not until you've signed on the dotted line."

Monsarrat could not argue with his rectitude. "When does the job start?"

"The clock ticks over at zero-dark hundred plus one on the first of June."

"It stops thirty days later?"

"At twenty-three fifty-nine hundred on the thirtieth of June."

"If I accept," Monsarrat summarized, "I fly somewhere, where I either babysit a person of interest or whack him. Either option, I collect your generous payment, plus a possible bonus. If I decline, I keep the listening fee, go back to my office, and never hear from you again."

"In a nutshell."

"Who will you place into power in Abuja?"

"A group of Northern generals has agreed to lead the new government. The Agency can keep chasing the Salafists across the desert sands, but the raison d'être of the new government will be oil profits."

"You prefer the status quo ante?"

"The only thing I prefer is my salary, right up to the day I retire and start collecting my pension."

"The person of interest? What's his role in the new government?"

"Remember the dotted line," Palmer admonished.

Monsarrat asked the only question that mattered. "Why me? I'm a dilettante. Why not hire a professional?"

"I wondered how long it would take you to ask that question."

"How long will it take you to answer?"

"About five seconds after the ink on the contract dries."

When Monsarrat had served as a warrior for the Holy Order of Langley, the Agency had dispatched him on assignments with fewer details than Palmer had provided, but his faith had since lapsed. He now fulfilled the role of dean, swaddled in the wraps of academia. "I need more information. It's thin gruel you've offered."

"You recruit the person of interest, you get rich. You whack him, you get rich. What else do you want to know?"

He wanted to keep him talking to give himself more time to weigh his options. "What are your plans for the new government?"

"Would it ease your social conscience if I told you the generals will turn the government over to civilian control after six months?"

"The junta is transitional? They'll hand the palace keys to a democratically elected government, turn off the lights, and go back to their barracks?"

"The scenario isn't quite so Elysian," he admitted. "A civilian puppet will go through the motions of establishing a democracy but will be controlled by the generals."

"Who will be controlled by you."

"You're a fast study, Nathan."

"I hang out with professors."

Palmer shifted his weight on the bench. "It was difficult for the consortium and the generals to agree on a candidate to play the role of president-on-a-string. For obvious reasons, no one from the North was acceptable, but they finally settled on a venal, easily manipulated candidate from a politically and financially weak tribe in the Delta. The international press portrays the tribe's people as a persecuted minority. The new leader will give the civilian government instant respectability."

"Don't keep me in suspense. Who have you anointed?"

"The Amanyanabo of Bonny: impressive title, royal lineage, zero political influence."

The name surprised Monsarrat. It conjured memories of Sanhedrin. "Rehovoth Okeri will be the next president?"

"One and the same."

He rose from the bench. "You'll need to find someone else. I don't want the job."

"You've come this far, Nathan. Don't you want to hear the rest of the pitch?"

"You can tell me on the way back to your car."

As they retraced their steps to the center of the town, Palmer continued speaking in his leisurely fashion. "The future president doesn't trust the junta. He's afraid the generals will change their minds and assassinate him, despite his royal lineage. He wants protection supplied by people of his own blood. By one blood relative in particular, with whom the consortium has an unfortunate history, but with whom you have influence."

"I could be his Sunday confessor. I still don't want the job."

"The person of interest is a thug. He only understands brute force, but despite his social shortcomings, he's not stupid. However, he is extraordinarily greedy. His incentive will be all the money he can steal and all the women and children he can rape."

Uncharitably, Monsarrat again thought of Sanhedrin. "He sounds like the right thug for the job."

Palmer's face was as emotive as a death mask. "He's the estranged youngest son of the Amanyanabo. Okeri wants him by his side in Abuja, not only for protection, but to prevent the young man's peccadillos from staining his own international reputation."

"Maybe you should hire a psychiatrist as well as a babysitter."

"Last autumn, the youngest son became the head of a group of malicious killers posing as freedom fighters who cared more about rape and pillage than fighting for the rights of their people," he continued. "In January, the new government in Abuja brought him and his fighters into its Christian coalition, but tribal hatreds proved stronger than political considerations, and the partnership quickly fell apart."

Monsarrat thought that Palmer tiptoed along his own dotted line. "If I had swabbed the youngest son's ears with lead in Port Harcourt, would we be having this chat right now?"

Like a boxer pounding a heavy bag, one solid blow followed by the next, Palmer concluded his tale. "The youngest son believed that promises had been made to him by your former employers and, by extension, the new government. He believed he had been guaranteed the title of either minister of defense and general of the Army of the Delta, no matter that it existed only on paper. When the Christian coalition turned against the youngest son, he fled from the Delta with a dozen of his thugs."

"Okeri was unable to help his youngest son?"

"His father was not yet the darling of the oil consortium's eye."

"What happened to the people the youngest son left behind?"

"They were slaughtered," Palmer answered.

Monsarrat thought the tale followed a familiar script. "What happened to the youngest son?"

"He set himself up as a crime lord in a southern African country, where he has become quite powerful and even more wealthy."

Monsarrat felt acid churn in his stomach. "I have to know, Mark. Is Innocence your person of interest?"

Palmer held out his hand. "I believe that we understand each other, Nathan. Are you ready to sign?"

They turned onto Main Street, bustling with end-of-semester activity. Cars streamed away from the college, laden with the remains of an academic year. Monsarrat gestured toward the campus. "Your offer is very generous, Mark, but without your confirmation that we're talking about Innocence, our conversation just ended."

Palmer watched a brace of opposing cars stop before a crosswalk for a mother pushing a stroller to cross the road. "I've only told you the business part of the story. If I were in your position, I would listen to the personal part."

"I don't want the job. I'm not a mercenary. I'm a dean."

Palmer recognized an insurmountable obstacle and switched tactics. "My orders are to reveal the name of the person of interest only after you agree to take the job. It's not how I would play it, but my people insisted, so I can't confirm to you that Innocence is Okeri's son."

"What else can't you confirm?"

"That he's in Cape Town, a most beautiful city in a most violent country."

His rational mind insisted that Innocence remain an unfortunate incident locked in the basement of his past life, but his emotions demanded immediate vengeance. "You thought I would jump at a second chance to whack him?"

"I thought you might be the only man on this good earth he fears. After all, you sliced off a chunk his right ear, just after you killed Blessed."

"Let the police take care of him."

"He's bought them."

"Like I said, you're good enough, and you're proximate. Take care of him yourself."

"I've already made three runs at him," Palmer admitted. "The first time, I sent two of my boys to make him an offer. He beat them so badly they're still recuperating in a private clinic in Cape Town. The second time I sent a half-dozen boys to kidnap him, but Innocence captured them breaking into his villa. He personally executed four, tortured the fifth before decapitating him, and carved his name across the ass of the sixth. He filmed the entire ordeal and sent the survivor back with the recording."

"So it's personal now."

"It always has been personal, for both of us."

"What happened on the third run?"

"My people told me to hire local help."

"You mean mercenaries."

"I have associates in Cape Town, former Recces, small-team operators. I hired them to do a recon job. They sent me videos and photographs."

"Hire your South African friends to snatch him."

Palmer shook his head. "My friends have an understanding with the local authorities. They can take jobs at their discretion, as long as their *contra legem* activities take place beyond the country's borders."

He reached into his jacket pocket and withdrew a photograph. "I recognized the thugs from the Delta, but not the woman. Obviously, she's not one of the hookers hired to service the help. The picture nagged at me. Why would a Filipina be leashed to a pipe with a rope? Then I remembered your demand in the Delta that we rescue the nurse who saved your life. You were very insistent, until the doctor jabbed you with a sedative."

"Her name was Rosalinda Santiago."

Palmer passed him the photograph like a shark playing a trump card. "Is this the woman?"

Monsarrat absorbed the picture. A small woman whose thick, black hair had turned grey, secured by a thick rope leash around her neck to a pipe set in a square of stained concrete. She looked twice her actual age. Her face was deeply lined, and her almond-brown eyes were red and swollen. Raw tribal markings lacerated her forehead. Her nose appeared to have been broken and set poorly, and her lips drooped downward. The silver Saint Agatha medal no longer hung around her neck.

The date stamped into the corner was recent. "Where is she?"

"Well, Nathan, that's the difficult part."

"Difficult in that you don't know, or difficult in that you won't say?"

He answered bluntly. "If you accept the assignment, the woman is your bonus."

Monsarrat understood Palmer had eliminated his options. "I have your word? I deliver the person of interest, and you give me Rosalinda?"

"You have my word," he promised.

Monsarrat considered the ploys he had used during his career with the Agency to convince good people to undertake bad actions. "If you doctored the photo, Mark, I will hunt you, and I will kill you."

"You'd have every right."

"If I reject your offer, what happens to Rosalinda?"

Palmer dropped his pretenses. "That's a question for Innocence to answer."

"Any ground rules?"

"Absolutely none," he replied. "You carry out the mission in any manner you choose. I don't care how many bodies are dropped along the way. My only concern is Innocence."

Monsarrat again admired Palmer's professionalism. He had flushed and trapped him over lunch and a stroll in the park. "Where in Cape Town do I find him?"

Palmer supplied the address as they entered the parking lot. "My employers want Innocence in Abuja, but he killed people I was paid to protect, and I'd rather place him in an unmarked grave than by his daddy's side."

"If Innocence dies, what happens to Okeri?"

"I'm willing to gamble that Okeri will serve as president and steal as much oil wealth as he can stuff into his deep pockets with or without his son, but if he does balk, I'll send him back to Bonny Island in a casket fit for the Amanyanabo."

"You don't want options. You want Innocence dead, and your employers just provided you with the perfect cover."

"Like I said, you're a fast study."

Monsarrat prayed at the altar of the once bitten, twice shy. He neither trusted Palmer, nor fully believed his story, but he agreed that it was time for Innocence to die. Even more importantly, he needed to free Rosalinda, if she truly were a captive of Innocence in Cape Town. "Half up front, Franklins delivered next Thursday."

They shook hands. "I'm looking forward to working with you again, Nathan."

Monsarrat gave him the address and the time for the delivery. "Anything else I should know?"

"One more thing," Palmer agreed. "In Port Harcourt, Blessed was upset when he saw there was no money in the Vaduz bank account, which made me wonder what happened to the cash he and Innocence carried to Lichtenstein."

"The original deposits into the account. I've also wondered about that," Monsarrat admitted. "There should have been no increase to the account balance, since the money for the Nok was transferred directly to Sanhedrin, but it should not have been empty."

"Maybe Sanhedrin stole the funds."

"Hacking into a Lichtenstein bank would be difficult even for a man of his dubious talents."

"Then consider this scenario," Palmer offered. "When Blessed and Innocence flew to Vaduz, they set up two, not one, joint ownership transfer accounts at the Vaduz bank, but only Innocence understood their actions. In fact, he told Blessed it was all business as usual. Before they left Liechtenstein, Innocence set up online access but didn't bother to tell Blessed. He shifted the money from the first account to the second account. When you arrived in Port Harcourt, you became the perfect patsy, and Innocence blamed you for the theft."

"Are you speculating, Mark?"

"Not at all," he replied. "My employers made a few phone calls. The secret bankers in Vaduz were quite eager to curry favor with the consortium."

"The story has serious implications. It means Innocence is actually highly intelligent."

"It is a fact you would do well to remember," Palmer agreed.

When the door to a crimson Ford F-150 opened, the light inside the truck remained dark. Palmer was a very careful man. "Watch your back, Nathan. You're about to have your choice of enemies, and not all of them live on the other side of the Atlantic Ocean. Some of them are as close as Langley."

LYING TO A NUN

All his adult life, Monsarrat had shaded the truth. With Doris, he felt as if he were lying to a nun. When he asked her into his office, his tongue swelled with mendacity. "I'll be away next month, for personal reasons. We'll have to postpone the recruitment trip."

"Did your brother hurt himself again, Dean?"

"Not my brother. Me. For surgery. And physical therapy. An old football injury."

"When will you go on the recruitment trip?"

"Right after the fourth of July, just as soon as I'm strong enough."

He drove his Jeep through the quiet streets of the college town and parked in front of Ralph's. The eponymous neon sign illuminated the front window. Inside, the bar was cool and dark. Ralph extended his hand across the bar. "Long time, Dean. How've you been?"

Monsarrat shook his hand. "Academically engaged, Ralph. Yourself?"

"Alcoholically engaged."

"Business is good?"

"It might be better if I catered to the professional crowd, but I wouldn't feel right abandoning these rummies."

He took his usual seat. On the elevated plasma television, the Red Sox trailed the Tigers. He tilted his head in greeting toward the regulars. "A double shot of Wild Turkey and a Corona, please."

Ralph poured the shot with a neat, economical motion. He pried the top off the long-necked bottle. "You want it with a wedge of lime, like they serve at the Cantina?"

"Hell no, Ralph. Just let me enjoy the damn beer."

He swallowed the bourbon, turned the shot glass upside down on the bar, and shook off the offer of a refill. "How's Tiny these days?"

Ralph's younger brother, a former 265-pound pulling guard for Louisiana State University, had collapsed from dehydration during a pre-season practice session in his senior year, the bayou heat having boiled away his body fluids. Packed in ice, trainers rushed him to Baton Rouge General Hospital. After months of therapy, he regained most of his motor skills, save for a slight stammer and lack of hand-eye coordination when exhausted or under duress, but never again played football.

"He's well, thanks."

"Still working the bar on weekends?"

"Gives me the occasional Saturday or Sunday away from here."

Monsarrat tilted the long neck of the Corona and felt the cold liquid sting his throat. "Would he be okay running the bar for a few days?"

Ralph shrugged. "Don't see why not."

"Maybe a week. No longer than a month."

"What's on your mind, Dean?"

Monsarrat wanted to entice, not overwhelm him. "Guy I know offered me a job, maybe twenty-four hours of work, maybe thirty days, no more."

"A guy you know well?"

"Same old song and dance, Ralph."

"What else did this guy you know well say?"

"The job includes travel to far-away lands."

Ralph supplied the well-worn punch line. "Meet exotic natives. Shoot them dead."

Monsarrat held up his Corona in salute. "You remember the old days?"

"Tough to forget 'em."

"You want a chance to relive your youth?"

"You need some help, Dean?"

Monsarrat remembered Palmer's dotted line. "I can tell you only so much until you agree to come on board. I don't mean to be difficult. It keeps me safe and gives you deniability."

Ralph glanced at the autographed photograph of Chuck Norris next to the cash register. "That's a sucker's game, Dean. Maybe guys in Langley like those rules, but I don't. You want my help, come clean."

He admired Ralph's no-bullshit, leatherneck approach. "Would you like to make some extra money?"

"Depends on the money. And the job."

"Fair enough," Monsarrat agreed. "I need a minder."

"What's a minder, in non-spook English?"

"Someone to watch my back."

"Go on, Dean."

"Twenty-four hours, thirty days, the money's the same."

"In which far-away lands?"

"Africa, but if all goes according to plan, you won't shoot anyone."

"What if the plan goes straight to hell?"

"If not, then not."

He looked around the bar, observed the locals, the silent television, the two small *ki'i* wooden statues guarding the space between the bar and the bottles. He wondered if Ralph tired of the familiarity, or if it were his *puuhonua*, his personal place of refuge.

"Why don't you tell me about the job first, then we can talk about the money."

"You fly to Cape Town, set yourself up in a hotel."

"The one in South Africa?"

"Affirmative," Monsarrat confirmed. "You secure commo gear and wait to receive my messages."

"I'm no communications expert, Dean."

"The gear is basic: a pay as you go cell phone, a dependable laptop. Buy the phone at a big chain store where they won't ask too many questions, the laptop at another."

"How do we stay in touch?"

"You set up a new e-mail account, use a fake name, give me the address before you leave town, and trash it after the job. I call you or send a text, you don't see a number. You get an e-mail, you don't see a return address. You contact me, you don't see recipient data. My gear is black."

"I buy my phone and laptop in South Africa?"

"It eliminates the possibility of airport snafus."

"What do I use for money?"

"In Cape Town, exchange dollars for rand. Don't use your credit cards in-country."

"Hotels want credit cards at check-in."

"Go online, reserve your tickets and a hotel, something large and anonymous, somewhere your accent won't make you the center of attention. At the airport, pay for the tickets with dollars. At the hotel, give them rand."

"I use my own name?"

"Unless you have a clean passport with a false name," Monsarrat answered.

"I'm just a jarhead, Dean. I don't play super-duper spy games."

"It's more common sense than rocket science."

Ralph popped the top of a Budweiser, made a notation in a ledger, and passed the bottle to a patron. He didn't bother to offer a glass. "When would I leave for Cape Town?"

"In one week," Monsarrat replied. "On Memorial Day."

"No can do. It's one of the biggest holiday weekends of the year. I can't leave Tiny by himself."

Monsarrat thought the objection reasonable. "How about the next day, Tuesday?"

"Yeah, that would work."

"The South African Airways flight leaves New York at 1115 hours. You change planes in Johannesburg and arrive in Cape Town at 1215 hours the next day, Wednesday. No visa necessary, just your passport with six months validity. You good with that?"

"Even jarheads take foreign vacations. My passport's good for another few years."

Monsarrat checked off one hurdle. "First thing, familiarize yourself with the city. Walk around. Establish your tourist bona fides."

"Am I familiarizing myself with any particular neighborhoods in the city?"

Monsarrat appreciated the quality of Ralph's questions. "Start at the harbor. Focus on tourist areas. Radiate into the business areas."

"What am I looking for while I'm radiating?"

"Thugs. Muscle," he answered. "Cops. Pimps. Whoever's on the streets."

"What do I do when I find them?"

Monsarrat decided he had shown enough thigh. "Are you on board, Ralph? I can't take you any further without a handshake."

"Sounds reasonable so far, but tell me about the salary."

Monsarrat offered the terms in a half-now, half-later proposal. "Twenty-five thousand dollar cash advance, to cover your expenses, plane ticket, hotel, food, phone, laptop, taxis, whatever you need. Costs refundable upon completion of the mission. A second twenty-five thousand dollar payment upon conclusion."

Ralph's stare could have leveled a barn. "It's a lot of money, Dean. What kinda trouble do you expect?"

"I don't expect any," he replied, "but if I'm wrong, you'll earn every dollar."

"If shit happens over there, Tiny gets it, like a life insurance policy?

"Of course, but shit won't happen."

"No offense, Dean, you guys in the field were great, but every spook I ever met lobotomized his sense of right and wrong. You may be retired and a good guy, but I'm gonna need a promissory note. You supply the second payment of twenty-five thousand dollars, you get your piece of paper."

"I'm glad you're thinking straight, Ralph. I'll bring the note and the cash advance to the bar on Monday evening."

"Cutting it kinda close, aren't you?"

Monsarrat had seen cash pervert the virtue of saints as easily as sinners. He didn't want the money in Ralph's closet, tempting him. "Don't worry about the timing. You have any other questions?"

"Yeah," he answered. "Why me?"

Monsarrat answered bluntly. "I don't want to worry about the guy watching my back. I need him to be loyal and dependable."

Ralph offered his hand. "I'm flattered, Dean. Tell me about the job."

Monsarrat felt the strength in his grip. "Welcome aboard, Ralph."

He shared only logistics, not objectives. "Each day of the op, I check in, an e-mail, a text message, a telcon. A method of delivery, a word or phrase, an exact time tailored to each specific day, according to the matrix I'll give you. Three specific boxes to check each day, starting the first and ending the last day of June."

"What if we go over into July?"

"Last day of June, we're wheels up, different flights, different destinations, gone and not going back, job finished or not."

Monsarrat enjoyed the clarity of planning an operation before it launched, and the best laid plans caromed like errant pinballs outside the pen. "On Monday, the day before you go wheels up, I deliver the twenty-five grand, the matrix, and a phone number to call in case of emergency with a simple sentence to recite. I brief you on a special purchase you'll make in Cape Town. We don't speak in person until the Fourth of July celebration on Main Street."

"What special purchase?"

"Details to come."

He asked questions as if he were playing a game of pepper. "Will I have problems carrying that much money through the airports?"

"Don't flash it. Don't declare it."

"I'm a tourist, no agenda, just drink the wine, eat the food, meet the girls?"

"You're on vacation," Monsarrat agreed. "Check into your hotel. Go shopping. On June 1, I initiate contact."

"How do you contact me? I won't know my number before I buy the phone."

"When I deliver the cash, we set a date, time, and place for you to pass the number and the purchases."

Ralph served another beer to a patron and added a new notation to the ledger. "Can you give me an example of a message?"

It was a fair request. "Let's say on June 1 the word is green. Maybe you'll see green grass. Maybe green beans. Maybe just the word green."

"The message matches the matrix, I know all is well," Ralph said. "What if the word is green but I get blue? What if the message should be an e-mail, but I get a text? What if the time is 1700, but it arrives at 2000? What if I don't get diddly?"

"If the matrix is violated, you follow your orders. Don't deviate. Don't improvise."

"You trying to frighten me, Dean?"

"I'm trying to make sure you come back home to spend your money."

Monsarrat waited for him to hand out more beers before continuing. "If the matrix is violated, even slightly, you bug out immediately. Check out of the hotel, flag a taxi, call the emergency number, recite the sentence, and disconnect. At the airport, buy a ticket on the first plane to anywhere that doesn't require a visa. Strip the phone and laptop of their data. Toss the equipment into separate garbage bins. You go wheels up, chill out for a few days, check your back, and return home nice and slow."

"What if you make a mistake? You wanted to write pink but you sent purple? You don't want me to wait around and see if you get back on schedule the next day?"

"Fallbacks are for Hollywood. We follow big-boy rules with big-boy penalties and big-boy rewards."

"All I know is I can't watch your back if I'm running away."

Monsarrat appreciated that Marines left no one behind. "As long as you dial the emergency number and pass the message, you're doing exactly what you need to do."

"Okay, Dean, I'll do it, but I won't like it."

Monsarrat placed his right hand upon his heart for emphasis. "I won't make a mistake, Ralph. If the matrix is violated, it means I'm blown. A lot of pain can rain down on my head if you don't call the emergency number immediately."

"Your ball, your rules, Dean."

Monsarrat checked off a second hurdle. "There's also an abort word. You receive it, no matter what time, no matter by phone or e-mail or text, you follow the same orders as if the matrix was violated, only you do not call the emergency number, because I'll be racing you to the airport."

"What's the word?"

He chose it easily. "I say Felix, you abort."

"Matrix and Felix. Sounds like a pair of superheroes from Greek mythology," Ralph noted. "Anything else I need to know?"

Other than not declaring cash at the airport, Monsarrat's instructions had been above board, but he needed to prepare Ralph for the prospect of spending time in a foreign prison. "The drop location is the fast-food chicken joint in the food court of the V & A Waterfront. On Friday, June 1, at zero-nine-thirty hours, order a meal, find a table, put the package with the special purchases on the chair across from you, eat your food, and walk away without the package."

"Where will you be?"

"I'll have eyes on you. When you leave the table, I'll sit down, retrieve the package, and depart in the other direction. We maintain zero contact."

"I'm not a fan of fast food, Dean."

"Food courts," Monsarrat explained, "are my favorite places to service a drop. They're busy, and they're anonymous."

He laid an Andrew Jackson on the bar and departed for his home. The remainder of the week, he searched online Cape Town newspapers for stories on violent criminal gangs. He studied reports on Rehovoth Okeri and the political situation in Abuja. He read until his eyes throbbed.

Thursday offered blue skies, cool breezes, and warm temperatures. At half past ten, he parked the Jeep on the north side of the Mohawk Trail, across from a diner overlooking the Hoosic River. He wore faded jeans, work boots, and a University of New Hampshire sweatshirt. Inside the diner, he ordered black coffee and a slice of apple crumb pie and sat at a table with a view of the highway.

Thirty minutes later, tall Paul walked through the door wearing sandals, designer jeans, and a grey tee shirt that clung to his torso like an epidermal layer. A pair of sunglasses sat atop his brown crew cut, and he carried a blue backpack on his right shoulder. He blended into the woodsy atmosphere of the diner as smoothly as oil floated on water.

His outfit was relaxed, but his grip was as calloused as a lumberjack's. "You're looking well, Dean Monsarrat. More comfortable than the last time we met."

"Call me Nathan, and welcome to the Berkshires."

Paul took the chair opposite Monsarrat. He glanced at the entrance before placing the backpack on the floor. "As you requested, Franklins only."

Monsarrat prodded the heavy bag with his toe. "Would you like a cup of coffee, Paul? Something to eat"

"Just coffee. Black with sugar, please."

Monsarrat walked to the counter and returned to the table with a white porcelain cup. "The owners bake their own pies here, and the grilled cheese sandwiches on rye bread are excellent."

Paul had twisted in his chair to watch the traffic flow on the highway. He turned back to Monsarrat. "I really need to return to the airport. I fly back this afternoon."

"Fast trip," he sympathized.

"Mark sends his regards and asks how you're progressing?"

"Tell him there's no cause for worry."

"He'll be glad to hear it."

Monsarrat felt a familiar cold, prickling sensation. "Is there a problem, Paul? You seem distracted."

"I'm just a bit tired. The flight was long, and the ride from Boston zonked me."

Monsarrat didn't believe the explanation. "Are you expecting someone?"

Paul leaned forward. "Nothing I can prove, I haven't seen anything, just a feeling that I have a shadow. Maybe I'm paranoid, but it's like I stepped off the plane and picked up a tail."

"You didn't see anyone?"

"Like I said, it's just a feeling."

"You have these feelings often?"

"The Gulf, South Asia, Africa."

"They're accurate?"

His lips curled. "I'm still alive."

"You have the feeling now, Paul, one hundred percent?"

His voice was flat. "I didn't make a vehicle. I didn't make foot surveillance. But I know I have a tail."

Through the window, Monsarrat surveyed cars flashing by the two-lane Mohawk Trail. "Drink your coffee. We'll shake hands, you'll saunter out of the diner. Stroll toward your car. What are you driving?"

"A Chevy Malibu, blue, Massachusetts plate 421EM7, sticker expires in September. Two hundred yards on your nine, this side of the highway as you step out the door."

"Give yourself five minutes between leaving here and starting your car. Check out the river. Examine the bottom of your sandals. By the time you put the key in the ignition, I'll be outside, hunting your tail."

Paul finished his coffee, stood, and shook Monsarrat's hand. "Good luck, Nathan."

Monsarrat watched him turn left out of the door. He picked up the backpack, paid the bill at the register, and dropped the change into the tip glass. He followed Paul's route, scanning the highway. He watched the blue Malibu turn onto the pavement and head east toward Boston. Neither a car nor a truck slipped behind the Chevy, but a professional would have waited further down the highway, out of sight from the diner. After a few minutes, he hoisted the backpack higher onto his shoulder and walked to his Jeep.

Doris was not at her desk when he entered his office. He opened his e-mails and saw Palmer's address at the head of the list of unread messages. He glanced at the subject line, "Smooth Sailing," the two words followed by a single question mark. He typed a brief reply, "So far, so good," and hit the send key, leaving Paul to explain his concerns to his employer.

Doris had still not returned when he departed the office. He scribbled a few words in capital letters across the top of her note pad, "BACK BY 2:00 P.M.," and placed the pad on her chair. She took umbrage when others touched items on her desk. The chair could be another tot for her list of grievances.

He drove his Jeep slowly through the college town. Beyond his house, he made a U-turn in the street, pulled into the driveway, and performed the kabuki of the alarm system. In his bedroom, he squeezed the cash into the safe.

He had not made vehicle surveillance teams, nor had he seen static surveillance posts. No one had followed him from his office to his home, but he still could not discount Paul's certitude. Western Massachusetts had become a spook's Mecca.

The next afternoon, he drove to meet Abby in Manhattan. She described herself as a city girl and claimed the trees she saw on her daily commute from Arlington to Langley satisfied her need to commune with nature. "I do like the Berkshires, baby, just not enough to spend a holiday weekend there," she had explained. "Let's stay in one of our favorite hotels with a view of Central Park. Food, sex, shopping, it'll be decadent."

"In that order?"

"You can put sex before food, but shopping is number one!"

He feared the answer to his question. "Are museums on your list?"

"Of course, it's a long weekend in New York. MOMA, The Met, the Guggenheim, the Cloisters, we'll see them all! The Lincoln Center, the ballet, the opera, the philharmonic, Broadway. It will be wonderful."

"Sounds like there won't be time for sex or food," he had grumbled.

On Sunday morning, he won the breakfast coin toss and chose a small restaurant on the Lower East Side. They stood in line for twenty minutes, waiting for a table. Once seated, Abby ordered a Florentine omelet with home fries and wheat toast. Monsarrat chose a large stack of cinnamon pancakes. They both drank coffee. "If I were an operative," she confided as she cut into his pancakes, "I would choose a high-society cover. I much prefer caviar and bliný over eggs and potatoes."

"Does that mean you wish you were eating brunch in the hotel?" Monsarrat deadpanned.

She wore a zippered Greylock College sweatshirt over a blue, cotton tee shirt that matched her eyes, black jeans, and tooled cowboy boots. Her blonde hair hung in a ponytail. Her dimples were deep, her cheekbones sharp, and her smile brilliantly white. "Any meal with you is pure Beluga, big boy."

Monsarrat wanted to spend the rest of his life with her, but she was not ready to quit the Agency, and he would not return to it. He reached for her hand and stroked her long fingers. "I agreed to do a job. I leave tomorrow. I may be back in three days. I may be back in thirty days."

Her blue eyes searched his face. "Do you mean your student recruiting trip, Nathan?"

"I'm freelancing, Abby."

"Are you working for Felix again? You know you can't trust him, baby."

He did not share his suspicions that his former boss would slither from his nest beneath a rock sooner rather than later. "He's not part of the plan."

"If you're not working for Felix, who hired you? Another three-letter agency?"

"I can't tell you, Abby."

"Did one of your old friends in the oil business hire you?"

He knew mentioning the payment and the bonus would be a mistake. "I just wanted you to know I'm leaving the country."

"Who has your back?" she asked.

"A good person. I trust him."

"Do I know him?"

"He's from the town."

"Can you at least tell me where you are going?"

He turned over her hand and traced the lines in her palm with his index finger. "When I was in the Delta, a woman took care of me. She kept me alive."

"I remember," Abby replied. "Her name was Rosalinda Santiago. You said that the rebels killed her."

"I thought she was dead," he admitted, "until a few days ago, when someone showed me a photograph."

"Are you sure it was proof-of-life? Computers can create the most realistic pictures."

"I don't have a choice, Abby. I need to prove it to myself." He failed to add that he needed to fix the mistake he had made in Port Harcourt.

"Is finding her the job?"

"She's personal. The job is to locate a person of interest."

She placed her right hand against his cheek. "You're a fool, Nathan, if you think you can step back into the game after a two-year hiatus. You're not a tough as nails spy anymore. You're just an academic."

"I don't have a choice, Abby," he repeated. "I can't abandon her."

"Hire someone to see if the picture's real."

He knew she was right. "I'm sorry, Abby. I need to do it myself."

She balled her left hand into a fist. "Don't give me your macho bullshit, Nathan. You don't need to do it. You want to do it."

He wrapped his hand around her fingers and lowered them to the table. "Need. Want. They're the same for me."

She pulled away from him. "You're going back to Africa, aren't you? You're going after that son of a bitch from the Delta."

He tossed fifty dollars onto the table and led her out of the restaurant. "I have to see for myself if she's alive, Abby. You can understand that, can't you?"

"What about us, Nathan? Did you consider me before you accepted the job? What happens to me if you die over there?"

He squeezed her hand tighter. "I'll be back in time to watch the Fourth of July fireworks with you."

Tears gathered in her eyes. "I buried my husband. I don't want to bury you, too, baby."

"I swear to you, Abby, this is the last time. I do this final job, and I go back to being a dean in the Berkshires."

The next morning, he helped pile her purchases into a taxi. "Did Amtrak add a special shopping train for you?"

She kissed him hard on the lips. "Be careful, Nathan. Take the full thirty days, if you need them. Just come back home safe."

He missed her already. "You can't say anything to Felix. You know I don't trust him."

He drove back to the Berkshires. In his house, he showered and packed a duffel bag with the few items he would need for Cape Town. Anything else, he would purchase locally. He tossed the bag into the Jeep, drove to Ralph's, and parked before the entrance. The bar was crowded with local patrons celebrating the Memorial Day holiday. Flags and bunting hung from the ceiling and covered the windows. Ralph and Tiny staffed the bar.

Monsarrat shook their hands. "How's everything, Tiny?"

"It's all good, Dean," the large man answered. "Next term, I'll finish my bachelor's degree at the state college. After that, who knows? Maybe I'll join the family business."

Ralph slapped him with a bar towel. "Go bus the tables."

When he was beyond hearing range, Monsarrat slid an envelope across the bar. "Cash and promissory note."

The envelope disappeared. "Get me up to speed, Dean. What else do I need to know?"

Monsarrat passed him a folded sheet of paper. "Memorize and destroy it. If the matrix protocol is violated, call this emergency number, deliver this sentence, and bug out."

Ralph read the words. "Nephew's in Cape Town deep in Delta shit."

Monsarrat had crafted the message carefully. "Deliver it word by word, no ad libs. Don't expect a reply, just hang up and go."

"Who's the guy I'm calling? Is he dependable?"

"The less you know, Ralph, the happier you'll be."

"I've heard that story before."

He passed a book of matches and a thick pad of paper across the bar. "You're familiar with flash paper?"

"Yeah, spook stuff. Never used it though."

Writing covered the first thirty pages. The remainder was blank. "Look at the first page."

As he read the notations, Ralph's expression changed from confusion to disgust. "Je1. Zero Seven. Thunder. Three. I'm not good with games, Dean. What's it mean?"

Monsarrat explained the code. "Je is June followed by the date. The first of June is Je1. The fourteenth of June will be Je14."

"Got it."

"Zero seven is 0700, the time the message will be delivered," Monsarrat continued. "Thunder is the code word. It will change every day."

Ralph flipped through the pages. "Thunder. Storm. Lightening. Rain. Snow. Hail. Meteorological, aren't you, Dean?"

Monsarrat ignored the jibe. "The method of delivery follows. One is a text message. Two is a telcon. Three is an e-mail to your new address. Which is exactly what?"

Ralph wrote the information on the back of a paper coaster and passed it to Monsarrat. "Memorize it. Destroy it."

The expectation of movement, of an end to lethargy, settled upon him. "Give it to me, Ralph."

"June the first at 0700 hours. The code word is thunder. The delivery is an e-mail," the publican answered.

Monsarrat gave his pupil a gold star. "Just don't lose the flash pad, Ralph, and don't light a match to read it in the dark."

"What do I say if someone asks me about the gibberish on these pages?"

"You'll think of something."

He considered the advice. "Yeah, always have. Anything else I need to know?"

"Best for last, Ralph. Like I promised."

Ralph poured a shot of rye and handed it to a patron. He made a notation in his ledger.

"Can't wait to hear it, Dean."

"Remember the food court?"

"Fast-food chicken joint, first day of June at zero-nine-thirty. What's in the package?"

Monsarrat held up a single finger. "First, a piece of paper with your cell phone number, nothing more. Second, a sitrep with your intel assessment."

"Intel assessment about what exactly?"

"Remember the instructions to familiarize yourself with the city, walk around, start at the harbor, focus on tourist areas, establish your bona fides?"

"You told me to radiate and look for street life."

"I want you to write it down for me," Monsarrat said. "Scribble it on the back of napkins, or buy a quill, ink, and vellum. Don't worry about your penmanship. I'll decipher it."

"Part one and part two are good, but I have a feeling you're leading up to part three."

"Good instincts, Ralph," he admitted. "I need you to secure a weapon, something with enough kick to drop a very nasty individual."

"Jesus, Dean, you don't fuck around, do you?"

Monsarrat had expected the outburst. "Don't carry a piece into South Africa. I don't want to spend my time trying to pop you out of the airport jail."

"You got instructions on how to buy a piece in a foreign country without getting arrested? Something I can memorize and destroy?"

He didn't want to sour Ralph on the deal. "Cape Town is like the Wild, Wild West. You walk through the nasty neighborhoods of the city, look for a punk flashing too much money, someone wearing too much gold jewelry. You feed him a story, you get him alone, you take everything and make sure he can't come back after you."

"Why don't I just brace a scumbag, see if he has a cannon to sell? Tell him it's a birthday present, ask him to wrap it up nicely in pretty paper with a ribbon?"

"You don't want to leave any loose ends, Ralph."

"How am I gonna tell if the piece is any good? I can't field-test it."

"Take it back to your hotel room and inspect it. Clean it as well as you can. Pray you chose the right punk, because if I need to ram the barrel up the nasty individual's ass, I don't want to hear a click when I pull the trigger."

"Maybe you should ask the guy on the far end of the emergency number to secure a weapon for you?"

Monsarrat appreciated the question, so he supplied a blunt answer. "It's not that kind of a relationship. He's more of a call in one big favor to take care of the local authorities sort of a guy."

Ralph looked around the bar, as if he might not see it again. "I'm not clear on a coupla points."

"Anything you need to know, ask it now. I have to catch a plane."

"Does the envelope have enough cash to buy everything I need? I don't wanna go looking for an ATM machine if I'm supposed to stay under the radar."

"Twenty-five thousand, as promised. More than enough."

"Who knows I'll be over there, other than you?"

"No one, for your own safety."

"What are you going to do with the nasty individual?"

Monsarrat replied tersely. "You don't need to know."

Ralph leaned across the bar. "You guys have a different rule book. You don't trust anybody, not even each other. You fly solo, you don't share. I get that, I really do."

"What's bothering you, Ralph?"

"In my world, me with my brother Marines, we have each other's backs. Communication is king. This is a one-sided relationship. I gotta wait for you to contact me, but if anything goes wrong on my end, I'm up shit creek without the paddle. I got no way to get a message to you."

Monsarrat understood his frustration, two cultures clashing, Marines and spooks. "That's exactly what I mean by big boy risks."

"I'm just telling you, Dean, for your own good. If something happens to me, you'll never know that your minder's been compromised."

"I understand you're frustrated, Ralph, and no plan is ever perfect, but this one gives each of us a good chance of getting out of South Africa vertical if the shit hits the fan."

"Just cut and run, leave the other guy behind?"

"I know it's not how you were trained, but we're playing by spook rules now."

"I'm not gonna let you down, Dean. I'll watch your back, I'll pass you the package, and I'll monitor your messages. I just don't like it."

"You'll put my money in the bank, too. Fifty large will juice your retirement package."

"You got that right, Dean, but when we're back here, I want you to tell me just what the fuck went down over there."

Monsarrat knew it would never happen. He nodded toward Tiny and left the bar. He took a deep breath, climbed into the Jeep, and started the drive to the long-term parking lot at Logan Airport. He flew Business Class to Cape Town via London and arrived in South Africa the following day.

A BRILLIANT WESTERN CAPE AFTERNOON

The British Airways flight touched down beneath a brilliant Western Cape afternoon at Cape Town International Airport in Matroosfontein, less than twenty miles from the center of the city. Monsarrat cleared Immigration and Customs and bought rand, the local currency, at a Bureaux de Change in the arrival hall of the sleek glass and chrome terminal. In the men's room, he took an envelope from his duffel bag, filled it with his remaining dollars and a pad of flash paper containing the matrix, sealed it, and returned it to the bag.

He departed the terminal and strode to the taxi rank. More spook than dean, he absorbed the peculiar *potjiekos* stew of accents, the rounded vowels of Gauteng, the fearful pitch of African tongues, the chirping of Asian tonal languages, and the nasal complaints of European parlance. Unlike his prior trip to Port Harcourt under the worrisome auspices of Sanhedrin, he did not need bourbon to bolster his nerves.

When he reached the head of the queue he sprinted across the road to the public transportation island and bought a one-way ticket at the kiosk for the A01 express bus to the Civic Centre. He offered his ticket to the collector, carried the duffel bag onto the bus, and tossed it onto the overhead rack. From his window seat, he surveyed the activity of the airport. His back appeared clear.

The midday traffic flowed smoothly, and the trip to the Civic Centre on Hertzog Boulevard in the center of the city took fewer than thirty minutes over fast roads. He retrieved his duffel bag and stood on the bus quay, as still as one of the city's nineteenth-century statues. The cragged beauty of Table Mountain dominated the landscape, and the harbor's hotels and malls pulsed with movement. Like the diamonds sold in its markets, Cape Town was an African gem, brilliant but flawed. The city, enchanting yet weary, home to the continent's wealthiest families but burdened by poverty and laden with crime, was a canvas painted with the tired dignity of waning light.

He walked through the Central District toward Signal Hill and, on New Church Street, entered a youth hostel with a neat sign promising clean rooms and cheap rates. He sought anonymity among Australian backpackers, European elderhostelers, and Asian university students, to blend like a chameleon into the collage of foreigners, his voice lost in a babel of languages spoken too loudly, one atop the other, like a precarious verbal stack.

He paid cash for a week's stay in a single room with a toilet and shower and signed the register as David Clarendon, a peripatetic Canadian from Halifax, Nova Scotia. The name matched his passport, credit cards, insurance cards, and driver's license. Posing as a northern neighbor, with the same language and similar accents, was a favorite operational ploy.

The receptionist, a young man born to generations of backpackers and hippies, looked as if he had been plucked from a Peter Max poster. His name tag identified him as Rick, and his dirty-blond hair hung past his shoulders in a ponytail secured by a blue elastic band. He wore pink-hued granny glasses and a tie-dyed tee shirt. Monsarrat took the sealed envelope from the duffel bag and handed it to him. "Could you hold this in your safe?"

The young man stepped into a small office, his long ponytail bobbing as he filled out a form and taped it to the envelope. He ripped off the bottom third of the paper, spun a dial, and placed the envelope inside the safe. After closing the door, he spun the dial the opposite direction. He handed Monsarrat the receipt. "It's an extra twenty rand per night for the service."

"It's not so much to pay for peace of mind."

The austere room offered a view of Table Mountain and little else in the way of creature comforts. Monsarrat dropped the duffel bag onto the floor, stripped off his traveling clothes, and tossed them onto the single mattress. He squeezed into the minuscule bathroom and stood beneath the stinging jets of the shower. His fatigue absorbed the hot water like a sponge. He desperately wanted to sleep.

After five minutes, he turned off the shower, toweled dry, and wrapped the thin cotton towel around his waist. He punched a Pretoria number into the cell phone purchased, like the David Clarendon identity, from former colleagues who had traded the quaint notion of *pro patria* for the remunerative siren of black services. The device had cost him dearly, but its ability to function globally while disguising its identity and location made it an invaluable tool.

He listened to a faint buzz before the line engaged. The last time he had seen Bruce Wilson, the analyst had been perched behind a government-issue, wooden desk in a windowless embassy office in Abuja, two high-intensity desk lamps combatting the sickly glow of overhead fluorescent strips. The cement walls of the

office were bare, save for scars of masking tape, a cardboard Old
Glory, and a single sheet of bond paper bearing a sprawling
handwritten message in uppercase letters, GIVE ME SUNLIGHT
OR GIVE ME DEATH.

Wilson remained the same bilious genius who had years
earlier perceived a kindred spirit and a sharp intelligence in
Monsarrat. "You're not calling from inside the building, and not a
soul outside the embassy knows this number, so before the
security goons trace your call, track you down, and break your
bones, who are you and what do you want?"

Monsarrat suspected that his friend's bark might not be worse
than his bite. "You remember that placard I gave you? Vaguely
Patrick Henry? Vaguely subversive?"

The analyst's voice rasped. "I heard you had become mad or
quixotic or some such shit. I heard you were trying to make an
honest man of yourself. I shall name you Diogenes."

"You sound consumptive, Uncle. You should get outside more
often."

"What kind of games you playing, Nephew? Calling me on
some shitbird device that's screwing my identification system?
You're a blank on the trace."

The accusation pleased him. "Can I drag you out of your
mushroom cave and buy you a decent meal? When was the last
time you saw the sun?"

The analyst wheezed. "Food is vastly overrated. So is sunshine."

"Not exactly a healthy answer, Uncle. You need to take care of
yourself."

"Who are you today? My grandmother giving advice?"

"Just a concerned friend."

"There ain't no such thing in this world of ours. I would have
thought the Delta had cured you of your romantic beliefs in
fraternity and liberty and all that shit. Made you more like your
old Uncle Bruce. Suspicious maximus."

"Cynical."

"Questioning."

"Paranoid."

"Alive. Psyche intact."

In Monsarrat's memory, Wilson was a bear, shaggy with wildly
sprouting hair, swaying his girth as he walked. He remembered
his cynicism and distrust, the brilliance of his intellect, his
guillotine perspicacity, and the depth of his loyalty to the very few
allowed into his selective circle. "You traveling these days?"

"Home to office and back again. I live in an embassy shire, like
a hairy hobbit."

Monsarrat did not want to reveal his location. "You feel like a trip to Durban, warm sun, sandy beaches, beautiful bikini babes?"

"It's a good thing you retired, Nephew. Your spook powers of persuasion actually are for shit. Sun? Sand? Sex? For your old uncle?"

"What if I came to Pretoria?"

"Allow me a statement of pellucidity. I don't travel. Especially not to wherever you and your black phone are sitting. Neither do I entertain guests, not even if they bear costly gifts of diamonds, frankincense, myrrh, Russian intelligence, or some such shit. You want to talk, do it the grown-up way. Send an e-mail on the high side, and maybe I'll respond."

Monsarrat knew a wall when he ran into it. "You want the short or the long version?"

"What kind of shit question is that? You think I have time to read your fairy tales?"

"Not read. Listen. I'm going to tell you a story."

"You think I have time to listen to your shit stories?"

"You have time, because you know I would not call you on a black phone just to chat about your lousy health. You're just looking for a little foreplay."

"Cut to the chase. What do you want from my benighted life?"

It was a question Monsarrat had considered during the long flight over the Atlantic Ocean. "In Abuja, you took a particular interest in a son of a bitch named Innocence."

"The deputy sadist-in-chief to Blessed," the analyst agreed. "Sanhedrin, your shit-for-brains boss, negotiated your release from the FATA rebels with him. He was a thug, but he wasn't at all stupid."

Monsarrat heard the interest in his voice. "Are you describing Innocence or Sanhedrin?"

"Touché, Nephew. Tell me about your interest in Innocence. Is it vengeance, served cold?"

He had not changed, Monsarrat noted. Slow to warm, once interested in a story, he held forth with enthusiasm, if comfortable with his interlocutors. A suspicious Wilson, however, was a taciturn miser with the coin of his words.

The analyst did not give him the chance to answer. "Any validity to the rumor that Sanhedrin sent you back to the Delta a few months ago to take out Blessed? Something about being a small cog in the usual Sanhedrin extraordinarily complicated wheel?"

"Nothing I would admit."

"Hey, Nephew, it's me, Uncle Bruce, keeper of secrets. Talk to me."

Monsarrat spoke obliquely, given his friend's slavish adherence to recording conversations. "Blessed bought a bullet in Port Harcourt and died too fast. So I heard."

"I'm still listening, Nephew."

Uncle Bruce, Nephew Nathan, just like old times. Monsarrat sat on the edge of the bed. "I also heard that whoever took out Blessed could have taken out Innocence but didn't. Probably a mistake, in hindsight, but in one of those cruel oddities of fate, I've been hired to locate Innocence and make him an offer."

"Why do you think the shitbird's in South Africa?"

"The gentlemen who hired me possess excellent intel. Almost as good as yours."

Wilson snorted. "I doubt that."

"They told me Innocence has become a very successful criminal businessman in Cape Town."

"Like cream, he's risen to the top of the city's criminal groups, the Russians and the South Africans excluded."

"They also told me he has a bright future in Nigerian politics."

"Don't flirt with me, Nathan. There's no thing as a bright future in Nigerian politics, so tell me about your employers and their offer."

Monsarrat tugged at the hook, to be sure that Wilson had fully swallowed it. "My employers lack your analytical gifts."

"Are you playing the coquette, trying to untie my knickers?"

"I need the most recent intel on Innocence."

In Pretoria, the analyst sighed. "Talk to me, Nephew."

"My employers hired me to return Innocence to the warm bosom of his family. If he cooperates, he travels vertically. If he's difficult, horizontal is an acceptable alternative."

"Maybe you prefer the latter?"

"Horizontal works for me," he admitted.

"Justice delayed, judgment meted, death embraced, all that shit?"

"Nothing I would want to admit to your digital recorders."

"What's this to do with me?" Wilson asked.

"As I said, I need the most recent intel on Innocence. Where does he live? How does he spend his days? Who are his allies? Who are his enemies? What are his habits?"

"You don't want a little, do you?"

"I want to know about his muscle. I want to know the best way to approach him."

"Anything else while we're out shopping?"

"I also want to know if Sanhedrin is involved with him."

"For you, I should violate my holy vows of silence and risk my pension? If I tell you tales out of school, what do I get in return?"

Monsarrat understood that free lunches were as substantial as pixie dust. "Remember the coup in Abuja, not so many months ago?"

"It's vaguely familiar. The Agency crawled between the sheets with the oil companies."

"Just vaguely?"

"Nice try, Nephew, but you know my vaguely trumps everyone else's very."

Monsarrat admitted the fact. "What do you know about their post-coup divorce?"

"It was only a matter of when, not if."

"What do you know about the counter-coup the oil companies are about to launch?"

The analyst's tension ratcheted. "A counter-coup, you say? You have details?"

"I wouldn't waste your time, if I didn't."

"Maybe we should meet," Wilson admitted.

"I'll make it easy for you, Uncle Bruce. Lunch in Sandton at the Veneto Lounge in the Titian Hotel, Thursday at noon. We'll discuss old times, about Innocence, and about a counter-coup."

"It's a hell of a tease, but Sandton is miles away in Johannesburg, and you know I don't like to leave the office."

"Hire a cab off the streets, as far from the office as your fat feet will take you. Stay away from Agency vehicles and Agency drivers."

"Are you trying to end my magnificent career? Meeting a former spook turned rogue in flagrante delicto in Johannesburg could burn me."

"An odd word choice," Monsarrat replied. "Who says I'm a rogue?"

Wilson wheezed when he laughed. "I know more about you than your momma, your girlfriends, your shrink, and your Sunday confessor combined."

"Nothing recent, though. I'm a private citizen."

"You know better than to believe fairy tales. No one ever leaves the Agency."

"We have a contract until death do us part?"

"Not even then," the analyst chided. "One more point, Nephew. If you're working in the private sector, you make more in a fortnight than I do in a year. You'll pay for lunch."

Monsarrat ended the call and tossed the cell phone on the pillow. He pulled on a pair of shorts, spread the towel onto the floor, propped himself above the cloth in push-up position, and lowered himself slowly until his elbows hovered parallel to the floor. He executed one hundred push-ups, feeling the burn in his muscles. He flipped over and began five sets of one hundred sit-ups, each set focused on separate muscle groups.

He dressed in blue jeans, a grey tee shirt, and black sneakers. He pulled on a black, hooded sweatshirt, closed the door to his room, and locked it. In the fading light of the early evening, he followed New Church Street to the Civic Centre. Come the fulsome night, the Central District would shed its staid, diurnal character to become an urban jungle of miscreants, recidivists, and deviants, denizens of the dark seeking prey in its fields of asphalt, offering nocturnal lures of sex, drugs, and violence. The raven Cape Town night would serve as a natural habitat for Innocence, and his muscle would terrorize the darkened streets as they had once preyed upon the defenseless villages of the Delta.

Monsarrat had hunted his enemies in the deserts of the Middle East and the jungles of Africa, in the great cities of Asia and the quaint villages of Europe, and across the vast swathes of Russia. Locating an unsuspecting Innocence would be a stroll in the park. Capturing him would be a pleasure. Killing him would provide a marrow-deep satisfaction.

"More spook than dean," he intoned.

THE RHYTHMS OF THE STREET

Monsarrat woke before dawn on Thursday, eager to meet his old friend. He had spent Tuesday night and all Wednesday wandering the Central District and its adjoining neighborhoods among beggars, prostitutes, and hustlers, observing the rhythms of the street and the ebb and the flow of human tides. He noted the markings of the different tribes and listened to pidgin boasts and threats. Cape Town, at land's end, attracted the continent's detritus, like a magnet pulling flesh, blood, and disease. Wherever he stepped, he had seen the footprints of Innocence.

At the South African Airways counter in Cape Town International Airport, he purchased a round-trip ticket with rand. The security formalities were conducted politely and quickly. He boarded the plane and settled into his window seat. Slightly over two hours and 750 miles later, the flight touched down at O. R. Tambo International Airport in Johannesburg.

In the elevated station above the airport terminal, he bought a Gold Card for the Gautrain. He passed through a glass barrier and boarded the waiting train for the twenty-five-mile trip. In Sandton, he rose from the bowels of the underground station like a vigilant Lazarus and, at the intersection of Rivonia Road and West Street, turned toward Nelson Mandela Square and the Titian Hotel.

His eyes scanned the urban landscape for potential threats, but when he turned suddenly and doubled back, no one reacted to his abrupt movements. He espied neither Palmer and his sidekicks, nor Sanhedrin and his chorus of heavy hitters. In the hotel, a lobby pianist clad in a black dinner jacket sat at a Steinway Baby Grand. Dark runners of silk adorned his pressed trousers. He wore a black bowtie and a pleated cummerbund of silk. His fingers danced across the ivory of the piano, filling the open space with strains of Chopin's "Revolutionary Etude."

Between two arc windows in the Veneto Lounge, Bruce Wilson, large and shaggy and disheveled, sat at a table for four. He rose when he saw Monsarrat and covered the distance between them like a mother bear lumbering to protect her cubs. He shook

143

Monsarrat's hand as if he were pumping water from a well and pinched his cheek between his thumb and index finger.

"You're looking well," he announced. "No worse for wear after leaving the cold embraces of the Agency."

Monsarrat clamped him on his broad back. "You look like an orangutan. Did you lose weight?"

"Flattery, Nephew," Wilson deadpanned, "will get you absolutely nothing. Save your charm for some shitbird who doesn't know you so well."

Monsarrat paid homage to the analyst. "Your social skills may be vestigial, Uncle, but you know more about Africa than the rest of the Agency combined."

"That is true," he agreed, "but only because when it comes to the Dark Continent, the Agency pushed its ugly head up its puckered asshole a long time ago."

"Kept it there, too."

An Indian waiter dressed in white livery offered menus and took their drink orders. Wilson watched him walk toward the kitchen before turning back to Monsarrat. "You have a nice stroll around Mandela Square, Nephew? Enjoy the statues? See anyone you know?"

Monsarrat acknowledged his acuity. "No one at all. Best of all, I didn't see Sanhedrin."

"How is the shitbird? Still the scariest son of a bitch to feed at the public trough?"

"We're not on the best of terms right now," Monsarrat explained. "Last time we met, his sniper planted a bullet next to my foot. Ten minutes later, the grey suits busted him, something about cultural heritage infringements, counterfeit cash, and money laundering."

"You put the FBI on him for currency violations? Shame on you."

"After what happened in the Delta, I thought it was apropos."

"Someday when I have more time, you'll have to tell me all about Sanhedrin and your misadventures together. You can even tell me about your new career at your college. For now, start with what you want from me."

The liveried waiter returned with two squat bottles of Windhoek Draught, the green glass beaded with condensation. He poured the contents into schooners with a studied aplomb. "Gentlemen, would you like to order luncheon?"

Wilson handed him the menus. "Bring us two of your *braaivleis* specials. Lots of meat. Lots of starches. Lots of sauces. Something not at all healthy."

"A steady supply of beer, too," Monsarrat added. "My hairy friend needs to drink the blood of German hops."

Wilson again waited until the waiter had moved beyond hearing distance. He spoke without his earlier jocularity, and his words rang more as an order than as a request. "Tell me about your counter-coup, Nathan, the one the oil companies are about to launch against the interests of the Agency. Or some such shit."

Monsarrat welcomed the shift in names. It showed Wilson had focused the full power of his formidable intellect upon the situation. He shared the intelligence Palmer had provided without naming the specific source. Wilson, a consummate professional, did not inquire. "On a scale of one-to-ten, how much of this is familiar to you?"

"None of it," he admitted. "I don't sit in Abuja, I don't follow those issues anymore, but American oil companies turning against Uncle Sam? I would have heard. Maybe some people are jerking your chain?"

"If so, they're paying a lot of money for the pleasure."

The liveried waiter approached their table. Wilson remained silent while he placed the large plates before them, set two full bottles of Windhoek on the table, removed the empties, delivered a polite *bon appetite*, and departed. "I'll ask you once again. What exactly do you want from me?"

"Intel on Innocence and his playmates."

"I'll brief you, but nothing written, no notes."

"That's not all."

"Why am I not surprised?"

Monsarrat explained his fallback system. "By the first of next month, when you haven't received a call, forget we ever discussed these contingency plans."

"If I do receive a call from your minder?"

"Send the hard boys, and send them fast. I figure Innocence will take his time with me, so there's a slight chance I'll still be breathing when they break down the doors."

"Although you may not be in one piece."

"You might want to put medical assets on standby."

"Anything else you need from me?"

"I want Innocence."

"Of course, you do." Wilson settled into his seat and lifted his eyes to the ceiling, as if reading from a celestial notebook. "Innocence plays the untamed jungle beast, but he's not quite the illiterate savage he pretends."

His voice took on the charm of a military briefing. "He's the third and youngest son of the Amanyanabo of Bonny, Rehovoth

Okeri, the titular leader of the Ibani nation. Since his father wanted a highly educated son to help drag the Ibani into the twenty-first century, he attended boarding schools in Suisse and received a bachelor's degree in economics from New York University. He earned a master's degree and was almost granted a doctorate in statistics from the London School of Economics."

Monsarrat wondered if Palmer knew Innocence's background and had chosen to withhold the information. "I'm impressed. I thought the son of a bitch was inbred."

"It's a role the shitbird's chosen to play. Magnificently, I would say. Oscar worthy."

"What happened in London that prevented him from receiving his doctorate?"

"He was a strong student. Academically, he showed great promise," Wilson began. "Socially, he did not play nicely with others. Okeri kept buying off the problems, until the police arrested Innocence on kidnapping, pederasty, and child pornography charges."

"No surprise."

"He knocked a young mother unconscious and dragged her blond-haired, blue-eyed toddler from a park in central London. In the back seat of his BMW, he stripped the little boy and took pictures with a cell phone camera. By the time he decided to bugger the toddler, a crowd had smashed the windows of the BMW, pulled him from the car, and beat him badly. His first night in a London jail, awaiting trial, he was beaten again and, in a fine example of poetic justice, raped. It could have been his cellmates, or it could have been the police, but it was brutal, and it was repeated until the sun rose on the new day. His father tried to extricate him, but Innocence was so deep in the shit that Okeri couldn't pay enough bribes to buy his release. After three weeks, the Brits finally allowed the Amanyanabo to pay off the little boy's family. They deep sixed the trial and deported him."

"Hard justice."

"The prodigal son refused to return home. Word is that he blamed his father for his serial tuppings in jail. He drifted down to Port Harcourt and wandered its mean alleys until he joined FATA. The rest you know."

"With such bad blood between father and son, why would Okeri insist that Innocence sit by his right arm? Why not the two older brothers?"

"He doesn't have enough chicken claws and frog blood. His juju isn't strong enough."

He pushed away his plate. "Enlighten me."

"You don't like the food?"

"It doesn't go well with your story."

"You now have an academic conscience?"

He wondered how many more people would ask the question. "Go on."

"Purity, Okeri's number one son, died of malaria. Diligence, son number two, died from too much palm wine. He plowed his car into the wall surrounding the French Embassy, took out the guard booth, and killed two sleeping policemen, in addition to his own self."

"So Okeri doesn't have a choice? It's Innocence or nothing?"

He finished the last crumbs from his plate. "Expense account, Nathan, right?"

"Cognac, coffee, dessert, from anything to everything."

Wilson signaled for the liveried waiter. "Bring us snifters of Remy Martin Louis XIII."

He waited until the table was cleared before continuing. "Okeri is paranoid, for good reasons. He understands his remaining son's limitations, but if he's going to be the next ruler in Abuja, he'll need Innocence by his side. You know the adage, keep your enemies close but your friends closer."

Monsarrat acknowledged his familiarity.

"Except for Okeri," the analyst concluded, "it has an addendum, keep your last son entwined like a DNA strand."

The waiter placed the two snifters of cognac on the table. "Enjoy, gentlemen."

"Remy Martin without an H. Upmann is like sex without a partner," Wilson grumbled. "The anti-smoking laws are more draconian here than back home."

Monsarrat swirled the cognac in the snifter. He watched the oily legs drip down the pear shaped bowl. "Cut to the chase, Bruce. When I find Innocence, what should I expect?"

The analyst finished half of his cognac. "I never learned the art of polite sips."

"What's bothering you, Bruce?"

The analyst leaned across the table. "Your story stinks, Nathan. Either you're lying to me, someone is lying to you, or you're so hot for payback you've shut down your shit detectors."

"I'm not lying to you."

"Then I fear you are about to step into a deep sinkhole of South African shit."

"I need to know."

"You've always been persistent, especially when you shouldn't be. It's part of your misbegotten charm."

"Compliments are always welcome."

"Innocence is in Cape Town, but you know that because you arrived from Matroosfontein this morning."

He thought his friend was fishing, but he admired the accuracy of his cast. "Tell me where he lives. Tell me about the muscle he keeps with him."

The analyst finished his cognac and placed the snifter on the table. "Yes to all the above. He lives in a fortress on The Ridge at Fourth Beach in Clifton with enough muscle to concern his Russian competition."

"Where does he go when he leaves his castle?"

"Anywhere and everywhere in a pink BMW Alpina B7 with heavily tinted windows, reinforced up to an AK47. Bodyguards front and rear seats. The driver carries, too. He's all over the city, although I'd watch for him in the Central District and the Waterfront. You know that already, don't you, because you've spent the past two days shuffling the streets like a lost urban cowboy."

The accuracy of the charge unnerved him. "You've been watching me, Bruce?"

"There was no need," he growled. "Either you're too damn predictable, or I know you too damn well."

"I've seen his thugs. They don't talk with the South Africans, and they stay far away from the Russians," Monsarrat said.

"You'll need to be careful," Wilson warned. "Nasty scumbags work the streets of Cape Town. I don't want to see your pretty face and other body parts on the evening news."

He had Palmer's explanation but wanted Wilson's opinion. "If Innocence is so bad, why don't the police toss him into prison and lose the key?"

"Has academia made you fey? Innocence has bought them or scared them so badly they stain their shorts when he cruises by in his pink Beemer."

Monsarrat pushed his snifter across the table. "You have anything else I can use?"

"Are you going virtuous on me? Salvation Army, teetotaler, abstinence?"

He ignored the question. "Does he stick to a schedule? Monday here, Tuesday there, a favorite restaurant at noon, a friendly strip joint at midnight?"

"Now you see it, now you drink it." The cognac disappeared in a single swallow.

"I need everything, Bruce."

"He's a shitbird. He's all over the map, all the time. He's a flesh-and-blood chaos theory."

Monsarrat pantomimed signing the bill for the liveried waiter.

"You want to give me your coordinates? So I can hover above and watch over you?"

"It's probably best if your knowledge of me is less than zero."

He accepted the leather case, glanced at the bill, and passed rand to the waiter. "Twenty percent for yourself. Very nice service."

Wilson waited until they were alone again. "I know you're based in Cape Town."

"You say so, Bruce. Not me."

"How do I pass you intel? Call our consulate? Ask for an occasionally retired spook named Monsarrat?"

"They wouldn't take the message."

"So I file this conversation, unless I get a frantic call from your minder?"

"Close enough."

The analyst sighed. "They're your body parts."

"One more thing."

"Of course, Nathan, for I have been placed on this Earth to serve your needs."

Monsarrat noted the slight sibilance of his words. "You used the term rogue, as in an all-American former spook turned rogue."

"Good memory."

"What have you heard?"

Wilson took the napkin from his thighs, dabbed his lips, and tossed it between the two snifters.

"You're stalling."

"Yeah, I'm stalling," he agreed. "I want to believe you so badly I'm betting my retirement on your bona fides."

"What's bothering you, Bruce?"

"The version of the story I heard about you and Sanhedrin ends with you failing to kill him on a back road in western Massachusetts, or some such shit. Nothing about a sniper. Nothing about the grey boys from the Bureau."

Monsarrat's response was a cocktail of equal parts bitter, nasty, and acidic. "You know better than that. If I wanted to kill Felix, he'd be dead."

"I also heard your former boss told the Mandarins you wrote a super-secret spook book."

"I'm a dean, not a professor. I don't have time to write novels."

"Sanhedrin claims you're planning to tell all to the talking retards on the cable channels," he continued. "He wants the Mandarins to toss you into one of their deep, dark holes to protect the Agency. Nowhere popular, like Gitmo. Somewhere no one will look for you, like Arkansas or al-Anbar."

"Do they believe him?"

"They believe what suits them. If they think you will bring unwanted attention to the Agency, they will burn you alive and toast marshmallows at your auto-da-fé. If they think I'm covering for you, my final hours on this mortal coil will be spent buried up to my neck in the South African *veld* with my head covered in honey and an army of fire ants munching my eyeballs."

Monsarrat winced at the image. "Is the Agency watching us now?"

"The rocket arrived forty-eight hours ago. All stations from Paris to Pretoria and in-between."

He had not mentioned South Africa to Abby, leaving the list of informers who could have alerted the Agency to his Cape Town adventure at two. He could not believe Ralph Sanders had talked out of class, which left Mark Palmer as the prime suspect, but neither could he understand why Palmer would want to scuttle his own mission, bought and paid with money from his employers.

He rephrased his question. "Are we alone now?"

Wilson nodded. "Your reputation on the *djembe* grapevine is lower than bat guano. If I asked permission for today's tête-à-tête, Chief of Station would have transferred me to the Public Affairs Office and trussed you like a turkey for a black flight to Langley."

Monsarrat knew her as a bureaucrat who bled ink. Her field experience consisted of weekend trips to London, Paris, and Rome. He asked the question that had troubled him since their telephone conversation. "If I'm a rogue, why did you agree to meet me?"

"I like you, Nathan," he admitted, "and I don't like Felix. I don't like the chief of station either, but right now I'm stuck with her."

"I'm grateful, Bruce," Monsarrat replied, "and I would be even more grateful if you gave me your digital recorders before you return to Pretoria."

Wilson tapped his head. "I didn't bring them. I've memorized our chat."

A conversation with Wilson was a duel without seconds. "What will you tell Chief of Station when you return to the embassy? She'll be suspicious, you leaving your office for the first time during working hours, right after Langley fired a rocket up my ass."

"Don't worry, Nathan. I won't say anything about you to the Chief. If she feigns interest and asks about my perambulations, I'll praise the *braaivleis* and describe my adventures in the wicked brothels of Sandton with leggy Bantu girls."

"What will you report about the coup?"

"Nothing yet. I have to dig further before I pry the lid off that jar of snakes."

"Keep the lid on the jar until the end of June."

"Understood, but come the first of July, Pandora and I pop it open."

"Come the first of July, I'll be back in the Berkshires in my role as dean."

"There's something I want you to do for me, Nathan."

Monsarrat heard the heavy thud of Wilson's other shoe dropping onto the gleaming, wooden floor of the Veneto. "I'm listening."

He pulled a pen and a crumbled scrap of paper from his pocket, scribbled for a moment, and pushed the paper across the table. "The woman who answers that number is smarter than me, meaner than Innocence, better looking than you, and more devious than Sanhedrin."

Monsarrat read the name and telephone number. "Why should I call Masha Krupnik?"

"Because she's the nastiest *vor* to ever suckle vodka from her momma's teat."

"How do you know her?"

"You know better than to ask me such shit questions."

Monsarrat had no intention of contacting the Russian. He didn't want a corkscrewed umbilical cord connecting him through her to Wilson, and from the analyst to the Agency, especially during the hot and humid summer months, when idiocy sprouted around Langley's bureaucrats like mold on wet walls. He ripped the paper into shreds and dropped them into Wilson's hand. "No, thanks. I don't like Russians."

"If you're going to hunt Innocence, you'll need a powerful friend, and Masha Krupnik is the most powerful Russian in Cape Town. You call her and say that *Dyadya* Bruce sends his love."

He shook the shreds into an empty snifter. "Don't do anything that can bite me in the ass, Nephew. You remember how I worry about my pension?"

The problem with being a former spook, Monsarrat decided, was that the Agency followed you into retirement. He liked Wilson and trusted him as far as he could trust anyone associated with Langley, which was not very far at all. He knew that Uncle Bruce felt the same of him.

THE FAR EDGE OF THE AFRICAN CONTINENT

Monsarrat woke to the sounds of Cape Town greeting the new day. He looked forward to seeing Ralph, although contact with his Berkshire neighbor would be limited to passing each other in the sticky aisle of a food court. Still, the meeting would provide proof that his minder at the far edge of the African continent was alive, well, and watching his back.

He shaved, showered, and dressed in blue jeans, a white tee shirt, black running shoes, and a black, hooded sweatshirt. He departed the hostel in the pale, golden light of Cape Town's dawn. In a bakery on Bree Street, he sat at a small table amongst office workers and students with a cup of black coffee and a blueberry muffin. He accessed the Internet on the black phone and logged into an untraceable e-mail account. He typed Ralph's address onto the send line and a single word, Thunder, onto the subject line, checked his watch, and at exactly 0700 sent the message.

He closed the phone, sipped the coffee, and picked at the muffin. Thirty minutes after sending the message, he left the bakery. Two hours remained until he would retrieve the package from the food court. At the intersection of Mechau Street and Bree Street, he flagged a taxi and directed the driver to the King Charles Hotel. The glass and steel Cape Town International Convention Center on Coen Steytler Avenue slid from view as they entered Dock Road.

His eyes swept the hotel entrance. Inside the lobby, he examined the tourists and businessmen, seeking the out of place. He sniffed the air for the rancid scent of tension that watchers emitted with their sweat. A hard coil of paranoia lodged in his throat, so thick it threatened to choke him. He exited the building, his pace, despite his taut nerves, casual. He pointed the cell phone's camera at the sights of the city, hitting his blocks in his role as a tourist.

He reached the food court with an hour to wait and strolled through the upper level. Kosher and hallal food stands, vegetarian and meat and fish, abounded. He bought a black coffee and a slice of cheese pizza, took a complimentary copy of a local arts magazine from a wire stack, and sat at a table by the outer rail.

He sipped the coffee, chewed the pizza, and leafed through the magazine while his eyes scanned the area for the arrival of Ralph and any tails he might drag in his wake.

Fifty-five minutes later, he spotted him walking across the food court as if it were a hill to be taken, a white shopping bag with a brilliant red logo and braided silver handles from a local gourmet market in his right hand. He appreciated his efforts to blend into his surroundings, but thought he bore the stamp of a Marine as boldly as if he had wrapped himself in patterned fatigues and Old Glory.

Monsarrat scrutinized the ebb and flow of people in the lower level of the food court, as well as those crossing the upper level, but no one exhibited an unwarranted interest in Ralph. He threw his half-eaten pizza, coffee cup, and magazine into a trash bin and rode the down escalator. He entered the fast food restaurant and took his place at the end of the line.

Ralph chose a white table with red swivel chairs anchored to the laminate floor. He placed the shopping bag on the seat across from him and pecked at his food on the plastic tray like a child separating unwanted peas from unloved carrots.

Monsarrat ordered a black coffee and chicken nuggets from a bored teenager with ketchup stains on his tunic. He added a wad of paper napkins to his tray and walked toward the table, suspecting that Ralph, a stranger in a strange land, would be as pleased to see a known face as he would be relieved to surrender the contents of the paper bag.

Ralph did not as much as nod but stood and carried his tray to the trash receptacle. The package remained on the chair. They passed within inches, but might have been ships on different oceans for all the attention they paid to each other.

He sat on the vacated chair, sipped his coffee, and arranged the chicken nuggets into geometric patterns. After ten minutes, he stood and reached for the braided silver handles of the bag. Its weight was an expected gift. Walking to the trash bin, he noted his knuckles were white with tension.

Egress from the restaurant was an exercise in muscle memory, a *pas de deux* for one. He departed the food court and strolled beneath the morning sunshine, as if burdened by neither cares nor worries, toward Portswood Road. He crested a hill and headed toward the Admiralty Hotel. Inside the building, he crossed the lobby, exited through a side door, and walked down the hill until he reached Beach Road. His pace faster, he followed the square, blue signs with the large, white capital "H" to the ellipses of the dun turreted Portsmouth Hospital and entered the building beneath a brown and white striped awning.

In the Visitor Center, he bought a bouquet of flowers and a teddy bear. The cashier, an elderly woman with a Kimberley accent as hard as a Northern Cape diamond, placed his purchases into a red bag endorsed with the hospital's blue insignia. "Is it your little one you're visiting today? Or your big one?"

"Not so little, not so big," he replied. "Just the right size."

In the men's room off the lobby, he threw the flowers and stuffed toy into the trash bin and dropped the white, paper bag into the red hospital bag. It was a small change but even minor disguises were preferable to maintaining the status quo. He waited another five minutes before walking outside.

A battered, white sedan taxi with black lettering on its doors idled at the arch of the ellipses. The driver held a spiral notepad in his thick left hand and a photograph in his right hand, his eyes darting from the picture to the rearview mirror and back again. Sirens of paranoia exploded in Monsarrat's tympana. Like the seasons of Ecclesiastes, operations demanded times for patience and times for action, as well as times to evade the enemy hidden and times to engage the enemy known.

He walked around the front of the taxi, absorbing the driver's features through the windshield. Heavy, chocolate jowls hung from his cheeks, and purple bags bulged beneath his eyes. Brilliantine slicked the knots of his thick, grey hair. His nose was crooked, and scar tissue decorated his cheekbones, two indications of a mediocre boxer with hands too heavy to hold at the level of his face. His shoulders were broad, and his legs were squat. He wore a green and gold Springboks rugby jersey and blue jeans so worn they were translucent.

He opened the passenger door of the right-hand drive vehicle and slid onto the bench. He noted the name on the license, Philip Matlinga, and that his picture matched the visage of the driver. "Drop me on the street outside the Mount Nelson Hotel, by the columns. No need to go up the drive."

The driver pushed the photograph beneath his jersey. When he spoke, his basso profundo voice sang in smooth notes. "The Pink Lady, my friend. Are you an American? You talk like a Yank."

Monsarrat allowed David Clarendon to flash his irritation. "Haven't met many Canadians, have you?"

"A Canuck? Welcome to Cape Town, my Commonwealth brother. Is this your first trip to our fair Mother City?"

"Not nearly," he replied. "Take Granger Bay Boulevard. There'll be fewer lights."

Four locks closed in unison as the driver steered the taxi onto Beach Road. "Were you visiting family in the hospital, my brother?"

His lungs ached, as if he had held his breath for too long. "My mate drank one too many and fell off the balcony."

"Ah, it's a hard life when you place your faith in liquid sin."

He entered a rotary, passed the Granger Bay Boulevard exit, and continued to traverse the circle onto Fort Wynyard Street.

Monsarrat leaned forward until only thin air separated them. "You're off route. Get onto Granger Bay Boulevard."

The driver provided melodious assurances. "Road construction, my brother, up ahead by Sonneberg Road. We'll take Portswood Road instead. It'll be faster. Save you some time and rand."

Monsarrat had not seen signs warning of construction. "Don't worry about my rand, Phil. Just do as I say."

Matlinga pulled the taxi to the side of Fort Wynyard Street, shifted the gear into park, and twisted in his seat to face Monsarrat. Black hair sprouted from the gnarled knuckles of the fist he waved at his passenger. "Now listen to me, Canuck. No one speaks to me with disrespect. Not in my hack."

Monsarrat heard the heavy click again. Three doors opened, and a hard shove from his left rocked him. As his shoulders rolled with the force of the blow, he dropped the bag between his feet. A pair of hands on his right pulled him toward the middle of the bench, and two men wearing faded jeans, stained tee shirts, and steel-toed work boots joined him in the rear of the cab, one to his right, one to his left. The thug on his left easily weighed more than 250 pounds of hard fat. The thug on his right was tall but sinewy and sixty pounds lighter than his partner. A third man wore identical clothes, but his body-builder physique stretched the fabric across his chest and biceps. He sat in the front of the taxi.

The driver locked the doors. "Bloody cheeky bastard, you deserve what's coming to you."

Monsarrat looked forward to burning the caustic mixture of stress and exhaustion and tasting the nectar sweetness of swift violence. "You guys all go to the same haberdasher?"

The body builder served as their leader. "He's a wise guy. Teach him a lesson."

Monsarrat felt the fat thug's elbow jab into his ribs. He grunted as the cotton sweatshirt absorbed the blow's force. "Not enough torque, fatty. Lemme show you how it's done in a cramped space."

He pulled back his thumb and slightly curled his fingertips while twisting his forearm and turning the palm of his right hand toward his face. He raised his hand until his fingertips were even with the crest of his cheekbone and scythed the hardened ridge of his outer palm toward the sinewy thug. He felt the soft flesh of the throat and the stiff edge of the windpipe and heard him gurgle in surprise before gasping in pain, his hands reaching for his throat.

Monsarrat leaned forward, lifting his left arm until his fist was beneath his chin, and drove his elbow fast into the narrow crescent between the upper lip and nostrils of the fat thug. He felt the bone crack and heard him scream.

As body builder twisted in his seat, Monsarrat's left fist moved toward him. The protruding knuckle of his middle finger penetrated the socket of his right eye and drove the back of his skull into the windshield. He reached around the headrest, twisted his neck, and crashed his forehead against the hard edge of the dashboard. Blood poured from an ugly gash above the ridge of his eyebrows. "Always wear your seat belt, mate."

The driver dropped his eyes from the rearview mirror to the unconscious thug on his left. "What the bloody hell?"

Monsarrat grabbed a fistful of his brilliantine hair and yanked his head backward, exposing his throat. "Do as I say, Phil, or I will snap your neck."

His voice squeaked. "Yes, my brother, I don't want any problems."

"Too late for that, Phil," he mocked. "You're already in a world of shit."

"Whatever you want, sir. What's mine is yours."

Monsarrat released his grip. "Turn off the engine, leave the key in the ignition, get out of the taxi, and pull the sack of shit on the front seat onto the street."

When the driver pulled the body builder through the front passenger door, Monsarrat leaned across the sinewy thug and pushed open the door. He shoved him out of the taxi, followed the inert body onto the sidewalk, took careful aim, and stomped on his head. He moved to the other side of the taxi, pulled the fat thug onto the street, drove his knee into his crotch, then kicked him in the stomach.

The driver was frantically searching the pockets of the body builder when Monsarrat reached him. He squeezed his throat until the purple bags beneath his eyes bulged. "My brother, tell whoever hired you I won't be so generous next time. I'll leave him with four dead stooges. Now run home fast, Phil, and report."

When he bounced his head against the frame of the taxi, brilliantine smeared the metal. He popped open the trunk of the sedan and shoved the body builder inside. "Soon, mate, we'll have a nice chat, and you'll tell me who sent you and the three stooges."

He closed the trunk, slid into the driver's seat, started the engine, pulled a U-turn, and drove toward the rotary. In the rearview mirror the driver waddled in the opposite direction from his broken colleagues.

He followed the M6 toward Sea Point Promenade. On Beach Road, across from the squat, candy-striped ziggurat of Mouille Point Lighthouse, he parked in a handicapped space before a concrete bungalow. He turned off the engine but left the keys in the ignition, grabbed the bag, opened the trunk, and threw the thug onto the asphalt. In the public toilets, he shoved him into a handicapped-designated stall and locked the door behind them.

Monsarrat placed the bag onto the floor and raised the lid of the toilet. He shoved the body builder's head into the bowl and held him beneath the sloshing water. When he struggled for breath, Monsarrat lifted his head out of the toilet and smashed it against the concrete wall. The thug slumped onto the wet floor.

Monsarrat removed a flick knife, a cell phone, a ring of keys, a dirty handkerchief, and a wallet from his pockets. He pried the plastic back from the cell phone and snapped the SIM card into two pieces. He placed the flick knife into his back pocket, removed rand from the wallet, and pushed the bills next to the knife.

He read the name on the thug's driver's license, Thaddeus Clintock of London Road in Cape Town, then pulled him upright. He slapped him in a slow left-right-left cadence. "Wake up, Thad. You answer my questions, and I'll take you to the emergency room."

When Clintock raised his hands in a boxing feint, Monsarrat bent his right wrist. The bodybuilder howled, and Monsarrat slapped him again. "Sit on your hands and tuck your ankles behind you, knees forward. Don't move unless I give you permission."

"Fuck your mother, mate. I did it last night."

"I'm glad you're a tough guy, Thad."

Monsarrat reached into his back pocket, stepped to the side of the toilet, twirled the flick knife, pushed the steel into Clintock's left nostril, and snapped the blades upward. The sharp edges sliced through the soft flesh. He clamped his hand over the thug's mouth as blood spurted onto the wall. "You won't be very pretty, but you'll live. If you feed me shit one more time though, it'll be your jugular vein that I'll slice."

He cut a strip of cloth from Clintock's tee shirt and stuffed it into his bleeding nostril. "Cooperate with me, Thad, and I'll fix you up. Screw with me, and I will fuck you up. Nod if you understand."

The bodybuilder bobbed his head.

"Who sent you after me?"

Blood and phlegm thickened Clintock's voice. "He called yesterday, didn't say his name, I didn't ask. Told me to get a crew together, pick up a visitor, a foreign chap. Rough him up, bad, teach him to mind his own business. Deliver a warning."

The timing of the call fit Monsarrat's visit to Johannesburg. "Was he local?"

"He was a wanker, a bleeding Yank poofter. Told me to go to the Central Library in the Old Drill Hall at ten minutes before closing."

"Repeat his instructions. Verbatim."

Clintock squirmed on his hands. "I don't get you, mate."

"Word for word, Thad. What did he tell you to do?"

"He told me to go to the gents. By the main entrance, last stall."

"Was he waiting for you?"

"Bloody hell, no! He told me to lift the cistern cover, there'd be ten thousand rand in a zippy bag taped to the inside. First half of a two-part payment, he said."

Monsarrat felt insulted. He thought he was worth more than a few thousand dollars. "What else did the wanker tell you?"

"I told you what I know, mate!"

"Tell me the warning."

"You're to go home, stay there, don't come back. That's it. Word for bloody word."

He had hoped for more substance. "What else was in the zippy bag?"

"A bloody snapshot of you traipsing around the City Center, dressed like now. A name on the back of the paper, David Clarendon, like the hotel chain."

The revelation angered Monsarrat. He had kept the Clarendon identity private, and he had watched his back in both Cape Town and Johannesburg, but someone good enough to avoid his surveillance had tailed him from the moment he landed in South Africa. Someone who had hired the four thugs. Someone who believed in violent warnings. He suspected Sanhedrin, but his former boss knew nothing of his arrangement with Palmer, unless he had traded intelligence with the oil wallahs or Palmer himself, who he suspected had leaked the details of his Cape Town trip to the Agency, had informed Sanhedrin.

"Show me the photo, Thad."

"I don't bloody well have it, mate. Philip needed it to recognize you."

He remembered the taxi driver at the ellipses, glancing from picture to mirror. "How did you know I'd be at the hospital?"

"The poofter called, said you were on the move, said to wait for instructions, called again, said you were heading for the Portsmouth, said to pick you up."

Monsarrat increased his pressure. "You're boring me, Thad. I get upset when I'm bored. When I'm upset, I get violent. Tell me the rest, and maybe I won't cut out your eyes."

"I know nothing more!"

"How do you collect the second half of the payment?"

"I finish the job, I call a number, I go back to the same stall and collect."

"What's to stop the poofter from stiffing you?"

"Not gonna happen, mate. Nobody stiffs me in this town."

He tossed the flick knife onto the floor. "Take my advice, Thad. Don't underestimate the poofter. He has a nasty temper and likes to vent it on foreign idiots like you. Piss him off, you'll remember our time together as friendly foreplay."

Monsarrat smashed the back of the thug's head against the wall, and Clintock slumped onto the floor. He picked up his bag, opened the stall's door, and walked into the sunshine. He crossed Beach Road, passed the lighthouse, entered the Promenade, and strolled along the cobblestoned path. Below him surged the blue waters of the Atlantic Ocean.

He felt like the dark circle of a bull's-eye. Since his movements had been observed, he had to assume that the exchange with Ralph had been noted and his best laid schemes blown in the first moments of the operation, hardly an auspicious beginning.

A deep-cover operative survived by the grace of skill and luck. Once exposed, each minute brought his death closer. Circumspection was a false luxury. Only direct action could save him. His black phone might also have been compromised, but he opened the bag, withdrew the sheet of paper, punched a number into the pad, and hit the green button. He willed the call to connect.

Ralph answered on the first ring. "I'm listening."

The muscles of Monsarrat's jaw were clenched so tightly, he feared the abort code would not pass through his lips. "Felix," he blurted, and ended the call.

He had no intention of racing his Berkshire neighbor to the airport. He snapped the SIM card in half and dropped it into a trash receptacle. The black cell phone splashed into the Atlantic Ocean. He left the Promenade and walked toward the City Centre. On Somerset Road, he stopped at an electronics store and purchased a prepaid cell phone.

At the corner of Long Street and Riebeek Street he entered a deli. With the lunch rush over, few patrons remained in the restaurant. He sat in the rear at a table with an unobstructed view of the entrance and ordered coffee and a roast beef sandwich from a waitress who looked as trodden as he felt. From the bag, he withdrew Ralph's report, composed by pen on lined A4 paper. The publican's script was compact and clear, as if he were listing accounts in the ledger between his *ki'i* wooden statues.

I. Four groups dominate crime in Cape Town: black South Africans, white Afrikaners, Russians, and West Africans. The Southies and the Afrikaners know each other well, and, for the most part, if they do not cooperate with each other they do not antagonize each other. There are three sub-groups of Russians, one from Moscow, one from Vladivostok, and one from St. Petersburg, which seems to be the first among equals. They're newer players and mostly maintain a peace with the Afrikaners, but not so much with the Southies and even less with the West Africans. A recent turf war between the Russians and the West Africans caused much disruption to business, and while there is now a fragile peace, relations remain strained and another turf war could break out easily, which would force the police to intervene and hurt business. So the Southies are working to keep the West Africans quiet, and the Afrikaners are trying to keep the Russians docile.

II. The leader of the West Africans is named Innocence. He is vicious and scarred with tribal markings and missing a chunk of his right earlobe. Before his arrival in Cape Town there were dozens of small groups of West Africans working apart from each other due to ethnic rivalries and language differences. The situation changed when Innocence arrived with his followers. He approached the leader of each West African group and made the same offer: work for me or die. The first groups refused, so he wiped them out.

III. Innocence forced the West Africans to work together and took them from petty street crime and hustling to protection and prostitution and drugs, which brought them more money and more power. He upped the ante when he began to sell guns and then heavier weapons, which led to the recent turf war with the

Russians. *The Southies and the Afrikaners got involved because too much blood attracts police attention and is bad for business.*

IV. The West African leadership consists mostly of Innocence and his supporters, since he killed most of his rivals. He acts like he's a star in a Hollywood goombah movie. He dresses like Superfly and drives an armored pink BMW with bodyguards who carry serious weapons. He packs a pair of pink, pearl-handled Colt .45 Peacemakers in a tooled gun belt with cowboy holsters. He lives in a compound on Fourth Beach where he throws nightly parties with girls and booze and drugs.

V. Intel is from the streets, paid for with money and old fashioned arm twisting. Nothing is verified.

VI. The .44 Special has been well maintained and cleaned of identification. You should hear boom and not click when you pull the trigger. The city is minus one punk.

VII. Semper Fidelis, brother.

Monsarrat finished his food and paid the bill. He left the deli through the rear entrance and followed the signs to the men's room. Inside a stall, he tore the report into small pieces and flushed them down the toilet. From the bag, he withdrew a box of ammunition and a Smith and Wesson .44 Special with a four-inch barrel and a nickel finish, stained and chipped with age and use. He sniffed the barrel for the odor of cordite, loaded six bullets, spun the chamber, snapped it shut, and tucked it beneath his belt at the small of his back. He dropped the box of ammunition into the bag.

He hoped that Ralph had reached the airport. He needed an adytum to hide in plain sight until nightfall, when he could retrieve his envelope from the hostel under the protection of darkness. He recalled the poofter's instructions to Thad. The Central Library would offer suitable protection.

Graced with the gift of a rare memory, he closed his eyes and saw a detailed street map of Cape Town. He stepped onto Riebeek Street and walked toward Adderley Street, searching storefront windows for reflections of unwanted attention. He turned onto Darling Street and passed the Houses of Parliament and City Hall. The Old Drill Hall, a fin-de-siècle building designed to represent the strength of the British Empire, stood across from Parade Street. Its clock tower resembled the spike on a Kaiser Wilhelm helmet.

He needed to secure the Smith & Wesson and its ammunition before attempting to pass through the security scanners of the Central Library. On Castle Street, at the rear of the Old Drill Hall, he launched a silent thanks into the blue Cape Town sky. Wooden horses and orange cones blocked the service entrance of the library. Construction materials for use inside the building were in neat piles.

Deception was theater, and he needed a stage prop. He shoved the bag inside his sweatshirt and walked into a convenience store. He bought a liter bottle of Coke and a small bag of potato chips and retraced his steps, eating and drinking. He wished his clothes were dirtier. At the construction site, he filled his mouth with potato chips. In his right hand, he carried the bottle of Coke and the bag of chips. With his left hand, he picked up a one-gallon can of wood glue.

A foreman with a clipboard grabbed the sleeve of his sweatshirt. His Cape accent was as thick as his beefy arms. "You bleeding idiot! No entry without hard cover."

Monsarrat cursed himself for overlooking the obvious. He prayed the sodden mass of potato chips in his mouth would disguise his American inflections. "Left it inside, boss."

The foreman shoved him through the doorway. "Pull your brain outta your arse. Hard cover all the time."

A garbage bin received the Coke and chips. He dropped the glue in front of the bin and climbed a flight of stairs to the main floor. On a bulletin board, a notice provided information for the monthly poetry meeting. He followed a hallway adorned with posters of South African authors to a reading room. He tugged the hem of his sweatshirt lower, entered the room, and took a seat in the last row. Two dozen students and appreciators of literature glanced at him. The poet, a thin, middle-aged man with splotched skin, lank hair, rheumy eyes, and the morosity of a university professor wore bell-bottom blue jeans and a paisley shirt with wide, pointed lapels. He leaned against a wooden podium, as if the recitation of his verse tore the energy from his soul.

After ninety minutes, the audience stood and applauded. The poet acknowledged the ovation with a wave of his hand. A docent thanked him for his creativity and generosity. Students jostled each other in their eagerness to speak with him.

Monsarrat stepped into the hallway and followed signs to the periodical room. As the light streaming through the windows waned, he flipped the pages of magazines at a reading table until a recording announced the imminent closing of the library. At ten minutes before eight o'clock, he departed the building through the main entrance, holding his bag tightly. The security alarms, designed to scan entries, remained quiet. Darling Street was deserted. The velvet night was an amulet, and the weight of the

Smith & Wesson provided comfort. Returning to the hostel entailed risks, but he needed his envelope in the safe to begin the endgame, and so set off for New Church Street.

AN ELECTRIC SHOCK OF EXPENSIVE COLOGNE

The hippie behind the reception desk wore the same pink-hued granny glasses and tie-dyed tee shirt. Monsarrat placed the bag on the counter, passed him the receipt, and signed the required forms. "Can you prepare my bill? I'll be leaving in a few minutes."

"So soon, Mr. Clarendon? We don't give refunds."

He offered a lewd wink. "The girl I'll stay with is worth the money. She's loaded, all around."

In his room, he rechecked the load of the Smith & Wesson and the box of ammunition. From the envelope, he removed his remaining dollars and placed them into his wallet. He separated the sheets of the matrix and struck a match. The flash paper dissolved, leaving puffs of dust on the floor. He prepared his duffel bag, tossed his clothes onto the bed, and carried the .44 Special into the tiny bathroom. In the shower, he closed his eyes and soaked beneath the jets of hot water until an electric shock of expensive cologne jolted him.

He closed the taps and wrapped a towel around his waist. The snout end of the Smith & Wesson led him out of the bathroom like a grunt on point. A young man in a blue suit, white shirt, paisley, silk tie, grey socks, and cordovan loafers, handsome in the androgynous manner of a fashion model, sat on the bed. He crossed his legs at the knee and plucked at the crease in his trousers. Save for his chestnut ponytail and the kitchen match he rolled in the corner of his sneering lips like a celluloid gunsel, he belonged more at an oval conference table in a corporate boardroom than in a New Church Street hostel.

Next to him stood a chiseled slab of granite twice his age with eyes the color of cobalt and the density of diamonds. His hands were as thick as cast-iron skillets, and his knuckles protruded like the knobs of an old oak tree. Cyrillic prison tattoos in faded, green ink adorned his fingers and thumbs. Both his skull and his face were clean shaven and pitted with scars. He wore a blue blazer, grey turtleneck, grey trousers, grey socks, and black wingtip shoes with welts sturdy enough for road work in Siberia. He stood so still he did not appear to breathe.

The young man spat the wooden match onto the floor. "I could never be a Scot. Go into battle in a kilt with your balls flapping in the wind? Not for me. Give me BDUs and lots of Kevlar."

Monsarrat aimed the barrel of the .44 Special at his nose. "Give me a good reason not to splatter your pretty face across the wall."

He swung the Smith & Wesson toward his companion. "Nice and slow, old man. Show me your palms, then put them under your thighs and sit on the bed."

The granite slab's shrug could have lifted a bus.

The young man translated the instructions into Russian. "*Yah z'naiu, Sasha, noh, d'vai.* Do it anyway. We are his guests."

Sasha lifted hands with a palpable force, like the breeching of a humpback whale, and held his palms open for a long minute before slipping them beneath his thighs and sitting on the edge of the bed. His cold eyes stared at Monsarrat with a Zen serenity.

"Do you speak Russian, David?" the young man asked.

His paranoia ratcheted. "How do you know my name?"

"This is your room, *da*? So you must be David Clarendon." He smiled indulgently. "In any case, Sasha has followed your request. After all, we are in your home. So to speak."

Monsarrat suspected that eternity would end before the older man blinked. His own hand ached from the weight of the Smith & Wesson. He usually employed a two-handed grip, but he rarely held a towel around his waist. He vowed to shoot the first Russian who smirked. "You, too, *pizdyuk*. Sit on your hands."

"There's no need to be insulting," the young man answered. He slipped his hands beneath his thighs. "Maybe you do speak Russian?"

Monsarrat crossed the room and pressed the barrel of the Smith & Wesson into his left ear. Waves of hostility from Sasha crashed against him. "Whoever you're looking for, you've got the wrong man. I'm not that David Clarendon."

"You're the David we want. Sasha and I are here to help you."

He heard the traces of St. Petersburg when he spoke. "Sasha speaks English?"

"Like you speak Russian but less. Not the first word."

"Tell him if I think he's going to flinch, I'll add a final pockmark to his facial collection."

"Are you sure you want me to translate that directly? Maybe I can soften your language? Sasha has had a hard life, and he is sensitive about his appearance."

He increased his pressure on the four-inch barrel. "*D'vai, pizdyuk.*"

"You have no need to be vicious, David. We really are here to help you."

Monsarrat patted the young man's suit, felt beneath his collar and inside his socks. He did the same to the granite slab. "Russian thugs without weapons? This must be a special occasion."

"Maybe you'll believe me now? We mean you no harm."

"He's Sasha," Monsarrat acknowledged. "Who are you?"

"My friend is Alexander Stefanov Poyarkov. He is called Sasha. He is my *byk*. My bodyguard."

"He's a *zek*."

"*Da*, he spent many years as a prisoner in the Kolyma gulag. He is also a loyal lad of St. Petersburg."

"He's Sasha. Who are you?"

The young man apologized for his lack of manners. "I am Nickolai Ivanovich Balashov, also of St. Petersburg. You may call me Nicky. Never Kolya. Nicky is jolly. Kolya is a Russian bear with its paw in a trap, too dark, too dramatic, too much like my home city's simpering Dostoyevsky characters with dripping noses and furtive expressions."

"You're a literary thug." He considered holding a mirror beneath Sasha's nostrils to check for exhalations of life. "Why are you in my room?"

The young Russian leaned forward against the pressure of the Smith and Wesson. "Our *vor v'zakonye* invites you to dinner tonight."

He flicked the barrel. "Why should I dine with a Russian mafia boss, *pizdyuk*?"

"Stop calling me scumbag. Also, please remove the revolver from my ear."

Monsarrat shifted the Smith & Wesson to his left eye. "Happy to oblige, *pizdyuk*."

Nicky flinched. "Our boss is a good friend of your *Dyadya* Bruce. Your uncle asked her to pass a message to you."

He had expected Wilson's name to enter the conversation. "I don't have an Uncle Bruce."

"Please, David, let us have a reasonable discussion."

"Does your boss have a name?" Monsarrat continued.

"Of course. She is Masha Yakovlevna Krupnik."

"*Skazhite mne*. Tell me the message."

"Masha only gave orders for us to drive you to the *dacha*."

"Where is the *dacha*?"

"In Constantia, fifteen miles south of us in the wine country. It is very picturesque."

"How did you find me?"

Nicky looked puzzled. "She told us."

Monsarrat wanted to learn Wilson's message, even if he remained uncertain of his old friend's loyalties. He held the Smith & Wesson level with the young man's forehead and stepped away from the bed. "Tell the *razebaistvo* to lie facedown on the floor and interlace his fingers behind his neck."

"Sasha is a very sensitive individual, David, but he is certainly not a screw-up."

"Tell him if he wants to be a hero, I'll shoot both of you."

The young Russian passed the message. Sasha's smoldering anger, like a flow of angry lava, heated the room. He expected the *byk* would enjoy a final reckoning, sooner rather than later.

"Now you, Nicky. Next to Sasha."

"Can I take off my jacket? Merino wool wrinkles so easily."

"Do as you're told, and I'll pay your dry cleaning bill."

Monsarrat dressed quickly, feeling extraordinarily vulnerable. Sasha could snap his neck like a dry twig as he pulled on his pants. He imagined his obituary: "American Dean of Undergraduate Studies Killed Naked in Cape Town by Russian *Byk*." Sanhedrin would chortle.

He slipped the wallet and passport into a rear pocket and held the .44 Special in the sweatshirt's pouch like Doctor Zhivago warming his hands against the frigid Russian winter. He gestured for them to stand. "We'll go out in a conga line. Sasha leads. Nicky, you're in the middle. I'll follow."

The lobby was empty. "Where's the hippie? Did you whack him?"

"You think we are animals? He is probably taking a piss." The young Russian pointed toward the door. "*D'vai*, David. The vehicles are waiting."

Three black Mercedes G63 AMGs with fully tinted windows idled on New Church Street. Sasha opened the rear door of the middle vehicle, and Monsarrat followed Nicky into the Mercedes. Sasha climbed into the front seat. When he turned toward Monsarrat, his smile displayed generations of Soviet dentistry, and his granite fist held a nine millimeter Berretta Px4.

Nicky offered the introductions. "David, our driver is Pavel. He is the master of the Mercedes."

Pavel was cut from the same quarry as Sasha, dressed similarly although younger, taller, and broader. Like Sasha, he did not speak. He followed the lead Mercedes into traffic.

"Give Sasha your pistol, David. Fingertips. Barrel pointed down."

Monsarrat supposed the G63 contained a small armory.

"Now your cell phone."

"Do I need a claim check?"

"*D'vai*, do it, David. It is impolite to keep our boss waiting."

"It's a lot of muscle for a dinner date."

"Masha speaks softly but carries very many large caliber sticks."

The small convoy departed the City Center and followed De Waal Drive toward the southern suburbs, skirting the flank of Devil's Peak and following Edinburgh Drive into Constantia. Cloistered behind the darkened windows of the big Mercedes, Monsarrat imagined gum trees lining wide boulevards, the leafy trellises of hilly vineyards, and the ocean's tangy salt air.

The convoy climbed a long, uphill slope. Pavel leaned the big vehicle into curves and accelerated into the straight sections. After five more minutes, he braked, drove forward, and stopped the Mercedes.

"Masha takes our security very seriously," Nicky explained. "Not everyone in this country appreciates us, our culture, and our approach to business."

The four doors opened, and yellow floodlight spilled into the Mercedes. Monsarrat saw a security pen, a tracked gate in front with a matching gate behind. A burly Russian gripped a Sig Sauer P516 pistol while he inspected the interior of the vehicle. A second Russian restrained an Alsatian on a short, chain leash. A third Russian pointed a Mossberg twelve gauge shotgun at them. Each dressed like Sasha and Pavel and, despite the hour, wore sunglasses. When the first Russian spoke into a microphone attached to the cuff of his blazer, the tracked gate slid open. The doors of the Mercedes closed, and Pavel drove slowly out of the pen.

He stopped before the entrance to the *dacha*, wide, stone steps leading into a three-story, Mediterranean villa encircled by manicured lawns. Trellises flanked the albarium stucco walls, and wrought-iron railings protected the tall windows.

Monsarrat stepped out of the Mercedes. "What's the view during the day?"

"Tokai Forest and Hout Bay," Nicky replied. "You must sample our Chardonnay. It's fermented in French oak barrels. We're thinking of expanding into the American market."

Pavel handed the young Russian a Berretta Px4. "For you, *pakhan*."

Monsarrat admitted his mistake. "I thought you were just a *pizdyuk*, Nicky. You didn't say you're the second-in-command."

Inside the *dacha*, slats of wide mahogany covered the floors. Paintings by Repin, Malevich, Maximov, and Serov shared the walls with illustrations by Bilibin and eighteenth century *lubki* woodcuts. A diamond encrusted samovar stood on a jappaned side table.

"No icons?"

"Our boss does not believe in religion," Nicky replied. He opened a pair of French doors with beveled glass and zinc and led him to an Empire armchair of gilded Karelian birch beneath a self-portrait of Orest Kiprensky. "Sasha will remain with you to make sure you are not bored."

The older Russian sat in a carved Svirsky Bergère chair of gesso and gilding, his granite hands folded demurely in his lap, the index finger of his right hand resting lightly on the trigger guard of the Berretta. Neither the pistol's sights nor his cobalt eyes wavered.

When he attempted to rise from the armchair, Sasha spoke his first words. His voice sounded like boulders in the throes of a rockslide. "*Nyet. Ne vstavayte.*"

Monsarrat did not want to argue with a nine-millimeter pistol. He held up his hands. "Where'd you get your prison tats, Sasha? Butyrka Tyur'ma or Matrosskaya Tishina?"

Sasha's expression did not change. "*Pehtuch.*"

"A prison bitch? Was that your job in the gulag?"

Nicky's return precluded Sasha's reply. "Our boss will see you now, David."

Monsarrat followed the young Russian up a curving staircase with steps and balustrades carved of the same mahogany that lined the floor. He felt Sasha's presence behind him. On the third floor, Nicky led him down a hall flanked with marble busts of Romanov royalty. "Our boss is a connoisseur of Russian history in all its glories and humiliations."

"But not religion. Not a very Russian trait."

Nicky knocked on a set of double doors. A strong voice proclaimed, "*Vkohdit!*"

He pushed open the doors. "David Clarendon is here, Masha. Would you like me to stay with you?"

"It is not necessary, Nicky. I am sure that Mr. Clarendon is a gentleman."

Monsarrat stepped inside, and Nicky closed the doors behind him. Metal, glass, and leather Bauhaus furniture filled the room. Soviet-era paintings proclaimed the triumphs of the proletariat, bountiful agricultural harvests, feats of factory production, and garlands of athletic medals. In the corner of the room a small

Klykov bronze statue of Marshall Zhukov stood on a granite pedestal the color of dried blood.

She noticed his interest. "The statue was a study for the larger monument now at the Resurrection Gate in Moscow, at the northern entrance to the *Kreml.* Georgy Konstantinovich was a brilliant soldier and a great man. Compared to the Marshall, the wax dummy's mausoleum in *Krasnaya Ploschad* is an insult to the history of Red Square."

Her feet were bare, and her pedicure shined with the colors of Joseph's coat. She stood six feet tall and exuded confidence and power like perfume scented other women. She wore makeup lightly, and crimson lipstick sparkled from the light of a silver candelabrum. A matching crimson coated the nails of her fingers. She wore jeans and a silk tee shirt with a single gold necklace.

She walked toward him and offered her hand. Her fingers, long, tapered, and unadorned by jewelry, belonged to a pianist on the proscenium stage of the St. Petersburg Conservatory. "Your *Dyadya* Bruce speaks fondly of you. It is a rare emotion in our world."

Monsarrat felt the strength of her firm grip. "Which world is that, Ms. Krupnik?"

She asked questions. She did not answer them. "Please sit, Mr. Clarendon. We have many items to discuss."

A leather and aluminum couch cost more than his annual salary at the college. "I look forward to our conversation."

"Would you like a drink before we begin? I believe you enjoy bourbon?"

Monsarrat had never known Wilson to be garrulous, but the beauty of a younger woman had inspired many older men to share their secrets. "Neat, please."

She crossed to a sideboard, poured three fingers of Maker's Mark into two tumblers of cut crystal, and handed him one. "A toast, Mr. Clarendon?"

"To peace and friendship?" he suggested. "*K miru i druzhby?*"

"Better to profits and free markets, plus expeditious partnerships."

Her skin was pale, and her thick, black hair luxuriant. Her Slavic cheekbones were high and sharp, and gold flecked her emerald eyes. He thought her strikingly beautiful, but knew pulchritude had not won her position as *vor v'zakonye.* "You have a message from our mutual friend?"

She sat on the far edge of the couch with her legs tucked beneath her thighs and placed her tumbler on a matching side table. "I do not usually run errands for the Central Intelligence

Agency, but I am as genuinely fond of your *Dyadya* Bruce as he is of you."

"Thank you for your kindness."

"A Krupnik is generous to her friends, Mr. Clarendon."

Monsarrat understood the warning, a Krupnik is dangerous to her enemies. "Please, I'm David."

When the *vor* smiled, stage lights burst through velvet darkness. "Now we conduct business, Mr. Clarendon, not make friendships, but perhaps after our work is concluded, we will reconsider our relationship."

He raised his tumbler. "I look forward to it, Ms. Krupnik."

Her index finger chastised him. "Twice you have assumed that I am not married."

"Should I address you as Mrs. Krupnik?"

She chose not to respond. Instead, she examined him like a curious schoolmistress. "Assumptions are reckless. They cause people to die. Are you reckless, Mr. Clarendon?"

He thought it a good question. He should have been recruiting students for the college, not sipping bourbon with a beautiful Russian *vor*. "To survive in our world, you need to trust your instincts."

"You would rather trust your instincts than the opinions of your experts?"

"Experts are usually enamored of their own thoughts."

"And your instincts, Mr. Clarendon?"

"I've failed them more than they have failed me," he replied honestly.

"*Yah soglasen.* I agree. We must have trust in ourselves, not only to survive in our world, but to flourish and rule."

He felt as if he had passed an unannounced test.

"Bruce did not trust the Central Intelligence Agency to pass to you his message. He is an analyst, but he also has instincts."

Monsarrat swallowed bourbon. He understood the value of silence.

"He says it is very important you know that Mr. Franklin Seleucid has arrived in Cape Town to recruit inexperienced students for study in the United States."

He focused on Wilson's word choice. Inexperienced. Innocent. Innocence. Like the proverbial bad penny, Sanhedrin turned up in the most unwanted places. "Did he offer more specific information?"

When she shook her head, thick, black hair twirled around her pale throat.

He asked her the same question he had posed to Nicky. "How did you find me?"

"Bruce has a great many friends in Pretoria for whom he conducts favors. These friends may be called upon to repay his generosity."

"Friends in the security services?"

"*Da*. Friends in the *sluzhba*."

Monsarrat understood that locating him under his work name had posed few problems for Wilson. The analyst would have reviewed the footage of international arrivals, working backwards from the day they met in Sandton, chosen a dozen faces to disguise his primary target, and passed the identification request to his South African friends. The name David Clarendon would have been on his desk within an hour. "Was it difficult to locate me at the hostel?"

"Bruce said you would like to stay, he used the expression, under the radar."

"Did he mention the reason for my visit to Cape Town?"

"He quoted the Lebanese saying about friends and enemies."

"The enemy of my enemy is my friend," Monsarrat recited.

"We Russians believe so also. *Droog poznayotsya v bedé*."

He supplied the translation. "A friend is known in trouble."

She looked at him with a new respect. "Bruce did not tell me that you speak our language so well. To truly understand the soul of Russia, you must first speak her tongue."

He suspected the *vor* was working toward a goal. He settled into the couch and waited for her to reach it.

"We have a mutual enemy, Mr. Monsarrat," she began.

Hearing his name stunned him. Wilson had become more than garrulous. He had abandoned loyalty for betrayal.

"*Da*, you are Nathan Monsarrat of Massachusetts in the United States. You are Dean of Undergraduate Studies at Greylock University."

He did not correct her. "Our mutual friend is usually more reticent."

"*Nyet*. Bruce only wants to help you. He is worried for you," she explained. "We have done business many times. He knows I am trustworthy."

He wondered if Wilson saw him as the means to the end of unknotting the *vor*'s knickers. He knew very smart men who had done very stupid things for women far less beautiful than Masha Krupnik. "Should I believe in your goodwill?"

"You should believe I offer a solution to the problem you want to resolve."

He finished the bourbon. "You mean Innocence."

"*Da.* He is a violent animal. He does not understand how to conduct business. Also, he is grasping. You say so?"

"Greedy," he agreed. "I would add psychopathic."

"*Soglasen.* He is abnormal."

She refreshed their drinks and returned to the couch. "Bruce said you have an unpleasant history with him."

He offered a sanitized explanation for his presence in Cape Town. "Innocence has pissed off many people. Some of them would like to speak with him. I've been hired to make it happen."

She absorbed his explanation. "Where will this conversation take place?"

He shaded facts. "After I secure him, I make a phone call and receive instructions."

"If he refuses to cooperate, do you have a second option?"

"The people who hired me prefer that Innocence travels vertically, but horizontal is acceptable as a last resort."

She used the Soviet term. "*Chehpeh.*"

"*Chrezvychainoye proisshestviye.* In an emergency situation."

"In such a situation," she continued, "you would facilitate the death of Innocence?"

"You make it sound like a kindness."

She sipped the bourbon. "More of a justice."

Her proposition was pellucid. "We are in an American win-win situation, Mr. Monsarrat. Kill Innocence, satisfy your obligations to your employers, and receive their payment. I also will pay you to kill the animal. Everyone wins."

Monsarrat did not tell her that he had never planned to deliver a vertical Innocence. "What do you win, Ms. Krupnik, if Innocence dies?"

"Satisfaction, Mr. Monsarrat."

"Can you place a monetary value on satisfaction?"

"Like health and happiness, it can not be measured in dollars. Still, I will provide you with the satisfaction of a quarter million dollar deposit into your bank account."

"For killing Innocence?"

"*Da*, for killing Innocence," she agreed. "For me, it is a sound business investment. For you, it is an opportunity to receive two payments for one job."

Monsarrat asked her the same question he had asked Palmer. "Why don't you kill him yourself? I'm sure Sasha and Nicky are more than capable."

She preferred to discuss her proposal. "I will place immediately $100,000 into your bank account. I will provide the additional $150,000 when I have positive proof that Innocence is dead."

Monsarrat weighed the quarter million dollars against his distrust of Russians.

"What were your plans, Mr. Monsarrat, if I had not invited you to my *dacha* for this chat?"

He appreciated the perspicacity of her questions. "I would observe him, and when the opportunity arose, I would remove him."

"I am curious. How would you remove him? He is a most paranoid individual."

Lacking an answer, he repeated his own question. "Why do you need me to kill him?"

"If I were brutal like Innocence, I would kill him and everyone with him, but I consider business to be a chessboard not a battlefield, and I am a grandmaster not a general. I do not want war. I want him dead, and if you kill him, I am blameless."

"You want to consolidate your territory without repercussions?"

"Your reputation is of a very resourceful man, Mr. Monsarrat."

She once again illuminated the room with her smile. "Also, my quarter million dollars, plus what your employers will pay you, is not insignificant."

"Do you have a specific proposition, Ms. Krupnik? Something more substantial than just wanting me to kill your competition?"

"*Da, konechna*, of course," she answered. "Innocence must die far from Cape Town. If you kill him here, I will be accused. There will be a war. I will triumph, but the violence is not good for my business."

"A dead Innocence is good for business?"

"Very much so," she agreed. "A dead Innocence is good for my bottom line."

"When does he need to die?"

"Within the next forty-eight hours."

"Why so soon?"

"He will travel tomorrow morning by car with his bodyguards to Rosh Pinah in Namibia to discuss a contract with a business associate. I want you also to travel there."

He suspected that her offer was an ultimatum: accept and be rewarded, decline and be punished. With finality. "Your intelligence is very good."

"I also have excellent friends in the *sluzhba*."

"How will I travel to Namibia?"

"Nicky will take you to Vioolsdrif, but you will enter Namibia alone. In Rosh Pinah, you kill Innocence."

"I never been there," he protested. "I'd be operating blind."

"I believe in your reputation."

Monsarrat wished he were as confident.

"For proof of his death," she continued. "You will shoot him in the head and show me the mutilated ear."

He played for time, to evaluate his options. "How can I do that if I'm in Rosh Pinah and you're in Cape Town?"

"Nicky will provide the necessary arrangements."

"If I choose to decline your generous offer, Ms. Krupnik?"

With a single sentence, she reduced his options to none. "If so, Mr. Monsarrat, or if you accept my money but fail to kill Innocence, I will send Nicky to you."

He entertained the image of a Brighton beach dumpster. "In that case, when do I leave?"

"At dawn. Your account at the hostel will be settled, your possessions will be disposed, and your cell phone and revolver will disappear into False Bay. New items will be provided. The *sluzhba* will erase all evidence of David Clarendon entering and exiting the country. You will return to South Africa neither as Clarendon nor Monsarrat."

He understood the perils of questioning a *vor's* orders.

"Do you have any more questions, Mr. Monsarrat?"

He had many questions she would never answer and few she might entertain. He proposed one of the latter. "Will I also have to kill the man he's meeting?"

"If it is useful."

She walked to her desk and reached into a drawer. She returned to the couch and passed him a thick envelope. "Ten thousand dollars for expenses."

He considered the Russian aphorism about dining with the devil. He would need a very long spoon with Masha Krupnik. She was one of the coldest, most efficient, women he had ever met.

She delivered a warning as subtle as a sledgehammer. "You speak our language and understand our culture. Remember that secrets are sacrosanct to Russians, more precious than diamonds."

He nodded his understanding.

"*Otlichno.* Excellent. I am confident of your success."

He wished he shared her optimism.

She held out her hand. "We are in agreement, *da?*"

"I have a condition."

She nodded her assent like royalty granting a request. "*Yah slushayu.* I am listening"

He shared Palmer's intelligence on Rosalinda Santiago with her. "After Innocence leaves Cape Town, I want you to rescue her from his villa. She'll be ill. I want you to arrange for her recuperation in a private clinic here. When she's strong enough to travel, I want you to give her a passport and send her home to Manila. Or to Massachusetts. Anywhere she wants to go."

"You are a loyal man, Mr. Monsarrat."

"I am," he agreed. "I am also very careful. Before I shoot Innocence in the head and show you his mutilated ear, I want to see Rosalinda. I want to hear her voice."

"What will you do if I am unable to free her from the villa?"

"I doubt that will be a problem for a woman of your abilities," he answered. "Also, I want you to open an account in her name in one of your Swiss banks and deposit the quarter-million-dollar fee into it."

She studied him, as if she had discovered a *yurodiviy*, a holy fool, on her couch. "You are a very generous man."

"She saved my life. I owe her."

"I give you my word," she agreed.

"I believe you, Ms. Krupnik, but I also give you my word if anything happens to Rosalinda, I will return to Cape Town and your *byki* will not stop me from killing you."

"I do not scare, Mr. Monsarrat."

"*Yah ponimayu.* I understand," he said. "As I do not make empty threats."

She offered her hand, and he shook it. "Bruce was correct. You are a rare man."

He slipped the envelope into his sweatshirt. "Is our business concluded, Ms. Krupnik?"

"*Nyet.*" She stood and walked to the double doors. "Nicky, come inside please."

The young Russian entered the room. "*Da,* Masha"

"Mr. Monsarrat will stay with us tonight. Prepare the Pushkin Room."

She waited until the young Russian departed. "Are you hungry, Nathan?"

The switch from the professional to the personal caught him by surprise. "I am."

"*Chornoiy ikra*? The caviar is Beluga."

"Of course."

She crossed to her desk and punched a button on the phone. "Oleg. I require dinner for two. *Prinesi minye chornoiy ikra. Dlya dvukh chelovek. Toxe dva stankhana i butylku Bison. Plyus dva omarov iz* Maine. Broil the lobsters."

She glanced at Monsarrat. "Serve me in forty-five minutes, Oleg. Make sure the bottle of vodka and the two glasses are very cold. You know how I like Bison."

She disconnected the intercom. "You do not mind me ordering, Nathan?"

"Vodka, caviar, and lobster? I am in your good hands, Ms. Krupnik."

"Business is concluded," she admonished. "I am now Masha."

During his career with the Agency, the *sluzhba* had been the enemy, eager to entrap him with the siren exchange of sex for secrets. As dean, he no longer possessed secrets, and Masha Krupnik was a *vor*, not a spy.

She sat next to him on the couch. Her long fingers reached for his sweatshirt. He helped her pull it over his head. His tee shirt followed the sweatshirt into the floor. He pulled her silk tee shirt over her head, dropped it on top of the growing pile of clothes, and unclasped her bra. Her nipples were pink and thick atop her white breasts. A thin, blue vein throbbed in her neck. He lightly bit her throat.

"*Nyet*. I am not a fragile American woman. I do not break so easily." She shoved him onto the cushions and sank her teeth into his pectoral muscles. She pulled off his running shoes and socks and tossed them onto the floor. His jeans and underwear followed.

Emerald eyes flecked with gold surveyed her conquest. "As I suspected. *Otlichno*."

Monsarrat wrapped her in his arms and reversed their positions. She lifted her hips. He unsnapped her jeans and dragged them down her legs. Her lace underwear was crimson, the color of her fingernails.

"Use your teeth," she commanded.

He bit the waistband, pulled it off her hips, and spit the lace onto the floor. He looked down at her face, framed by waves of her thick, black hair. He ran his fingertips over her crimson lipstick and spread it across her high Slavic cheekbones. He felt her sharp nails dig into his back. She wrapped her long legs around his waist, bit his neck and lips. She gripped his ears and guided his head between her legs. Her mons was bald. Her *amor Veneris* was swollen. He tasted her salty stickiness.

Her wet softness wrapped around his hard flesh. She moved her hips against him greedily. He thrust slowly and then more quickly as her breathing rasped.

"*Da*, now, *vmeste*! Together!"

She reached for his hair and pulled his face toward her. She bit his tongue and climaxed. Monsarrat felt his body spin, tethered by his flesh to the woman beneath him, and shuddered as her breathing slowed and deepened.

They lay side by side on the couch, their bodies coated in a sheen of sweat. She ran her fingers over her breasts and pressed them to his lips. Monsarrat wondered if she sealed all her business deals on the couch.

After a few minutes, she stood and pulled on her lace underwear. "Dress now, Nathan. It would be impolite to be naked when Oleg arrives to serve us dinner."

He followed her instructions. He suspected it would be safer than the alternative.

DAWN IN THE PUSHKIN ROOM

Monsarrat woke in the darkened Pushkin Room, its windows covered by drapes as thick as blackout curtains. He felt along the wall for a switch, and a dozen bulbs from a crystal chandelier hung from a scalloped ceiling illuminated the room. Gold foil covered the walls, and pamphlets, drawings, and notebooks garnered from Alexander Sergeyevich's apartments on the Moika Embankment in Saint Petersburg and Sadovaya Street in Tsarskoe Selo lined bookshelves of red oak.

In the bathroom, he found clothes that fit his frame, plus the necessities for his ablutions. He shaved, showered, and finished dressing minutes before Nicky knocked on the door. For the ride to the northern border, the young Russian wore jeans, sneakers, an unbuttoned Oxford shirt, and a beige, linen jacket.

He brushed by Monsarrat and drew the curtains, allowing sunlight to flood the room. "*Dobroye utra*, David. Good morning. It is a beautiful day."

"Good morning to you, Nicky. Is today casual Saturday?"

The young Russian ignored the question. "Prepare yourself for departure, please. Our drive will be long."

He followed Nicky past the kitchen and smelled the aroma of coffee freshly brewed. "Do we have time for breakfast?"

"We have coffee and many varieties of croissants in the car, plus black bread, butter, *chornoiy ikra*, and vodka. It is a moveable picnic feast."

The three black Mercedes G63 AMGs idled before the entrance to the *dacha*. Sasha and Pavel waited in the front seats of the middle vehicle.

"No good-byes from your boss, Nicky?"

"She sends her best regards, I am sure."

During their dinner, Monsarrat had waited for her to comment on his encounter with the four stooges, but she did not broach the subject. By the end of the evening, he knew she had not dispatched them. Buffoonery was not her style. If she had wanted to send him a message, she would have ordered Sasha to shatter his fibula.

He followed Nicky onto the rear bench of the G63. Pavel trailed the lead Mercedes as the convoy drove through the streets of Plumstead on its way to Kromboom Parkway. North of Settler's Way, it turned east onto Table Bay Boulevard and followed the road until it joined National Route Seven for the 420-mile trip to Vioolsdrif and the border crossing into Namibia. At Melkbosstrand Road, the route narrowed to a single lane.

As the convoy's speed slowed, Nicky turned on the bench. He took a wicker hamper from the rear cargo area and passed it to Sasha. "*Priyatnova appetita*, my friends."

He set a second wicker hamper on the rear bench and repeated the wishes for a good appetite. "Dig in, David. Napkins, silverware, cups, plates, everything necessary for our picnic."

Monsarrat ate a butter croissant and drank a cup of strong, black coffee while the young Russian sipped herbal tea and nibbled a plain piece of toast, his manners dainty for a stone killer. "Coffee's too strong for you, Nicky?"

"I imbibe no caffeine, no nicotine, no alcohol, no drugs. I am a paradigm of virtue."

"I wonder if you're really Russian."

"I am a patriot. Do not doubt my loyalty because I live outside the *rodina*."

Monsarrat saw the neat bulge of the double holster and brace of Px4 pistols beneath the linen jacket. "Only a fool would doubt you, Nicky."

He closed his eyes and considered Sanhedrin. If Wilson was correct and his former boss was in Cape Town, the dots connected themselves. When Sanhedrin was involved, suspicions became a necessary substitute for proof. He knew in his marrow Sanhedrin had hired the four stooges. His decision to hire cut-rate thugs like Thad and Philip had been based more on parsimony than philosophy. His next probe would be more professional.

The Mercedes crunched gravel and rough pavement beneath its tires and stopped before a line of gasoline pumps. Nicky opened the door. "We will refuel here. If you need to relieve yourself, I will take you to the pissoir. It is dangerous for you to roam the South African wilderness."

Monsarrat followed him out of the vehicle. "Gas, lousy food, and dirty bathrooms. It looks like a rest stop to me, not the high veld."

"*D'vai*. The *vannaya* are over here."

He took in the possible escape routes from the men's room, if he were foolish enough to try to outrun a gaggle of heavily armed *byki* in a G63 convoy. He stood before a urinal while Nicky loitered behind him. When he washed his hands, Nicky stood next to him.

"You want me to watch your back while you take a leak?"

The young Russian prodded him. "Walk to the Mercedes, David. We have far to go still."

"No hands, Nicky. We'll stay the best of friends if you keep your hands to yourself. Same for Pavel and Sasha."

He doubted that an iota of fear pulsed in the young Russian's veins.

At the gas pumps, he listened to Nicky instruct Sasha to subdue their guest if he attempted to escape but not to harm him. The older man grunted. Monsarrat, who understood the difficulty of following orders that conflicted with personal desires, empathized. Still, the Agency had hardwired him with an antipathy toward Russians. "You and Pavel need to piss, Sasha? Take it out, hold it for each other, just like old times for a couple of *suki* prison bitches?"

Pavel possessed less discipline than the older man. He stepped toward Monsarrat, but Sasha placed a hand on his arm and spoke a single word. "*Vskore.*"

Monsarrat understood the implications of the promise. Soon.

On Nicky's return, the convoy regained National Route Seven. Signs for Western Cape towns flashed through the tinted windows. The convoy crossed into the Northern Cape, and at Springbok, in the shadow of the Copper Mountains, they stopped again for fuel. Monsarrat followed the young Russian out of the Mercedes and stretched his sore muscles in the afternoon heat. "How much longer to the border?"

"One hundred miles, maybe less, not more. You must have patience, David."

As the convoy rolled north, the African sunshine lit the dun hills. After an hour, they crossed the first bridge over the Kowiep River. A sign for Vioolsdrif flashed by like a card trick. With little else to do until he stepped onto Namibian soil, Monsarrat reviewed his plans and contingencies.

The brown waters of the Orange River demarked the border between the two countries. The South African facility was clean and well organized. Nicky pointed out the separate chute for pedestrian crossings. "You take from Sasha the new backpack we bought you. It is full with water and sandwiches and clothes and necessities, like toothpaste. You wave good-bye to us like excellent friends sad to see each other depart. You enter the chute for foreigners with your passport in your hand. Do not bother to wave to us again. We will be on the road out of this dump before the *apparat* is done with you."

The convoy halted outside the entrance to the facility. Nicky reached into the pocket of his linen jacket and passed a cell phone to Monsarrat. "This phone is a burner. The access code is four zeros. All passwords are Clarendon with a capital letter. A Cape Town number and an e-mail address are programmed into the contact list."

He leaned across Monsarrat and pushed open the door. "You have forty-eight hours to contact me. Use the video program so I will see you as well as hear you. Two sad events will occur if you fail to follow instructions."

"Only two?"

"One, your phone will go dead. Two, you will also go dead. Sasha and I will find you and kill you."

Monsarrat thought it might have been his first truthful sentence. *"Yah ponimayu,* but you should also understand something."

"What would that be, *moy druhg?"*

"First, I'm not your friend. Second, if I don't see Rosalinda, I won't kill Innocence. Third, if I ever smell your sweet perfume again, I'll put a bullet between your eyes."

The young Russian's smile was lupine. "I hope we meet again soon, David."

Sasha lowered his window and dropped the backpack onto the ground. Monsarrat stepped out of the Mercedes, retrieved the bag, and walked toward the border crossing. He heard the crunch of the heavy vehicles as the convoy reversed direction toward Vioolsdrif, where the Russians would await his call and final instructions from their *vor,* mission accomplished, return home, or mission aborted, kill him. He hoped their orders would not be mission accomplished, kill the patsy.

The pavement baked in the heat. As a buffer against the air conditioning in the Mercedes, Monsarrat had worn his sweatshirt. He stripped it off and stuffed it into the backpack. He entered the crossing facility and followed the signs to the men's toilet. Inside a stall, he placed the water, sandwiches, fresh clothes, and toiletries on the lid of the cistern. He arranged the new work gloves, watch cap, and wool scarf on the toilet cover and inspected the empty bag. He suspected the Russians had added bugs to the cell phone but did not possess the technical skills to discover them. He returned the items to the backpack, slipped the cell phone into the back pocket of his jeans, and exited the concrete structure for the pedestrian chute.

Foot traffic was light, and he passed through the South African formalities quickly. He crossed the bridge over the Orange River. Beyond its north bank, a white sign stained with red dust directed him to the Republic of Namibia's Border Control Office. A sergeant and two corporals cradled AK-47s behind a boom barrier. The sergeant stepped forward with an expression of contempt. Middle-aged backpackers offered scant opportunities for confiscations.

He accepted the David Clarendon passport and flipped through the pages. He jerked his head toward a hand-printed sign, Immigrations and Customs, and beckoned one of his assistants. In the tin shack, he shook the contents of the backpack onto a lopsided card table while Monsarrat emptied his pockets and the corporal rubbed the stock of his AK-47.

The sergeant examined the sweatshirt, work gloves, scarf, and watch cap before dropping them onto the table. He waggled his long, black fingers. His voice was deep and smooth. "You realize that you are in Africa, Mr. Clarendon?"

"I come from a cold climate."

"How long will you stay in my country?"

"A week or so. I want to visit Windhoek. Walvis Bay. Etosha. The Skeleton Coast."

"I suggest Caprivi, also."

He stamped his passport an entry notation and a temporary visa valid for ninety days. "The visa is of no charge for Canadians, but I must collect an on-site processing fee of five hundred South African rand."

"Of course," Monsarrat agreed.

He walked along a rutted, single-lane road, past a second stained, white sign welcoming him to the Karas Region. At a gas station outside the border town of Noordoewer, he bought a warm Coke and a soggy candy bar from a compact old man in a grey tee shirt that had once been white. The faded letters across his chest proclaimed "Herero and Proud." He stood an inch above five feet with nappy hair pressed against his scalp in tight, grey ringlets. Cauliflower ears framed his square face. His eyes were black, and his nose was squashed across his broad cheeks.

Monsarrat ignored the Russian cell phone in his back pocket. He laid a thin stack of one hundred rand bills, each blue note graced on the obverse with a portrait of Nelson Mandela and on the reverse with a Cape buffalo, on a dusty counter. "I need to use your telephone."

The old man stood on his tiptoes to examine the bills. He craned his neck upward when he spoke. "Where cell phone?"

Monsarrat found himself slipping into the Herero's rhythms. "No cell phone."

The old man clucked as he stacked the bills neatly. "Where you call?"

"International."

"America?"

"Port Harcourt."

"How long talk?"

"Two minutes. Maybe three."

The old man shook his head. "One thousand rand more."

Monsarrat enjoyed a good jawing. "Five hundred."

The old man passed him a pencil marred with teeth marks and a scrap of paper. "Eight hundred."

Monsarrat jotted the number for Mark Palmer's cell phone and passed it to the old man with an additional eight hundred rand.

The Herero placed a rotary telephone on the counter. On his tiptoes, he spun the zero. The dial clicked loudly in the small space. "Missy, I call Port Harcourt. Here number."

The old man passed him the receiver, and Monsarrat stepped closer to the counter. He smelled the odor of onions and sweat. "I need privacy."

The Herero turned his back, sat on the stool, and placed his fingers in his ears.

Monsarrat listened to clicks and hisses and then the voice of Palmer. "It's your academic friend. I'm visiting Namibia. Let's get together tonight."

Palmer's reply was faint, as if the distance from Port Harcout had weakened his words.

"I'll be in a mining town called Rosh Pinah. It's small. You'll find me."

He listened again before answering. "Our host will have guests, so bring a couple of well-dressed friends to balance the table."

Palmer spoke loudly, as if the connection had suddenly been amplified by telephone pixies. "Watch your back. Rosh Pinah borders the forbidden zones. It's an African version of the Triple Frontier, with a booming black market in diamonds and a busy trade in women and children."

The old man twisted on the stool and tapped his wrist.

"How long until you get here?"

Palmer's voice faded. "I need to arrange logistics. As soon as possible."

Monsarrat replaced the receiver onto the cradle and handed the rotary phone to the Herero. "I need go Rosh Pinah."

The old man spoke the international language of finance. He held up his right hand and rubbed his thumb across his fingers. "Ten thousand rand."

"Three thousand rand. Private car. No taxi."

The Herero placed his hands behind his back. "Eight thousand rand."

Monsarrat passed him the money. "I need duct tape, hand towels, hunting knife, and flashlight. Can you get?"

"Two thousand rand more."

Forty minutes later, Monsarrat pulled on his sweatshirt and settled into the passenger seat of a vintage, four-cylinder Audi 80 held together with baling wire. The headlights were yellowed. The clattering of the car drowned out the sounds of the desert. He placed the backpack between his feet and looked for the seat belt.

The Herero laughed. "Noordoewer. What expect?"

At fifty miles per hour on Jan Haak Road, the Audi rattled like an angry diamondback. The Herero sat on a pillow and drove with his fingers of his left hand on the steering wheel, chain smoking with his right hand, lighting each new cigarette from a dented Zippo after flipping the red coal of the old butt out the window. The temperatures plunged as the sun dipped beneath the horizon. In the dark mountain passes, the headlights barely illuminated the road.

An early moon rose over Ai-Ais and Fish River Canyon. The soft lunar glow bathed the Richtersveld. The Audi crossed the confluence of Orange River and Fish River. Monsarrat imagined fish eagles patrolling the skies, peering at the clattering vehicle with avian suspicion.

At Sendelingsdrif, Jan Haak Road became Route C13. Rosh Pinah spread across a rift in the Hunsberge like an oasis devoid of water. The dunes of the Namib Desert lapped at its western edges. Three miles past the town, the aviation warning light atop a cell phone tower blinked like the bloodshot eye of Polyphemus. Beyond the tower, the granite and limestone Roter Kamm Crater lay to the north. The Audi surmounted a series of speed bumps as the old man turned left on Lood Street, then left again on Kokerboom Street. He steered the car into an unpaved parking lot. Along its far edge, spotlights on tall poles cast yellow pools. A building with a portico stood at the end of a short gravel walk.

The Herero spoke his first words since leaving Noordoewer. "Lodge. Rosh Pinah only."

Monsarrat stepped out of the Audi. His back ached, and his kidneys felt as if he had been kicked by an African ostrich. He leaned through the open window into the driver's seat. "Drive carefully, old man."

When the Herero spun the wheel of the Audi, the tires churned gravel. Monsarrat shouldered the backpack and walked toward the portico. He passed a pair of black Cadillac Escalades flanking a BMW Alpina B7 with heavily tinted windows. Its South Africa license bore a Cape Town designation.

The reception area of the Rosh Pinah Lodge had been carefully maintained. He noted the utilitarian décor, the rough-hewn furniture, and the ocher color of the sunbaked tile floor. A hand printed sign at the registration counter advised him to tap the call bell for service.

As the chime echoed through the empty lobby, a fluorescent bulb in an office beyond the counter flickered, and an unshaven, middle-aged Afrikaner wearing a flowered shirt, blue jeans, and unlaced work boots shuffled forward. His voice was gruff from sleep. When he yawned, his breath smelled of beer and cigarettes. "Welcome to the Rosh Pinah Lodge, mate. You need a room for the night?"

Monsarrat didn't want to remain in Rosh Pinah a moment longer than necessary. "One night should do it. What time is check out?"

The Afrikaner placed a registration book on the counter and passed Monsarrat an index card and a pen. "Noon, but we're flexible. No need to worry about buses full of tourists demanding rooms."

"What's the charge?"

"One thousand rand includes VAT, breakfast, and gratuities. Private loo and telly in your room. Laundry machines and ice venders in the back. Breakfast starts at 7:00 a.m., coffee, bread, meats, eggs."

He scribbled David Clarendon's information on the index card and offered the Afrikaner his passport and two thousand rand. "I'm already hungry."

The Afrikaner filled out a receipt, tucked it into the passport, withdrew a key attached to a plastic shoehorn from a rack beneath the counter, and handed the items to Monsarrat. "We don't get too many foreigners. Most work with the mining companies or service firms. Tourists tend to stop for fuel and food and keep on traveling to Aus and beyond or one of the border crossings."

He recalled Palmer's warning of the area's denizens. "I'm for Lüderitz, but my ride had to turn back. Problem at home. He should pick me up tomorrow."

"That's a pity, but we're glad to have you. Our rooms are clean, and the food is simple but good. Townsfolk are friendly, too."

"Good food and friendly people sounds okay."

"Packets of soap and shampoo are on the bed. Towels, too. Anything else you need?"

"I'm fine. Looking forward to some rest."

"You and me both, mate. Except I have to wake up early tomorrow for a match against the wankers from the market."

Monsarrat feigned interest. "Football?"

The Afrikaner replaced the register beneath the counter. "Nah, we're for rugby. Football's too finesse a sport for this lot."

The Rosh Pinah Lodge offered forty rooms on two branches of a single floor. Monsarrat followed the signs to the West Wing. The key to Room 137 opened a solid door lacking a peephole. Inside the room, he flipped the lock, set the chain, emptied his backpack on the bed, and sat in the lone chair before the black screen of a thirteen-inch television set. After eating the sandwiches and drinking a bottle of water, he brushed his teeth, shaved, stripped, stepped into the shower, and soaked beneath a slow, tepid spray. He toweled dry and dressed in the clothes Nicky had supplied.

He examined the folding knife and the other items the old Herero had procured for him in Noordoewer. The sharp edge of the blade bore rasp marks and an oily sheen. He dropped the knife into his pocket, returned the other items to the backpack, and added two hand towels from the bathroom. He turned off the lights in the room and sat on the edge of the bed, modulating his breathing as his vision adjusted to the darkness and his hearing attuned to the sounds of the night. After a few minutes he stood, shrugged on his sweatshirt, and trod softly out of the room, listening for the click of the lock. In the quiet hallway, the overhead lights burned brightly.

Careful to not disturb the Afrikaner sleeping in the office, he entered the empty reception area and flipped the pages of the registration book from the back until he found his own entry, then turned another page and carefully scanned the names of guests. Three men with the same Cape Town address shared Room 105. Four Afrikaners from Windhoek resided in Rooms 107 and 108, two to each room. Innocence Okeri of Cape Town resided in Room 104, and Allegiance Ireko of Windhoek slept in Room 106.

Monsarrat loved the dawning of clarity. He noted the familiar sibilance of the given names and the mirrored spelling of the surnames. Allegiance and Diligence. Ireko and Okeri. Allegiance Ireko and Diligence Okeri, Innocence's twice-named older brother, the number two son of Rehovoth Okeri, who despite Wilson's insistence had failed to die in a car crash from too much palm wine, a missed curve in the road, and a wall. He admitted the possibility that an Allegiance Ireko, who was not Diligence Okeri, might have passed through Rosh Pinah during the same hours that Innocence had chosen to visit the town from his South African redoubt, but he did not believe in coincidences. Nor did he care to assail the Gordian knot that bound Diligence and Innocence.

He opened the plastic file box and studied a five-by-seven index card. Innocence had arrived earlier on Saturday with a planned departure for the following day. He pulled Diligence's card and saw identical arrival and departure dates. He reinserted the cards and returned the box and the book to their places.

He removed the roll of duct tape from the backpack, dropped it into the pocket of his sweatshirt, and shoved the work gloves into the back pocket of his pants. In the East Wing, a weak pool of light and muffled music spilled from beneath the door of Room 104. The lack of the peephole made his task easier. He knocked softly, then slightly harder, careful to not attract the attention of the bodyguards in the room across the hall.

A muffled London accent seeped through the door. "What do you bloody hell want?"

Monsarrat spoke softly in his best Afrikaner impersonation. "I'm sorry to bother you at such an unacceptable hour, Mr. Okeri, but there are two gentlemen in the reception area who have asked to speak with you."

"Tell the idiots to come back in the morning."

"I tried, Mr. Okeri, sir, but they insisted."

"Call the bleeding authorities."

"I can't do that, sir. They are the authorities."

The chain dropped, and a middle-aged woman wearing a towel, a flaming red wig, and enough foundation to withstand the footlights of a Broadway theater opened the door. Behind her, using her bulk as a shield, Innocence stood in a halo of light, clothed in a pair of silk boxer shorts and a tooled-leather holster belt with a dozen bullets fitted into loops. He gripped a brace of pink, pearl-handled Colt .45 Peacemakers with seven inch barrels, like an overweight Buffalo Soldier caught in a bordello.

Monsarrat thought he had added at least thirty pounds of fat since their last meeting. His tribal scars stretched wider across his forehead, and his long, jagged fingernails had been clipped. He saw confusion followed by a bloom of recognition in his eyes.

The seconds of mute disbelief cost Innocence dearly. He slowly raised his hands, but Monsarrat flung the woman aside as if we were still a linebacker playing football for his university in Iowa and struck him in the throat with the tensile ridge of his right hand, between his thumb and index finger. He kicked the back of his knees, first the right, followed by the left.

Innocence dropped the revolvers and collapsed onto the floor, his hands pulling at his mouth and his lungs fighting for air. Monsarrat kicked him onto his back, pushed the two Peacemakers out of reach, and locked the door. He placed his running shoe on his throat.

"Remember me? I'm the guy you tortured for eighteen weeks in your filthy Delta compound. I'm also the guy who sliced your ear in a cheap Port Harcourt hotel room. It's just like old times, you and me together again. Have you gained weight? Even so, you're looking well."

On the floor by the bed, the hooker pulled at the towel. "I swear to Christ, mister, he just hired me for the night. I don't even know his name!"

Monsarrat gestured toward the bathroom. "Get dressed. If I hear a sound from you, what's going to happen to him will happen to you, too."

She grabbed her clothes and ran into the bathroom. He heard the click of the lock.

He ripped a long strip from the roll of duct tape and wound it around Innocence's mouth. He secured his wrists and ankles with duct tape, then rolled him onto his stomach. He wound duct tape around the frame of the bed and wrapped a sticky, grey collar around his throat. Satisfied with his handiwork, he removed the empty holster belt.

He retrieved the revolvers, opened the cylinders, checked the loads, and slid the Colts into the holsters. "Two Peacemakers, Innocence? Are you planning to shoot a herd of elephants? Or just have some bloody sex with your lady friend?"

He turned off the radio and searched the room. A room key and a pink cell phone went into his pockets. He pulled the blankets off the bed and, beneath a pillow, found a wallet thick with rand. He took the watch cap and work gloves from the backpack and jammed them into the back pockets of his pants. He slid one Peacemaker into the holster and dropped it, along with the remaining duct tape, into the backpack.

Innocence lay like a beaten dog tethered to the end of a short rope. Grunts filtered through the duct tape covering his mouth. Monsarrat snapped the barrel of the revolver against his scarred ear. "Your wound's healed nicely, but you'll lose more than a lobe if you make trouble."

He grunted again, and Monsarrat kicked him in the head. "Where are your manners, Innocence? I need to speak with your lady friend."

He knocked on the bathroom door. "Are you dressed, darling? It's time for you to go home."

She stepped out of the bathroom as if she expected each breath to be her last. "Can I really go, mister? I swear to Christ I won't say a word to anyone about you or him. Ever. You can trust me. I'm dependable."

"What's you name, darling?"

"Sandy."

He pressed the wallet into her hand. "Okay, Sandy, take his money, go home, and convince yourself that I'm a figment of your imagination, because this is a small town, and if I hear a siren, believe me when I say that I will find you quickly and kill you slowly. Tell me you understand."

"Oh, my sweet Christ, I understand, mister. Can I just go home now?"

He opened the door and watched her run down the hallway. He knew he should have bound, gagged, and locked her in the bathroom, but since the Delta, he had grown adverse to kidnapping women. He locked the door again, crossed the room, and turned off the light.

On the house telephone, he called the room of the three bodyguards and spoke in his best Afrikaner accent. "I'm sorry to bother you at such an unacceptable hour, but Mr. Okeri has been rushed to the health clinic on Lood Street with chest pains. The clinic's quite close, around the corner, in fact."

He heard two sets of footsteps approach the room and an insistent knock on the door. The knob rattled, and a voice called, "Mr. Okeri, sah! Are you in need, sah?"

The knob rattled again. "He nuh be in de room. We gun go tuh dis place and talk wit' de ductah man."

A second voice cursed. "He in de room but nuh can talk. De witch woman put de bad juju on massah!"

"We guh wake Moses. He gun tell us de right ting tuh do."

Monsarrat listened as the footsteps of the bodyguards receded. "Back in a minute, Mr. Okeri."

He placed the Colt into the waistband of his jeans, tugged the watch cap over his hair, and closed the door softly. In the parking lot, he placed the backpack on the pavement and unfolded the knife. When he pulled on the work gloves, his hands were steady. "One hundred percent spook," he whispered into the night.

A bodyguard ran from the entrance of the lodge toward the pink BMW Alpina. Monsarrat approached him silently, placed his gloved hand over his mouth, and pulled his head back, exposing the soft flesh of his throat.

He thrust the blade of the knife into the jugular vein and pushed the body onto the ground. When he opened the driver's door, the light pierced the night like a beacon. A switch on the dashboard released the trunk. He closed the door, heaved the bodyguard into the open space, and stepped to the side as he removed the knife. Blood spurted in a crimson geyser.

He wiped the blade on the dead man's clothes and crouched against the far side of the Alpina. The remaining two bodyguards arrived at the car and stopped before the open trunk. Monsarrat swung the butt of the Peacemaker and caved the skull of the first man. When the second bodyguard charged, Monsarrat leveled the barrel and shot him in the forehead. The boom of the Peacemaker sounded like a howitzer in the still night.

Monsarrat recognized the three men from the FATA compound. When he spoke, he no longer bothered to whisper. "Payback, you bastards."

He heaved both corpses into the trunk. From the backpack, he removed a towel, cleaned his clothes, and tossed the bloody cloth on top of the bodies. He closed the trunk, slipped the Colt into his pants, and picked up the backpack.

In the driver seat, he placed the backpack and the Peacemaker onto the passenger seat, started the engine, and shifted the BMW into gear. He drove to the C13 and turned north. After three miles, the car's headlights illuminated the cell phone tower. At the edge of a mining road, he turned onto the pitted asphalt and drove in low gear until the pavement ended at the entrance to a sealed mine. He backed the BMW next to the door of a dilapidated shack, popped the lid of the trunk, and transferred the bodies into the shack.

Monsarrat threw the towel onto the floor, shook the expended brass from the Peacemaker onto it, and reloaded the revolver. Before departing, he confirmed the strength of the Russian cell phone's reception.

At the lodge, he parked the BMW in the empty space between the two Cadillacs, slipped the Peacemaker into jeans, shouldered the backpack, and walked to his room, where he washed the remaining dirt and blood from his clothes. He dried himself with toilet paper and flushed the soggy mess.

He stopped before entering the reception area as four Afrikaners with skulls as polished as cue balls stepped into the lobby. He noted the bulges beneath their bush jackets. A compact man with the physique of a middle-weight boxer walked between them. He wore a blue business suit and a white, silk shirt open at the neck. In his right hand, he held a leather attaché case. His closely cropped hair was ash grey, and tribal scars marked his forehead. He appeared an older, neater, more contained version of Innocence.

An Afrikaner placed three room keys onto the counter, and the group exited the lodge. Monsarrat heard the rumble of the Escalade engines and the crunch of gravel beneath tires as the two Cadillacs pulled out of the parking lot. He waited another minute, then walked quickly to Room 104.

Innocence writhed on the floor of the dark room. Monsarrat kicked him hard in the ribs. "Your brother and his bodyguards checked out. Your three thugs are dead. You're alone, and I'm your only friend."

He heaved him into a kneeling position and pulled the duct tape from his mouth. Altering the facts bothered him not a whit. "Your buddy, Mark Palmer, arrives from Port Harcourt soon. He prefers to take your corpse back with him, but if you talk fast and tell me what I need to know, I'll cut you loose. If you lie to me, though, I will fillet your lips and give you to Palmer."

Innocence's voice was strained. "Sojah man kill Sunday? Kill Goodfriend and Moses? Suffah man evil man!"

"Was pidgin the language of instruction at the London School of Economics?"

A baneful energy flickered in Innocence's eyes. Contempt and a London accent replaced his pidgin. "Assuredly not. May I use your Christian name, or shall I call you Mr. Monsarrat?"

Monsarrat answered by flicking the knife against his lips. "We have much to discuss, Innocence, and little time. Start by telling me about the Nok. Why did you deliver it instead of your father?"

"Would you mind releasing my wrists? The pain is impeding my ability to concentrate."

The plea reminded him of Sanhedrin in Greenfield. "Impeding? A terribly well-educated bloke, aren't you, Mr. Okeri?"

Exasperation laced his voice. "I see no need for barbarity."

Monsarrat again tapped his lips with the knife. "I asked why you delivered the Nok instead of your father. Would you like to answer me?"

He repeated his request. "Will you release my wrists?"

Despite Palmer's assurances, Monsarrat saw that Innocence feared him not at all. "You're stalling."

"My wrists or my silence, Mr. Monsarrat. The choice is yours to make."

Monsarrat placed the tip of the knife against his eyelid and slowly pressed against the blade. "There is always a third way, Innocence."

"When I learned Rehovoth had agreed to meet a buyer for the statue, I took it from him. After all, your boss at the CIA originally promised me the money."

"Sanhedrin didn't know that you stole the statue from your father?"

"You've lost me. Who is Sanhedrin?"

"De big, big CIA man," Monsarrat explained. "Your benefactor at the Agency."

"He told me his name was Fineghan Scarnagh," Innocence claimed. "After you delivered the Nok, he became so perturbed that he flew to Port Harcourt to lecture me. He said that if you were not such a burned-out case, you could have checkmated his plans and ruined his career. He was so upset, I thought he might shoot me, but at the time I was too valuable an asset to waste."

"Because you were to become a general and a minister in the new government?"

"The Army of the Delta and the Ministry of Oil. To his credit, he kept his word, but the positions turned out to be temporary. The new government turned on me, and I had to leave the country with just a few of my good friends. I believe you know the rest of the story."

"Close enough."

"As punishment for stealing his statue," Innocence continued, "my father insisted that I fulfill my filial duties in Cape Town."

"What did he want you to do?"

"Rehovoth uses his hereditary position as the Amanyanabo as a cover for what Americans would call his real job, the head of a business empire dealing in diamonds, drugs, weapons, and human trafficking. He personally controls our markets in the Maghreb, the Sahel, West Africa, and Central Africa. Diligence, my elder brother, oversees our Southern Cone markets in diamonds and weapons from Windhoek. I control drugs and human trafficking from Cape Town."

Monsarrat suspected that Rehovoth Okeri, once anointed as president, would pull his own strings, despite the best efforts of the oil consortium. "How's business?"

When Innocence laughed, the sound erupted in a blistering howl. "Business is divine. You do not know my father, Mr. Monsarrat, but he is a man of powerful religious convictions. He believes the Lord chose him to be the Amanyanabo, as He chose Abraham and Jesus and Mohammed to lead His peoples. He also believes the Lord wishes him to gather obscene amounts of wealth."

"Didn't your arrival in Cape Town upset your brother? He had to share his business."

"Diligence is as successful as Rehovoth, albeit in a smaller geographic area. When our father saw his second son's genius for business, he sent me to Cape Town to prevent him from growing too powerful. Rehovoth fears Diligence will become his Absalom. He suspects my brother does not wish to wait for him to succumb to old age before supplanting him as Amanyanabo."

Monsarrat connected the dots. "Your father sent you to South Africa to spy on your brother?"

Innocence laughed again. "Nothing so prosaic, I assure you, Mr. Monsarrat. My father sent me to Cape Town to one day kill Diligence."

Successful interrogations, like recruitments, were luxuriant affairs, but the impending arrival of Palmer pressured Monsarrat. "If your father needs you in Cape Town to check your brother, why will he bring you to Abuja when he becomes president?"

Innocence demanded, "Release my wrists! The pain is unbearable."

"I hope so," Monsarrat answered. "Answer my question."

"Rehovoth believes I am viscous but weak. He wants to use me as a shield against Diligence, but I refuse to play pawn to his king."

"Why doesn't he bring back your brother and keep him under wraps in Abuja?"

Innocence shook his head. "Not another word unless you release my wrists."

The knife sliced his lower lip before he finished speaking. Blood flowed in a crimson cascade over his chin and onto his thick chest. He thrashed against the duct tape, but his scream was muffled by the blanket Monsarrat pressed over his mouth.

"You don't have bargaining chips, Innocence."

A pouting injustice replaced the contempt in his voice. "My father fears the ambitions of my brother. He dreads a palace coup, with Diligence as Zeus and himself as Kronos."

"Why doesn't Rehovoth just kill him?"

"He needs the money Diligence earns from weapons and diamonds," he explained. "His plate is too full to run the entire Southern Cone by himself, and he won't turn the operations over to me. He tells me I'm a failure. He says I'd rather fuck my own whores and snort my own coke than pay attention to his bottom line."

Monsarrat decided Innocence enjoyed his explanations, as if he climbed a rung toward his freedom with each answer. "Your father needs Diligence to run his empire, but he doesn't trust him. He doesn't want him to become too successful, so he took half of his markets and gave them to you, but you're a failure in business, so he's decided to use your only gift, your violence. He wants to keep you by his side to protect him not only from his enemies, but from his second son."

"Bravo, Mr. Monsarrat. I would applaud, but my hands are taped together."

"Who will run the Cape Town operations if you're in Abuja?"

Innocence spat blood onto the rug. "I'm sure my father wishes Purity, his eldest son, were still alive, but unless he is able to raise the dead, he will return the operations to Diligence. However, this conversation is academic, since I refuse to return to Abuja."

Psychopaths, Monsarrat knew, often told the best stories. "Tell me why your father faked your brother's death."

As his lip swelled, he began to lisp. "When my elder brother survived the crash, Rehovoth saw opportunity in his good fortune. Diligence Okeri received a death certificate so Allegiance Ireko could be born, live in Windhoek, and expand the family business without arousing suspicions."

"But you kept your name in Cape Town."

"I am not as malleable as my elder brother. I like my name, so I kept it. I especially like the way it rankles my father. It's a nagging reminder to Rehovoth that I am still his son."

The Okeri family drama tired Monsarrat. He ticked the penultimate item on his list. "What are you and Sanhedrin planning?"

"You mean Scarnagh? He's a dirty, little thing. I don't trust him. I only hire him to do dirty, little jobs."

Monsarrat noted his use of the present tense. "When did you last see him?"

"Not so long ago, he came to Cape Town with Mark Palmer. He tried to convince me to go back to Abuja to help my father, but I refused. Scarnagh spoke for both of them. Palmer only smiled. Until I made my counter-offer, and then he said yes."

The response rocked Monsarrat. If Innocence spoke the truth, the two men had traveled to Cape Town before Palmer trekked to the Berkshires. If Innocence did not lie, Palmer's tale of the divorce between the Agency and the oil consortium was as phantasmagoric as his own goodwill and Sanhedrin's honesty. It also explained how the Agency knew he would travel to Cape Town and how Sanhedrin had been able to track him so easily.

"What did you hire them to do?"

"I'm a very successful South African businessman, and I'm about to become even more successful," he boasted. "I paid them to kill my brother, half up front, half upon completion."

The story had been told thousands of times prior, a younger brother plots to kill his older brother to gain profit and power. "When will it happen?"

"Fast, sojah man," Innocence mocked. "Rehovoth will become president, and I will remain in Cape Town in charge of not only drugs and whores, but also diamonds and weapons for the entire Southern Cone."

"I underestimated you," Monsarrat admitted. "Until recently, I thought you were an illiterate thug."

"It's a role I perfected," he acknowledged. "Now do you understand, Mr. Monsarrat? Scarnagh and Palmer sent you here, and they're coming to implicate you in the death of my brother. Neither will harm me. I doubt you can make the same statement without having your Pinocchio nose grow longer."

"They're going to kill Diligence and pin the murder on me?"

"You're a very smart man, Mr. Monsarrat. You'll understand their anger if they arrive and find me dead and unable to pay my extremely generous fee. They may decide to kill you instead of Diligence."

"How do you know they're coming?"

Pity graced his answer. "I know, because I planned it, Mr. Monsarrat."

Monsarrat felt a tinge of compassion for Innocence. Blinkered by the shortcomings of the psychopath, he was unable to contemplate the possibility that anyone could be more devious than himself. "Why don't you kill Diligence yourself?"

"I find the notion of fratricide abhorrent."

"You're a paradigm of virtue," Monsarrat agreed in a voice heavy with sarcasm. "Tell me how they plan to frame me."

"It's very simple. You retired from the Central Intelligence Agency to become an assassin for hire draped in the robes of academia. Having intimate knowledge of your effectiveness, I paid you a generous fee to kill my brother. You succeeded in your mission, but unfortunately for you, my brother's bodyguards killed you."

Monsarrat recognized another shortcoming of the psychopath, the enormous capacity for self-delusion. "In that case, I suppose I'm out of options. I should cut you loose."

"Yes, Mr. Monsarrat, immediately. Then you should flee, although I would like to watch Scarnagh and Palmer chase you and catch you and engage in a struggle where only one of you will survive. I think I might bet on you as the winner."

Monsarrat could no longer tolerate his prisoner. He wanted to execute him and finish the grisly business. He showed him Palmer's photograph of Rosalinda. "You have one chance to stay alive long enough to make that wager, Innocence. Tell me where you are keeping Rosalinda Santiago."

He squinted to see the photograph. "The nurse woman that Scarnagh insisted Blessed remove from the oil rig so she could care for you in the Delta? Nothing has changed. As I told you in Port Harcourt, Blessed killed her the day we released you."

Monsarrat thought the question had surprised him. He returned the picture to his pocket and struck him hard with his right fist. When he toppled onto the rug, he pulled him upright and struck him again with his left fist. He stared into eyes, full of fear and yellowed by malaria, and pressed the edge of the knife against his jugular vein. "The picture is recent. She's your prisoner with a rope around her neck, just like in the Delta."

"She's dead, I swear it," Innocence blubbered. "Blessed killed her fifteen minutes after he received the ransom money. He said she was no longer of use to him."

He did not want to accept the explanation, but it matched the story Sanhedrin had provided and Innocence verified almost three years earlier, before the Nok turned his life upside down, while Palmer's photograph could have been created in a digital laboratory with the sole intent of bringing him to Cape Town.

He took the pink cell phone from his pocket. "What's the code?"

"Will you call Palmer to beg for mercy?"

When Monsarrat again flicked the knife, it sliced his upper lip. Blood once more flowed, and Innocence again thrashed, while Monsarrat smothered his screams with the blanket. "Tell me the cell phone code."

His voice was a wail of mourning. "Six four times. The devil but one better."

Monsarrat punched the numbers, and the pink cell phone unlocked. He stuffed it and the bloody blanket into his backpack.

He opened the folding knife, sliced a fresh strip of duct tape, and placed it over Innocence's bloody lips. When he severed the duct tape around the bedframe and hauled him to his feet, he smelled his fear. "How do you like being on the end of a leash, Innocence?"

In the parking lot, he popped the trunk of the BMW. Innocence struggled, but he brought the butt of a Peacemaker onto the back of his skull and heaved him into the trunk. He pulled the blanket from the backpack and tossed it over the inert body. "Pleasant dreams, you son of a bitch."

He closed the lid and drove out of the parking lot. On Lood Street, he turned left and pulled into the loading area behind the market. He parked the BMW between a dumpster and a delivery truck. Ten minutes later, he sat at a breakfast table in the Rosh Pinah Lodge, watching the first fingers of dawn break through the windows of the lobby.

THE HALLOWED HALLS OF BERKSHIRE ACADEMIA

The lodge's staff set out breakfast at quarter to seven. Fifteen minutes later, as Monsarrat drank black coffee at a table for four, Felix Sanhedrin entered the reception area. Mark Palmer walked next to him, followed by Frank and Joe, his assistants from Port Harcourt.

Monsarrat raised his cup. "Coffee, gentlemen? Breakfast is on me."

Sanhedrin took the chair to Monsarrat's right. He exuded good cheer. "How are you, Nathan, old buddy? How long has it been? Since Greenfield?"

Monsarrat absorbed Sanhedrin's designer jeans, alligator boots with silver toe caps, silk shirt, paisley ascot, and cream smoking jacket. "Sartorially splendid, as always, Felix. Or are you Franklin today? Maybe Fineghan?"

Sanhedrin tensed. "I was surprised when Mark told me you were in Namibia. Rosh Pinah is a bit removed from the hallowed halls of Berkshire academia."

Monsarrat considered him. A thoroughly deceitful person, Sanhedrin wouldn't recognize a truth if he tripped over it on a church pew, but although a terrible liar, he thrived in the trenches of the Agency. "I'm surprised to see the two of you together. Last time I spoke with Mark, the oil wallahs and the Agency Mandarins were feuding."

Palmer sported he same outfit he had worn in the Berkshires. He sat on Monsarrat's left and offered his hand. "You're looking energized, Nathan. Is the torpor fully gone?"

Monsarrat registered the strength of his grip. "You arrived quickly, Mark. Were you in South Africa when I called?"

Palmer spoke as if Sanhedrin were in another country. "Felix had personal business to conduct. We could have been here sooner, but the man moves at the speed of cold molasses."

Monsarrat hid his distaste for Palmer beneath a veneer of banter. "Felix has never rushed an expense account lunch."

Frank and Joe, dressed identically to Palmer, sat silently at a table behind them.

"Your bosses know you're working with the Agency? Or are you following orders again?"

"It's a brave new world, Nathan. Enemies yesterday, allies today, who knows what tomorrow will bring?"

"Profits, I expect."

Sanhedrin offered Monsarrat his warmest smile. He reeked of menace like other men smelled of after shave. "Where's Innocence, old buddy? I'd like to speak with him."

"He's indisposed."

Sanhedrin flashed impatience. "What does that mean, Nathan?"

Monsarrat gestured at the empty breakfast nook. "Keep your voice down, Felix. You'll disturb the guests."

He crossed the reception area and handed one thousand rand to the desk clerk, a young woman with a blond Price Valiant haircut, violet eyes, and a scattering of freckles across the bridge of her pert nose. She wore a man's dress shirt with the top four buttons open, exposing her tanned cleavage. The script of her nametag identified her as Rebecca. "Breakfast for my four friends. Plus a tip for your troubles."

He returned to the table. "Get some food, at least for appearances."

Palmer gestured to Frank and Joe. "Bring two plates for us from the buffet, also coffee, and get some food for yourselves."

Sanhedrin repeated his question. "Where is Innocence, old buddy?"

Monsarrat enjoyed his discomfort. Sanhedrin remained an easy man to annoy. "Did you bring a planchette, Felix?"

"What's that?"

"It's a helpful tool for communicating with the dead."

Sanhedrin patted Monsarrat's arm. "Nice try, Nathan, but I trained you. I know when you're lying."

Palmer glanced at his watch and coughed discreetly.

"When I learned you were working for the oil consortium against the Agency's interests, I was a tad upset," Sanhedrin continued. "So I'm sure you can appreciate my relief that we're all on the same side now."

Monsarrat turned to Palmer. "Are we all on the same side, Mark?"

Sanhedrin didn't allow him to answer. "The oil consortium realized its plans would piss off its friends in Washington. Short-term gain but long-term loss. Reassessment is the name of the game. Now we're all pulling on the same oar, in the same boat, in the same direction."

Monsarrat thought the description a recipe for traveling in wide circles. "That's how your bosses see it, Mark?"

"Don't ask me, Nathan. I'm kinetic. You want analysis, call Port Harcourt."

Sanhedrin was magnanimous. "The consortium didn't need to beg for forgiveness. The Mandarins didn't seek retribution. We kissed. We made up. We're moving forward."

"How sweet," Monsarrat said. "Just like in the movies. Agency gets oil consortium. Agency loses oil consortium. Agency and oil consortium make up and get rich together."

Sanhedrin rolled his eyes. "Just give us Innocence."

"Do I get a gold star for slinging your bony ass out of the fire again?"

"You're a tad low on respect these days, old buddy."

Joe set full plates of food on the table. "Plenty more where this came from."

Frank put down mugs of coffee. "Bon appétit, gentlemen."

When Monsarrat addressed Palmer, he allowed himself the luxury of anger. "I don't care if the Agency surrendered or the oil consortium capitulated. You hired me to return Innocence, preferably vertical, but horizontal was also acceptable. Circumstances dictated that I go with the second option."

Palmer sipped his coffee. "Our deal's still good."

Sanhedrin interrupted, "I traveled to this Namibian shithole to protect the Agency's interests, and I speak for the Mandarins. We want Innocence hale and healthy."

"I can't help you, Felix. He's in a shallow grave deep in the Namibian desert. Maybe if you boys had presented a single set of instructions, I wouldn't have whacked him."

"I hope you're joshing, Nathan. I'd hate for your remaining days to be spent in Gitmo."

"How would that happen, Felix?"

His former boss addressed him as a father might rebuke a recalcitrant son. "Innocence is set to play a vital role in ensuring the national security of our country. Allowing your personal desires to interfere in that endeavor would be the basic definition of treason."

Monsarrat thought Sanhedrin was desperate to protect his investment. "You're miscast as an offended virgin, Felix."

"If you did whack Innocence, old buddy, you've created the biggest shit storm of your tarnished career. You really should stick to counseling confused coeds."

"Still the master of alliteration."

Palmer pushed away his plate of food. "Whenever you're ready, Nathan, I'll take Innocence. Vertical, horizontal, I need him or his corpse."

"You may want to wait a minute before you order Frank and Joe to rob desert graves," Monsarrat advised. "Since Innocence is dead, you have no reason to kill his older brother, but you can send Diligence to Rehovoth in his place."

Palmer maintained his poker face, but Sanhedrin showed surprise before covering it with skepticism. "How's that work, old buddy? Diligence died when he slammed his car into a wall."

Monsarrat enjoyed trumping his former boss. "Diligence walked away from the crash, and Papa Rehovoth created a new identity for him. He's alive and well and on his way to Windhoek."

"Why would you think so, Nathan?"

"Innocence told me interesting stories before he died," Monsarrat confided. "He thought he could buy his life if he spilled his guts."

"Pray tell, old buddy. What kind of interesting stories?"

"Don't you ever get tired of playing both ends against the middle, Felix?"

Palmer exchanged insistence for politeness. "It's been nice catching up with you, Nathan, but if you could give me the coordinates for that desert grave, I'll exhume the body and return it to Port Harcourt."

"Keep quiet, Mark. I'm not through with him," Sanhedrin snapped. He waved a bony finger at Monsarrat. "Which interesting stories did Innocence tell you?"

"You know Diligence is alive, because Innocence hired you to kill him, right after you and Mark asked him to sit at the side of Rehovoth. It must have taken you all of five minutes to concoct your plan to take his money, send me to Africa, and pin his murder on me."

Sanhedrin tasked. "The problem with our work, Nathan, is that some of our partners are too fond of hearing their own voices."

Monsarrat thought Sanhedrin was guilty of his own accusation. "You set me up to be your patsy for the murder of Diligence. You were going to let me rot in an African jail for the rest of my life, so that you could cash a check."

"It's just business, old buddy. Nothing personal."

"It's personal for me, Felix. It's my life," Monsarrat countered. "I don't care about your business, I don't care about the Agency's coup, and I don't care about the consortium's profits."

Sanhedrin's interest was avuncular. "What do you care about, Nathan?"

"I came here to take Rosalinda Santiago home with me."

Sanhedrin, unlike Innocence, was not surprised by the name. "The Filipina nurse? I told you three years ago that she was dead, but you wanted her to be alive so badly you shut down your bullshit deflectors and gobbled our story."

Monsarrat admitted the accuracy of the assessment. "You told Mark to feed me a fuzzy story and show me a doctored photo of Rosalinda to get me back here."

"You're too soft hearted to be a spook, Nathan," Palmer advised. "It's a good thing that you quit and became a dean."

"Your employers did not tell you to stand down, Mark, because you lost too many of your own people hunting Innocence in Cape Town. They ordered you to back off after they reached their agreement with the Agency, but your need for vengeance demanded that Innocence die, so you gave me a nod and a wink and sent me to kill him. You don't give a damn about the coup. You get payback and keep your pension."

Palmer used the words Innocence had proclaimed earlier. "You're a very smart man, Nathan, but I still need the location of the body."

Monsarrat remembered the promise he made to Palmer in the Berkshires. "You used me."

"It wasn't personal, Nathan," Palmer stated, "and you were never in danger, although Felix thought he had won the trifecta. First, Innocence pays us, second, I put a bullet into your skull and leave your corpse next to Diligence, and third, we deliver Innocence to his father and make the Mandarins and the wallahs happy, but I knew it wouldn't go down so smoothly. I knew you would whack Innocence, and after that sick bastard was dead, we'd have no reason to kill you."

"Felix didn't know about your deal with me."

"He knows less than nothing."

Sanhedrin listened to the interchange with mounting frustration. "You made a deal to kill Innocence and let Diligence live, even though I wanted the opposite?"

Monsarrat never tired of the show, Honor Among Thieves. "Maybe the oil wallahs will be satisfied, Felix, but you know how the Mandarins hate bumps in their smooth coups. Your next promotion might not arrive until the Second Coming."

His thin body shook as his anger vented. "The next time you want to talk smug to me, old buddy, you should remember who your girlfriend works for."

Monsarrat understood that Sanhedrin, contrary to his physical appearance, was the most dangerous man he knew. He could not allow his threat to pass unchecked. "You read my medical reports, Felix. After my time in the Delta, I'm a potential threat to myself and others."

Sanhedrin rose and stepped away from the table. "I trained you, Nathan. You can't make a move without my knowing it, so don't try to scare me."

He turned to Palmer. "Let's go. It's a long trip to Windhoek, and I have a lot of prep work to do if I'm going to convince Diligence to join his father in Abuja."

"What do we do about Nathan?"

"Leave him," Sanhedrin snapped. "He doesn't present a threat to us, he's too well trained to talk about any of this, and we no longer have a viable scenario for his death. Lord knows what kind of safeguards he put into place before leaving Massachusetts."

Monsarrat enjoyed Sanhedrin's anger. "How'd it turn out with the statue and your Russian friends, Felix?"

Sanhedrin strode toward the exit. He turned when he reached the door. "Neither of us ended up in a Brighton Beach dumpster, Nathan. I'd chalk it up as a successful conclusion to a difficult business arrangement."

"One last question, Felix?"

Sanhedrin pressed his fingers against the door. "Make it fast, old buddy."

"Why did you hire those clowns to brace me in Cape Town?"

"I'm sure I don't know what you're talking about, old buddy."

"The four thugs? The Central Library in the Old Drill Hall? Twenty thousand rand? A warning to go home, stay there, don't come back?"

Sanhedrin answered as he pushed open the door. "I don't give warnings, Nathan. Ask Bruce. He's gone native, I understand."

Palmer watched him leave the building. "We don't always get to choose our playmates."

"Oil and water, you and Felix."

"Truer words," Palmer agreed. "Is Innocence really dead, or was that song and dance routine for Felix's benefit?"

Monsarrat felt no compunction. "Thoroughly dead."

"I'll need proof before I can pay you the rest of the money."

During his career with the Agency, betrayal had been as natural as breathing and as necessary as eating. He was not surprised that his former boss would plan his death as casually as he would toss a poker chip onto the baize, but he had felt a kinship with Palmer and was disappointed that he had chosen to sacrifice him for his own gain. In the secret world, blood feuds were the yin and the yang, and betrayal demanded retribution. In a time and a place of his choosing, he would take his vengeance upon both Sanhedrin and Palmer.

"I'll send you an e-mail with photo attachments."

Palmer offered his explanation. "You're a hard man, Nathan, with very few chinks in your armor. I could have used your friend Abby to blackmail you, but it's always a messy process, and, anyway, I didn't want to involve a civilian, so I chose the second option, Rosalinda. She was dead, so there was neither harm nor foul, but your guilt over her passing in the Delta guaranteed your acceptance of my offer."

"I understand your need for Innocence to die, but I expected better from you."

"Men like us are not meant to drink from the milk of human kindness. Men like us have allegiances, not friendships."

"Just don't try to stiff me with the payment, Mark. You'll only piss me off even more."

"It's not my style. Send me the proof, and I'll make sure your funds are deposited immediately."

"What will you do about Diligence?"

"Other than split Innocence's very generous retainer with Felix?"

"Other than that."

"I'll explain the death of Innocence and the resurrection of the second son to my employers. Like I said, they won't be upset. Diligence may give us more or fewer or different problems than his younger brother, but at least he didn't kill any of my people."

"What happens to your plan if Diligence refuses to leave Windhoek?"

"Personally, I think we should bury him beneath a sand dune on the Skeleton Coast, but knowing Felix, if push comes to shove we'll drag him to Abuja against his will."

"You're sure Rehovoth will accept Diligence?"

"I doubt the father will protest too loudly. He's a survivor and a pragmatist. He knows he needs family by his side, and with Innocence gone, Diligence is the only son left standing"

Palmer rose and signaled for Frank and Joe to follow him. "I have one more question for you, Nathan."

Monsarrat considered refusing to answer but knew he would gain nothing more than a momentary satisfaction. Making an enemy of Palmer would lead to serious problems, and he wanted the remainder of his payment securely deposited into his bank account before he initiated his vengeance. "Go on."

"How did you track Innocence to Rosh Pinah?"

He offered an expurgated tale devoid of Marines, analysts, and Russians. "He left slug marks across Cape Town."

"A Boy Scout could have followed him," Palmer agreed.

Monsarrat's answer served as a warning. "I'm no Boy Scout, Mark."

"Get me the photos, Nathan, then check your bank account."

Monsarrat watched them exit the lodge, then walked to Innocence's Room. As he opened the door, strains of Afrobeat erupted from the pink cell phone. A single word, Diligence, filled the screen. The music faded, and the blare of trumpets announced a voice-mail message.

He punched in the code, pressed the icon, and listened for the first time to the voice of Diligence. His accent bore only the faintest traces of pidgin. "An American calling himself Fineghan Scarnagh has contacted me, little brother. He addressed me by my birth name and said you provided him my number. He says it is urgent that we speak short time. Why did you share my personal information and not introduce him to me yourself? Answer me very fast, little brother."

Monsarrat considered responding, Shades of Banquo, fear Fineghan Scarnagh, for he is the man who murdered me. He decided to put the message to more practical use.

He examined the room for compromising evidence, tossed the key onto the dresser, and shut the door quietly. In his own room, he emptied the contents of the backpack onto the bed, inspected the items, and returned them to the bag. At the reception desk, he bought bottles of water and sandwiches, although he knew he would not be hungry for a long while. He handed his own key to the young woman with the violet eyes. "You run a very nice lodge, Rebecca."

"Thank you, Mr. Clarendon, but my dad owns it. I just work here."

The streets of Rosh Pinah were empty in the quiet morning hours. He entered the loading area behind the local market. The stench of an abattoir leaked from the BMW. When he opened the trunk, Innocence blinked in the sudden light. "Good morning, sleepy head. Pleasant dreams?"

He closed the trunk, settled into the driver's seat, and turned the air conditioning to its highest setting. The big car covered the distance to the cell phone tower in minutes. He turned left and jounced along the pitted road, enjoying the thought of his passenger's discomfort. Although returning to the scene of the crime engendered risks, he needed to add Innocence's corpse to the bier of bodies to uncomplicate matters for the Namibian authorities.

When he parked next to the dilapidated guard shack and stepped out of the BMW, he inhaled the rotting odor of human putrefaction. He hauled Innocence from the trunk and dragged him toward a rock outcropping. He balanced the Russian cell phone on a shelf of shale jutting from the face. From the backpack, he removed scarf, gloves, blanket, sweatshirt, and a single pink, pearl-handled Colt .45 Peacemaker. He wrapped the scarf around his mouth to muffle his voice, slit three holes in the hood of the sweatshirt to align with his eyes and mouth, and donned it backwards. He pulled on the gloves and slipped the Peacemaker under his belt. He entered the code into the Russian cell phone, pulled up the sole entry in the contact list, and pressed the video conversation icon.

After a moment, Nicky accepted the call. "You are dressed for your Halloween party, *moy druhg?*"

"No names," Monsarrat warned. "Where's your boss?"

"You need not be concerned," the young Russian answered.

He understood plausible deniability. "The woman I mentioned? Show her to me."

Nicky spoke as if expecting an apology. "We visited the villa but saw so sign of her. We asked a few of the African scum for her location, but they swore upon the wombs of their mothers no one of that description had ever resided there."

Monsarrat accepted, once and forever, that Rosalinda had died in the Delta. "*Yah ponimayu.* Open the bank account in my name, deposit the money, and send me the information. Do you have a pen and paper?"

"*Da.* Give me the information."

He issued the instructions with a warning. "You and your boss don't want me as an enemy, Nicky. Deposit the money, and you won't need to watch your back for the rest of your life."

He wrapped himself in the filthy blanket like a Saturnalian toga and slipped on the work gloves. He grasped Innocence by his throat and lifted his head. "Can you see us? I'll only do this once."

Excitement throbbed in the young Russian's voice. "*D'vai, moy druhg.* Do it."

"Do you recognize him?

"*Da.* It is him."

Innocence strained against his bonds. Beneath the duct tape, he grunted bestial sounds. Monsarrat's own voice, filtered through the scarf, seemed distant. "Struggle all you want, you sick son of a bitch. This is for Rosalinda."

He struck him with the butt of the Peacemaker. He dropped the revolver onto the sand, leaned forward, and spoke into his damaged ear. "In the Delta, I promised to kill you and your buddy, Blessed, very slowly, with my fingers around your throats. Shooting him broke my heart, but I'm going to enjoy strangling you."

He heard Nicky urging him to finish the task. He remembered Blessed bleeding into the carpet of the hotel room. He remembered how easily Sanhedrin had used him, first to launder a quarter million Agency dollars and later to dispose of Blessed. He remembered Palmer's sincerity when he revealed the doctored photograph. He remembered Rosalinda soothing him in the thatch hut and imagined her death in the Delta, alone and frightened, far from her home and family.

Innocence weighed more than the iron Monsarrat lifted in Holbrooke Gymnasium, but hatred and rage fueled his strength. He jerked him vertical and slammed his knee into his crotch, yanking the tape from his mouth as he doubled over and vomited into the sand.

When his retching subsided, Monsarrat stood him upright and turned his face toward the cell phone. His pulled the gloves from his hands, encircled Innocence's throat, and slowly increased the pressure against his trachea. As he squeezed harder, he lifted him until his bare feet cleared the sand. He squeezed still harder and felt the muscles of his throat collapse. He saw saliva bubble on his lips and heard the breath escape from his lungs. He kept squeezing until the final spark of life drained from his body and, in the obsidian vacuity of his death, he saw his own reflection in his lifeless, black eyes.

Nicky's voice carried across the sand. "*D'vai*, finish him!"

Monsarrat dropped the body onto the desert floor, picked up the Peacemaker, and pressed it against the back of his skull. He repeated, "For Rosalinda."

When he pulled the trigger and the heavy slug exited through his forehead, a geyser of blood and gristle soaked the sand. Bright green flies settled quickly onto the crimson pools. He spit out a single word toward the cell phone. "Satisfied?"

"*Khorosho*. Very good," Nicky answered. "My boss will be pleased. Your money will be deposited in seventy-two hours, as you instructed."

Monsarrat ended the call. *Khorosho*, he agreed. The execution had surely been a bloody horror show.

He smashed the Russian cell phone with the butt of the Peacemaker, snapped the SIM card in half, and threw the chaff across the sand. He covered the bloody corpse with the blanket and tossed his sweatshirt, scarf, gloves, Peacemakers, and holster belt on top of it. He added the pink cell phone to the pile. In a just world, Diligence's recorded message would spawn complications for Sanhedrin.

He wiped his fingerprints from the folding knife and dumped the rest of the backpack's contents, save for the water and sandwiches. As a younger man, he had enjoyed hitchhiking the open road. Aus was one hundred miles distant, another hundred miles to Keetmanshoop, and the final leg of the trip to Windhoek would cover three hundred miles. He planned to check into the city's finest hotel, exchange his return Cape Town ticket for a first class seat on the next flight to Europe with a connection to Boston, buy a change of clothes, sit for a shave and a haircut, soak in a hot bath, and eat an excellent meal. He might run into his former boss and Mark Palmer. The possibilities shined as brightly as the Namibian sun.

He stepped lightly across the desert. He passed the cell phone tower and gained the C13 toward Aus. His luck held, and he raised his thumb high as a Volkswagen bus emerged from a cloud of dust on the southern horizon. Dents and chips of rust marred the blue and white paint of its bug-eyed fascia. It rolled to a halt, and the driver stuck her head out the window. "Did you have an argument with your mates, Mr. Clarendon?"

He took in her blond Price Valiant haircut, violet eyes, pert, freckled nose, and her tanned cleavage. "Hello, Rebecca. Have you come to save me from the desert?"

"Only if you call me Beka."

"I'm flattered you remembered my name."

"We don't have too many Canadians stay with us. Leastwise, not like you."

Monsarrat doubted she was as guileless as she appeared.

"I'm for Witputz to see my boyfriend. Where are you headed?"

"Windhoek. I fly home tomorrow."

"The big city! I haven't been in years." A wicked gleam played in her violet eyes. "What do you say, Mr. Clarendon? You pay for my benzene back and forth, and I'll drive us there."

He studied the Volkswagen. "Will the bus make it over the mountains?"

Her grin was brilliant. "If not, we'll tramp together."

"What about your boyfriend?"

"Have you ever been to Witputz? It's a farmstead full of manure and flies."

"Do you have friends in Windhoek who can put you up?"

The wicked gleam grew brighter. "I was thinking I could stay with you. I don't snore, but I don't think you'll want to sleep much."

Grieving assumed many forms. "I'm older than your father."

She opened the passenger door. "Don't worry about him, Mr. Clarendon. I'm a big girl."

Monsarrat climbed into the bus and dropped the backpack between his feet. "Only if you call me David."

She put the bus in gear and pulled onto the road. "Do you have a middle name, David?"

He shook his head. "My parents couldn't agree."

Her wicked gleam erupted into starbursts. "I do. It's Electra."

The next morning, Monsarrat awoke alone in the empty hotel room. Beka had left a note with her cell phone number and e-mail address. He shredded the paper and flushed it down the toilet. He took the telephone directory from the nightstand and found the listings for the Namibian Police Force. At the reception desk in the lobby, he bought a Telecard and received directions to the hotel's public telephones. On a wall beyond the cloakroom, he slid the card into the slot and dialed the commander for the Karas Region. He delivered the message twice, in case local gendarmerie in Keetmanshoop had not yet fully wakened.

Outside the hotel lobby, beneath a sky as brilliant as a polished Namibian diamond, the doorman ushered him into a taxi for the airport.

IV. THE BERKSHIRES

THE FIRST DAY OF THE NEW ACADEMIC YEAR

Fields of green covered the Berkshire campus. Flowers waved in the late August breeze like Mother Nature's banners. From his office in Campbell Hall, Monsarrat watched the bustle of the annual ritual, the first day of the new academic year. For some, it offered the opportunity to learn. For others, it was a party with a steep cover charge.

Beneath the soft morning sun, freshmen and their parents walked apart, separated by an embarrassed generational gulf. Upperclassmen threw Frisbees. Gentler souls sat beneath the shade of oak trees, joined by the umbilical cords of earbuds. Effusive students drank beer, smoked joints, and danced to music booming from speakers balanced in dormitory windows. He suspected some of them would stand in the docket of future Disciplinary Committee meetings.

Lately, Doris had greeted him with a smile and hummed catchy pop tunes throughout the day. A satisfied lilt lifted her voice, and disapproval no longer darkened her visage. Each morning, she set daisies, buttercups, and petunias in a clear glass vase on his desk. To mark the special day's festive occasion, she sported a beehive hairdo, a silk skirt and blouse combination, patent leather sling pumps, and a necklace of freshwater pearls. He suspected the newly hired instructor of English 101 as the motivation behind her mood shift. Since the prior month's faculty orientation, the freshly minted PhD had spent more time by her desk than in his own office.

The evening following his return from Windhoek, Monsarrat had burned all traces of David Clarendon and scattered his ashes across his backyard, like the remains of a cremated brother. The next morning, he received a telephone call from a discrete bank in Zurich to finalize the details of his new bank account. Two days later, he flew to see Abby. They spent the weekend on the Mall, exploring the Freer Gallery, the Sackler Gallery, and the American Art Museum of the Smithsonian Institution. They watched children bobbing on the wooden horses of the carousel in front of the Arts and Industries Building. The calliope music sounded like summer.

"We should see a ball game," Monsarrat offered.

Abby had been distant since his arrival. "We should talk, Nathan. Would you like a cup of coffee?"

They crossed Independence Avenue and walked toward the Potomac River. On Sixth Street, they stepped into a coffee shop. Monsarrat ordered two lattes. They sat by a window and watched families hurry toward the L'Enfant Plaza metro station.

Abby began slowly, as if she were preparing to divulge state secrets. "Felix never includes me on his messages, but Friday morning he blind copied me on an e-mail he sent to the Mandarin collective."

If Sanhedrin had sent a message directly to the Mandarins, he had broken the Agency's rigid lines of protocol. "He must be sure that whatever intel he possesses is pure gold," Monsarrat mused. "His superiors won't be happy that he went around them."

She removed the plastic cover from the cup and sipped the foam. "He didn't go around them. He vaulted right over them. He told the Mandarins that he possessed intel of an extremely sensitive nature. He waved all the flags of national security and said he would speak to them and only them. He did not allow any intermediaries."

Monsarrat understood well the machinations of his former boss. "Did he describe the nature of the intel?"

"He mentioned oil, al-Qaida, and treason," she answered. "Specifically, he informed them of the treason of a former valued member of the Agency. He named you, Nathan."

Her announcement did not surprise him. He had anticipated the dropping of Sanhedrin's second shoe. "Did he say what I was to have done?"

"Felix claimed that you scuttled an Agency operation to bring a friendly, democratic government to an oil-producing West African nation. He called it "Operation Blessed Innocence." He said you assassinated the number one and number two men in the democratic opposition."

Despite her concern, Monsarrat smiled at the thought of Blessed and Innocence in any government, democratic or despotic. "Felix is being Felix. He's covering his ass with one hand and asking for medals with the other."

She was not mollified. "I worry about you, baby. You don't know Felix like I do. He's driven, like he's trying to avenge the insults he suffered as a boy."

"Did he mention who paid me to scuttle his op?"

Tears leaked from the corners of her eyes. "He claimed you took hundreds of thousands of dollars from Yahya al-Masri, the financial genius of al-Qaida. He accused you of complicity in setting up a government based upon Shari'ah law that would sell its oil only to our enemies and our competition."

Monsarrat suspected Sanhedrin had coordinated his story with the oil wallahs. With their support, the Mandarins would consider his charges seriously. If they chose to act upon them, he would know soon enough, immediately after they shoved a black hood over his head and bundled him aboard a rendition flight to Gitmo. "Felix thinks I jilted him when I retired. He takes my new life in academia as a personal insult."

"What happened when you took your trip? Did you go back to the Delta?"

Monsarrat chose his words carefully. "Not the Delta, Abby. South Africa and Namibia. That's where Sanhedrin popped up. He brokered a reconciliation between the Mandarins and the oil wallahs. They worked together to put a puppet into power in Abuja. Felix's supposed number two man in the democratic opposition was the son of the puppet, and the father wanted the son by his side. The son was the psychopath who held me captive in the Delta and killed Rosalinda."

"You're sure she's dead, baby? You said the photograph was doctored?"

"I'm sure, Abby. The picture was created by software," he explained. "Rosalinda died three years ago in the Delta. In Namibia, I had to make a choice, let the psychopath live or kill him for what he did to me and Rosalinda."

"So you executed him?"

"It was an easy decision," Monsarrat admitted, "but it pissed off Felix, and he wants his pound of flesh from me, as punishment for interfering with his plans."

He failed to add that Sanhedrin had forgotten neither his humiliation in Greenfield nor the money he had paid to transport the terracotta statue from Port Harcourt. He also suspected that Palmer had provided his former boss with details of the oil consortium's generous fee. Sanhedrin may also have learned of the Russian's quarter million dollar payment. A grasping man of combustible jealousies, the knowledge would have infuriated him.

Abby's instincts were on target. "Felix wants you to know what he's doing, and he's using me to play messenger."

Monsarrat did not want to share Sanhedrin's parting threat in Rosh Pinah. "Don't worry, Abby, but if Felix starts acting stranger than usual, let me know."

"I'm not good at these games, Nathan. I don't want to be the messenger. I just want to be with you and do my job."

Monsarrat hated the thought of surrendering to Sanhedrin's blackmail but refused to allow his former boss to use her as a hostage. "On Monday, tell Felix you're not seeing me anymore. He'll leave you alone as soon as he's satisfied you've told him the truth."

She slammed the table so hard that her latte spilled. "Absolutely not! He doesn't run my life! I will not let him come between us."

He walked to the counter and returned with a handful of paper napkins to blot the coffee. "It's the smart thing to do, Abby."

Frustration and anger laced her reply. "Like quitting the Agency was the smart thing for you to do? You have so many unresolved issues, Nathan."

He agreed but did not want to hold the discussion in a coffee shop. "You know no one walks away from the Agency clean."

If she knew, she was not in the mood to concur. "Felix scares me, baby. He wants so much, and he wants it so fast."

"I'm not working against him, Abby. I just want him to leave you alone and stay far away from the Berkshires."

"Your Nipmuck agreement?" she laughed. "You're too trusting, Nathan. Felix never met a handshake he didn't violate."

After he returned from Washington, Monsarrat visited Ralph to fulfill his financial obligations. "As promised, Ralph. Cash for the promissory note."

The Marine passed him the note but ignored the envelope. "I didn't earn it."

Monsarrat shredded the paper and burned the small pieces in an empty pretzel bowl. "With all respect, Ralph, take the money."

"Can't do that, Dean."

Monsarrat tossed the envelope to Tiny. "Maybe your brother's smarter than you."

He grabbed it from Tiny's huge hands. "You're a good man, Dean. Stupid with your cash, but a good man."

"To clean thoughts," Monsarrat responded, raising his shot glass of bourbon.

"And dirty deeds," Ralph answered.

The conversation confused Tiny. "What are you two talking about?"

His brother snapped him with a wet towel. "Go clean the tables, Tiny. I ain't paying you to stand around and look pretty."

When he moved away, Ralph asked, "What happened in Cape Town, Dean?"

Monsarrat shook his head. "Spook shit."

"Why the bug out?"

Monsarrat continued to scythe the air, like a pendulum gathering force. "Enjoy the cash, Ralph. You earned it. Just don't mention it to the IRS."

"My momma only raised one fool, and he's wiping down tables with a dirty rag."

Monsarrat dropped a twenty dollar bill on the bar. "Semper Fi, Brother."

The next week, to Doris's delight, he traveled on his recruitment trip through the Southern states. Upon his return, the long summer days passed easily. He slipped into the comfort of his routine like an old man donning his favorite slippers, but he had angered too many scrofulous people to allow the slow pace of the college town to lull him. He kept the five round .38 Smith & Wesson Special locked in the Jeep and the Glock 30 hidden in his briefcase, in addition to carrying a seven round .22 Magnum Smith & Wesson in a leather holster on his hip. With its two-inch barrel, it weighed less than a pound and was easily hidden.

On the Friday morning prior to the start of the new semester, he received a call from Solomon Grinnell. The former yeshiva *bocher* spoke elliptically. "You used to work for my father. He never appreciated your advice. He saw you as an affliction to his authority."

"As do so many others," Monsarrat responded. "*Shabbat shalom*, my friend."

"*Shabbat shalom.* Peace be upon you, *habibi.* How are you faring these days?" Even at his most solicitous, Grinnell sounded like a Brooklyn thug.

Monsarrat answered truthfully. "Actually, I am very well."

"I'm happy to hear it. The affair with my business associate worked out smoothly?"

"The large Russian?" Monsarrat asked.

"Who works for the art collector."

Monsarrat had experienced his fill of Russians. "As smoothly as any venture involving our mutual friend can work out."

"Which brings me to the reason for my call," Grinnell responded. "You asked me to let you know if I heard anything about him and the Russian community."

"Has he pissed off the wrong people again?"

"Only the wrong people? Since when has he been so discriminating?"

Monsarrat pictured him enjoying a Talmudic moment. "Give me some good news, please. Did one of your friends take out a contract on him?"

"Just a buzz in your ear, *habibi*. Our mutual friend has been spending quality time with the art collector he worked for previously. The one to whom he delivered a very valuable statue. Word is that our mutual friend has been retained to find another national treasure."

Monsarrat absorbed the information. "Any thoughts on the location of this treasure?"

Grinnell admitted he could not divulge details. "Although I have heard the words icon, Vladimir, a large dollar figure, and a tight deadline used in the same sentence."

"How large a dollar figure?"

"Rumor has it in the eight-figure range."

"I'm impressed," Monsarrat admitted, "but I haven't heard from our mutual friend. I hope to keep it that way."

"*Insha'allah*. If I learn more, I'll let you know." Grinnell promised.

The festivities on the **campus** grew more raucous. A Frisbee sailed by his window. He opened his e-mail to find a message from Wilson, sent from a private account. Nephew, my retirement from our mutual employer is imminent, at the conclusion of this fiscal year. I hope to see you again soon. In fond regards, Uncle.

Monsarrat deleted the message. He wondered if their lunch in Johannesburg had influenced Wilson's decision to retire. He suspected Sanhedrin had feted him in Pretoria before arriving in Rosh Pinah. His instincts warned that complications trailed the analyst like a dirty bridal train.

The institutional beige telephone on his desk chirped. He still awaited a replacement handset. He pressed the speaker button and launched another salvo in his charm offensive. "Thank you for the lovely flowers, Doris. Your pearls are very becoming, too."

Flustered, she answered, "Oh, thank you so much, Dean. You're very kind to mention it."

An electronic silence hung between them. "May I help you, Doris?"

To overcome her embarrassment, she spoke breathlessly. "You have a call on your private extension, Dean. Mr. Franklin Seleucid from Educational Placement Services. He wants to discuss a potential student. He's the same man who called last year."

Her memory impressed Monsarrat. Perhaps there was more to Doris than what met the obvious eye. "Did he say anything else?"

"Just that he wants to speak with you."

Monsarrat patted the .22 Magnum on his hip. He could instruct Doris to never accept calls from Franklin Seleucid and Educational Placement Services, but Sanhedrin would simply show up at his office. He could order the college's security to remove him from the campus, but his former boss would somehow force a meeting. The best he could do would be to dictate the terms of engagement.

"Put him though, Doris. Persistent bugger, isn't he?"

"Did his student enroll in the college this term, Dean?"

"Unfortunately, no. He wasn't able to travel."

"That's too bad," she said. "I'm putting Mr. Seleucid through to you now."

Monsarrat waited for the call to transfer. He felt strong enough, ready to defeat Sanhedrin. He felt, at long last, more Monsarrat than dean, more Monsarrat than spook.

CPSIA information can be obtained at www.ICGtesting.com
Printed in the USA
LVOW07*2119240216

476601LV00003B/10/P